THE
LAST SECRET
OF
WICKHAM
GRANGE

Also by Zoe Manlow

No Common Wench

THE
LAST SECRET
OF
WICKHAM
GRANGE

ZOE MANLOW

First published in the UK in 2026 by Bedford Square Publishers Ltd,
London, UK

bedfordsquarepublishers.co.uk
@bedfordsq.publishers

ISBN
978-1-83501-426-4 (Paperback)
978-1-83501-427-1 (eBook)

2 4 6 8 10 9 7 5 3 1

Typeset in 10.9 on 13.75pt Garamond MT Pro
by Avocet Typeset, Bideford, Devon, EX39 2BP
Printed and bound in Great Britain by
CPI Group (UK) Ltd, Croydon CR0 4YY

The manufacturer's authorised representative in the EU for product safety is
Easy Access System Europe, Mustamäe tee 50, 10621 Tallinn, Estonia
gpsr.requests@easproject.com

*For my family, with all my love — and for Mungo,
the original Shenstone Hound*

Part One
2006

Prologue

Even here, even now, she couldn't escape the house.

Raising her eyes from the heap of earth at her feet, Caroline could see its upper windows, as dark and empty as the hole in front of her, staring down blankly as if they too could not believe that Frances was dead. The undertakers were ready, their leather-gloved hands folded like bats; the long canvas straps lay under the coffin, and Caroline, ever practical, couldn't help wondering how they'd be retrieved afterwards. The vicar, a middle-aged black woman with a kindly face and beautiful voice, was saying something, but Caroline wasn't listening. All she could think was that none of this seemed remotely relevant to Frances, to who and what she had been.

She wished she'd worn boots and thicker tights; the spring earth was cold and damp under her feet, an unwelcoming bed for her grandmother's rest. Shifting uncomfortably, she glanced across the grave to see how her mother was doing, but Betty's head was bowed, hidden by the brim of what should have been a ridiculous hat but somehow wasn't. She'd paired it with a long cream wool coat that she'd painted with hundreds of tiny black roses, which made her look rich and exotic. The folds of the coat hung to her ankles; she wasn't particularly tall, but then again, she had the kind of poise that gave the illusion of height, so she could carry it off. Caroline looked from her mother to the tiny coffin thinking, not for the first time, that wherever Betty had sprung from, it wasn't from the delicate bones that were now being lowered into the darkness.

The vicar bowed her head. Caroline muttered a belated amen, a split second behind everyone else, and realised that it was over. The little group shifted and stirred and began to move away, leaving Frances to the earth and the silence.

It was only a few hundred yards back through the churchyard and up the hill to the house. Caroline went slowly, grateful that after a swift understanding glance her friend Ruth went ahead with the others, picking their way through the scattered memorials, under the lychgate and up the lane. A car went past, and Caroline looked enviously at the couple inside, going anywhere that wasn't Wickham Grange.

She slowed down as the road curved, partly to catch her breath, but partly because this was the moment she always dreaded. The first sight of the gates.

God knows when they'd last been shut. Somehow they'd been missed during the two world wars they'd seen, and Maud had joked they'd been made of melted-down Spitfires, but they were older than that, solidly Victorian along with the rest of the house. Once, Caroline supposed, they'd been locked every evening by a gardener or someone, but now they were welded open, fixed to the wall with ivy and laurels and other damp and creeping things.

And behind them was the house. It stood some way behind the gates, a riot of gables and chimneys at the top of a gravel sweep, as sturdy and confident as the Victorians who had built it. Once, it must have been almost rural, until West Wickham had begun its creep up the hill, so now only the neighbouring churchyard stood between it and the 1930s villas of the suburb below. Halfway up the lane, neither town nor country, Wickham Grange had been left to stand aloof and isolated, an oddly formal relic of a dead age.

'Why don't you sell up?' Caroline had asked once. It must have been in the 1980s, when Frances had announced that she was retiring and converting the Grange into flats. 'You'd be able to buy something smaller and much easier to manage.'

Frances had shaken her head. She did not look up from her desk, but even in profile Caroline could see the sudden tension on her face. 'I've got to stay here,' she'd said. 'I can't leave.'

Caroline had not stopped, then, to wonder. 'Of course you can,' she'd said. Oh, how arrogant she must have sounded, though at the time it had felt like confidence. 'Maud wouldn't have minded, surely. And the market's improving, I know there's Mr Harris but we can—'

'No.' The word had rapped out and Caroline had been startled by the force with which Frances said it. 'I can't leave. Don't ask again, Caro. I mean it.' She had taken a deep breath, and it would have been then that Caroline first realised that her grandmother had grown old. 'Trust me,' she had said. 'I know what's right. What has to be done.' And then, quietly, as if to herself, she'd added, 'There's really no choice.'

And so builders had quoted and architects had planned, and the old house was carved into flats, new bathrooms and doors and kitchens going where once there had been narrow beds and despair.

But throughout it all the gates had remained fixed, unyielding, just as Frances had done.

'For God's sake get a caterer.' Betty had been adamant when Caroline rang about the funeral. 'It'll be bad enough without having to faff around with vol-au-vents.' She had paused, the empty air between them heavy with things waiting in vain to be said. 'I take it you're not staying at the house?'

God, no. Caroline had shuddered then and she shivered now as she went through the heavy oak front door. If you knew where to look you could see traces of the old rooms, faint lines on the walls showing where things had been moved and bricked and plastered. Across the hall, the door to what had once been the drawing room, and then Frances's flat, was open, and she could see a couple of women in black polyester blouses handing round plates and glasses. Mr Harris was hunched over a teacup like a vulture shielding prey, talking to Betty who was gesturing vaguely over her shoulder; Caroline could not help but think they were talking about her, what she was going to do. It was more than she could face, so she shrugged off her coat and hung it on the newel, smoothing it more carefully than she usually would just to give herself a few precious seconds. The dark wood of the staircase curved up like an ampersand into the gloomy reaches of the upper floor, its heavy carpet held in place by brass rods. Overhead, the big hanging lantern had been switched on, but even that seemed dim, as if it too were in mourning, and the hall itself felt empty and echoing, despite the murmur coming from the gathered guests. It was a wide space, wood panelled, and it could once have been welcoming but today was cold and formal, like a waiting room at some once-fashionable private clinic. On the landing, she knew, doors led into other, smaller rooms and Caroline couldn't help wanting to run upstairs and hide herself.

'Want a drink?'

She turned, warm with relief. Ruth was coming across the hall's tiled floor, carrying two glasses of what turned out to be fairly respectable white wine. She tilted one in toast.

'To Frances.'

'To Frances.' Caroline took a sip, then looked back up the staircase. 'Is it me, or does it feel like any minute now she's going to come out and tell us to go outside and play?'

'Or make ourselves useful and take the dogs out or take someone down to the shop to buy sweets.' Ruth sat on the bottom stair and Caroline — mindful that she herself had none of Frances' delicacy — took the one above. There was a low, almost embarrassed laugh from the group around the table, Betty's rising high and clear above the others. Beside her, a thin, elderly woman — God, what was her name? — looked faintly disapproving. Caroline sighed. A few more minutes and then she'd have to go and join them. But not yet.

Ruth's clever, dark eyes were sympathetic. 'You okay?' she said, and of everyone who'd asked that question since Frances died Caroline felt she actually meant it.

'I think so. It just feels – weird. It was the same when Maud died, but at least then Granny was still here to carry everything on. Now it's like everything could collapse any minute.'

'I know what you mean,' Ruth said. 'Wickham Grange without Frances. It's not natural.' She glanced into the drawing room. 'Your mum seems to be doing all right, though. Doesn't she mind about the place coming to you?'

Caroline shrugged. 'She says not.'

'I hope it's okay. You know what they say, where there's a will there's a relative.' Ruth swirled her glass thoughtfully. 'Though surely it's good for you? I mean, you can sell up, set up on your own now.' She looked suddenly guilty. 'God, sorry, it's Frances' funeral and here I am being an insensitive cow.'

'You, insensitive? When I had to call a cab to get us home when we went to see *Ghost* because you'd cried so much you couldn't see?'

'You can talk. You can read the end of *The Railway Children* without crying.'

'They should never have been allowed on that track without adult supervision.'

They grinned at each other, and Caroline felt a sudden rush of warmth. Whatever else had happened in this house, it had brought her a best friend and that was something, surely, to be glad of, even on a day like this.

She finished the wine. 'I'd better go in. You coming?'

'Sure.' Ruth got up, held out a hand so Caroline didn't have to heave herself to her feet. 'Chin up. It's nearly over.'

But it wasn't. It hadn't even really started.

She got up and followed Ruth across the hall and into Frances' – her – flat. Caroline looked at the cracked Art Deco clock and was startled to find they'd only been been back for half an hour; it felt like she'd never left. She shook her head at a tray of canapés, knowing she'd regret it later and would end up wolfing down a tepid burger on room service.

Betty beckoned her over. She was sitting on one of the sofas that flanked the fireplace, next to Mr Harris and the thin woman. They looked up warily as Caroline approached.

'There you are, sweetie,' her mother said. She was wearing black eyeliner and had managed to get a perfect flick on both eyes. 'Mr Harris here was just asking if you've got any plans for the house.'

'Mum—'

'I think they've got a right to know, darling.' Betty patted an empty space beside her. The two old people moved further apart, as if to make clear that they were not together in any sense other than being here at the same time.

'I haven't really given it much thought.'

'Do you have any plans to sell?' The woman's voice was clipped, no nonsense, straight to the point. Caroline felt a stab of annoyance.

'There's a lot to consider,' she said. 'Tax, for a start.' Well, that was true enough, in a way, though the complicated calculations she'd had to plough through were something she'd rather not have to think about.

The old man said sharply, 'We're protected. Your gran sorted it all out when she gave us the flats. Protected. She said.'

'We have all the paperwork.' The woman – Caroline still couldn't remember her bloody name – was sitting very erect. 'I can assure you it's all in order.'

'I'm sure it is.' Caroline put her glass down. The room was suddenly very hot. 'We can talk about it once probate's all sorted out. It's not appropriate now, surely you can see that.' From across the room she could see Ruth looking sympathetic and it was too much, she could feel her voice crack and she was buggered, absolutely buggered, if she was going to cry here, in this room, this house, which had already seen so many tears. 'Look, Mum, I'm going to head back to the hotel. D'you want to share a cab? I'll be outside.'

Without waiting for an answer she turned and went out, picking up her coat and dragging the front door open, not really hearing the so-familiar squeal as its corner caught the floor tiles. It had got colder, the chill making her fingers fumble as she called the cab company, her breath misting as she paced the gravel for the promised ten minutes it would take the car to arrive. It would only be a fifteen-minute drive back into the centre of Croydon, so within the hour she could be alone, something she suddenly desperately craved. She resolutely kept her back to the house, as if for fear that if she turned she would see Frances and Maud and her mother and Connie and everyone, everyone else, watching her and waiting for her and wanting her to do – what?

The car arrived. Betty had not appeared. Caroline climbed in, leaned back against the seat and closed her eyes, not opening them until they turned out of those damned gates, heading back to lights and a minibar and bland, corporate rooms. She opened her bag, checked her phone, read messages from work that were for once welcome and affirming.

But at the bend in the lane she could not help it. She twisted her head, knowing what she would see: Wickham Grange, stark and implacable, waiting for her to return.

1

Caroline

The distant mewl of a siren came whining up the hill, carried on a sharp-toothed wind. For a moment Caroline thought it was the sound of children playing; but, like her, the children that had once lived here were long gone.

In front of her, the old house was watchful and silent, its familiar huddle of gables and chimneys streaked with rain and its windows dully reflecting the clouds that sulked overhead. It was late September, and from somewhere came the tang of one of the first bonfires of autumn, its smoke mingling uneasily with the heavy smell of damp, dead leaves. The car engine ticked quietly as it cooled.

She lifted her case out of the car and hauled it across the drive, swearing as the wheels snagged and jolted on the gravel. A row of plastic doorbells sprouted like fungi beside the front door, typed labels announcing that flats 2 and 3 were home to Harris (caretaker, in neat brackets) and Fairfax. Ah, that was the old woman's name! Caroline had distant memories of Mr Harris, an unsmiling man always ready to chase a child away from the greenhouse and shed. There was no name beside number 4, and she guessed that the last tenant had been evicted by death or dementia.

Alleyn, Miss F, was at the top of the list. Flat 1.

Caroline fumbled for the key, a mundane Yale on a plastic keyring rather than the chain and iron hoop that her grandmother had carried. Dead leaves blew in behind her, and one, still with its stalk, went skittering ahead, looking for all the world like a mouse running across the floor. Caroline stepped on it, more firmly than she had meant to, crumbling it into a hundred tiny ghosts that drifted away out of sight.

She stood for a moment, oddly reluctant to go further. The house felt chilly and neglected. One or two letters had been left on the hall table, and a garish pizza menu sat some distance from them, as if it were being shunned for its lurid colours. Dusty sepia photographs on the wall showed the house when it was surrounded by newly planted trees, its walls and gates unencumbered by ivy, the lane just an earth track instead of the tarmacked road it had become. Even the trees in the churchyard looked young and gawky, not the shaggy yews they were today. From somewhere above came a familiar tune: the Radio Two traffic news jingle. Despite the quiet, she was not alone.

The door to her grandmother's flat opened silently, like a well-trained servant. Tall French windows let in what was left of the afternoon's light as Caroline dumped the case beside the refectory table that ran down one side of the room, and pulled a sheet off one of the chairs so she could sit down. Once the Grange's drawing room, it had become a living room when Frances carved out a home for herself. She had only been gone for a summer, but even now the place felt empty and lost without its guardian.

Her mother, as was to be expected, had not listened to the suggestion that she come to help. *Good lord no, darling, I'm sure you'll manage and I've got such a lot to do here… just sort out her stuff, will you? Get rid of anything you don't want, see if Ruthie wants any little memento. Got to dash, darling, I know you'll do it all splendidly.*

And why should Betty have thought any differently? After all, until half an hour ago Caroline herself had been expecting nothing other than the chore of sorting old clothes and getting the house ready for sale. But now there was a piece of paper and a last message, and she couldn't shake the sense that everything was about to change.

*

She'd headed up the motorway from Oxford and into West Wickham expecting everything to be utterly straightforward. The will had been clear, although Frances's decision to leave her the house had been startling, to say the least. And so, safe in the knowledge that probate was almost done, she had sat in the lawyer's office with a calm expectancy that the firm would be as briskly efficient as her own. The solicitor, a small, plump man with a stripe of grey in his beard and wearing an immaculate three-piece suit with an actual watch-chain stretching across his waistcoat, had offered coffee, made a few professional pleasantries, lawyer to lawyer, mixed in with the usual polite enquiries about weather and traffic. Yes, your grandmother was a formidable lady. My condolences. If you could just sign here? Then that's probate all complete.

Nothing at all to warn her of what was coming.

'Thank you, Mr Akbar.'

'Please. Call me Geoffrey.' He must have seen the flicker on her face, and smiled. 'My father adored cricket. Hoped I'd end up playing for the county.' He patted his tummy comfortably. 'Alas, athleticism and I had little to say to each other.'

Caroline smiled briefly, shifting in her chair, finding it disconcerting to be on this side of the desk. 'I hate to seem rude, but I've had a long drive up from Oxford. If I could have the keys?'

Mr Akbar nodded. 'Of course. Of course. Here you are.' He slid the ring across the desk. Then he hesitated slightly, tilting his head to one side, and said, 'May I ask if you have any plans for the property?'

Caroline shrugged. 'I intend to sell – it's far too big for me, and I want to use the capital.' She looked around the neat, plain little office, the family photo on his desk, the dark wood bookshelves. It was orderly and welcoming, and she felt a sudden pang of jealousy. 'I hope to set up in practice on my own,' she said, with a faint smile. 'But it's not cheap.'

'As I know only too well.' Geoffrey folded his hands on the desk. He paused, as if trying to decide what to say.

'Is there some problem?'

'Well…' He took a deep breath.

A thought struck her. 'Has my mother complained about anything?'

'What? Oh no. No, nothing like that.' He looked momentarily alarmed. 'Do you think that's a possibility?'

'No.' Of course Betty wouldn't do any such thing. It would be too much work, for one thing, and besides, she'd been quite clear that she had no interest in the house. They'd met the solicitor just after Frances' death, when he'd told them about the legacy. He'd been embarrassed, clearing his throat when he got to the tricky bit. Shares, jewellery, an insurance policy to Betty; the house to Caroline. 'I hope that's not a shock,' he'd said apologetically. 'Do you have any questions?'

Yes, Caroline had wanted to shout, what the bloody hell was Granny thinking? But instead she'd looked at Betty, who had just shrugged. 'God, no, darling, why would I want that old pile?' she'd said. 'I always told your gran I didn't want it. Gloomy old dump, I couldn't get out of there fast enough.'

That was certainly true. Caroline frowned, partly at the memory and partly at what the solicitor was saying. 'So there's some other difficulty?'

Mr Akbar opened a drawer and took out an envelope. Caroline immediately recognised her own name, in Frances' precise copperplate, neatly central. Another line that she couldn't make out.

'It may not be problematic,' the solicitor said. 'And I did not think it was appropriate to mention it until probate was complete and the house was formally your own. But your grandmother was quite clear. In the event of you inheriting the house, and deciding to sell, I was to give you this.'

Caroline took the envelope from him. It was light, as if it only contained a few sheets of paper. Frances had signed across the flap, which was sealed with yellowing sticky tape.

'Do you know what it is?'

Mr Akbar shook his head. 'I'm afraid not. Miss Alleyn – Miss Frances Alleyn, that is – she just brought it with her and asked me to keep it with her papers. It was only to be given to you in the event that you decide to sell the house.' He leaned forward, earnest and kind. 'Would you like to read it now?'

Caroline glanced at her watch. 'No. No, thank you. I want to get to the Grange as soon as possible. I'll have a look tonight and then if there are any queries I'll come back to you.'

'Of course, of course.'

And with a handshake and further expressions of sympathy he had shown her courteously to the door.

So now she was here, sitting back in this room, back in this house. She lay the envelope on the table, sliding it gently back and forward on the polished wood. Frances' writing was clear and stark, bold capitals stating that it was to be read by the addressee only.

Caroline Alleyn.

And below that, slightly paler, as if the ink had been about to run out:

Caro, I beg you, ask them to forgive me.

2

The shout was a sharp bark that made her bang her elbow on the corner of the car door. The contents of the box she held jangled in protest.

'What are you doing here?'

Two old women and an equally old man stood at the front door. She recognised Mr Harris and Miss Fairfax, the elderly woman she'd met at the funeral, who were staring at her with identical expressions of suspicion and hostility.

'I'm sorry,' she said, trying to sound pleasant. 'I didn't mean to disturb anyone. I've come to sort out Frances – Miss Alleyn's flat.'

'Nobody told us you were coming today.' This was Miss Fairfax, wearing a neat jumper and a pair of what she would certainly have called slacks. At her side, a small indeterminate dog stared hungrily at Caroline's ankles.

'I'm sorry,' Caroline said again, trying to damp down a spark of annoyance. 'I didn't mean to scare you.'

'It would have been courteous to let us know.' Miss Fairfax spoke again. The smallest of the trio seemed to be hanging back a little, as if she had been detailed to leap for the panic button should Caroline make any sudden moves.

'I was only able to finalise the dates last week,' she said. She took another look. 'Mr Harris, isn't it?'

'Ain't seen you here for a while,' the man said. 'Not since your gran's burying back in the spring.'

Instinctive mitigation, born of guilt, made her say: 'I saw her as often as I could. But I – well. I'm here now.' She held out her hand, determined to get the encounter back under control. 'It's nice to meet you—?'

The other woman was introduced, briskly and quickly, making it clear it was none of Caroline's business: 'Miss Tanner, who is staying here in the spare flat for a while. She's been ill, I hope you won't be disturbing her.' When Caroline took their hands it was like handling kittens, they were so soft and fragile, but still with the threat of sharp little teeth should the grip be too firm. Afterwards the three of them regrouped, standing shoulder to shoulder and resuming their scrutiny. Caroline had the feeling they were all waiting for her to go so they could wipe their palms.

'I'm going to pop down to the shops tomorrow,' she said, feeling the silence begin to itch. 'Can I bring you anything back?'

'No,' they said in a short unison. 'Sainsbury's deliver,' Mr Harris added. His tie peeped over a hand-knitted pullover. 'We ain't ready for meals on wheels just yet.'

'Well, just let me know if you ever need anything,' Caroline said. 'I'll see you later. I'm sure we'll have things to discuss.'

She picked up the box again, giving an ungainly little stumble as the gravel turned under her boot. She nodded briskly to the stony-faced trio, then slammed the car door unnecessarily hard, as if she were putting a forceful full stop to the encounter. She took her time to put away bath oil and shampoo, and when she came out again for the next box she was relieved to find that her interrogators had gone.

By the time she had finished unpacking the day had, in the sudden way of early autumn, become quite dark. Caroline switched on the standard lamp and drew the curtains, realising as she did so that the service station sandwich she had eaten halfway through her journey from Oxford had dissolved long ago. Her stomach suddenly growling, she went back out into the hall and picked up the pizza leaflet. From somewhere upstairs the dog gave a sharp yap, and she could hear the low back and forth of voices, but couldn't be sure if they were the tenants or a television. Either way, they snapped into sudden silence as her footsteps clicked across the tiles.

There was a brief and undignified interlude, during which Caroline had to spell out the name Wickham Grange three times and the postcode twice, but by the time the moped sputtered away down the lane she had turned on the heating and opened a bottle of wine. She took the pizza and sat down at the table, where the letter lay like a flare on the mahogany. When she'd opened it, little furry wisps of old manila had scattered across the table like ash, and she brushed them aside with the side of her hand. She wished she could brush away what the letter had said with the same ease.

She had just picked up the first drooping slice of pizza – olives? She hadn't ordered any damn olives – when her phone chimed. Ruth's voice sounded bright and modern, a very welcome intrusion.

'Hey, you, how's it going? Is the place still standing?'

'Like we'd never been gone. I've taken off all the dust sheets and it feels like Gran's still here, just popped into the garden or something.'

'Dust sheets? Who has dust sheets these days? But you're okay, that's the main thing? I've been worrying about you.'

'Yes,' Caroline lied, pulling a string of mozzarella off her lip. 'I'm okay.'

'How are the old dears?'

'Spiky. Acted like I was already sending in the bailiffs. There's a new one, too, some little old lady I've never heard of. Mum must have let her have the keys to the empty flat, though she never said anything about a new tenancy. I'll have to check her paperwork, if there is any. Something else to sort out.'

'Grim. Have you made a start on your gran's things?'

'I'm planning to do that tomorrow. Shouldn't take too long.' So there would be enough time for the rest of it, she thought. She'd only read her grandmother's letter once, but already she was thinking of how to deal with it, get it over and done with, be rid of it.

'Hmm.' Ruth didn't sound convinced. 'Well, you know you're welcome here if it all gets too much.'

'Don't think I'm not tempted. But I need to get things sorted and I can't do that if I'm just lolling around with you.' Caroline looked around the room, its shapes and corners so well known to her that she almost didn't see it at all.

Ruth blew out a breath. 'I always loved going to the Grange,' she said. 'It's nice here, but Dad was always so busy, or in hospital, and when Eddie was at school… anyway, Mum used to say we came to see you for a break. The most peaceful house she knew, she called it.'

'Seriously? Even back then? There must have been, what, eight or nine kids at any one time.' Caroline remembered those summer days; the memories as delicate as the daisy chains she and Ruth had made, sprawled out on the lawn with whatever other children were around at the time, squealing with delight as they tried to stop the dogs stealing a lick of homemade orange squash ice lollies.

'Yes, but that's what made it fun, wasn't it? All those tree-houses and dens. Creeping over the wall into the graveyard, shitting ourselves in case we got caught.'

'I don't think I'd be able to get over it these days.'

Ruth laughed. 'Me neither. Though it seemed back then it was about ten feet high.'

'Everything feels huge when you're a kid.' Caroline looked at the letter, lying white and stiff on the table in front of her, and thought about telling Ruth what it said. But before she could speak—

'What? Oh for God's sake.' There was a muffled exchange and then Ruth's cut-glass vowels came back. 'I've got to go. Eddie has just informed me that four guests have become vegans since they booked and neglected to tell us. Why do people do that?'

'Who've you got in tonight?'

'Christ knows. It's either some bricklaying awards or a creative writing retreat. Anyway, just call if you need anything. I mean it.'

'I will. Hope you've got plenty of lentils.'

'God help the plumbing. Nineteen-twenties pipes weren't built for all that fibre.'

Caroline smiled, knowing how much Ruth loved the rambling Shenstone Hall, set in its Wiltshire downland.

'Let me know how you get on, okay? And I'm always here. You know that.'

Caroline did. It was the most comforting thought she'd had all day.

Later, her head too full for sleep, Caroline stood at the French windows, watching a fox contemptuously spitting out the olives as it licked at the pizza crusts she'd thrown onto the lawn. Her childhood bedroom was long gone but even so, when she eventually turned out the light, she did not need the faint glimmer from the street lamp in the lane to show the path to the bedroom; she could have found her way just through the feel of carpet, tiles, and coir matting underfoot, the subtle shift of scent, the texture of the wallpaper. The bedding she had brought with her smelled new and artificial, and for a moment she missed the striped Bri-Nylon sheets and cellular blankets of her childhood.

Wrapping her dressing gown around her, she went over to draw the curtains. The grass and flowerbeds were mottled with yellow light from the upper floors. It was a view which would have been familiar to Maud Shenstone herself, and to Frances on that unimaginably distant day when she had arrived here, never to leave.

Something moved. For a moment Caroline thought it was another fox — maybe even that rarest of urban creatures, a hedgehog? She looked again. It was a shadow cast from above, from one of the upper windows. There was the faint sound of restless, pattering footsteps but she couldn't tell where they were — in the hall? In the room above?

The shadow moved. Someone else was looking out. Someone else was awake. Were they watching her? Waiting for her to go to bed, to be alone in the dark?

She shivered suddenly. The thermostat must have turned

everything off. She got back into bed, pulled the duvet around her, turned off the lamp, looked at her phone. Gone midnight. She'd arrived here yesterday already.

The footsteps above paused.

And the light from that upstairs bedroom winked out too.

3

The next day the weather turned sharply to the east. Caroline was woken by the wind bumping and booming in the chimneys, while rain threw itself against the windows and beat the last remaining leaves into a defeated pulp. A good day, then, to put off the charity shop run and tackle the office instead. Maybe start getting a few valuations.

And to decide what to do about her other, unforeseen challenge.

She went out of the flat and across the hall, which was chill and shadowy. Mr Harris was coming down the stairs, a shopping bag in his hand, but only grunted in reply to her greeting as he shrugged himself into a mackintosh and a flat cap and hauled open the door. A sluggish waft of damp air crawled into the house, winding around her ankles like a wet dog.

It was with a faint sense of trespass that she unlocked the office door and let herself in. It was a small room, situated off the main entrance hall, separate to the flats now but once intended as a sanctum where the ladies of the house could check laundry lists or scribe dutiful letters to distant relatives. Oak shelves lined the walls, and a roll-top desk stood below the window, its surface dull with dust. Every inch of space was covered in papers, files, folders… Caroline opened the nearest one, the carbon paper dented with type. Something about – she squinted, then turned on the light – oh, a reference for a landlord. *Dolly Collins has always been an exemplary tenant… highly recommend…* Granny's signature. *P.p. The Hon. Maud Shenstone. March 1973.*

Not long before the old girl died. Caroline had liked Maud, a fat, inquisitive figure always in baggy tweeds that were covered in dog hair. She had smelled of mints and cigarettes, and her hands had been surprisingly deft, ideal for helping a little girl whose mummy was too busy – if she was there at all – to put her hair in bunches ready for school. It had been Caroline who found Maud one evening, sitting on a bench in the garden, her eyes staring blankly at the churchyard. One of her beloved hounds had been lying beside her in silent vigil, its head motionless under her cold stiff fingers. Caroline had looked for a long moment, then gone in and fetched Granny; that had been the first and only time she had entered this room without knocking.

Until today.

Now she sat at the desk and checked through its pigeonholes and drawers. A box of cards and letters was in one, but the others bore witness to Frances' flair for organisation: bills in one file, bank statements in another, a third for documents dealing with household insurance and maintenance. A practised glance at these showed that on the surface at least everything was pretty much in order, and Caroline carried them into the flat to read later. She had something else to do first.

The letter was in her pocket. She'd read it so many times by now that she could have recited it, but she took it out nevertheless, enjoying the smooth thickness of the paper and the steady flow of the copperplate. Her grandmother's words were as crisp and practical as if she were sitting at the desk beside her.

My dear Caroline,

I am in my eighties now and in the natural course of things I must expect some increasing frailty. Audrey recently referred me for some tests, but to be frank the outcome was far from positive and so I need to put my affairs in order. I have put it off too long, not wanting to face up to the situation I have created. Please do not think me a coward.

You are the only one I can trust to do what is necessary. Everyone else is too old, too closely involved, too vulnerable. I do not even know if some of them are still alive, so, Caro, it has to be you. Forgive me.

Firstly, I know it will have surprised you to learn that I have left the house to you and not to your mother. I did not do this to slight Betty; on the contrary, I have always admired her determination to live her own life in her own way. I wonder, sometimes, how things would have turned out had I had some of her courage.

But I have to face the fact that she would not be the right person for this task, and it is too important for me to risk failure now. And besides, it is too late to undo the past, something of which I become more painfully aware the older I become.

You will have already seen the other document that I will place in this envelope. I do not know how you will react; with irritation, I suspect, that there will be an obstacle to the sale of the house. Believe me, my dear, I wish things could be otherwise, but this is the only way I can think of to ensure that innocent people are protected.

I believe the correct term is a restriction — no doubt if I have misunderstood you will know the proper terminology — but I am assured that the effect will be that the sale may not go forward without the permission of the people named on the form. You will not know them. They are women whose lives were blighted here many, many years ago. It was because of me, and decisions I took then, that they have had to live in fear for so long. This is my last chance to look after them before it is too late, which is why I need your help.

Caroline, you will need to speak to them — to Grace, Harriet, Vera, Jane and Maggie. They will not want to hear the name Wickham Grange but you must tell them that I am dead and that they can prevent the house from being sold. That they can protect themselves if they wish. They will know what that means.

Above all, tell them that I am sorry. It was my decision to bring Lizzie to the Grange that sparked everything; I failed her when I lost her, and that is a terrible grief to me. And although she was innocent, her presence here was the catalyst for so much. Some of it, to be truthful, has brought great joy, but to my shame it meant these women have lived under a shadow that could still darken their last years. I want to prevent that, I want them to die in peace, so I need you to give them this chance to keep things hidden, as they have been for nearly seventy years.

If they do consent, then so be it. I have tried. If they do not, well, they too are old now, and nature will one day take its course. I can only ask you, in that event, to be patient.

I always tried to do my best for the women we helped, but I have one appalling failure, one soul that I let down, and she haunts me as I write. If anyone should have been safe here, it was that poor child Lizzie Sixpence, but I failed her when I lost her, and that is a terrible grief to me.

I know that above all you will do what you think is right. You have always had such a burning sense of justice; although we do not share blood, I hope that in some small way it is something I have passed on to you.

Thank you, Caroline. I am more proud of you than I can say.
My fondest love,
Your grandmother, Frances

4

Caroline stared at the letter for a long time. Dated the previous year… she remembered making a promise to visit, and had honestly meant to come, but the case she had been working on, and its awkward barrister, had taken up her every moment. On the day it concluded, Frances had had the first of several strokes, and although Caroline rushed to see her, her grandmother could never tell anyone anything ever again.

Betty had only just made it over from Spain before Frances died. As they sat in the hospital Betty's face had been taut and white with shock, and Caroline remembered wondering if her own features had the same stricken look. To see Frances – tough, indomitable, utterly practical Frances – reduced to this crumpled heap of a being was an insult, an affront to the order of things.

When they'd finally left, ushered out by nurses promising to call if there was any change, they had stood at the front of the hospital, suddenly rootless and uncertain. Traffic grumbled and whined and from somewhere came the sharp stink of cannabis. As if answering a challenge, Betty had lit up her own cigarette, ignoring the NHS prohibition on the wall.

'I've booked us into a hotel,' Caroline had said. 'It's not far—'

'As long as there's a bar,' Betty said. She shivered, wrapping her thin Mediterranean cardigan around her. 'Where do we get a cab around here?'

They found the rank, and sat in silence for the ten-minute journey. Around them, Croydon unfurled in a blur of lights and shouts, like a down-at-heel fairground. The hotel seemed eerily quiet and orderly in contrast, the receptionist barely glancing up as she tapped her screen and handed over key cards. Caroline checked her phone. Nothing.

She followed Betty into the bar, finding a couple of velour bucket chairs that were shaded by huge ferns in pots, so artificially glossy that it took her a moment to realise they were actually real. Betty ordered them each a large glass of Pinot Grigio.

'Are you all right?' Caroline had asked cautiously.

Betty raised an eyebrow.

'I suppose so. How are you supposed to feel when this sort of thing happens?'

Caroline didn't know. 'It doesn't feel real,' she said.

'Mmm.' Betty had taken a cautious sip of wine, then on finding it reasonable, a larger mouthful. 'Daniel not coming?'

Caroline kept her voice even. 'We broke up. Six months ago. I did tell you.'

Betty shook her head. 'Another one bites the dust,' she said. 'You've got to be careful, sweetie. A career and a business are all very well, but they won't keep you warm at night when you're old and alone.'

'You were hardly a role model for happy families, Mum.'

'I've not done so badly. At least I've got Mateo.' Another tilt of the glass. 'You'll have to come over and meet him. When – when all this is over.'

Caroline had made a non-committal noise. 'Maybe. I've got some big cases coming up—'

'Of course you have,' Betty had said drily. But then Caroline's phone had buzzed: the hospital, telling her that they were sorry to say that everything was indeed over.

That had been in the spring, what she had always thought of as the saddest time to die. Now the death of the year had brought her back to the Grange.

Thinking of her mother... she tapped out a text. *Hi, mum, here safely. The tenants nearly called the police, thought you said you'd tell them I was coming?*

No response.

She remembered the piercing guilt she had felt when the old man had questioned why she hadn't been a regular visitor. It had been a painful reminder, like a stone in a shoe or a wrinkle in a mattress, that she had not come as often as she could – should – have done. There were too many reasons she'd rehearsed too many times: work, the journey, the weather – and, of course, her own complicated feelings about the house and the childhood she had spent there. She'd seen too much, too young, and it had left its scars.

Whatever. She'd dismissed enough psychiatric reports to know that the workings of the mind cannot be pinned down and dissected. All she knew was that she would have to do as Frances had asked. She would make the calls and ask the question. If it meant she could break free…

Remember the house you fled to? Can I sell it please?

She picked up the photocopied Land Registry form that had been in the envelope with the letter. Five names, in Frances's orderly print. No addresses, but Frances had written neatly in the margin: *Addresses in the cabinet. The key is in the top drawer of my desk.*

Harriet Barker was first. Caroline unlocked the filing cabinet, setting the paper cradles rocking. Abbott, Ali, Anderson, Baker, Barker.

The thin file was held together with a fraying treasury tag. The cover bore just Harriet's name, and dates which Caroline assumed referred to her stay at the Grange: *8th November 1946 – 26th March 1947.* Inside was a single sheet, bearing the briefest of contact details – updated over the years, by the looks of things, as there were three addresses, all in the North West, two struck through in pencil. A phone number was only shown beside the last one.

'Okay, Harriet,' Caroline said out loud. 'Let's get you ticked off.' She paused. Harriet had left here in 1947… so the chances of her still being alive were not great, and it was still less likely she'd want to talk to someone phoning out of the blue. *Hi, I'm calling from Wickham Grange, do you remember when you were hiding here after your husband/father (and once or twice, wife) had tried to kill you? Great, let's relive old times!*

Only one way to find out. She got out her laptop, thankful that she'd persuaded Frances to have broadband installed – no wonder the old trouts were able to get their shopping delivered – and checked the code for Barrow-in-Furness. A long way to go, she thought; how bad must things have been to send someone to the other end of the country at a time like that? Wasn't 1947 the worst winter ever? She was almost sure she'd seen a documentary. Frozen seas and no coal, that sort of thing. Hand-knitted balaclavas.

Her mobile rang. A breathless, husky voice, born of cigarettes and raucous laughter.

'Darling? Just saw your message, you should have called. How are you?'

'I wasn't sure if you'd be awake.'

'Oh, sweetie, not even I'm in bed at – what is it, half eleven? I've been up for at least an hour.' There was the rumble of traffic in the background, and the sound of church bells. 'Anyway, you say you've seen the old dears?'

'Yesterday. They weren't happy that you hadn't told them I was coming. And you didn't mention that there's a new tenant.'

'Is there? I thought the solicitor was sorting everything out. It all totally slipped my mind, darling. Sorry. I'm sure you put it all right, though. It must be nice, seeing the old place again.'

Caroline could hear the clicking of a lighter. 'Oh come on, Mum. It's not like it was a happy family home, is it?' She broke off, not wanting to go there.

'But you saw that lawyer chap? You can start to get it all sorted out?'

'Yes.' No need for details. 'I'm going to get the estate agent in, and I'll need to get a survey done—'

Her mother sighed. 'Oh God, it all sounds terribly boring. Well, sweetie, see what you can do and then maybe you could come out here and have a break? Wouldn't that be lovely? It's still warm, the pool will be gorgeous.'

Caroline gritted her teeth. 'I'd love to, Mum, but I've got to get back to work when I'm finished here. I can't just go on holiday straight away. I'm going into West Wickham later, I can get the estate agent to come round later this week.'

'Darling, don't you think that's a bit too soon?'

'Mum, it's my responsibility, I can't just ignore it. If nothing else I'll have to sort out the tenants, surely?'

'Maybe. Look, I have to go—' *Of course you do*, thought Caroline grimly – 'I've got a show tonight, and the gallery's nowhere near ready. You'll be fine, darling.'

It was the best she was going to get. 'Okay. Oh, and, Mum?'

'Yes, darling?' One thing you could say for Betty, her good nature was unshakeable.

'I don't suppose you remember anyone called Lizzie Sixpence, do you?'

'Lizzie who? Sixpence? What an adorable name. A friend of yours?'

Most people's mothers know the names of their daughter's friends. Then again, most people's mothers know the name of their daughter's father. 'No. I came across the name in some of Granny's papers, that's all.'

'Doesn't ring any bells.'

'Look, if you do remember, can you drop me an email?'

'Of course. Anyway, must dash. Adios, sweetheart.'

The line went dead. Caroline laid the phone down and rubbed her eyes, as if she too were in the bright sunlight of Barcelona, the latest stop on her mother's artistic meanderings. At least Betty actually could paint, Caroline thought, otherwise she'd be a walking stereotype, the girl who ran away to follow a dream and ended up breaking her neck. Instead she'd fallen on her feet every time, even getting an interview on *The South Bank Show*. People had asked Caroline if she was proud.

She hauled herself back to autumn in West Wickham. Dialled. The line buzzed three, four times.

'Hello?'

An elderly voice. Caroline tried to sound gentle and friendly. 'Hello, is that Harriet Barker?'

A long pause. Then: 'May I ask who is calling?' Definitely wary. The clipped consonants of a generation who had a 'telephone voice'.

'My name is Caroline Alleyn. I'm calling on behalf of my late grandmother, Frances Alleyn. I believe you knew her?' There was silence, broken only by what sounded like a gasp. 'Frances left instructions asking me to contact a few people and let them know that she has passed away.'

The silence stretched. If it had not been for the wavering sound of breathing, Caroline could have sworn that the old lady had hung up.

'Miss Barker, are you all right? I'm sorry if this is a shock. Only my grandmother was quite specific that she wanted me to tell you that she had died and that she was sorry. Does that make sense? Miss Barker?'

'Thank you.' It was said with effort. There was an awkward pause. 'Ay'm most grateful.'

'Anyway, there was one other thing, then I won't hold you up any longer. I've inherited the house and I'd like to sell, only Granny left instructions that the house can't be sold without your permission. You and some other ladies.'

Caroline couldn't be sure, but she thought she heard a whispered, 'Oh God.'

'Please don't worry,' she said kindly. 'It shouldn't be very difficult – I wonder if I could send you the paperwork?'

'Sold?' Harriet sounded dazed, as if she had just heard terrible news.

Caroline tried to sound sympathetic. 'I'm afraid the house is much too big for me. If I can just get your consent it can all go through quite smoothly.'

There was another silence, deeper and heavier. Then the old lady's voice, when it came, was raw and naked, stripped to its marrow. 'No. You can't. You mustn't.'

'It's quite straightforward – all I need you to do is—'

'I said no!'

Caroline clenched her fingers around the handset. 'Miss Barker, please, it's not anything difficult. I appreciate it must be a surprise, and I know a lot of people find legal issues alarming, but I promise you it's quite straightforward. I would happily fund any advice you might want to take—'

'Shut up.' The old woman spoke with a force that made Caroline blink. 'I said no and I mean no. That damned house has to stay as it is. Do you understand?' Her voice was rising, the words becoming sharper until Harriet was almost spitting. 'It must be left alone!'

'Please, Miss Barker—'

But the old lady was shouting furiously and did not hear. 'You leave me alone!' she screamed. 'Leave me alone and leave that place alone!'

The phone slammed down with such force that Caroline jumped, dropping her own handset and having to fumble for it on the floor. When it rang in her hand, it startled her so much she almost dropped it again.

'Hello?'

'Did you just phone my grandmother?' A man's voice, rough and angry.

'Yes. I'm so sorry, I didn't mean to—'

The man's voice faded for a moment. 'It's all right, Nan, I'm telling her.' Then he was loud in her ear again. 'You don't call here again, you understand? Do you hear me? She's an old lady and I won't have her scared.'

'As I say, I'm really sorry. I'm just calling from Wickham Grange—'

'You what?'

'Wickham Grange. Your grandmother knew my grandmother.'

'I don't know what you're talking about. But you just listen to me.' He had pulled the receiver closer to his mouth so his words were muffled and rasping. 'If you call here again, if you make the slightest effort to contact my nan again, then I'll bloody well make you regret it. I'll be watching out for you, you hear me? Now fuck off and leave us alone.'

The phone was slammed down. Caroline put her own phone back in its cradle, realising as she did that she was shaking. The fury in the old lady's voice, and the hostility of her grandson, had been as violent and unexpected as a punch. She felt a little sick, the shock leaving a taste as rancid as sour milk in her mouth.

As she always did, she sought order and control, and clicked to start a spreadsheet. Name? Harriet Barker. She carefully typed in the phone number. Address. Outcome? None. She toyed with heading a final column 'Told to fuck off, Y/N' but decided against. She was annoyed with herself for feeling as disconcerted as she did; she had somehow imagined that Harriet would just agree, not react with such horror. But she was only one of five, and maybe she would change her mind if the others agreed. It had to be worth a try. *Pull yourself together*, she thought, *get it over with. Five old ladies, it's hardly taking down the bloody Krays.*

Grace Brown was next on the list. Caroline lifted out her file, as thin and uninformative as Harriet's, her dates too printed neatly on the cardboard. *18th January–26th March 1947.* Odd. Caroline frowned. Unusual. From what she remembered – but probably just a coincidence. Surely. Maybe they'd travelled together, gone on to – she flipped open the cover – hang on. Harriet had gone to Barrow, Grace to Coventry. So roughly the same direction.

There were four or five other addresses for Grace, the last one in London. That went onto the spreadsheet, and Caroline decided to get the rest of the files out to get them listed all at once, save time, get it over with sooner. Lee, Mortimer, Norman. Nothing under S for Sixpence. So Lizzie, whoever she was, hadn't stayed here. Was that what Frances had meant when she mourned Lizzie's loss?

But these folders… each one held just a single sheet of addresses. None of the usual detail that Frances, usually so meticulous, had kept as a matter of course. No letters, no cards, no nothing. Caroline couldn't shake the sense that this was strange, odd, out of place, that there was something about these five women that marked them out as different to the others who had been swallowed up by this house over the years.

Vera, Jane, Maggie, Grace, Harriet. All left on the same day, 26th March 1947, and as Caroline sat at her grandmother's desk she realised that that was what was itching. She'd seen countless families come and go, felt their rootlessness and fear as they picked up whatever it was they'd been able to salvage and walk out of those gates, but however much she thought back, she could not remember a single time when more than one or two people had gone on the same day. For five of them to leave at once was surely…

Coincidence. Again. She thought about the documentary. Twenty-sixth of March would have been at the end of the bad weather. They'd been snowed in. They'd taken the chance and gone at the first thaw. Surely?

But there was something else, something closer, something too close. Her mother had been born in this house, taking her first breath upstairs in one of the vanished rooms. Caroline had been vaguely surprised when she'd dug out Betty's birth certificate for the probate forms, and saw the neat typescript naming her place of birth as the Grange. For some reason she'd always assumed that Betty had been brought here by some desperate woman who had left her behind a few weeks later.

Abandoned her baby.

An act that had haunted her ever since she had been old enough to understand. Frances had been matter of fact, Betty hard and brittle, but each in her own way had said the same thing.

Your real granny isn't here any more. She couldn't stay here, she had to leave.

My bloody mother just cleared off. She couldn't be bothered.

Of course, in the end Betty had done pretty much the same. She just took longer.

Caroline went to rub her eyes, then stopped, as if for fear that the grief and despair of these meagre pages could somehow leach into her own mind. Thoughts jostled in her head, shrieking for her attention. One of them slithered to the front, seeping into her mind like venom.

Her real grandmother.

Was that vanished being one of these vanished women? Was that why Frances had made this last desperate attempt to find them and keep them connected to the house? Twenty-sixth of March… she clicked open the calendar on her laptop and counted. Betty had been born on the 12th. A tiny baby, just a newborn, left behind and seemingly forgotten until Frances had for some unimaginable reason taken her for her own.

My bloody mother just cleared off.

Caroline had given up, years ago, wondering about where she came from. It had become, not exactly irrelevant, but unimportant, something she couldn't solve and therefore wouldn't waste her time on. The truth, that Frances was not a blood relation, that she had taken on the role of mother and then grandmother, had been introduced to her slowly and carefully, as if it were some dangerous secret a child could not be trusted with. But now, with the loss of Frances and the appearance of these five women, the question started to flicker in her head, nebulous and fragile, a frail flame she could feel herself being drawn towards.

And a hard, pragmatic part of her that she was rather ashamed of couldn't help thinking, *If one of them is my grandmother then maybe she'll let me sell… maybe she'll help persuade the others…*

She put the files back into the cabinet, careful to place them correctly as Frances would have done. The last one snagged on something, and she pulled the drawer further out so she could free it. An envelope had fallen to the bottom, rucked up from years of being dragged backwards and forwards by the cardboard cradles. It must have fallen out of someone's file, and Caroline felt she could make up for her earlier shame by putting it back in the right place.

The envelope was unmarked, so she opened it in the hope that she'd find a name. Instead she saw it contained a single yellowing newspaper clipping, dated from, she guessed, some time in the 1950s, a black and white blurry image of a fat man and the headline *London gangster trial collapse*. Kenny Clapton, who'd been facing a ten-year stretch for armed robbery, kidnap and extortion, was waving to someone on the steps outside a court building. The article hinted at corruption and jury nobbling.

Nothing under C for Clapton in the files.

Caroline sighed. Just another puzzle in a day that was starting to feel like some kind of fairground ride, the house of mirrors or ghost train, full of twists and distortions. She clearly needed coffee.

She went back across the hall and into the flat, switching on the machine and savouring the smell as the drink brewed. The rain had stopped, but the wind still bounced around the trees, like a dog that wants to continue playing. The house was utterly silent, as if it were listening carefully to discover what she would do next.

She looked at the heavy marble mantel clock. Half eleven.

Grace Brown lived in Hackney.

She could be there by one.

5

Betty, 1966

Oh shit, oh shit, oh shit.

I've lost count of the days. I know Frances doesn't believe me, but it's bloody hard work studying, and who can blame me if I want a bit of a social life on top? I think she's stuck back in the 1950s, when I was happy to just play with the kids who were at the house. Not that I got the chance to do much else, what with her constant watching and warnings about who I could talk to and where I could go, but I'm grown up now, for crying out loud, who wants to be climbing trees or stealing strawberries or reading *Mallory Towers* at my age? I want—

Yeah, well, the one thing I crave is the one thing I can't have. Ironic, when you consider that the bloody place is crawling with mothers. There are two here at the moment, the usual pale and shaking women who look surprised if someone laughs. I feel sorry for them, honestly I do, and I catch myself wondering, was she like you? Did she sit like that, as if she would shatter if she moved?

I'll never know.

If it really is the eighteenth then I'm a fortnight late. Oh Christ, let me think. The fourth was Jake's party. We were drinking that wicked Polish vodka flavoured with quince. It went down like lemonade, that's all I can remember. Then we had the life class on the tenth, when I did that really good charcoal and the model was the woman with the glorious white hair. I did a babysitting stint here on the eleventh, so Mrs Whatsername could be taken out to get her train tickets and so on. She went the next day. And that was last Thursday and it's Thursday now and I should have come on at the start of the month.

Oh shit.

What if I am? I mean, I can go to a doctor in London to find out for sure, that's not the problem. I'm sure as hell not going to that old cow Audrey, she'd blab to Gran the minute I walked in the door. And I can probably pinch someone's driving licence or bank book if I have to pretend I'm married. I did that when I went to get the cap. Bloody waste of time that will turn out to have been if I really am—

Pregnant. There, I said it.

Whose? Who else? To be crude about it, my knickers went down as easily as that quince vodka. He only had to look at me and smile and that was it. Off to the bedroom, under the pile of coats. Under him. And I can't even blame the fact that I was drunk, because the only thing blurring my brain was desire. I couldn't believe he was even talking to me, let alone taking my hand and leading me up the stairs. He's new but he's already the centre of the crowd, and here he was, wanting me. I didn't stop to think.

So what am I going to do? I bet Frances knows someone who knows someone, but I can't face that. I'll have to go through with it.

I'll have to stay.

Oh God. Stay at Wickham Grange, to be surrounded by all that misery. To be woken up by other people's nightmares.

To have a child I'm not ready for.

Just like she did.

My mother.

Whoever she was.

6

Caroline

Number 28 was towards the end of the neat Victorian terrace, its front door painted a sensible navy and its curtains drawn back to allow in what little sunlight there was. Caroline hesitated for a moment, trying to smooth down her hair and get her breath back; she had misjudged the distance from the Tube and had had to walk briskly along what felt like dozens of identical little streets. But she was here now, and pushing open the gate she went up the tiled path and rang the bell.

'Yes?'

The young woman who answered the door was short and stocky, with cropped blond hair and at least a dozen rings in each ear. She looked at Caroline with a lack of curiosity that bordered on hostility.

'Is Mrs Brown at home please?' Caroline gave her a bright smile.

'No Mrs Brown here.' The girl had an Eastern European accent and wore a blue nylon tabard over a Pride T-shirt.

Shit. The smile snapped off as Caroline took out the form and checked. 'This is Levington Terrace?'

'Yes.'

'Number Twenty-eight? I'm looking for a Mrs Grace Brown—'

'Martine? Martine, who is it?'

'Someone looking for a Mrs Brown. I tell her to go?'

There was a long silence. The young woman turned and called back down the hallway. 'Mrs Edmunds? Mrs Edmunds, are you okay?'

A figure appeared in a doorway. Caroline took a step forward.

'Grace? Grace Brown?'

The old woman who had appeared in the hallway was standing very still. She was black, with fine white hair, wearing a long linen dress and a sensible cardigan. 'Nobody has called me that in a long time,' she said quietly.

Martine frowned. 'I tell her to leave, if you want, Mrs Edmunds?'

Caroline leaned round so she could see over the younger woman's shoulder. 'Please, I just need to talk to you.'

Grace started, her hand going to her throat.

'I'm sorry – I don't mean to alarm you.' Caroline took a small step forward, holding out her hand. 'I'm Frances Alleyn's granddaughter. From Wickham Grange.'

'Oh – just for a moment you reminded me of someone…' Grace gathered herself. 'It's all right, Martine,' she said. 'I can spare Miss Alleyn a few minutes.'

The younger woman looked dubious, but stepped aside. 'I will bring tea,' she said. 'And you shout if you need me, you promise?'

'Of course. Please, Miss Alleyn. In here.'

Caroline followed her into a neat lounge. The furniture was clearly antique, even to Caroline's inexpert eye, and there was no dust on the small television that stood in a corner. Bookshelves filled the alcoves on either side of the fireplace, and photographs of what Caroline assumed to be children and grandchildren smiled down from the walls. The room smelled of polish, and the sweet scent of some late autumn roses in a cut-glass vase.

'Sit down.' Grace pointed with her stick and Caroline took an armchair that proved to be surprisingly comfortable. The old woman herself took the sofa, looking across at her with watchful brown eyes.

'Frances's granddaughter, you say?' she said. Her voice had the thin clarity of age, but still with the lingering lilt of the Caribbean.

'Yes. Caroline.'

'Ah. I see. And what can I do for you, Miss Caroline Alleyn?'

'I'm sorry to just drop in like this. But – well, I'm really sorry to have to tell you that my grandmother died recently.'

Grace reached for her pocket and brought out a handkerchief, which she dabbed under her eyes. 'I'm so sorry to hear it. She was an extraordinary woman and I owe her a lot.'

'Thank you,' Caroline said. Maybe this was the right way to do it, in person, gently, not a phone call out of nowhere. 'Did you know her for long?'

'A few weeks. A long time ago.'

The door swung open and Martine brought in a tray which she set down on a side table. 'Everything all right, Mrs Edmunds?' she said as she lifted the teapot. 'Would you like me to stay?'

'No, dear, thank you.'

'You are upset.' Martine looked fiercely at Caroline.

'I'm fine, thank you, my dear. Miss Alleyn just told me some sad news. An old friend.' The hanky fluttered again. 'Only to be expected at my age. So few people left…' Grace looked up at her. 'Maybe you could make a start on the ironing? I find it so hard, standing for any length of time…'

'If you are sure.'

'She's such good girl,' Grace said when Martine had gone. 'My son pays her to look in on me twice a week. She's training to be a physiotherapist. She'll be good at it. Strong hands.'

Caroline looked at one of the photographs on the wall. 'You were a nurse?'

Grace glanced up at her younger self, hair in an immaculate French pleat under a stiff white cap. 'Thirty years,' she said. 'Matron. Or chief nursing officer, as we became.' Her eyes flicked back to her guest. In the sudden quiet Caroline could hear the faint burble of a radio from somewhere further back in the house. 'Please,' she said, 'tell me what you want.'

Caroline put down her cup and brought out the photocopied form. 'Well,' she said. 'It's this. My grandmother left me Wickham Grange, and I would like to sell it.'

'Wickham Grange.' Grace shook her head. 'Oh, that house…' She let her voice drift and her eyes went to the window, staring out at the grey, sulky sky.

'I know why you were there,' Caroline said quietly. 'I know it must have been very hard for you.'

'Do you?' Grace said. 'Can you begin to imagine what it was like, to be young, alone, black, in a world that saw you as different and unwelcome, even though you'd come here, in the middle of a world war, to serve the same country that despised you? And then to find that the one person you should have been able to trust and rely on was the person you were most afraid of in all the world? Can you really understand that?'

'No,' Caroline said. 'No, I can't, and I'm grateful that I can't. But I grew up there and I saw what had been done to the people who came there. I do understand some of it. Please believe that.'

Grace let out a long breath. 'I think you should go,' she said.

'Please. Just a moment more.' Caroline held out the letter. 'Like I said, I want to sell the place. But for some reason she – Frances – left things so I can't do that unless I have your consent. And that of some other people.' She was watching the older woman intently, and thought she saw a little pulse start to jump in her neck. 'I don't know why she did this,' she went on. 'She left me a letter – here, please read it.'

Grace scanned the first few lines, then put the paper down abruptly, pushing it away so forcefully that a corner got folded and creased under her saucer. But already the pulse was slowing and when she took another drink her hands had stopped shaking. 'Presumably you would like that consent.'

'Well, yes. I want to set up—'

'No.'

'But—'

'It's too much.' The old lady's fists were clenched in her lap. 'It's too much, I don't understand what you want…'

'Mrs Edmunds, please—'

'What does it matter? Your grandmother was right. Give it five years and you will be able to do what you like.' Grace turned her head fretfully on the cushions. 'Please. Call Martine and ask her to show you out. I am very tired…'

Caroline looked intently at Grace. 'Nobody came to Wickham Grange because they wanted to,' she said. 'I know that. Jesus, even I couldn't get out fast enough. My own grandmother, my real grandmother, she left the place when my mother was a baby – I don't suppose you know anything about that?'

Grace shook her head. 'No,' she said. She smiled faintly. 'I think it is safe for us to assume that you and I are not related, my dear.'

'But was she one of these women?'

'No.' Grace said it very quietly.

'Fair enough. But whatever crap you'd been through, whatever appalling things had driven you there, you survived. Even though you had to start again from scratch it didn't stop you building a whole new life for yourself.' Caroline nodded at the nurse on the wall. 'You got to the top of your profession, and believe me I know that that's a tough climb even in this day and age, and I've only had the sexism to deal with. You were even brave enough to get married again, by the sound of it.' She leaned forward and put her hand on Grace's. 'All that takes balls, Mrs Edmunds, if you'll pardon my saying so, so forgive me if I don't buy the fragile old lady routine. Shall we start again?'

There was a long silence. The clock on the wall let out a melodic chime. Then Grace sighed.

'You have a lot of your grandmother – Frances – in you,' she said. 'She could be hard, too.'

Caroline shrugged. 'Don't pretend you don't know how to play rough.'

That brought a faint smile. 'I learned the hard way.' Grace reached for the teapot and topped up their cups. 'As you say. Things were bad. For many years.'

'But you're here now. You survived. Can we at least talk about the house?'

'No.'

'But—'

'I am sure that to you it seems perfectly simple, but believe me, there are some things you don't understand.'

'I don't understand anything.' Caroline spoke more forcefully than she meant to. 'I don't mean to be rude. But you must see this is incredibly frustrating.'

'I'm sure it is.' Grace hesitated, then asked, 'Have you spoken to anyone else on that list? Maggie? Vera, or the others?'

'I called Harriet. You remember her?'

'I do. A kind, efficient lady.' Grace took a sip of tea. 'And I suspect she too will not discuss matters.'

Caroline remembered Harriet's fury, and added sugar to her tea as if it would take the taste of the memory away. 'She refused to talk to me. Can you at least tell me why? Is it something financial?'

Grace made a sound that might have been the beginning of a laugh. 'Oh no, child, it's not money. It's far more than that. Far, far more.' She sat up a little straighter. 'So. I am sorry but I have said everything I mean to say. You do not have my consent to sell. If you wish, I will put that in writing. And for the record, no, I don't know anything about your real grandmother.'

Caroline hadn't expected that to sting as much as it did. 'Is there nothing I can do to change your mind?' she said.

'Nothing.' Grace looked at her. 'Frances might have been hard, when she had to be, but above all she was fair. I think that fairness will have passed to you, too. I think you will respect my wishes.'

'Do I have much choice?'

'Not really, no. And I will save you some time. None of us will give you permission. I can tell you that with absolute certainty.' Grace got up, leaning heavily on her stick, and held out her hand. 'I found out who I was at Wickham Grange,' she said. 'I meant it when I said I owed your grandmother a lot, and for her sake, I am glad to have met you. And I am sorry that I can't help you. I truly am.'

Caroline held out her own hand, which Grace clasped tightly. 'Maybe you'll never understand,' the old lady said. 'I don't know. But I promise you, it is for the best to just leave things as they are. Please believe me.'

Caroline hesitated. 'Can I ask you one more question?'

'Enough. I have said enough.' And now the old woman suddenly did look tired, as if she were being weighed down by something old and hard and eternal.

Caroline followed her into the hall. 'There was another woman. Lizzie Sixpence. Frances spoke of losing her. Do you know——?'

Grace looked her full in the face. Martine was coming out of the kitchen, her expression stern. 'You should go now,' she said, opening the front door. But Caroline didn't move, just stayed looking into that old face that wore the lines of all its secrets like a labyrinth. 'Please, Grace,' she said quietly.

Pity shone on Grace's face for a moment. 'Lizzie was a victim,' she said quietly. 'More than any of us. I still pray for her.'

'Do you mean she's dead?'

But the young woman interrupted. 'You need to go. Mrs Edmunds, you come up for a rest.' Martine turned furious eyes on Caroline. 'You go,' she said again, 'or I call Mr Edmunds. I call the police.'

Caroline knew herself defeated. 'All right, I'm leaving. Grace? May I leave my details? In case you change your mind?'

She left a card on the hall table, and went out. The day had darkened again while she was in the house, and rain was starting to spit down from the tatty clouds that skulked over London Fields. The rows of bay windows seemed to stare at her accusingly as she walked past. A tortoiseshell cat stalked along a wall, pointedly ignoring her attempt to stroke it. She felt rebuked.

She had achieved nothing, learned nothing. Her footsteps seemed to beat out the words as she headed back to the main road. Nothing, nothing, nothing.

A black cab trundled past and she stuck out her hand more in hope than expectation, but it chugged to a halt and she climbed in. The driver was middle aged and luxuriously bearded. 'Charing Cross? Course, love.'

She leaned back in the seat. It was beginning to feel as if she was never going to be free of Wickham Grange, never going to be able to move on, make those changes that had seemed so close but now felt impossible—

Something buzzed against her thigh. She almost left it, not sure what would be worse, a text from work or her mother, but the thought that it might be from Ruth made her open her bag and rummage for her phone.

She tapped the screen. An unknown number appeared above words that seemed to spike at her eyes.

She could imagine Grace's long, capable fingers moving methodically across a keypad.

Please don't look for Lizzie Sixpence.

7

'CAN I HELP YOU?'
The library assistant smiled. She was young and slender, wearing a hijab of bright turquoise and emerald green; against the dull municipal furniture she looked like a jewel set in MDF. The place was surprisingly busy, with children running around and older women sitting in a circle around a table that was piled with coffee cups and knitting wool. The reference section was the only area that felt like a library, quiet and almost empty, the only other user being a man sitting alone at a table, a heap of old newspapers open in front of him. He was writing in a huge, battered notebook and did not look up.

'I'm looking for the local newspaper archives,' Caroline said. 'From the 1940s?'

The assistant frowned. 'Quite a lot were destroyed in the war,' she said. 'Do you have any particular years in mind?'

'Nineteen forty-seven, please.'

'Ah, you should be all right then. Just down here. Do you know how to work a microfilm reader?'

'Yes, thanks. Oh, and is there internet access?'

The librarian smiled. 'Sure is.'

'Great.' Because that was something else she had to sort out. Once she'd decided to go to Hackney she'd wanted to check which Tube station she needed, but the browser had stubbornly refused to load. No internet connection… she'd checked the cable, checked the plug, and eventually hunted out the router only to find its shelf empty, the wire dangling forlornly.

She'd looked up the stairs, but the doors were shut and the house was silent.

So now, exasperated and frustrated in equal measure, she was sitting here and taking out the legal notebook she'd brought with her. First things first: she'd see their Sainsbury's and raise them Ocado, quickly doing an online shop, choosing the essentials for the two weeks she'd taken off work. Not that she intended to be in the house for that long. She was tempted to sniff her clothes, to see if its smell – wax and dust and long dead dogs – had somehow seeped into her clothes.

Then, feeling faintly ridiculous, she threaded the first spool of film into the machine and wound it through the viewer. She watched as history blurred in front of her eyes. The end of the film flapped as she wound it, like the beating of wild goose wings.

She almost missed March. Stories about the snow, stories about shortages, power cuts, floods, a brave little photo of the West Wickham WI holding an Easter cake competition – hoarded rations, the caption made clear. And the edition of the 26th was just the same. Nothing to indicate why five women would suddenly leave, all at once, as if driven away by some unseen predator.

'Bugger!' Caroline let the word out before she could stop herself, more loudly than she'd meant to, then looked around guiltily, expecting to see a row of disapproving faces. But the Baby Bounce and Rhyme Time class in the next room was successfully masking anything she might say, and she went back to the desk, where the librarian was sorting through a stack of magazines.

'I don't suppose you have any other local papers, do you?'

The girl looked up. A tiny ruby winked in the side of her nose. 'Not many. Different boroughs hold their own archives. Were you looking for anything in particular?'

Caroline shook her head, realising how tenuous everything would sound. 'Just family stuff.'

'Was it definitely in London? Well, you've a couple of options. You could look in the *Evening Standard*, that would cover more than just this area. There might be something in there. Or you could go to the National Archives. It'd mean a trip to Kew but it's brilliant, I did a placement there and you'd never believe the stuff they've got.'

'It's not available on film? Online?'

The girl shook her head. 'Sorry. Not yet.'

'In that case I'll take the *Standard*. Thank you.'

The newspaper's logo showed crisp on the reader's screen as Caroline wound through to the end of 1946; nothing useful, but there was a stern letter to the editor, lamenting the breakdown of family life since the end of the war:

There has been a sad decline in the normal, decent life of this country. Men returning from the front must be able to come home to domestic stability, where they can take up their roles as head of the household, with women once more in their rightful sphere of kitchen and nursery, no longer the trousered harpies we have come to know.

Yeah, yeah, Caroline thought. She wound the spool back to the start of the year, skimming through rationing, strikes and the health service, her eyes getting tired with the tight print.

Nothing. No mention of Wickham Grange, no mention of Kenny Clapton, the man who'd been waving outside a courtroom ten years later, no mention of anything that would explain the sudden flight of five women so long ago.

By one o'clock her neck was starting to ache and she was getting hungry. She had tucked the last film back in its box and was just about to reach for her coat when a shadow fell across the table.

'Sorry to intrude,' the librarian said.

'What? Oh, are you closing?'

'No. Not at all.' The young woman smiled and sat down. 'Only I was talking to Rob over there.' She looked across at the man with the notebook, who gave an awkward little wave. 'I told him you were looking at the old newspapers and he asked if he could maybe help. Didn't want to come across himself, in case it looked a bit – well, you know.' She smiled. 'He's really nice,' she said confidingly. 'If you're looking for something in particular, he could point you in the right direction.'

Caroline thanked her, feeling a little as she had done in 1983 when a friend had breathlessly informed her that 'my brother fancies you and says will you dance with him?' She could almost hear Spandau Ballet start up the opening notes of 'True' as the librarian beckoned the man over.

He was big, with a dark beard that was speckled with grey. When he reached the table he held out his hand. 'Hope you don't mind,' he said apologetically, 'only Layla told me you were looking into some local history stuff and I thought I might be able to help. Rob Sayers. Er, do you fancy a coffee?'

After a split second, she nodded. He waited politely while she packed up her things, and maintained a friendly silence as they walked downstairs and out into the chilly afternoon, finding a small café in the high street that had by some miracle escaped being swallowed up by the big chains. She took a table next to an elderly man who was systematically cutting a muffin into chunks and feeding them to a dog that nestled inside his coat. Its black eyes were bright with enjoyment.

Rob came back with two flat whites, then sat down opposite her and proffered a bag.

'Cannoli?'

She shook her head. 'No, thanks. So, you're a researcher?'

'Sort of. By rights I'm a history lecturer.'

'Which university?' she asked.

He grinned. 'No such luck. I teach A level at a sixth form college, but I get a day off a week to do research for my PhD. Hence being in the library today.' He was dunking a pastry as he spoke, sending a flurry of crumbs down his jumper. 'Suburban London, post-war social structures and the impact of change thereon, 1945 to

1955. Demobilisation, women being forced out of the workplace, the introduction of the NHS and the crime wave, all that stuff. Layla helps me get old parish magazines, that kind of thing, and as you were asking about the same era she thought I might be able to point you in the right direction. What is it you're looking for, exactly?'

Caroline shrugged. 'I'm not really sure. I'm just going through some old family papers, and found a few things I want to check up on. People who were in our house in the 1940s. What happened to them.'

'You mean your family tree?'

'No. No, these are people my grandmother would have—' She hesitated for a moment, feeling a strange protectiveness towards Harriet and Grace and the others. 'Worked with,' she said at last. 'I was wondering if they'd been in some sort of trouble.' With a kidnapper and armed robber? It seemed outlandishly improbable.

'Lawless times,' he said. 'You sure you don't want one?' He proffered the bag again. 'Okay. Well, everyone thinks that after the war it was all bunting and the New Look, but really things were a bit shit. More than a bit, to be honest. Rationing got worse, not better, there were power cuts and shortages, people were royally pissed off – you get the picture.'

Caroline thought back to the letter in the *Standard*, and nodded.

'Do you know what kind of trouble your grandmother's friends were in?' he asked.

'I think,' she said carefully, 'that they'd left their husbands.'

Rob was looking at her with shrewd brown eyes. 'Battered wives?'

She was impressed. 'Yes.'

'I'd not be surprised. You had thousands of men coming home, most of them traumatised, trying to fit into families who had got used to them not being around. And, of course, there were no mental health services or anything like that. Plus it was still patriarchal back then, though my daughter would say it still is.

Anyway, if these women did leave, they'd be treated as the ones who'd done something wrong and the pressure on them to go home would have been immense. And the courts would almost always find in favour of the husband, especially if kids were involved.' He suddenly noticed the crumbs and brushed them away with a tut of annoyance. 'Do you have any particular years in mind?'

'Nineteen forty-six. Up until the 26th March 1947.'

He raised an eyebrow. 'That's specific.'

She fiddled with the lid of her cup. 'I know this sounds silly, but my grandmother wanted me to contact five women, and when I went through her papers I found that they'd all left her house on the same day. I know it doesn't sound much but it was unusual, and it ties in with – with some other family things. I thought there might be something in the papers from that time… some, I don't know, some disaster or government scheme or something that had made them go—'

'Like packing orphan kids off to Canada?'

'Maybe, but there isn't. Or at least nothing I can find. Is there anywhere else I can look?'

'What is it you want to find out, exactly?'

'What happened to make them all leave at once? What else was going on?' *Was one of them my grandmother? Would she let me sell the place?* 'Those old papers I was looking at, they were full of reports of burglaries and con men. Was there a lot of crime back then? Gangsters, if that's not being melodramatic?'

Rob raised his eyebrows. 'Not melodramatic at all. Did you know that the Sweeney was formed after the First World War because of the explosion in crime? Well, it was the same in 1945. All through the war, actually. Have you heard of the blackout ripper? Killed women under cover of darkness. Acid Bath Haigh, he was in the forties, I'm sure. Looting, desertion, prostitution, honestly, you name it, it went on. Why do you ask?'

'I'm not sure. Oh, God, this is all so bloody tenuous, I'm sorry.'

'History is tenuous. Full of what-ifs. Go on, if you want to.'

'I found this.' She took out the clipping about the collapsed trial of Kenny Clapton. 'This was in my grandmother's papers, I've no idea why. And it says this Clapton guy had been convicted of a robbery in Croydon, so not a million miles away, and I just wondered—' She shrugged. 'I couldn't see anything about him in those old papers that might connect him with the women. It's probably nothing.'

He thought for a moment. 'The assizes files are all at Kew, but they're not digitised and it'd be the proverbial haystack.'

'It might be worth a look,' Caroline said doubtfully, although the rest of the calls meant that she already thought she knew that wherever she went she would not find any easy answers.

I'm afraid Maggie doesn't want to speak to you. I did pass on your message, but she became very distressed, I'm afraid we had to call for the nurse. Please don't ring again. Our residents' welfare must come first. Goodbye.

Rob finished the last bite of pastry and dropped the bag into his empty cup. 'Look, I don't know of anything off the top of my head, but I'll ask around. You're definitely looking at 1946, 1947?'

'Yes. The winter of 1946 through to March. They all ended up at my gran's house in West Wickham, were there at the same time.' He looked curious, so she carried on. 'It was a sort of unofficial refuge, run by one of those bossy aristocratic women who headed up little units and committees during the war. Gran was her secretary, and I was clearing out her things when I came across this – mystery, I suppose you could call it.' She shrugged. 'I just want to know,' she finished, aware that it sounded weak, but not ready to mention the restriction, the sale, or the way that Harriet had reacted to her call.

Or to think about Vera, who had spoken in a soft Welsh accent. 'I'm terribly sorry to hear about your grandmother, but I have never known anyone of that name. I was never at that house and I certainly do not consent to anything. You're mistaking me for someone else. Leave me alone. I will be speaking to my solicitor.' Click, buzz, dead.

'And you think they might have been involved with this Clapton guy?'

'I suppose so. But there's some – some family stuff that makes me think that March is significant.'

She didn't want to remember Jane, either, who had been laughing when she answered the phone, only to hiss at the words Wickham Grange: 'Consent? Don't be ridiculous. I don't know what you're talking about. I shall be blocking your number and reporting you to my service provider.'

Rob nodded. 'Well, I can't promise anything, but I moonlight for the OU and I've got a colleague there who studies post-war crime. She might at least know where you can look.' He took out his phone. 'D'you mind if I take a picture of this?'

'Not at all.' Caroline held the clipping straight so the text could fit in the shot.

'Great. Have you got a number I can call you on?'

'Oh – sure. Hold on.' She scribbled on the back of one her work cards. 'That's my personal mobile. I'm only here for a fortnight, so if you don't hear anything by the ninth then don't worry. There's probably nothing to find, anyway.'

'We can but try.'

She held out her hand, thanking him. He looked surprised at the formality, but shook it amiably enough before picking up his bag.

'You know,' he said, suddenly sombre, 'you might uncover some nastiness. I know you probably see that kind of thing all the time in your line of work—' he waved her card – 'but they were very different times. Just thought I should say.'

Nastiness? Caroline watched him go, his burly figure squeezing between the tables. There would almost certainly be plenty of that. After all, it was what had brought women to Wickham Grange in the first place. It was nastiness that earned her a living.

The thought was unexpectedly unpleasant, like biting into a rotten fruit. She took a last mouthful of now-cold coffee, and let its bitterness sweep over her. It was oddly comforting.

*

Irritation at what felt like a wasted morning lasted throughout the drive back. She'd ended up with nothing new except a vague promise from a stranger, while all the time there were drawers and bookshelves waiting to be emptied, old clothes to be bundled up, cupboards to be cleared, shelves to be wiped and meters to be read. She'd stop off, shop for some proper food while she waited for the delivery – the pizza had repeated all night, she could still taste those sodding olives – then get on with the ritual chores of death.

West Wickham hadn't changed much, she thought as she emerged from Marks and Spencer's some half hour later. A couple of banks, a Wimpy – God, how many Saturday afternoons had she and Ruth spent in there? – Clarks, scene of many a strop over school shoes – it was like a tapestry of her past rolling out in front of her. She half expected to see her younger self emerging from WHSmith, clutching a copy of *Jackie* or *Smash Hits*.

Well, her younger self was long gone. In its place, the older Caroline walked briskly over the road and into the estate agents. It took just a few minutes to arrange the valuation; the woman behind the desk might as well have had a neon sign saying *Commission!* over her head. Would Monday morning suit?

It would suit very well. Caroline thanked her and left, but as she struggled to pull the door shut behind her one of her carrier bags gave way and a French stick slipped out of its wrapping. It went rolling across the pavement and into the gutter, where it was almost speared by the end of a walking stick.

'Mind yerself! Damn near had me over. I've had one hip done, I don't want the other one buggered just yet!'

'I'm so sorry.' She had bent to stuff other escapees back into the bag, and so didn't immediately see his face, but when she straightened up Mr Harris was looking at her coldly.

'Oh, it's you,' he said.

A stout woman with a shopping trolley tutted loudly and Caroline moved out of her way. 'I am sorry,' she said again, then, trying for a pleasantry, 'These bags, they don't hold much, do they?'

He ignored her, instead pointing his stick at the display of houses for sale. 'What you doing in there?'

'Just arranging for them to come out to the Grange,' she said, stung by his rudeness. 'I need a valuation.'

'You can't turf us out,' he said. 'You know that, don't you? Protected, we are. Your gran always said so.'

'Well, it's early days,' she said briskly. 'Can I give you a lift back?'

'Protected,' he said again. 'And no, you can't. I can get a bus, same as I always do. We'll manage just fine on our own. You'll see.'

'Fine,' she said, her smile evaporating. 'I'll see you back at the house.' A spiteful little impulse made her add, 'And we can have a look at your tenancy agreements. See exactly where we stand.'

He gave a little barking laugh. 'Good luck with that, love. I been at that place more'n seventy years, you ain't getting me out except in a box.'

'Let's hope that won't be necessary, Mr Harris.' She started to walk away, and then his words hit her.

She swung back round to find he was still looking at her.

'Did you know Lizzie Sixpence?' she asked abruptly.

He blinked, slowly, his wrinkled eyelids making him suddenly look like he had sighted prey.

'Now why would you be asking that?'

'Something my grandmother said.' She was watching him closely, ignoring the people passing beside them, the cars, the smell of rain on the air.

Mr Harris nodded. 'Ah. Well, now. In that case you're going to be disappointed. I never heard of nobody called Lizzie Sixpence.' He leaned in a little closer. 'And if you'll take my advice, miss, you'll forget that you ever heard that name an' all. For your own good, like.'

'If you've never heard of her, why are you warning me?'

'Best let it be. That's all I'm saying. Now, if you'll excuse me, I've got me bits to get.'

He turned before she could say anything else, and began to walk away. Caroline had a fierce urge to call him back – further questions, my lord! – but he had squared his shoulders and was already moving past tables optimistically set outside a new café.

'You're sure you don't want a lift?' she called after him; but in reply he only raised a hand in what could have been a wave.

8

Jesus, why had Frances kept that? Caroline ran a finger over the pencilled words at the top of the page. *My Family.* She remembered the teacher setting them the task – no consideration given back then to kids in care or kids who dreaded going home – and even more clearly remembered the teacher's face when she read what Caroline had written. Betty had been summoned to the school to be confronted by the headmistress, who had said very politely that whilst she understood it was the 1970s, and that things moved on, she'd been perfectly willing to have an illegitimate child in her school, even one with her – cough – family history of promiscuity. But, she went on sternly, it was simply not acceptable for Caroline to broadcast the fact that she was – and at this point she had lowered her voice, as if about to swear in church – born out of wedlock. It was nothing to be proud of, in fact she thought the child needed to be taught a proper sense of shame.

Caroline had sat swinging her legs, wondering what family history meant and whether it was something to do with the Tudors. Betty, however, had simply blown a nonchalant smoke ring and announced that at least she'd had a man willing to give her the time of day, and being a tart was better than being a shrivelled old bitch who needed to learn to mind her own business; come on, sweetie, let's get an ice cream on the way home.

There was something to be said for a rebellious mother after all, perhaps. Caroline could remember that walk home, her mother for once holding her hand, Caroline enjoying the strong, warm grip and the sense of closeness that had even then become a rarity. It had been a sunny day, nearly the holidays, and she had been wearing new sandals.

Betty had stopped suddenly, outside a little café. 'I said we'd have an ice cream,' she said, and Caroline, scarcely able to speak for a sudden bubble of happiness, had taken a seat on a red and white checked cushion and been allowed to have strawberry sauce.

'Do you want some, Mummy?' She'd pushed the thick glass bowl across the table.

'Just a taste.' Betty had dipped the spoon from her coffee into the glutinous red and white blobs. 'Yum.' But she had been distracted, pushing her cup round and round in its saucer. 'Did Miss Doherty tell you off?' she asked suddenly.

Caroline shook her head. 'Only a little bit.'

'Cheeky bitch.' Betty tapped ash. 'Bad enough having her looking down her beaky nose at me, let alone having a go at you.'

Caroline had accepted the scolding as part and parcel of grown-up irrationality, and was more interested in something else. 'What does beaky mean?'

'You must have noticed. When she turns sideways she looks like a budgie.'

Caroline giggled in delight. 'Budgie! Miss Doherty's a budgie!'

'Yes, well, don't tell her I said so.' Betty took a sip of the froth on her coffee. 'And don't tell Granny either, okay?'

'I won't.' Caroline licked a stripe of ice cream off the handle of her spoon. 'But why would she tell me off? Why didn't she like what I wrote?'

'Because some people are judgemental old cows.' Betty said it loudly, and a woman in a headscarf who had been staring at them looked away, affronted. Then, quieter, 'Because some people want everyone to be the same as them, and look down their noses when you do something they don't like.'

Caroline thought about it. 'Is that why Granny says I mustn't tell anyone where I live?'

'Maybe. I don't know. She always used to say that to me too. God, I wasn't even allowed to go to the shops by myself until I was a teenager.'

'Why not?'

'Oh, something about being safe. You know what she's like.' Betty was stirring her drink again, then said wickedly, 'You must be careful. You don't know who might be taking the wrong sort of interest in you. I would much rather you were prudent.'

The vivid impersonation made Caroline laugh with pleasure. And then, heady on sugar and sunshine and her mother's attention, she said: 'Why haven't I got a daddy?'

For one awful moment she thought she'd spoiled it all. But Betty had put her head on one side, consideringly.

'You're seven, right?'

'And a half.'

'Oh, you've got to know sometime.' She waved to the waitress, asking for another coffee, and Caroline waited, ice cream forgotten until a cold drip landed on her wrist. Betty leaned forward, took her hand – again! – and sighed.

'You haven't got a daddy because he wasn't very nice,' she said. 'I thought he was a good person but he wasn't, and he didn't want to be with us.' She squeezed Caroline's fingers. 'I'm sorry, maybe I should say it better, but that's the truth and it's right that you know.'

Caroline thought of the new friend who'd arrived at the Grange last week. 'The boy who came on Friday says his daddy hit his mummy and hit him. Did my daddy hit you?'

Betty stared at her. 'Jesus, you go straight to that? That bastard house – no, darling, he didn't hit me. He wasn't around for long enough.'

'That's good.' Caroline had another mouthful of ice cream. Then she said, tentatively, 'Did you have a daddy?'

There was a long silence and Caroline suddenly felt the sugar in her stomach curdle. She opened her mouth, began to say, 'I'm sorry, Mummy,' but to her surprise Betty shook her head.

'You've not got anything to be sorry for, sweetie. You're the only one who hasn't done anything wrong.' She pushed a strand of hair off her daughter's hot little face. 'God, it feels like only five minutes since your granny was having this talk with me.'

'Did you have ice cream?'

'Chocolate cake. And it wasn't even my birthday. I was fourteen,' she added, as if to herself. 'Four bloody teen.'

'What talk?' Caroline scooped out the last few sprinkles.

'About me. And my mummy and daddy.' Betty took a deep breath, leaning forward to speak quietly. 'Granny told me that she is not my real mummy. My real mummy left me behind at the house. And I don't have a daddy.'

Caroline's eyes were wide. 'Who's your real mummy then?'

'No bloody idea, darling.' Then she had sat back, watching the little girl who was sitting very still, thinking.

'Mummy—'

'Shall we leave it for now, poppet? I want to get back. I've got to do some work.' Betty paused, and Caroline, knowing the moment had passed, put her spoon neatly back in the bowl. Then Betty said suddenly, 'You do know that not everyone is nasty, don't you?'

Caroline had agreed, wanting her mother to go on, but the bill had come and Betty had not taken her hand again. Instead she went back to France the next week, leaving Caroline alone with her grandmother and nothing had ever, ever quite been the same since.

The exercise book went onto the *Keep* pile, a smaller heap than *Throw Out* and *Oxfam*, both of which were sprawling across the floor in a rash of bin bags. Books were stacked on the table, mostly *Reader's Digest* and Jean Plaidy, but with the occasional Agatha

Christie or Georgette Heyer, left behind when their owners moved on. Caroline had even found a *Lady Chatterley's Lover* tucked primly behind a *London A-Z* from 1985. She flicked through it. No London Eye, no Shard; Tate Modern still a derelict power station. She caught herself wondering if any of her women would have recognised the London they might have known all those years ago.

Her women.

Harriet, Grace, Vera, Maggie, Jane.

Lizzie.

All leaving behind only a name on a sheet of paper and – maybe – a tiny baby.

She'd left the box file cards on the table, going through it in search of clues. Nothing. There were dozens of cards, Christmas, Easter, birthdays; the messages were usually brief but happy, thanking Frances and Maud for everything, we'd love to see you again; hope 1968 is happy and healthy; it's Jackson now, do come and meet him; saw Betty's paintings in the paper, wow! Some held snapshots of babies and weddings and holidays, faded colour or blurry black and white. Time frozen in cardboard.

Abruptly, Caroline turned back to look at the room. She was starting to feel as if she'd be trapped in the past forever. It had taken her all weekend to get this far, clearing out wardrobes and drawers until the flat looked bare and vulnerable, and she couldn't spare much more time today for nipping at the heels of shadows. The estate agent was due in an hour and with the place looking like this, a couple of grand would be knocked off the valuation before you could say conveyancing. Besides, she needed something to distract her from thinking of furious old ladies, snarling at the sound of her voice. Caroline grabbed a couple of the bags by the scruffs of their necks, and strode out to the car in a savage fit of determination.

Twenty minutes later the boot was full of black bulges and the faint smell of old lavender. Just the paperwork was left to tidy away, and then she could put some coffee on, make the place feel a bit more saleable.

She retrieved the office key from where she'd left it in a bowl on the table, and carried the box file down the hall. Opened the office door. Stood for a moment, trying to pin down the elusive flutter of fright that went through her.

She went in cautiously, not sure why she felt so alarmed. The room looked the same. The piles of paperwork, the books, the dust, Betty's painting on the wall, all still there. The chair tucked into the kneehole of the desk.

The filing cabinet.

The cabinet key hanging from its lock.

The key she had left in her flat.

Her locked flat.

She pulled open the drawer. The files swayed. Caroline noticed with a kind of surprise that her hand was shaking, because she already knew what she would find.

Harriet, Grace, Vera, Maggie, Jane. Women who were somehow connected to the lost Lizzie. Women who had vanished from this house seventy odd years ago, their secrets locked in this drawer and guarded by her grandmother.

And now their files had disappeared too.

9

Lizzie, 1944

The foot is still in its slipper. She can't see where the rest of him is, but a foot's not too bad. The worst is when there are faces. Sometimes she dreams of them afterwards, coming to tell her to give their things back.

She turns her eyes away and wriggles further into the ruins. It was a terrible squeeze getting in, but she can just about stand up here and now she can turn on her torch, though the batteries are dying. There's just enough light to see that she's in what's left of the kitchen. Good. These people would have lived in here, it's where they kept their stuff. She'd learned early that in streets like these you didn't bother with the front parlours. No, she knows what to get and where to find it and it'll be in here.

Sure enough, there's a dented tin that's got a bit of money in it. Rent, or for the man from the Pru. Ten shillings. Better than nothing.

She pulls open a cupboard door but it sends a shower of plaster and bits of brick pelting down around her. She shrieks, startled, then claps her hand over her mouth. Too late. She can hear Sid hissing from the gap he'd made in the rubble. 'Shut up, you silly little bitch. Get on with it before the wardens come.' It had been a bad night, they'd be a while, too many direct hits. Mickey is on guard at the end of the street, all the same.

She pulls a string bag out of her pocket, risks the cupboard again. Tins and jars are quickly taken out and stowed away. There's a bar of chocolate, too, something she hasn't seen in years. Yank, obviously. She sniffs, longs to take a bite, but knows that if Sid knew she'd so much as licked it he'd tan her hide. He'll have flogged it before breakfast to some poor sod who'll cough up a few bob just to have a sweetie for his kiddies. She wonders fleetingly what it would be like to have a dad like that, one who brought you presents, even if they were taken from a dead man's house.

There is a sudden groan from somewhere in the wreckage. A loud crack sounds overhead and a bigger, sharper cloud of dust and stone hits her, making her cough. She has run out of time.

She starts back down the passage. The ruins are shifting, she can feel it, something changing in the air around her, like the way the pressure plunges when there is a hit. Her foot slips on something soft, and she looks down, sees a tiny blackened toy dog. It has a pink velvet tongue and she can't resist, she stoops and picks it up, stuffs it deep into her pocket. After all, she is only thirteen, and she has never had any toys of her own. Maybe she can hide it so Sid won't make her sell it.

There is another crack. Louder. She can see Sid, silhouetted against the grey light of early morning. He is twitchy, looking up and down the street. She's on hands and knees now, dragging the bag behind her. She can hear Mickey's voice, urgent with panic. 'Hurry up,' he shouts. 'Quick, the place is going to collapse—'

Sid snaps at him to shut up and at her to give him the stuff.

She shoves the bag through the gap. Planks and bricks have fallen across it, barring her way out. She shoves at them, getting a deep splinter in her palm that makes her cry out, 'Sid, please, help me…'

He looks up from where he's counting the tins. 'For fuck's sake,' he says, and for one sickening moment she thinks this is it, this time he'll leave me to get flattened.

It is Mickey who moves, extends his hand and grabs her arm. He pulls.

And Lizzie Sixpence clambers out into the cold air of a gritty London dawn.

10
Caroline

The estate agent was standing by the fireplace in the drawing room, mentally measuring up, her eyes flicking from cornice to skirting board to pelmet. Period features. Character residence.

'You say there are tenants?' she asked, looking over her glasses. They sat so far down her nose that Caroline wondered why she bothered wearing them. Perhaps she thought they gave her an air of gravitas when talking about stamp duty and searches.

'Yes. The house was converted into flats when my grandmother retired – thirty years ago, maybe? I need to check their agreements to see exactly what the situation is.'

'And they're in their late eighties?' The woman left the implication hovering in the air like a gnat. 'Well, it's not impossible to sell with tenants in situ.' She smiled brightly and made a note. Her name badge was partially hidden by the scarf she'd knotted round her neck in an attempt to brighten up a navy suit; she could have been Karen, Kate, Katherine, Kay. 'Don't you think?'

Caroline dragged her attention out of the office and back into the room. 'I'm so sorry,' she said. 'You were saying?'

Ka gave that shiny smile again. 'The location,' she said patiently. 'Best of both worlds. Some way out of the hustle and bustle, but close enough for convenience. I think we could get away with calling it semi-rural, don't you? Good links to the shops, transport, half an hour out of central London, potential to modernise – you'd probably get planning permission for an extension if you wanted to—'

'Why?'

'I beg your pardon?'

'There are four flats already. Why would I want to extend?'

'Maximise your earnings. There's plenty of land.'

Build over the garden? Caroline hadn't thought of that. She looked out of the French windows, down the sweep of grass and over to the churchyard. The rain had stopped and a damp sun was pushing aside the clouds, striking a flash of gold from the weathervane on the stubby little steeple that was just visible over a stand of poplars. A blackbird was on the lawn, dipping for worms. The earth smelled rich and restful.

And something was moving behind the greenhouse.

'So what would your estimate be?'

'As it is?' The woman looked at her clipboard. 'I'd suggest an asking price of around one point six million. It's a big house and it looks like it's structurally sound. You'd get more without the tenants, of course, and – forgive me – it is all a little bit dated. But if you put in some new kitchen units, had the wiring checked, maybe installed some double glazing, you'd probably get quite a bit more.' She raised her neatly plucked eyebrows hopefully. 'So would you be interested in instructing us to put it on the market?'

'Not yet,' Caroline said. The bright cheeriness on Ka's face went off with an almost audible pop. 'But I'll certainly bear your valuation in mind.'

Had that been rude? Caroline wasn't sure she cared. The woman had driven off in a branded Smart car, having optimistically left a card with her name (Katerina, as it turned out) and a promise to 'check in when you've had a chance to mull things over'. Caroline didn't even bother to watch her go. She was turning away and heading for the garden even before the car had turned out of the drive.

She went down a path at the side of the house, ready without knowing it for the loose paving stone that still wobbled underfoot. Then through a little wooden gate, heading past the caretaker's shed and the vegetable garden, where sad tendrils of twine still hung limply from the runner bean canes. Plastic clothes pegs in faded pink and blue drooped from a line strung between two trees, damson and plum, their sour fruit always eaten too early, she and Ruth seeing who could spit the stones the furthest. Dead leaves slithered slickly under her boots, and then the stone wall of the churchyard was in front of her, a low green huddle across the end of the garden, its ivy shroud dripping as it stirred uneasily in the gathering wind.

Caroline stopped, her breath misty in the air. Beside her, the greenhouse looked like some great angular bubble, so fragile that the slightest touch would send it collapsing into shards; the panes were stained and mossy, and a long, savage bramble had lashed itself along the ridge of the roof.

She had thought it was someone tending a grave at first. And then, dispelling that idea, there had been two brief flashes as the sun caught a pair of binoculars, before the figure ducked away and out of sight. It had been so quick, so surreal, that now she was here she almost doubted herself. That quick gleam of sun had maybe caught a window being opened somewhere down the hill; could have been a driver flashing their headlights as they headed west; perhaps was the leaded lights of the church glittering as the last autumn brilliance flooded the nave.

Maybe, could, perhaps.

No.

Instead, someone had been here, watching, and from the smell – familiar from a hundred cells – he'd pissed up the wall, too, so he'd clearly been there for some time. And there hadn't been just that sudden twin flash. There had been another light, and it was still here, glowing richly red against the dank ripe earth. A cigarette end, the smoke still wafting lazily up into the sky.

It lay beside a mess of footprints left by heavy, ridged soles that had trampled the grass and scuffed the mud before heading across the wall, through the rows of leaning stones and away.

She looked around, suddenly conscious of how quiet it was, how alone she was. Nobody but the dead knew she was here.

And they could not say who else had stood in this place, or if even now he was still watching her.

11

Betty, 1966

I can't pretend any more. I can't go on saying it was a dodgy prawn that made me throw up, I can't pretend I didn't need any towels this month because I had some left over, I can't say I'm just bloated from too much booze.

Time's up. I've got no more choice than any of the other poor bitches who cower here.

So I go down to the office and knock. Frances doesn't say come in, she gives a vague sort of hmm? sound. Less intimidating, she says.

'Elizabeth. Come in, shut the door. Just dump that lot on the floor, sit down.'

Then she looks at me, straight on, her glasses reflecting the light so I can't really see her eyes. She sits very still.

Two words, but I can't get beyond 'I'm…'

My knuckles hurt and I realise I've been clenching my fists.

I manage preg.

I can barely speak for fear, shame, panic, loss. Words come trickling out of me, then eventually become a flood as I tell her about the way he looked when I told him, the panic that flared in his face before it was replaced with a flat, blank stare. For a moment I thought he was terrified and then he spoke.

'You're mixing me up with someone else. For Christ's sake, don't cry, people are looking. Look, this should sort you out. Ask Jen, she knows someone.'

He'd stuffed a shiny, greasy bank note into my hand. Five pounds. Walked away, only turning to hiss one last thing.

'Don't ever speak to me again.'

He had gone within the week. Transfer to Glasgow, someone said. He'd always had more talent than the rest of us.

Frances is not my mother, although it's her name on my birth certificate. Twenty years of letting people think she'd had a bastard. Twenty years of being shamed and judged.

I don't know if I can be that brave.

For just a second she tilts her head to one side, as if she is listening to something from long ago. Then she reaches forward and puts her hand on mine.

'My poor girl,' she says. 'How utterly bloody for you.'

And with that, my tears finally come.

12

Caroline

The weak sun had not lasted, and by the time Caroline got back to the house it had started raining again in earnest. She had gone out so fast she'd not bothered with a coat, and now her hair was slick against her shoulders, cold miserable snakes wriggling on her neck. She ran a finger through them, finding a leaf that was snagged like a fly in a web.

'You'll catch your death if you're not careful.'

'Who's – oh. Miss Fairfax. I didn't hear you.'

'It's Doctor Fairfax to you.' The old woman was coming down the stairs, encased in a waterproof so shiny she looked like some enormous beetle. The dog trotted beside her, wearing a jaunty yellow cape.

'I'm sorry.' *Audrey has referred me for some tests.* 'You were my grandmother's doctor?'

'For fifty years and more. Not that it's any of your business.'

Caroline decided to let that go. 'Did you see anyone out there?' She jerked her thumb towards the door. 'Out in the garden. There was a man, watching the house.'

'Can't say I did.' Dr Fairfax looked down at the dog. 'Barnaby here would have barked if there was anything. He's a very good guard dog.'

As if in confirmation, the dog bared yellow teeth and growled.

'Well, if you're going out, be careful,' Caroline said. 'I didn't see where he went.'

'You sure you saw him at all? Dark afternoon like this, you

being cooped up all this time with your grandmother's old things – maybe your mind's playing tricks.'

'I'm sure,' Caroline said shortly. *Yes, I saw him and I smelled him and I trod on his fag end. Don't try and gaslight me, you old witch.* 'By the way, did Mr Harris mention I'd like a chat about the tenancy agreements?'

'He did.' Dr Fairfax was opening the front door. 'And my answer's the same as his. I'm protected. All signed and legal. Your grandmother asked me to move in when she retired, and she wanted to make sure that we were both safe, whatever happened to her.' She pulled up a hood which hid her face and gave her a long, pointed silhouette. 'You'd best go and get out of those wet things, dear. Stay in the warm.' And with that, she stepped briskly out, Barnaby giving Caroline one last narrow-eyed look as he followed.

Caroline shivered as the wind sliced into the house, but not just from the chill on the air. There had been something unnerving in the way the woman spoke, her steely determination not to show the slightest sign of cooperation or helpfulness. Her flat overlooked the garden, the day had only clouded over in the last half hour or so – there was every chance that she'd have been able to see anyone there. She could have set bloody Barnaby on any number of intruders if she'd wanted to.

And if that little rat on a lead was such a good guard dog, how come he'd not heard anyone going through the office? Caroline took out her own key again, experimenting; the click of the lock was loud enough, surely, and anyway, whoever it was would have had to come through the front door with its dragging, squealing corner. Barnaby might be Wickham Grange's answer to Cerberus, but he'd missed this.

Assuming, of course, that there had been anything to miss. She threw a calculating look up the stairs, then went to get dry, change, put on some make-up. She wasn't facing this battle unprepared.

Flat 3 was rigid with tidiness. The coat hanging on the hallstand had been pleated into neat folds, the boots underneath had their laces tucked neatly inside, and the walking stick stood to attention by the door. The wallpaper was a surprisingly modern print, but the furniture was as solid and boxy as the television, which was showing some early evening quiz programme. There were no books, no pictures, just a copy of the *Mirror* lying on the coffee table. Even a couple of cork coasters were arranged in a straight line.

'I was just about to have me tea.' Mr Harris had one hand resting on the back of a dark wood chair. Even indoors he wore a tie, and his leather slippers were shiny.

Caroline stood on the square of carpet, breathing in the smell of frying onions, trying not to read the questions flashing across the screen. 'I wouldn't have disturbed you if it wasn't important. I won't take up much of your time.' She gestured to the sofa. 'May I?'

'If you must.' The old man stayed standing, and Caroline regretted asking. The sofa was hard, upholstered in some slippery green fabric, and she had to tilt her neck to look up at him.

'I think someone broke into my grandmother's office this afternoon.'

His eyes narrowed for a moment. 'Broke in? I never heard nothing.'

'They had a key. They must have taken it from my flat.'

'What makes you say that?' He was standing very still, only his eyes moving as they flicked from her face to the television.

'There was only one key, and that was on the set I got from the solicitors when I came. I'd left it in my – Gran's – flat when I went out.'

'I'm forever blowing bubbles.'

She stared at him. 'I'm sorry?'

'What song's associated with the Hammers. "I'm Forever Blowing Bubbles".' He nodded at the screen. 'Sports round.'

'Mr Harris, please. I'm trying to ask you—'

'Why'd you think I'd know anything?'

'You're the caretaker. You'd know whether anyone else had a key, surely? Maybe you've lost one?'

He chuckled thinly. 'I been retired these past fifteen years,' he said. 'You'd have known that, if you'd bothered to show your face here once in a while.'

She sounded sharper than she meant to. 'That's no concern of yours. The issue is that someone has stolen some items from the office—'

'Stolen's a big word.'

'Papers were taken out of the filing cabinet. Personal papers, relating to some of my grandmother's – guests. Private information.'

'Then you should have taken better care of it.'

'It was in a locked cabinet in a locked room.' She stood up, anger making it easier to get out of the soft cushions than she'd expected. 'Are you sure you didn't see anything?'

'Like what? I been in here all day. Ain't been out since you nearly had me over in Wickham.'

She changed tack. 'The Wi-Fi has gone off, too. The wire's been cut and the router's gone.'

'Router? That little box with the flashing lights? Ain't seen that in months. Mind you—' He leaned closer, and she had to stiffen every muscle to stop herself flinching. He smelled of soap and strong tea – 'You thought it might be rats? Wouldn't be surprised, meself. Often hear a skittering behind the skirting boards. Old house like this, must be full of 'em.'

Caroline tried not to think of the pattering footsteps over her head in the night. She shook her head, as if to scatter that scurrying, furtive sound.

'There's something else. A man, out there in the garden. Did you see him?'

'You think I ain't got anything better to do than stare out the window?'

'Mr Harris, I don't know why you're so hostile—'

'Hostile? I ain't being hostile, love.' He finally pulled out the chair and sat down, leaving her feeling big and threatening. 'Anyone round here's being hostile, it's you. Turning up out of the blue, poking about, talking about chucking us out on the street.'

'I haven't—'

Mr Harris chuckled, a sound as dry and humourless as dust. 'Pull the other one. I saw that daft little car, that woman in the scarf looking up and down at the place like she were counting the bricks. I told you before, and I'll tell you again, I've got protection. Here, have a look.'

He leaned back and pulled open the drawer of a big oak sideboard, tugging out a brown envelope. Caroline recognised her grandmother's writing: *Tenancy agreement, June 1985.* Just about when the flats had been put in. She'd done a quick bit of research before coming up and he was right, if the agreement pre-dated 1989—

There was a sharp electronic beep. 'There's me tea ready.' Without looking at her, he stood up and headed for the kitchenette. 'You can let yourself out,' he called over his shoulder. 'Make sure you shut the door properly, seeing as you reckon there's a looter about.' He gave that thin chuckle again.

She went across to the table, picked up the envelope. He'd left the drawer open and a splash of colour caught her eye, something vivid and somehow familiar. Quickly, she pulled the drawer out a little further, then let go sharply, as if the handle had burned her.

There was a clatter of cutlery from the kitchen. Turning on her heel, she almost ran across the room and out onto the landing, where the last light of the day was struggling through the stained-glass window that took up almost the whole of one wall, making smudges of dull red and orange on the carpet. She didn't stop until she was down the stairs and in her own flat, leaning against the door and sliding the chain into place. Then she went into the lounge, poured a large glass of wine and downed half of it in one, hoping that it would calm the unease that swirled in her stomach.

It didn't.

She sat at the table, head in her hands. She'd not been here a week, yet she felt like she was being smothered – by her grandmother, by the women, by the lost files, by the man in the garden. By Lizzie bloody Sixpence.

And now by Mr Harris. Nobody had come into the house, nobody had broken in. She'd seen more than enough liars in her time, and he'd been good, very good, but that flicker of the eyes, the attempt to distract, they'd given him away. Of course it had been him, with his caretaker's keys, coming into this room, finding the office key in the bowl and then removing the files. Who else?

But why? And why just those five files, those names on Frances' list? Had he seen her letter? He'd known the name Lizzie Sixpence, that was a given. Why didn't he want her found?

She took another gulp of wine, almost choking as it caught the back of her throat. The questions piled up like litter.

And now there was one more that stabbed at her mind.

The brightness in that drab oak drawer had seemed familiar for a very good reason. She'd seen it before, a hundred times.

Her own graduation photo.

13

Lizzie, 1945

There are crashes coming from the street, flashes in the night sky. It feels strange not to cower, to know that they are fireworks and not bombs, to stand outside and not go running for the nearest hole in the ground. God knows where the bangers and rockets have been kept for the past six years, and God knows why anyone would want to celebrate this chill November evening with yet more explosions. But Lizzie likes them; she looks up at them blooming across the sky and can't help smiling. She puts her hand in her pocket and cuddles the little toy dog. It's her best thing and she loves it.

'What you grinning about?'

Mickey smiles at her. She shyly pulls her dress down; they've done it a few times now, and it's nice, even though she knows it's risky. When they started, back on VE night, out here in the garden, well, anyone could have seen, and soon it will be too cold. But she liked lying beside the patch of blue flowers that were somehow growing in the rubble. Irises, Mickey called them, though how he knew that is anyone's guess.

When he puts his arm around her she leans into him gratefully. They'd had to run from a site this morning, disturbed by a copper, and she still feels shaky. Maybe it was her monthly coming. Not that she could tell Mickey about that. Even June, who had grudgingly provided her with safety pins and a Kotex last month when she had her first one, had made it clear that after that she was on her own with it all.

'They're pretty.' She follows a bright red star as it drifts down, and he thinks how young she is, out here oohing and aahing. 'I wish I could draw them. I used to like drawing.' All those years ago, in the other time, before she came here to be with them.

'Maybe we'll get you some crayons,' he says teasingly. 'We'll find a school and you can help yourself.'

She shakes her head. 'Nah. I ain't going in any school no more.'

'You'll go where you're sent.' They both stiffen as Sid comes out. He's grown more menacing these past few weeks, looking ahead with calculating eyes to the new world of peace and the chances it would bring. The bombs have gone and the sites are being cleared, but there will be other openings, other victims, and he wants to be ready. There is talk that he's been meeting with the leader of another gang, bigger, nastier, crueller. She doesn't want to think of how that can be possible.

Sid picks his way across the filthy yard to where Lizzie and Mickey are standing. Beyond the broken-down wall is a wide empty space that had once been a street, houses, a shop, a tram stop. It has been cleared, but bits of wood and stone are still scattered across it like bones.

Sid looks her up and down, his eyes unreadable in the dimness. When he speaks it makes her jump.

'How old are you now?'

She swallows. She's known this was coming, but had hoped it wouldn't be just yet, surely not, it's too soon. When she'd brought the Kotex June had said something about getting herself some French letters, and Lizzie had asked how she was supposed to learn French when she hadn't been to school since 1940. June had laughed so hard she'd almost choked. Then she'd explained, but Lizzie hadn't believed her.

Until now. 'Fifteen,' she says, not able to meet Sid's eyes.

'No tits, no arse. It'd be like screwing a plank.' He takes a drag on a fag. 'But enough for some. Plenty of dirty old men'd be up for a skinny little kid like you.'

Mickey flinches. 'Come on, Sid—'

Sid turns, gives him a considering look, and Mickey takes a step backwards. 'Come on nothing. Who are you, her bleedin' brother? She earns her keep, same as the rest of you, and now there's no houses to get into she'll have to do something else. You think I keep you out of charity?' He grips Lizzie's arm hard, but she knows better than to cry out. 'See all that?' A wide sweep of his Woodbine takes in the rubble-strewn emptiness. 'You want to go back? You want to go back to where I found you?'

'No, Sid,' she says, and she is telling the truth. 'I'm sorry.'

He looks back at her, lets his face soften into the nearest thing he has to a smile. 'You're a good girl, Lizzie, ain't you. You'll do as you're told. We'll look after you, you'll be all right.'

'All right, Sid.' She whispers it, but what else is there to say?

He nods, then lifts her chin with his fingers so she is looking up at him. The unfamiliar light from a street lamp washes over her face, making her features look flat and empty.

'You'll do, with a bit of work,' he says. 'Go find June. Tell her I told her to doll you up a bit. Not too grown up, mind, there's plenty out there as'll get a hard-on just looking at you if they think you're a kiddie. Have a wash, arms, legs, in between. There's bound to be a dress and a pair of shoes you can have. Wear ankle socks.' He grins suddenly. Then he bends and kisses her, holding her arm so she can't move away from his tongue as it squirms inside her mouth, his other hand squeezing her breast so hard she winces. When he is done he lets go as if he were dropping a piece of rubbish. 'For fuck's sake tell her to give you a brandy,' he says over his shoulder as he heads back into the house. 'I can't sell you if you're that bloody frigid. You've got half an hour, then we're going up West.'

She takes a tiny step after him but Mickey blocks her path. 'You don't have to do this, Liz,' he says urgently, his voice low and panicked. 'You don't have to go on the game, we can, we can—'

'We can what, Mickey?' She touches his face, very gently. 'He's right. There ain't nowhere we can go. And if we did he'd find us, then we'd be done for.'

'But Lizzie—'

'Sh. It'll be all right. We'll get away one day.'

'When?'

'Gawd knows.' She manages a smile. 'Maybe when we're old and grey. Darby and Joan. We'll go dancing.' Another firework blooms and she looks up. 'Dancing under the stars. I'd like that.'

June appears in the gap where the upstairs window had been. 'You coming or what?' she yells. 'You might not want to do any work tonight but some of us have got a living to get.'

'I'll come with you,' Mickey says. 'I'll keep an eye out, make sure you're safe.' He swallows. 'I'll always keep you safe, Lizzie. I promise.'

'Bless your heart, Mick. You're a love. But I'll be all right. You stay here and keep Sid sweet.'

He watches her forlorn little figure pick its way across the piles of rubble and roof tiles that mark where the other house in this terrace had once been. She lifts aside the boards that blocked the door, turns and gives him a small, resigned wave, and is gone.

14
Caroline

Caroline woke slowly, as if she were swimming up through thick, grey light. The rain had stopped, leaving just a mournful dripping that sounded like the beats of a failing heart, and a branch brushed against the window as if the garden were seeking a way into the house.

She sat up, feeling the headache that had started last night begin to throb again. She'd slept badly, despite the wine, kept awake by the rain as it battered the windows and by clicks and grunts from the radiators, all competing with the high-pitched, unearthly yelps of a lonely fox.

She'd eventually managed to calm her thoughts enough to fall into a restless, uncomfortable doze. The flat was darker than her home in Oxford, so when she woke suddenly it had taken a moment to get her bearings, to register the shape of wardrobe and dressing table, its mirror staring blankly at the wall. Her phone said two thirty; outside, the rain was easing into a softer patter, like faraway tap dancing.

She was just settling back on the pillows, closing her eyes, when the sound that had woken her came again. Muted, but unmistakeable, awash with despair, someone was weeping desperately, their misery seeping through the chill air of the night. Then a scream, high and sharp and panic stricken, and running footsteps, a door opening and closing, and sobs, low and desperate.

Caroline sat up, snapped on the light. The room bounced into stark focus. She got out of bed, went through the living room, stood by the door, suddenly and unreasonably afraid to open it. She pressed her ear to the wood, knowing that just a few inches away was the hallway, the stairs, the echoing space that was the rest of the house. She had heard so many tears here, but this deep and relentless misery had such a tang of pain to it that it was unbearable.

She shoved the chain more firmly into its socket, and went back to bed, but it was a long time before she finally fell into a sleep that was more dream than rest, a confused melee of images and sounds, Mr Harris and Grace screaming at her, Maud's hounds baying, and underneath it all, this bitter, unceasing weeping.

Now, as the flat, dull daylight plodded across the room she caught herself listening again, but the sound was gone. She picked up her phone, swearing as she saw that it was already gone nine.

There were two texts waiting for her, one from her PA asking her to call the senior partner:

Mr Dudley says it's nothing to worry about, just wants to know if you'll be back when you'd planned. He'd like a chat about the next year's company plan.

Caroline thought grimly that if Mr Harris was a rock, then Charles Dudley was definitely the hard place. Tall, urbane, with a dashing sweep of silver hair, he had two overriding interests in life: breeding wire-haired dachshunds, and trying to get Caroline to move from criminal to corporate law. Inheriting the house had felt like a chance to break away, to start up on her own, be free of Charles and the partners and everything else, but now it all seemed distant and lost. She couldn't face yet another argument, and texted back a simple message that she'd speak to him when she got back. Maybe by then she'd have her escape open again. Maybe by then she'd have a new grandmother.

The second message was more welcome, from Ruth:

Just checking in, hope you're okay. Got a wedding here today and the bride's already in hysterics, have suggested I send Flora up, that'd sort her out. Mum a bit brighter and sends her love to Frances and Maud, I said you'd tell them x

That made Caroline manage a smile, though it was shadowed with sadness for the bright and vivacious Connie she had once known. She, Frances and Maud had been an unlikely trio, sitting around the table sharing tea or gin or cigarettes, always with a faint air of conspiracy about them. She remembered Betty saying once that they were the mother, maiden and crone; it had not been until English A Level that Caroline had understood the reference, but even at the time she had picked up on a sense of connection between the women that seemed to go far beyond simple friendship. Connie had married into the Shenstone family, and her friend Frances had been Maud's secretary, so they'd been close since the war, but even so there had been something… and now, caught up in the tangle woven into Frances' last letter, she began to wonder if they had had some shared knowledge, some need for secrecy that even a ten-year-old girl had been able to feel.

She got out of bed, wrapping her dressing gown around her more for the comfort of its soft folds than to keep out any cold, for the radiators were pleasantly warm and the carpet, though faded, was thick under her bare feet. At least the house was silent now, not even the slow shuffle of footsteps above to show that anyone else was even alive, let alone awake. She went into the kitchen, and got down the biggest mug she could find. She was glad she'd brought her own coffee machine, needing that rich earthiness to remind her that there was a world away from Wickham Grange, a world where she had a job and a reputation and old men didn't hide her photograph in their drawer. The picture was nearly twenty years old – how had that happened? – taken when her hair had been as spiky as her ambition. She couldn't remember much about that day, only that the beribboned plastic tube she had been given to hold in the photo had been hot and sticky from other people's hands.

So why had Mr Harris got it? He'd known her as a child, true, but that didn't explain anything. He had just been a remote, grey adult presence, with his little bedroom at the back of the house and his shed full of mysterious tins and jars. She sipped her coffee, remembering the smell of turpentine and oil, the rattle of the lawnmower and the clanking box of tools. *Would you be so good as to ask your ladies to excuse me*, he'd say to Frances whenever he had to go upstairs, *I'd be much obliged,* and she'd gather them all together in the drawing room so they did not have to see him. They'd huddle together on the sofa or at the table, trying to chat, eyes constantly flickering to the door, while Caroline watched and wondered and grew another layer of determination. *This will not be me*, she had promised herself. *Never. I'll make sure I'm safe.* The law had seemed such a safe haven, with its certainties and order.

Feeling suddenly rebellious, she ran a bath, pouring in a tenner's worth of Jo Malone before easing herself into the slippery water. She could not quite shake a sense of decadence at the fact she was soaking herself at this time of the morning, when ordinarily she'd be at her desk, takeaway coffee at her elbow and already deep in – what had Rob Sayers called it? Nastiness. She wondered if he'd been able to find anything, but Jesus, surely there was enough weird shit going on without him dredging up some more.

Steam curled lazily around the room and fat drops of condensation dawdled down the tiles; she tipped her head back, staring at the ceiling and letting the heat draw the tension out of her shoulders. She knew she could take her time. The sound she was waiting for would not come until at least ten thirty.

When it did, she was ready.

15

How had she come to know this so soon?

It had only been a matter of days, but the squeal and clunk of the front door had already become part of some almost unheard background beat. Mr Harris could have been a metronome, ticking out the rhythm of the house, with Dr Fairfax a close counterpoint, one on his morning stroll to the shops, the other to the end of the lane and back, Barnaby pattering and piddling at her heels. God knows when the other one goes out, Caroline thought. She hadn't seen Miss Tanner since she arrived, and as she'd expected there hadn't been any record of the old lady taking up any kind of tenancy. Everything that had happened since had driven the matter from her mind. But now she had another idea: maybe it had been her, looking out over the garden the other night, watching, waiting, a shadow amongst shadows, or her screaming and sobbing in the dark.

The idea was unsettling. She picked up Frances' keys, flicking through the plastic tags until she found the one she wanted. Then, carefully, she opened her own front door and stepped out into the hall. She stood and listened for a second, but the house was as quiet as a corpse.

Once on the landing she went straight to the window at the far end to check, but the drive was empty, the only movement being the sulky shifting of the laurels in the wind. The orange tinge of the stained glass made her think of insects trapped in amber, and she turned sharply away and back to the door she wanted. One last glance around, and then she was in.

She did not waste time. She went straight to the sideboard, pulled open the drawer, seeing again that strangely familiar face that unbelievably was her own. She lifted the photo, careful not to disturb what lay underneath, seeing instantly that the nagging suspicion which had kept her awake last night had not been misplaced. Sketches, more photos, a news cutting – another one? – were all tucked neatly away. There was a pencil drawing of the house, and a nearly there portrait of Frances, both rather self-consciously signed *EA, 1962*. An uncertain picture of a sleeping baby cuddling a stuffed dog. Here was plump and ringleted Betty, glowering in ballet shoes, baggy white knickers hanging out of her leotard, then Betty at thirty, her cheesecloth shirt open past her breasts, eyes invisible behind enormous sunglasses. There was a yellowing snapshot of a poster for a Lilles art gallery, advertising *Aquarelles de Elizabeth Alleyn, Aout 13–25, 1993*. Then here was Caroline in Brownie uniform, school uniform, bridesmaid dress and fancy dress. The *Radio Times* listing for Betty's TV interview. Caroline counted twenty separate images before giving up.

And underneath them all, the hard plastic shape of the router, its wires flopping uselessly in her hand.

She stood for a moment, not sure what she wanted to do. The photos had unsettled her more than she had expected, but beyond that unease – why did he have them? What was his interest in her history, her mother's past? – came the uncomfortable awareness that there was, in practice, little action to take. She could challenge him, of course, and she was tempted to do so, but as soon as the idea took shape she knew she would not. She'd be met by that hooded stare, and he'd say, *It's only some old photos. Your gran gave them to me, as a keepsake of old times.* Or it would be, *I found them and was going to give them to you if you'd let me have half a chance.* He'd have any one of a dozen explanations. And then he'd go on. *The router? It was broken, I meant to tell you. I'm an old man, I forget things.* Before finishing with a threat: *You break into my flat, not a day after you accuse me of stealing? Maybe I should be calling the police… it's harassment, that's what it is…*

The thought was exhausting. There was too much else scrambling around in her head for her to have the energy for this. She'd leave it, tuck it away until she was ready to do whatever seemed to be the best thing.

She looked at the clock. She'd been here ten minutes. Long enough. With a final check that the drawer was as she'd found it — you didn't spend an unhealthy amount of time with housebreakers without learning from their mistakes — she slipped back down the stairs.

She had the key in her own lock when the front door opened. Dr Fairfax was struggling to control the dog and shake out her umbrella, and feeling that it was more than the old woman deserved, Caroline went to hold the door for her. The doctor spared her a fraction of a glance.

'Thank you,' she said curtly. Then, sharply, seeing the keys: 'Where've you been?'

'I needed something from the car.'

Dr Fairfax nodded. 'Hmm. Come on, Barnaby.'

But the dog was fixated on something across the drive. Hackles up, he bared his teeth, emitting a long, deep growl that made Caroline think there might have been something in the guard dog story after all. The doctor twitched his lead, but he refused to move, standing square on his four stubby legs, quivering with malice.

'For crying out loud,' the doctor was saying, 'come on, I haven't got all day.'

Caroline looked out, trying to see what had agitated the animal. 'Probably a squirrel,' she said, remembering how Maud's dogs would streak across the lawn in a frenzy at the sight of any such small intruder.

'He should know better. Come on!' Fairfax bent, scooping Barnaby up into her arms, where he wriggled furiously. Out on the lane, there was the sound of an engine; a van, turning in at the gates, sounding its horn at some obstruction. The driver leaned out of his window, yelling something Caroline couldn't hear; Barnaby threw back his head and barked with rage, and then a man plunged out of the bushes, throwing himself clear of the van's wing mirror, which threatened to clip the side of his head, before stumbling to his feet and running for the gate. She just had time to catch a glimpse of dark hair, round glasses—

Caroline swung round to the doctor. 'You see? There bloody well was someone – hey, you, get back here!'

But although he was stocky he was fit, she could tell from the ease of his stride, whereas she was a middle-aged woman whose running days were not so much over as extinct. She had barely made it across the drive before he was out of sight, rounding the curve of the lane and away.

'Did you see that?' The Ocado driver was climbing out of the van, coming excitedly across to stand beside her. 'I nearly hit him, didn't see him until the last minute, you'll be my witness, he was just there in the bushes.'

'I know.' Caroline leaned a hand against the wall, trying to steady her breathing.

'You want to call the police, he's a menace, probably going to break in.'

And then an anguished wail: 'Barnaby! Sit still! No!'

Caroline swung around, just in time to see the dog finally squirm out of Dr Fairfax's arms and launch himself at the gate. She made an ineffective lunge, her fingertips just brushing rough fur as he pelted past her and out onto the road. Dr Fairfax was coming across the gravel, her face stricken, the lead dangling from her hands.

'Can you get him? Barnaby! Barnaby, here boy, come on.'

'Oh for fuck's—' Caroline flung her arm in the direction of the house. 'Leave the bags in the hall. She'll show you. Barnaby! Get here!'

The road was still slick with rain and the mud that had washed down from its grass verges. Barnaby had slowed to a trot, distracted by smells and litter, his snout down and his tail flashing white against the tarmac, but he was yards ahead and moving steadily away. When he stopped to cock his leg she closed the gap, but he looked back at her and she could have sworn he grinned as he ran off again, up the bank and onto the footpath that led down to the church.

Shit, she thought, *if he gets in there I'll never catch him*. But sure enough, he scampered past the porch and down into the graveyard, leaving her to pick her way across the lumpy turf, following the dog's upright little scut as he meandered in and out of the stones. She called again, furiously.

'Barnaby! Barnaby, you little arsehole, get back here this minute!'

'Is he yours?'

A figure straightened up from behind a table tomb and for one blinding moment Caroline thought, *It's him, he's waited, he's here—*

But it was a tall black woman, her hands in gardening gloves and her hair hidden under a bobble hat. She wore a battered wax jacket and thick, sensible boots.

'No, he belongs to my – someone I know. He got out and ran in here. Can you see him?'

'He went down there. Don't worry, there's a wall, he can't get far. What's his name? Barnaby? Barnaby! Come on! I've got cheese!'

'Cheese?'

'Well, I can hardly offer him a bone, can I? Look, we can head him off. This way.'

She strode off with the confidence of someone who knew every rut and dip of the grass. Caroline stumbled after her, some obscure childhood superstition making her try to avoid stepping on the graves, but the woman had no such scruples, treading briskly on arms and legs and skulls, stepping over tumbled headstones and concrete kerbs, only pausing to right a fallen pot of plastic flowers. Barnaby stood watching them for a moment, then with a contemptuous bark disappeared into the tangle of ivy that curtained the wall between the churchyard and the Grange.

'He's in there somewhere,' the woman said, coming to a halt in front of a particularly dense curtain of leaves. 'I doubt he'll get over the wall, and anyway it just leads into a garden.'

'I know,' Caroline said grimly. 'It's my house. He lives there.'

The woman looked up. 'Oh! You're Frances' granddaughter. I was very sorry when she passed, she was a remarkable lady.' She caught Caroline's eye and shook her head. 'Sorry. I always forget when I don't have the badge of honour on display.' She unzipped the wax jacket to reveal the dog collar at her throat. 'I'm Mel Cooper. Vicar, as you can see.'

'Of course.' Caroline remembered a gently moving eulogy, but little else about that day.

The vicar smiled. 'I would shake hands, but—' She displayed muddy palms. 'Since we can't afford a gardener any more it's all hands to the pump. Your Mr Harris helps out, bless him.'

'He's not my—'

There was a sudden rustle. Mel made a grab for the dog, but Barnaby was enjoying himself too much and dodged away, going deeper into the thick, wet leaves. Caroline swore.

'I don't even know why I'm chasing him,' she said, plunging her arm in after the dog. 'I can't stand the furry little git. Get here, you – ah! Shit!'

'Are you all right?'

Caroline extricated herself from the ivy, then pulled up her sleeve and examined the long, deep gash on her forearm. Blood was beginning to bead along its edges and she knew that a vicious stinging pain was just biding its time. 'I think so. There's something in there, something sharp.'

'Well, watch yourself. You don't want to go getting lockjaw or something. I wonder what it is – no, let me.'

Mel pushed the vegetation aside, snapping off dead twigs and holding back the long, snaking branches. It flushed Barnaby, who came bounding out of the undergrowth, and Caroline, feeling that she had really, really had enough, lost all sense of kindness to animals and grabbed him by the tail. He reached round, snapping, but that brought his collar within reach and she snatched him up.

'Oh well done!' Mel said in delight. 'This might be long enough, hold on.' She fished a loop of twine out of her pocket and passed it through Barnaby's collar, but he made no effort to get down and instead nestled in Caroline's arms. 'He likes you.'

'The little bastard can smell blood, more like.' Caroline bent to look at the gap Mel had made. 'Can you see what's there?'

'Looks like a memorial of some kind. Odd, we don't usually have those in the churchyard wall. Much more common in the church itself. I've got a torch on my phone, if I hold him and shine it, can you take a look?'

Caroline handed over the dog, who sat down placidly at Mel's feet, licking himself. She bent, knees protesting. 'Move it to the left a bit,' she said, 'I can't really—'

The thin beam juddered as the vicar shifted position. It picked out a square of stone, set slightly proud of the wall, its edges jagged and sharp. But the lettering was still clear, shielded from the weather by its green shroud. Caroline blinked, as if that would change what it said, but no, there it was, telling its tale again after so many years.

In memory of
Lizzie, 1947

16
Betty, 1970

Whatever you decide, don't let it affect your education.

That's what Frances said, and although at the time I thought she was missing the point – I was having a bloody baby, for Christ's sake! – today I am so, so grateful that she insisted I went back to college.

Because there's an announcement on the art department noticeboard and I swear that as I read it I couldn't breathe for excitement. Two weeks, en plein air, oils and watercolour in the Dordogne. Oh God, I really want to go. I haven't been anywhere for so long. I've just been here or at home, not fitting in properly anywhere. At college I'm the part-time student with the kid, the one the others look at with raised eyebrows and that oh-so-quick glance at my left hand when I say that I can't come to the party, I've got to get home, I haven't got a babysitter. And at home I'm the one who's surrounded by other people's children, and mothers who call themselves failures, even if they can't say the word because they've had their teeth knocked out. I made vows in church when I married him, one of them wept last week, and even when Maud said yes, and so did he, the poor cow didn't stop crying. They've been taught that they're wrong for leaving a man. Everyone thinks I was wrong for not having one in the first place. I'm starting to think that women can't win.

Did my mother run from my father? Or could she just not face the consequences of having me? Is that why she left? I don't know which is worse.

But please God, just this once, could I be me again and not just a mother? Caroline will be all right. She's a funny little thing, solemn and wide-eyed. Nothing of her father about her, thank God. God knows what I'll say if she ever asks, but I'll cross that bridge when I get there, maybe I'll just say what Frances said to me. Anyway, she won't mind. She'll have Frances, and the dogs, and Maud, and maybe they'll ask Connie to bring Ruth over as well. They can play together, they've always got on like a house on fire.

Anyway. I've got the money, I've saved up, and I can lay it on with a palette knife about how useful it will be for my technique. Who knows where it will lead? I'm an artist, I can't not paint, I might as well try not to breathe. I'll ask Frances tonight. And then, you never know, maybe for two whole weeks I can be free.

17

Caroline

When Caroline opened the door to her flat, she was not entirely surprised to find Dr Fairfax sitting at the table. The old woman was very upright, her hands folded neatly in front of her, but her eyes jumped straight to the muddy, triumphant dog and she wasn't able to stop the catch in her voice as she called him. Caroline gratefully let go of the twine, and wondered if eleven in the morning was too early for a very stiff drink.

'You left your door open.' Dr Fairfax had Barnaby on her lap, where he was briskly licking her chin. 'I thought I had better wait in case you hadn't got your keys.'

'Thank you.'

'I've put your shopping away.'

Caroline eased herself onto a chair, wincing both from the ache in her arm and at the sight of the packets of Always Ultra that had been left stacked neatly on the kitchen counter.

'It seemed the least I could do, in the circumstances.' The doctor sniffed briskly.

'I'm just glad we caught him.'

'We?'

'Me and the vicar. She was clearing up some dead wreaths and saw him run past.'

'Well, I don't want you thinking I'm not grateful.' Dr Fairfax leaned forward suddenly. 'What happened to your arm?'

Caroline looked at the bloodstain on her sleeve. 'I caught it on something,' she said. 'It's all right, I think there's some TCP somewhere.'

'Let me have a look. Get down, Barnaby.' Dr Fairfax peered and frowned. 'That needs cleaning properly. Wait here.'

Caroline was too exhausted to stop her. She barely had the energy to move to the sofa, where she stretched out her back, feeling her muscles squawk. She could almost smell the damp chill wafting from her clothes and hair, as though she had brought the mould and decay from the churchyard into the house with her, and she wanted to scratch at her arm, in case fragments of stone had lodged under her skin and were even now creeping towards her heart.

Mel had been professionally tactful. She'd seen Caroline's face, had caught her as she jerked back in shock. 'Are you all right?' she'd said, even as she was bending down herself to look. 'Good Lord. How long's that been there, I wonder? Does it say 1941?'

'Forty-seven,' Caroline said. She was staring numbly at the wall. She shook her head as if she could jostle her thoughts into order.

'I've never seen it before. I'll have to have a look in the records, see what happened.' Mel looked at Caroline again and frowned. 'Are you sure you're okay? That cut on your arm looks really sore. Do you want to come in for a coffee, have a rest? I'm due one.'

'No. Thank you. I'd better get him back.' Caroline took the twine, and Barnaby heaved himself reluctantly to his feet, plodding along beside her as they headed back to the gate. 'Oh, so now you run out of energy,' she said. She could have sworn he winked.

The path was narrow, so they had to walk in single file, Caroline leading with the dog. Her arm was beginning to hurt in earnest, and when the dog stopped to sniff at a white marble cross she winced as the twine went taut in her hand, and turned around to pull him away. The cross looked out of place amongst the weathered old stones. A neat inscription said simply, *The lost dead*.

Mel came to stand beside her.

'Our civilian war memorial,' she said, reaching out to touch it. 'A V1 fell just over there by the wall – you can still just about see the crater – and lots of graves were destroyed, and of course, when they came to clear up they had no way of knowing which bit of body went where. So they were all reburied here.'

Caroline looked back to where Lizzie's stone was hiding. 'But you keep burial records?' she asked.

Mel nodded. 'Yes. Well, sort of. We keep photocopies in the vestry, in case the family history types come round, but the originals are held in the county archives. Fireproof boxes and so on, you know the sort of thing. Do you want to come and have a look?'

'Please.' Caroline was starting to feel light-headed, and not just from the pain in her arm. From a letter to a stone… *Lizzie Sixpence, what the fuck happened to you? And why would Grace warn me not to find you if you were dead?* 'Let me know when would be a good time. I don't want to interfere with—' She waved her good hand vaguely – 'churchy stuff.'

'Of course.' Mel nodded, her eyes bright and intelligent. 'Can you do this evening? I have to admit I'm intrigued. Come to the vicarage, you know where it is? I'll get the books for the late forties and we can look in comfort. No need to freeze our bums off sat in the church.' She grinned. 'Make it after six and we can have a medicinal gin.'

And so Caroline had gone back up the hill towards the house, Barnaby trotting unconcernedly at her heels, while she found herself constantly looking back, as if she would see a long-dead woman watching her go.

'Leave it alone!'

Caroline jumped guiltily, snatching her hand away from her arm. The door had opened and Dr Fairfax was coming across the room, carrying – Caroline had to look twice – a gleaming brown leather Gladstone bag. The old woman tutted in annoyance.

'You'll do more damage if you touch it. And I don't suppose you've washed your hands, have you? Didn't think so. Now sit still. This will—'

'Shit!'

'Sting. Well, it's better than an infection. There. Keep it dry. I'll write you a prescription for some antibiotic cream.' She raised her eyebrows at Caroline's expression. 'You don't get struck off for being old, you know.' She snipped off the ends of a bandage, tying them in a neat reef knot. 'Take a couple of aspirin and get some rest. You look frightful.'

'Thank you.' Caroline couldn't be bothered to keep the edge off her tongue. 'I was kept up by the crying last night. Did you hear it?' The old woman didn't answer, so she went on, more forcefully. 'And you must have seen that man hiding in the bushes out there. Do you believe me now?'

Doctor Fairfax clicked her bag shut. She stood up, clipping Barnaby's lead back in place. Only when she was at the door did she speak.

'I think you're imagining things, dear,' she said. 'All I heard was my friend, who's had an operation and needed a painkiller. And all I saw was some young lad going for a run.' She gave a cold little smile. 'If you want my professional opinion, you'd better lay off the red. It can't be doing your blood pressure much good, a big girl like you. Not if you're seeing and hearing things, now, can it?'

And with that she was gone, leaving Caroline to stare in disbelief at the door as it swung shut behind her.

18

St Anne's vicarage was a plain, modern house that stood awkwardly next to the gargoyles and stained glass of the church, like someone who has arrived at a party only to realise too late that they were supposed to be in fancy dress. But the windows glowed, and when Mel opened the door Caroline was met with a blast of unidentifiable pop music and the smell of something simmering deliciously in the background.

'Come in, come in.' Mel stood aside, gesturing with her glass. 'Sorry about that racket – Amy! Turn it down! Now, let me get you a drink. This is John, my husband. Darling, get Caroline a drink, would you? There you go. Ice? Lovely. Come on through, I thought we could go in here.'

She led the way into a book-lined study. A huge grey tabby cat was stretched along the table, idly twitching its tail as it watched Mel pull out a chair for her guest. 'How's the arm?' she asked, noticing the bandage.

'Not too bad. There's a doctor living in one of the flats—'

'Audrey Fairfax? God, she's terrifying, isn't she? She was retired when I came here, but stood in as a locum now and then. She looked after me when I had Amy. Real old school, told me to put whisky on her gums when she was teething. The health visitor had kittens, but I have to say it worked.' Mel smiled, then patted one of two cardboard folders that sat in the middle of the table. 'Anyway, that's all ancient history. And talking of which, I've been positively saintly and not looked at these yet. Honest.'

Caroline looked at the folders. 'These are all the burials? I didn't realise there'd be so many.'

Mel shrugged. 'This lot is actual funerals. These ones—' she nudged the smaller folder forward, disturbing the cat – 'well get out of the way, then, you stupid animal – these are burials and interments. Ashes being buried, people who died elsewhere, that kind of thing.' She opened the folder, so Caroline could see the neatly written columns of names and dates that ran down the first sheet. 'I was thinking, how about you take one and I do the other? You choose.'

'Sounds sensible. You're sure I'm not holding you up?'

'Not in the least. Frankly I can't resist something like this. I got the impression you were quite startled when you saw the stone?'

'You could say that.' Caroline took a mouthful of her drink, which was not so much a gin and tonic as a gin that had once heard a vague rumour that something called tonic existed. 'I've been trying to research the name Lizzie Sixpence. It cropped up in some of my grandmother's papers.' She put the glass down. 'I didn't realise you knew her. Gran, that is, not Lizzie.'

'Mm. Quite well. Blimey, John's overdone it a bit with the gin, hasn't he? You sure you're okay with it? Well, I say knew her, she was a very private woman, but I saw her quite often. She wasn't a churchgoer but I'd see her in the garden, have a chat, and she started inviting me in for coffee occasionally. She was—' Mel paused – 'a little lonely, I think.'

Caroline started to say something defensive, but found herself nodding. 'I suppose so. Especially once my mother moved abroad permanently.'

'Oh yes, she's a painter, isn't she? Frances showed me a few of her pictures. I don't know anything about art but they looked very good to me.' Mel stroked the cat, which had decided to butt its head against her hand. 'I think she missed you. And your mum. She often talked about you both. She was very proud of you, especially. She'd tell me about your cases. Fighting the good fight, she called it.'

'She should know.'

'What? Oh yes, the refuge. Before my time, but my predecessor – Ian, did you know him? Really nice guy – he told me a few stories when I was settling in, giving me the local flavour, that kind of thing. I think he really admired Frances. He used to call the Grange the House of Hope. I got the impression that he helped with things like finding jobs for people.' Mel paused, remembering. 'It must have been an amazing place.'

'I suppose so. Bloody awful in other ways.' Mel raised her eyebrows, and although the dog collar was nowhere in sight, Caroline found herself wanting to explain. 'It was where my mother was abandoned as a baby, which was hard for her I think, not that she's ever really talked about it.'

'God, really? That's so sad. For her and whoever her mother was.'

'That's what Gran said.' Caroline couldn't help a half smile. 'I must have been seven or so when I asked her about it. My mum just said her mother buggered off at the first opportunity, but later, when I was older, Gran said that sometimes tragedy just arrives and we have to do whatever we can to bear it.'

'That sounds like Frances.' Mel smiled too. 'Nothing if not pragmatic.'

'Oh, God, yes. So anyway, she for some reason said that my mum was hers—'

'Really? That's amazing. I mean, back then, all that stigma.'

'I know. I've never been able to work it out. Even when I was a kid she was still getting sniffy looks and snide comments from one or two old bats.'

'After all those years? Some people are just plain spiteful, aren't they? Not that I'm allowed to judge, but still.'

Caroline laughed, just for a moment. 'What I could never understand is why she didn't just adopt, if she wanted a child? The best I can come up with is that she knew the procedures would take forever and she might get turned down, being unmarried, so she did the next best thing and to hell with what the neighbours thought.'

'That's really brave.'

'It is,' Caroline said, and was surprised to realise that she'd never thought of it like that before. She shook the thought away. 'Anyway, I was born when Mum was still a teenager herself. Unmarried in the sixties and seventies – well, you can imagine. History repeating itself, blah blah. "Runs in the family," they'd say. I can remember asking her if that meant we'd win races. She had nowhere else to go, so she stayed at the Grange, and I think she resented it, which is why she left as soon as she could. Took her life back.' Caroline shrugged. 'So to me it was a house where my mum wasn't there and I was surrounded by people going through the worst possible times of their life.'

'Not easy for a little girl. Oh, I am sorry.'

The warmth of Mel's genuine sympathy was like balm, and Caroline took another drink. Surely it was just the gin that made unexpected tears prickle in her throat? 'It wasn't so bad when I was small,' she said. 'Always someone to play with, that kind of thing. But then eventually—' She paused. 'Eventually I realised what was really happening, what these women had been through.'

'It must have left its mark,' Mel said gently.

Caroline took a mouthful of her drink. 'Frightened the living daylights out of me, to be honest. Made me realise what can happen in people's lives. How dangerous other people can be.'

'But it was a place of hope, all the same?' Mel said. 'For the women, I mean?'

'I never saw it like that. Though I suppose so.'

'The first stage in their new lives. Wow, imagine walking through that front door for the first time – I know it startled me when I first went there.'

'At least you didn't have to run the gauntlet of Maud's dogs.' Caroline took a deep breath. 'Anyway, it was all a long time ago,' she said. 'I worked like mad to get good grades and left when I went to uni. Haven't really been back since.'

'Until now.'

'No. I know I should have come more often…'

Mel raised her hands. 'I'm not judging. You did what was right for you. Sorry, I know I'm interrogating, it's an occupational hazard. For what it's worth I can see how it would have been a hard place to forget, not that it's any of my business.' She patted the files. 'I'll shut up.'

'No need,' said Caroline, and meant it. There was something oddly reassuring about the conversation, as if by speaking she was giving the old hurts and fears a shape, a solidity, that made them tidier and easier to hold.

Mel smiled. 'Shall we have a look and see if we can find your Miss Sixpence?'

'Please.' Caroline pulled one of the folders towards her.

'Okay. For crying out loud, Zadok, get down. Well, shall we have a top-up to fortify ourselves before we start?'

<h1 style="text-align:center">19</h1>

The rich smell had turned out to be a casserole, served with chilli dumplings and a garlic bread of such ferocity that as she walked back up the lane Caroline imagined she could hear the thud of dying vampires plunging to the ground. She suspected that three more gins and no tonic probably had something to do with that.

The Coopers had insisted she stay for dinner, and then John had very simply and kindly said he would escort her home; whereas a week ago she would have politely declined the offer, now she was glad of his presence as they turned into the gates of Wickham Grange. She deliberately didn't look at the dark spot in the bushes where the man had been hiding, and didn't like to think that even now he could be somewhere, watching and waiting.

The evening at the vicarage had been full of laughter and chatter, the teenage Amy agog to hear about Caroline's work– had she met any serial killers? Did she wear a wig? Did she go to crime scenes? When the answers had all been no, she'd looked disappointed, only to perk up again when Caroline had taken pity and described her visits to cells and courtrooms, with judiciously edited anecdotes about some of her more salubrious clients. By the end of the evening Amy was googling law courses and Caroline, rather to her own surprise, had offered a week's work experience. Surrounded by the ordinary and the comfortable – the cat, the mismatched cutlery, *The Archers'* theme tune – she had felt herself relax for the first time in what seemed like weeks.

But now, back in the flat, she felt suddenly lost. She poured a glass of wine, but pushed it aside after one mouthful, its sharp fruitiness too much. Instead she made tea, knowing it would wake her up for a pee at least three times in the night, but not caring. She doubted she would sleep anyway. There were too many questions and puzzles batting at her mind, as Zadok had batted a ping-pong ball around the vicarage kitchen. It felt as though her head were full of snares that trapped her thoughts, and that they were struggling to get free, to line themselves up in some kind of order but slipping and writhing away again before she could hear or see them clearly.

Oh, Lizzie. She rubbed her hand across her eyes, leaving a dark streak of smudged mascara on her wrist. *How did Granny lose you? And how did she fail you?*

The ice cubes in her gin at Mel's had barely started to melt before she'd found it. Not the name Sixpence, but another, just as familiar, in neat block letters.

Mary White had been buried on the fifteenth of February. Robert Stourton had gone to his grave on the twenty-first. Caroline had a sudden image of chilled mourners, heaps of bomb debris scattered amongst the tombs, a gravedigger struggling to send his pick through frozen earth. But in the middle of March he had had an easier task. He must have been glad of it.

Installed memorial on West wall of churchyard, the note read. *Commissioned by The Hon. Maud Shenstone. Payment waived.*

Mel had shaken her head. 'It doesn't mean Lizzie's not buried there,' she said. 'Do you know who this Maud Shenstone was? She must have had some clout if they let her off paying for it.'

'She owned the Grange,' Caroline said. 'Left it to my gran when she died, back in the early seventies. Her nephew married Gran's best friend.'

'Bit of a tangle, then,' Mel had said sympathetically. 'Any connection you know of with this Lizzie? Was she a relation or something?'

'Not that I've found. She was just mentioned in some stuff I'm sorting out.' *And she's lodged in my head with the others and she follows me around, and even if she is dead she's steering my life into places I don't want to go.*

She felt a sudden fierce need to make something happen, to stop this sense of floating helplessness. She looked at the marble Art Deco clock that had stood on the mantle – no, the chimney-piece, she corrected herself, Maud's insistence on the correct terms lingering even now – for more than seventy years. Nine thirty. Add on an hour. The gallery closed at ten. She sent a quick text, then flipped open her laptop.

Betty's face, when it appeared on the screen, was tanned and glowing, her hair up in the sort of elaborate knot that Caroline could never manage. Peacock-blue glitter twinkled on her eyelids and her lipstick was deep and lush.

'Darling! What a lovely surprise, I was just talking about you when I got your text.' There were voices in the background, and Betty glanced over her shoulder. 'It's my daughter,' she said to someone unseen, 'yes, the lawyer. Oh, you go ahead, the prawns are in the fridge. Open another bottle, would you?' Then back to Caroline: 'Is everything all right? Are you okay?'

'I didn't realise you had company,' Caroline said. 'I'll call back—'

'Nonsense. It's just Mateo and a few friends who came to the show.'

'Oh. How's it going?'

'Super. Quite a few sales, and I think there'll be at least one commission in the bag if I play my cards right.' A man's hand appeared, handing her a brimming champagne flute. 'Bless you. So, darling, did you need something?'

For a blinding second, Caroline wanted more than anything in the world to whisper, *Yes, I want my mum.* She had longed to say it nearly forty years ago, when she had stood in this very room watching Betty getting ready to disappear, but then, as now, had choked it back down so all that was left was the faintest echo in her head. *Mum, please, Mummy, don't go…*

Disappearing women. Wickham Grange seemed to lure them in

through its heavy iron gates and then – where? A Spanish art show, an Oxford office?

A stone in a wall?

She swallowed another mouthful of wine. The tea already looked oily and unattractive, like a teenage boyfriend met again in middle age. 'Mum, I'm sorry if this isn't a good time, but I wanted to let you know about the house. The agent's saying it'll be snapped up by developers. I'm definitely going to sell.' *If I can,* she added silently.

'Did they say a price?'

'Well over a million. Even with the tenants.'

'Goodness. That's more than I thought. You'll be rich.'

'There'll be tax, Mum, and the place needs work…'

'Trust you to see the boring side. Think of the fun you could have!'

'I really just wanted to know what you think. If you think it's a good idea?'

Betty took a sip of her champagne. 'Oh, I don't know, sweetie. Are you sure? It's been part of the family for such a long time – we both grew up there, after all. What's the hurry?'

'I'm only here for another week, it'd be good to get it sorted out before I go back to Oxford.' Caroline let out a breath. 'I just think we should get rid of the place.'

'Why? There's nothing wrong, is there?'

'No, Mum.' *No, just weird sobs in the night and my pictures being hoarded by the caretaker and someone watching the house.* She glanced up at the ceiling. 'And it's not fair on the tenants. They're worried I'm going to throw them out.'

'Well, tell them you won't do anything of the sort. Is Mr Harris still there? I remember him teaching me to ride a bike. Poor old soul, I won't have him bothered.'

From somewhere inside Betty's house a doorbell rang and she turned, earrings swinging. 'Look, I have to go. You'll be fine, darling, honestly. Bye.'

The screen shimmered and went blank, leaving Caroline looking at a monochrome reflection of herself. The smudge of mascara made her eyes look huge and grief-stricken; and as if to match the thought, from far above came that faint and heartbroken cry.

20
Lizzie, 1946

'GOOD EVENING, SIR. GOOD EVENING, MADAM. THE restaurant is just down there to the left. Indeed, sir, but it's good for the garden. I believe the BBC said it will be fine by the weekend. Certainly, madam. Taxi!'

The doorman turns to beckon one of the cruising cabs and Lizzie takes her chance, pattering up the steps to slide past him, but just as she gets to the revolving glass door he turns and drops his arm to block her way.

'Sorry, love. Nice try.'

She tries her best smile, puts her hand on the polished brass bar that will spin her inside. Sid has made her practise this, but the sounds feel as artificial as rayon in her mouth. 'I beg your pardon?'

He looks around carefully, but the last diner has whisked through the doors and into the warm.

'You think I came down in the last shower of rain?' The doorman takes a small step forward. Water drips off the cockade in his top hat. 'Get out of it. More'n my job's worth to let a tom in here.'

She swallows an acidic bubble of panic. 'What d'you mean, a tom? I told you, I just want a drink,' she says, but she can hear the accent slipping and the man gives her a look that says it's all over.

'Yeah, and I'm Clement Attlee.' His eyes rake her up and down, not unkindly. 'You ain't foolin' nobody, love. You sound like Cary Grant and that coat looks like it needs a saucer of milk.'

Behind her, a taxi pulls up and a middle-aged man gets out, climbs the steps towards them. He is in uniform, leaning on a cane, and the doorman stands aside respectfully. The man limps up the steps and pauses beside them.

'Everything all right, Thomas?' She can't tell if it's a first or surname.

The doorman touches his forehead with a gloved finger. 'Good evening, Major. Nothing to worry about, sir. Just helping this young lady on her way.'

The major turns and yet again she feels male eyes wander across her. Even after all these months, she sometimes thinks that the hot, hungry stares are worse than the hands.

Nothing is as bad as the tongues.

Or Sid, when she gets back and finds out she hasn't turned any tricks, which is most nights. That's the worst. She can still feel his fingers all over her—

'Lost, eh? An orphan of the storm?' The man smells of brandy.

'Something like that, sir. Now come on, there's a good—'

But the major intervenes. 'Just a second. What's your name?'

Sid told her this, too. 'Lucille, sir.' She hates it. Loose Eel, something slippery and cold. Her lipstick tightens as a smile tries and fails to stay in place.

'Lucille, eh? And what's a pretty young thing like you doing trying to get into a dump like this?'

'If I may, sir—'

'Don't fret, man. Well, we can't have you staying out here in the rain. You'll get pneumonia. Let's get you somewhere warm. I know a place. Very nice. Thomas, get me another cab, would you?'

The major takes her arm, leads her back down the steps. As she climbs into the car she casts a desperate look down the street, sees that Mickey is still there, standing in the shadows, his thin shoulders hunched in cold misery. She wishes with all her heart that it was his hand gripping her elbow, his skin that would soon be burning on hers, but instead all she can do is give him a tiny wave, before he turns away, disappearing into the rain.

21
Caroline

'OH, ER, HI. IS THAT CAROLINE? It's Rob. Rob Sayers. We met at the library the other day?'

Caroline blinked and sat up. Shit. She'd only sat down to grab some lunch and now it was nearly three. Was she really of an age now where she had an afternoon nap? 'Of course. Hi. How are you?'

'Fine, fine.' He cleared his throat. From somewhere in the background she could hear young voices. 'Er, look, I hope you don't mind me ringing, but I spoke to that colleague I mentioned at the OU. She's sent me a few things that might be interesting. I can put them in the post if you like?'

'Oh God, that's really nice of you.' And it was; this sudden, casual kindness touched her more than she could say. It had been a long time since someone had done something like this for her, and she found herself not wanting to let the moment go.

'Or if you fancy meeting up I can talk you through them?' Rob said, rather hesitantly.

Caroline looked around the room. Bin bags lay like frog spawn all over the carpet. Frances' clothes, this time; Caroline had found the scarf that had been her last present, folded neatly in a drawer with a sprig of lavender lying on it. She had held it to her face for a long time, and found herself whispering, *I'm sorry, Granny, I'm sorry…*

The memory made the thought of escape irresistible.

'That'd be good. I can come into Croydon if you like? Or do you know West Wickham? It's only about fifteen minutes down the road from the town centre, there are some decent coffee places there.'

He hesitated. 'I'm teaching until five. D'you fancy a drink after work?'

So a time for that evening had been fixed and now she was sitting in the Wheatsheaf, with an entirely legal glass of white wine. Rob caught her looking at it, and she smiled ruefully.

'I used to come in here all the time with my mate Ruth,' she said. 'We used to psych each other up that we'd try to get served, then chicken out and ask for a Coke instead.'

'I remember you saying your gran's house was round here.'

'A mile or so up the road, yes.' She took a sip. The wine was sharp and clean, like frost. 'It was good of your colleague to help,' she said, looking at the brown envelope he'd fished out of his bag.

Rob smiled. 'Anything to distract her from what she's supposed to be doing,' he said. 'She's all right, Elaine, but dear God the woman's got the concentration of a gnat with ADHD.' He nodded his thanks to the barmaid as she leaned across to light a candle on their table. 'So, basically, I just said to her that you were looking for connections between five women who'd stayed in this area in 1946, 1947, that right?'

'Yes. Although I'm certain now that they were at the house in 1947.'

'Really? That's interesting.'

'Well, it's an assumption.' She fiddled with the stem of her glass. 'This is going to sound odd, but there was another name. One my grandmother said she'd lost. The missing women must have known her. And yesterday I was in the graveyard – don't ask – and I found a hidden memorial to her, dated 1947. But she can't have been buried there because Gran would have known.'

Rob looked at her. 'I don't mean to be unkind,' he said slowly, 'but your gran – if she was an old lady…'

Caroline shook her head. 'No. I see where you're coming from, but I spoke to her on the phone regularly before she had her first stroke. She was totally compos mentis. Someone else who used to know her said the same. And she's a vicar.'

'Who are we to argue with a woman of the cloth?' He grinned and she found herself smiling back. What was it about this man that made her relax like this? 'Well, anyway, Elaine had a look for me when she was at the records office. Now, I can't say she found anything concrete, but this was interesting.' He opened the envelope and pulled out some sheets of paper. 'No surprise if I tell you that there were just too many files to make looking through them for your women remotely feasible. Back then people were still looking for displaced relatives, bomb victims, deserters, you name it. So Elaine thought she'd have a look instead to see what else might have been going on. Anything that might have been a reason for your women to leave together, like you said. And when she looked at the records for round here, she found there'd been some serious shit happening.'

Caroline picked up one of the sheets. It bore the mug shot of a slickly handsome young man, one eyebrow raised and a sardonic smile on his lips. 'Sidney Parker,' she read. 'Theft, looting, affray, assault, immoral earnings, possession of unlicensed firearm – wow. He was a nasty piece of work.'

'Just wait till you see his mate.' Rob handed her another piece of paper. 'Your old friend, Kenny Clapton. I'm sure it's the same guy who was in the clipping you found.'

'He was round here?'

'He was all over the place, but Elaine recognised the court building you can see in the press photo and it's Croydon Town Hall, where they held the Assizes, and that made it easier to find him. Anyway. Young Sidney was quite a small fish in a murky pond, but he teamed up with Kenny after the war and moved into the big time. He'd always been more of an opportunist, breaking into bombed houses, that kind of thing, but with Kenny it became armed robbery, running a string of girls, protection rackets, you name it.'

Caroline frowned. 'And you think they were operating around here?'

'There's several arrests around that time in Bromley, West Wickham, Hayes and Beckenham, all the local town centres. A real crime wave. Housebreaking, protection rackets, so there was probably police collusion. And girls getting done for shoplifting who were also being nicked for soliciting. Not that any of them would grass, but from Elaine's research it looks like there was some kind of feudal system going on. Kenny would be at the centre of it all, with his – I don't know, what would you call them? Henchmen? – out in the suburbs, running their own little operations but on his behalf. As a matter of fact, it'd be a good move. Less chance of opposition from a rival gang, nice leafy suburb full of people with decent houses, less bomb damage, easy access to London—'

'You sound like an estate agent.'

He laughed. 'Maybe that's what they mean when they talk about good catchment areas on their ads. Not schools at all.' He tapped the photo. 'And Sidney had a few women in tow – here, have a look at June Fielding, proper gangster's moll, you wouldn't want to meet her in a dark alley, would you? – but Kenny saw them strictly as business assets. June was arrested for soliciting at least eight or nine times.'

Caroline saw a narrow, tight face under peroxide curls. 'In that case maybe they were victims. They hid at the house and ran away to escape him.' She looked up. 'Do we know what happened to Sidney?'

'You thinking of trying to track him down? No such luck, sorry. Elaine got the rest of his record and there's no trace of him since early 1947, when he was linked to a robbery in a hotel up west. No death certificate, but given his associates there's every chance he ended up at the bottom of the Thames or was killed and buried on a bombsite somewhere. Kenny finally got caught and died in Parkhurst in the seventies.'

'I can't pretend I'm sorry.'

'Me neither, if I'm honest. Don't get me wrong, I'm not a hang 'em and flog 'em merchant, but these two were brutal. I don't want to come over all he-man, but even if they were still alive I'd not be comfortable with you contacting them. Their kind is dangerous.' He stopped, looking sheepish. 'Sorry. I know you must meet that sort of thing every day.'

'Well, maybe. But it's nice of you to be concerned. Do you know if the gangs are still operating?'

'God, I hope not. Though that's naive. We've got people traffickers and drug dealers these days. Why do you ask?'

'It's nothing.' Nothing except the man watching her…

Rob raised an eyebrow. 'Famous last words. Come on, if I buy you dinner will you tell me?'

Caroline looked at the menu, chalked on a blackboard behind the bar. Everything came with either chips or custard, and suddenly the thought of comfort food, in a cosy pub with an interesting man was very, very attractive. And he was kind, with a warmth that somehow caught at something chilled and forgotten within her. She mentally stuck two fingers up at Doctor Fairfax.

'Oh, go on then,' she said.

22

He insisted on driving her home.

'Are you kidding?' he said when she'd protested that she could easily walk or catch the bus. 'You tell me there's some bloke hanging around in your shrubbery, and you think I'll let you go home on your own?'

'Honestly, it's only been twice. It'll all turn out to be a coincidence, he'll be the local twitcher or something.'

'Yes, well, I'd rather not read about you being found chopped up in a freezer, if it's all the same to you. "Axe Horror Lawyer Abandoned by Callous Teacher Who Couldn't Be Arsed to Drive Her Home", that's what the *Daily Mail* will have to say. It'll look bad on my CV. Come on, I'm parked over here.'

So he'd driven her home and been suitably impressed by the house, giving a low whistle as they went through the gates.

'Wow,' he said, craning his neck to look up at the riot of brickwork that formed the chimneys. 'It's – exuberant.'

That made her laugh, so she suggested coffee. He went around the flat, looking at the cornicing and the architraves with a genuine enthusiasm.

'You said it was built in the 1880s?' He was bending to look at the tiles on the fireplace. 'These are lovely. De Morgan?'

'I think so,' Caroline said. 'I know they had to be covered up to protect them when my grandmother had the central heating put in.'

'And this is where all those women came.' Rob took his cup and sat down. 'It must have felt like such a haven, mustn't it?'

'You're the second person to say that.' Caroline looked around the room, trying to see it with fresh eyes.

He said thoughtfully, 'They really seem to have got to you, these women.'

'One of them could be my grandmother. That feels – odd. I don't know why.'

'Well, you've just lost one. And now you think you might have found another one. That must be disconcerting, to say the least.'

She turned on the sofa to face him. 'But the person I can't stop thinking about is Lizzie. She's just a name in a letter but I can't get her out of my head. What happened to her?'

'You found a memorial,' he said gently. 'She was the one your granny couldn't save, even though saving people is what she did.' His eyes were very warm. 'Maybe that's why you think about her. I mean, you're a lawyer. Justice must be in your blood, if you see what I mean.'

She did, and it was too big a thought for the time of night and the place and the house. So, instead, she suggested another drink, with polite murmurs about the spare room – which neither of them believed. He'd told her he was divorced, living with his teenage daughter of whom he was clearly very proud, and she'd shown him Betty's paintings. Then there had been more wine and comfortable conversation, and now – she twisted her head on the pillow – he was lying beside her, snoring gently. She stretched, full of a warmth and satiety that she'd not experienced for a long time. Ingenious as the people at Ann Summers may be, they couldn't give you afterglow like you got with the real thing. She'd nip to the loo – that last glass had been a mistake – then drift off and get a decent night's sleep. For once the house was peaceful, no sobbing echoing in the dark or escaping dogs or hidden watchers pacing overhead.

She was just coming out of the bathroom when she smelled it. For a moment she thought it was Rob, awake and having a post-shag cigarette; then she breathed in again, and the thickening smoke scratched at her throat, making her cough, prickling her eyes, sending fear jolting through her body.

She almost tripped over her dressing gown as she ran back into the bedroom, shaking Rob awake with one hand, grabbing her clothes with the other.

He sat up, blinking at her. 'You want me to go?'

She threw his jeans across the bed. 'There's a fire,' she said, trying to calm both the hurt in his eyes and the panic in her voice. 'I need you to help me get the tenants up, get them outside in case it's serious. I'll call 999…'

He scrambled out of the bed, pulling on clothes while she shoved her feet into the trainers she'd kicked off only an hour earlier. 'How many of them?'

'Three. They're mobile but I don't know how well they hear — oh Christ!' The first shrill shriek of the smoke alarm was slicing through the silence. 'God, I'm sorry – this *fucking* house!'

Out in the hall, smoke was beginning to slink along the floor and up the walls, feeling its way across tiles and panelling. They went up the stairs, and she pointed him at Mr Harris's door, then went on down the landing to the doctor's flat, faint memories of Girl Guide safety lessons in her head: *Don't open the door if it's hot, that'll mean the fire's on the other side, come on, you mad old bat, answer the bloody—*

The door swung open and the old doctor was there, wrapped in a thick dressing gown and mackintosh, Barnaby on his lead and her Gladstone bag in her other hand. 'I heard the alarm,' she said, pushing past onto the landing, her glance going sharply to where Mr Harris was pulling his cap down over his head and brandishing his caretaker's keys. Caroline abandoned them, hurrying across the landing to the last door, pounding as hard as she could, wincing as pain shot up her injured arm. The smoke was with them now, an unwanted guest, dimming the light that Dr Fairfax had switched on, making Barnaby bark in agitation. Caroline raised her hand again, rattled the door handle, and then Mr Harris was there beside her, catching at her wrist, pulling her aside with a force that made her gasp.

'You go on down,' he said, 'I'll get her—'

'Mr Harris—'

There was a sudden muffled crash from downstairs and a fierce surge of heat. Caroline jerked in shock. Barnaby barked, almost masking the sound of a panicked shriek coming from inside the flat. Mr Harris pressed close to the door, calling through, his voice calm and confident.

'S'all right, love, you're quite safe, don't you worry, I'm here, we've got you.' Then his bony face turned back to Caroline, snarling, 'Get out of it, she won't come out with you all here gawping, go on!'

Rob appeared, his eyes red and watering. 'I've called the fire brigade,' he said, 'They're on their way. It's getting worse, we need to go.' He looked at the closed door, where Mr Harris was again calling. 'We should break it down—'

'Leave it!' Mr Harris yelled, his voice cracking. 'She's back in the Blitz, she's scared of the bombs, I'll bring her. I said I'll bring her!'

Caroline took a deep breath, then retched as smoke dived down her throat. 'All right,' she said, 'just hurry, if she won't come out then see if you can get in there and wait. Put a blanket or something across the door.'

Mr Harris had turned away and resumed his gentle pleading. 'Come on, love, it's all right…'

Caroline hesitated for a second more, but Rob had taken her hand and was pulling her back to the stairs. 'You can't make him come,' he said over his shoulder, 'and we need to go, quick, before it's too late.'

A great gout of smoke erupted in the hall below them, shooting up to where they stood. Thick and oily, it burst onto the landing, billowing around them, wrapping them in greasy darkness, slashing at their eyes and throats. Caroline took one last look but there was nothing, just that swirling, cloying mass, and she stumbled away, down the stairs, closing her eyes so she could not see the stooped old man as he called again and again and was not answered.

23

Doctor Fairfax was waiting on the steps by the open front door. Cool air swept in and filled their mouths like balm, and Caroline sagged against the door frame, gasping and sobbing with relief.

'Are they coming?' Fairfax snapped. 'Are they with you?'

Caroline twisted round, trying to see up to the landing, but there was just that cloud of smoke, writhing and snaking up to the ceiling. 'He was trying to get her to come out,' she said, her throat rasping. 'She wouldn't open her door—'

'That wretched girl.'

A piercing blue light swept across the drive, cutting through the dark like a laser. Even before the engine stopped the first fireman was leaping down out of the cab, his visor gleaming. 'Brian Mitchell,' he said, striding across to them, his eyes raking across the front of the house. 'Crew manager. Anyone inside?'

'Two. Two old people, a man and a woman. First floor.' Caroline pointed.

'All right. Steve, Rosie, you go up. Any idea where the fire's located?'

Rob spoke, his voice hoarse from coughing. 'Round the back of the house,' he said. 'I could see the light, something burning. I'm not sure exactly where.'

'What's there?'

'Kitchen, a courtyard where the bins are,' Caroline said. 'And there's a shed where the caretaker kept his stuff.'

'Gas bottles, oil?'

'No. It's all mains.'

'Right you are. Alan, Josh, you make the initial recce.'

There was a rumble behind them as the side of the engine was rolled up and the men disappeared.

Doctor Fairfax stood quite still, her gaze fixed on the front door, her hands clenched around the handle of her bag. 'Wretched, wretched girl,' she kept saying, her mouth moving in a thin, desperate line.

'You okay?' Rob put his hand on Caroline's shoulder.

'I think so. You?'

'More or less.' He looked down at her face, her eyes still fixed on the front door. 'It'll be all right. The crew'll get them out. They're trained, they know what to do.'

'But they're so old. And if she won't let them in…' Caroline swallowed, then choked, hawking up a great black blob that she spat into the bushes. 'Oh for fuck's sake, what if they die!'

Rob tightened his grip on her shoulder. 'Hey, come on. You know it's not your fault.'

'I should never have come back.'

Audrey Fairfax spoke sharply. 'Shut up! There's something happening.'

From the house there was a shout. They all took an unthinking step forward, as first two, then four figures emerged at the front door, silhouetted against the hall light. Mr Harris was led out first, but he twisted free, going back to take Miss Tanner's hand, holding it close to his chest as they came across the gravel, his thin body bending to shield her from the light and noise and cold. She looked impossibly frail, as if she herself were made of ash and would crumple into nothingness with a single breath of wind. Caroline dropped her head, covering her face with her hands, feeling a rough sob clogging her throat.

'House is clear, guv.' The woman firefighter pushed her visor back, wiping her hand across her face. 'Bit of a fire that had spread to the kitchen but Josh dealt with it and the smoke's clearing. These two are okay, I've radioed for an ambulance just in case.'

'No need. I can provide whatever care is needed.' Doctor Fairfax brandished her bag.

'I'm sure you can, but we'll get them checked all the same.' Foil blankets were being wrapped around the two old people, who seemed shrunken and diminished now they were out in the dark, clinging together like scared children. The doctor tutted, and opened her bag. 'Now come along,' Caroline heard her saying briskly, 'no harm done, have a drop of brandy – nonsense, officer, it'll be perfectly safe…'

'Caroline? Caroline, are you all right? I saw the engine – is everyone okay?'

Mel Cooper came running through the gates, sweeping Caroline into a hug. 'Oh thank God,' she said with simple sincerity. 'You're shaking like a leaf! What happened?'

'Don't know. They're just looking now.' Caroline saw Mel's eyebrows rise as she saw Rob, who was leaning on the wall, gladly taking Dr Fairfax's medical advice and swigging from her bottle. 'I'll tell you later,' she said.

'Make sure you do.' Mel took the foil blanket that Rosie was holding out. 'Get this round you.'

'I'm all right.'

'You're freezing. Don't argue.'

One of the firefighters came around the corner of the house, his helmet under his arm, saying something to Mitchell. The older man nodded. 'Okay, everyone, stand down. All under control.' He beckoned Caroline over. 'Looks like it started in the shed. Then when one of the paint pots exploded it broke the window and let the fire into the house. You want to come and see?'

Caroline, Rob and Mel followed him around the side of the house and into the small courtyard outside the kitchen. The air was hot and sulky with smoke, and a sharp chemical smell cut through the cold air like acid. Charred planks that had once been a shed hung together like drunks holding each other upright. A metal incinerator, the kind that looked like a dustbin with holes in the sides, lay gaping on its side in a heap of ash and spent extinguishers were resting against the wall, a last dribble of foam pooling around them.

'Thoughts, Alan?' Mitchell said.

'Someone's been burning stuff in this,' the firefighter said, nudging the incinerator with his boot. 'Didn't damp it down enough when they left it. You see there, that scorch mark on the ground? That's where a bit of paper or whatever fell or blew out. The shed door wasn't closed properly, and it's my guess that the paper, or a spark from it, must have caught some rags. There's cotton residue over there.' He pointed, his thick glove making his hand looking grotesquely swollen. 'They can smoulder for hours until they get hot enough and then whoosh, away we go.' He turned and nodded at the house. 'Smoke would have mainly got in through that airbrick, and that open fanlight there. And there's a broken window, must have been smashed when a tin of paint went up. They can make quite the bang. That would have let the fire pour in, especially if there was a net curtain or a blind in the wrong place. There's quite a bit of scorching in the kitchen, I'm afraid, but it's all out now.'

Rob was looking around at the debris. 'All this from a bit of paper?'

'You'd be surprised. I once saw a house gutted where the owner had tried defrosting the fridge by putting a tea light in it. Whole place went up in under ten minutes.'

Caroline turned over a pile of damp ash with her foot. It left greasy smears on her trainer. 'Do you know what was being burned?' she asked.

Alan shook his head. 'Nah. Paper, by the looks of things. Couple of bits of cardboard. Some kind of book, maybe. There's some left at the bottom here – hang on.' He bent and hauled the incinerator upright, reaching inside and pulling out a fluttering, crumbling wad. 'Old typed stuff. Most of it's gone, these are the only legible bits left.' He held them up to the light of a torch that Mitchell had unclipped from his belt. 'Can't see much. Vera, is that? And this looks like Bessie.'

'Maggie.' Caroline took the papers. Tiny fragments of letters were just visible under the feathery grey ash. Maggie and Vera. Jane and Harriet would be here too, she knew, with Grace. The last trace of them was flaking softly across her skin.

She took a few steps away, down towards the gate that led into the garden. Tatters of clouds were drifting across the sky, the dull orange glow of London a blur on the horizon. She closed her eyes, letting the wind stir the fragments in her hand. And then with a sudden flick of her wrist she threw the papers up into the air, so they could crumble and spin away into nothingness.

24

The Blue Drawing Room at Shenstone Hall was shabby and worn in the way that only a room used and loved for two hundred years can be. The mismatched lamps sent a gentle glow over the sagging sofas and the scratched tables; from chipped gilt frames, the faces of long-dead Shenstones looked down indulgently as Caroline and Ruth sat by the fire, a bottle of wine warming on the hearth. Two huge grey dogs stretched inelegantly on the rug between them, their paws twitching as they dreamed, while in a deep box beside them a heap of puppies squirmed and snuffled on a blanket. From somewhere in the house a clock struck eight, followed five minutes later by a deeper chime from the church in the parkland outside.

'Still out of sync with God.' Ruth yawned, swinging her feet up onto the sofa. 'Though aren't we all.' She cocked a bright blue eye at her friend. 'So. You were telling me about your handsome historian.'

'He's not my handsome historian. He's not even really handsome.'

'Don't split hairs. I'm delighted for you! Come on, how long is it since you had a man, in any sense? Ages. Is he nice? Are you seeing him again?'

'No idea. I mean, he helps me out, buys me dinner, then he's nearly burned to death. Hardly likely to bring him back panting for more, is it?'

'He might like dangerous women.'

'He's a historian. His idea of a dangerous woman is Typhoid Mary.'

Ruth laughed. 'You're doing yourself down, Alleyn,' she said. 'He must be interested, otherwise why bring you all that stuff about the spivs?'

'Maybe. Oh, I don't know. It's all just been so bloody weird. I don't know what I think any more. Rob said—'

'Ooh, so it's Rob, is it? Nice. Didn't you once shag a Horatio?'

'You know perfectly well his name was Henry. Shut up. *Mr Sayers* said maybe Gran was confused, but I don't think so, do you?'

'Not in the slightest. I know once she had her strokes she wasn't herself, but you say all this business was set up before she was ill?'

'Mm. I can show you the letter if you like.'

'And none of the people you spoke to were saying anything?'

'Not a word. Just clammed up completely. One even tried warning me off.' She held out Grace's text, and Ruth raised her eyebrows.

'Maybe Lizzie's not a person. Maybe it was some sort of code, or a what do you call it, a euphemism.'

'I thought that. But then why is there a bloody memorial, for crying out loud? Surely that means she's dead, poor soul. Gran said she'd lost her, and the text is trying to stop me finding out how she died.' Caroline stared at Grace's message, as if trying to will more words to appear on the screen.

'But why would someone be spying on you? That's the bit that bothers me.' Ruth bent and touched the bottle. 'Sod it, I can't be arsed to wait. Shift your arse, Flora. You too, Fingal, get out of the way, you daft dog. Pass me your glass, we'll have it cold. Eddie will do his nut but who cares.'

Caroline didn't want to think about that pale, wild face in the bushes. She went gratefully for the easier subject. 'How is he? I only saw him for a minute. Busy as ever?'

'He is, though don't tell him I said so. The estate doesn't get easier. Or cheaper to run. If we didn't have all the weddings and conferences we'd be buggered, I don't mind telling you.'

'I'm sorry.'

'Don't be. We do all right. And I can't complain, there's not many people get to live and work in a beautiful house, even if it is with their big brother.' She took a sip and pulled a face. 'Maybe he's got a point about warming this stuff. Anyway. The big question is, what are you going to do next?'

'I don't know. Honestly. I mean, some bits are straightforward, like getting cleaners in to sort out the smoke damage – that'll be easy enough, it's only really the ground floor that's badly affected and the flats are okay. Did I tell you there's an extra tenant? One I didn't know about?'

Ruth looked surprised. 'Didn't your mum say anything?'

'What do you think? Of course not. Something else she's left me to sort out.' Caroline took a mouthful of wine, and was inclined to agree about the temperature. 'A big part of me just wants to walk away and have done with it all. But—'

'But another part of you can't bear not knowing?' Ruth raised her eyebrows. 'Don't look at me like that. I've known you since we were in our prams, remember? You've always wanted to find things out. You want to know what happened, so you can fix it. You always do.'

'I can't fix this. If it's connected to the war then it's more than sixty years ago. It's over.'

'Well, clearly not if your gran left that restricting thingy. Something must be lingering, else why would it all kick off the minute you start asking questions?'

Caroline groaned. 'None of it makes any bloody sense. And it's all so – so small.'

'A house fire's not small.'

'True. But all the little things, the crying, the man in the garden, the pictures, tiny on their own, but together – it's like being smothered. And how are those old dears involved?'

'They're not on the form, so they're trying other ways to make sure you don't sell.'

'Obviously, but like this? Hiding family photos, pretending

they've not seen anything, burning things – Jesus, why not just rely on their tenancies? I mean, I've not really looked yet in any detail but I can't imagine Gran didn't get everything dotted and crossed.'

Ruth took another mouthful of wine, then sat up. 'There is one thing we can do,' she said.

'Go back and finish what old man Harris and his bonfire started? Hang on while I fetch a blowtorch.'

'No, you idiot. Honestly, I don't know why it didn't occur to me sooner.'

'What?'

Ruth put her glass down. In the soft lamplight her face looked suddenly sad.

'It might take a day or two,' she said. 'But we could always ask my mum.'

25
Mickey, 1946

It has been a dreary summer and now it's a dreary autumn. The rain has been relentless, as if the earth is in mourning for the wounds it suffered during the war; everything is grey and flat. Tonight the heavy wet air is cold, and when Mickey gets off the tram he can see the dank grey smudge of a smog beginning to hang over the city.

They'd moved out of the bombsite, that was one good thing. Kenny had seen to that. But Mickey is wary of this newcomer, his good suits and wide ties, his fat cigars and his polished shoes. His face, with its wide blue eyes and sweet rosebud mouth, is pretty, almost girlish, masking the steely ruthlessness of the man, his utter lack of concern for anything or anyone other than himself. Even Sid seems in awe of him, frantically eager to please, fetching brandy and cigarettes and ferrying him around, especially now they were planning these big jobs up West. He makes up for it once Kenny has gone, mind you, becoming harsher and sharper, not hesitating now to use his fists on anyone, the girls included. Mickey touches his own cheek at the thought, the swollen skin pulpy and soft under his fingers.

Their new place is a flat on the outskirts of Croydon. It bears the same scars as all the other gritty and broken houses, but Sid has contacts who make sure there's glass in most of the windows and, strikes or no strikes, always some decent coal, at least when Kenny is around. The rest of the time they make do with slack, or failing that wood from the shattered remains of the buildings that still slump on every street.

The power is on, for now, so fingers crossed there will be gas for the kettle as well. A cuppa, that's what he wants, a cuppa and to get rid of his takings for the day before he could get caught with them. Two wallets, a nearly new ration book, a handbag and a five-bob note. Best he could manage, people were staying in these cold evenings.

He turns down the road towards the flat. It's in an old house, one of a terrace that stretched away around the bend of the street. Gaps show like sores between the buildings, planks and tiles and rafters jabbing out into thin air, bits of curtain and carpet flapping forlornly in the wind. He shivers, and pulls his coat collar up. He can taste the smog, now, its yellow breath wrapping around his throat like a scarf.

The gate has somehow survived the bombs, although the wall, now just a pile of random bricks, has not. It swings open, catching the overhanging laurels that brush his bare head and send cold drops trickling down his collar. The branches rustle, sending shadows flickering across the path. One of them looks like—

'Who's there?' The shape comes closer and he squints into the gloom, then takes a step forward, grasping her arms urgently. 'Lizzie? That you? What you doing here?' He takes a rapid look up and down the street. 'Gawd, girl, I ain't seen you for weeks. Not since – well, you know.' He gives her a shy hug, remembering their beautiful, fearful stolen afternoons. 'Where's the major? Does Sid know you're here?'

She has been crying, he can hear it in her voice. 'Oh, Mick,' she says. 'You got to help me. I'm in trouble. Such terrible bleeding trouble.'

26
Caroline

She was looking over her left shoulder, holding a mass of blond hair up off her neck with one hand, the other lifting a string of what could have been diamonds to her lips. *Lady Alastair Shenstone, formerly Miss Constance Thompson, the newly married chatelaine of Shenstone Hall in Wiltshire* the caption read, and discreetly left it at that. Even from the black-and-white photograph, the viewer could tell that her lipstick had been a dangerous scarlet that matched her nails, and while a prim pie-crust collar introduced a note of propriety, the rest of the picture howled with sensuality. The readers had howled too; this was not, they complained, how they wanted to see their Girls in Pearls, brave new post-war world or not. Connie, unabashed, had laughed in delight, and kept the cover on the library table ever since, her beauty and vivacity winking unchanged at the world from inside a glinting silver frame.

Caroline put the picture down amongst its companions: Ruth as a baby, being gingerly held by an eighteen-year-old Eddie, brother and sister in evening dress, in mortar boards… God, and here was Wickham Grange, a very young Maud in long skirts and a boater, wheeling a bicycle through the gates with three of the ubiquitous Shenstone hounds loping at her side. Caroline caught herself looking at the black-and-white windows, as if she would see Mr Harris's baleful face staring back at her from across a hundred years.

There was a rumbling in the passage, and she opened the door so Ruth could push the wheelchair through. Caroline thought that every time she came here, a little bit more of the Connie she'd known as a child had vanished; she'd only seen her briefly on her arrival the night before, but even the space of a night had somehow eroded her further. Connie was still upright, still slender, and the eyes had kept their deep, rich blue, but the spark had gone, replaced by a gentle puzzlement. Her white hair wreathed around her skull like mist and when Caroline bent to kiss her, the pale skin of her cheek felt impossibly delicate, like a bubble of milk on a baby's lips.

Connie looked up, her eyes wandering before finding Caroline's own, and her uncertain smile wavered for a moment. The movement sent the morning sun dipping into the wrinkles and valleys of her face. 'Hello, dear,' she said hesitantly, 'have you come before?'

Ruth parked the wheelchair beside the sofa, so Caroline could take Connie's hand. 'I'm Caroline,' she said. 'Frances' granddaughter.'

'Frances?' Connie blinked, as if she were trying to hear a faraway voice. Ruth leaned forward.

'Do you remember, Mum?' she said gently. 'You were friends, teachers together, back when you were young. You were evacuated here with your school and all the children in the war. It's where you met Dad.'

'Dad?' Connie shook her head. 'No, love, my dad's been gone a long time.'

'You used to come and see us,' Caroline said. 'At Wickham Grange. With Alastair's sister, Maud.'

'Broad Maud.' Connie cackled. A broad smile suddenly broke out on her face and she started to sing. '*There'll be blue birds over the…*' Her voice wavered and she looked suddenly bereft. 'Can't remember,' she said. 'Bloody war. Bloody Germans. Hate that siren, Wailing Winnie. Never any bacon, never any hot water. Can I have a bath this week?'

'You had a bath this morning, Mum. You have one every morning. Mrs Grady comes to help you.'

'Does she?'

'Aunty Connie?' Caroline stroked that vulnerable hand. 'Aunty Connie, can you help me with something?'

'Homework? Ask your mum, sweetheart, Aunty Connie's having a little drinky.' She held out her hand. 'Gin and it, please.'

Ruth got up and made a great show of clinking the bottles on the sideboard. 'Here you are, Mum,' she said, handing her a glass of water.

'Bottoms up.' Connie drank, drops dribbling down her chin to fall on her blouse, where they bloomed on the fabric. Ruth wiped her mother's face gently but Connie batted her hand away, with a snarled 'fuck off!' and Ruth retreated, holding the napkin in clenched fingers on her lap.

'Oh, Ruth.' Caroline looked across at her friend. 'I'm so sorry. I didn't realise it was like this. I should come more often, I should help.' She swallowed. 'I should have done that with Gran.'

Ruth dabbed at her eyes with the napkin. 'There's nothing you can do. We have help, which is more than a lot of people get. We've got space, there's always someone to sit with her if I need to go to a meeting or if Eddie's had to go out—'

'Eddie? Who's Eddie? Is he my husband?'

'No, Mum. Dad died a long time ago. Eddie's your son.' Ruth looked at the sideboard. 'Fuck it, it's only half twelve but I'm having one. I need one. You? And Mum can have one as well. What harm can it do her now? Here you go.'

Caroline touched her glass to the one in the old lady's gnarled fingers. 'Cheers, Aunty Connie,' she said. The sharp smell of gin made her think of Mel; how could she believe in a God that allowed such a wreck to be made of someone like Connie Shenstone?

Her phone, lying on the table, gave an impatient buzz. Ruth looked down at it and raised her eyebrows. 'Oh I say,' she said. 'A gentleman caller. The not-your Mr Sayers. Call him. I shall avert my maidenly gaze while you converse.'

Caroline opened the text.

How you doing? I'm still coughing like a Victorian mill worker. If you'd wanted me to go home you could have just said, no need to torch the place. Fancy another dinner sometime? I'll bring asbestos underpants. R x

'You'll have to change your name,' Ruth said when Caroline showed her. 'Mary will suit you. Though don't go spreading your typhoid here, Environmental Health will be all over us.'

'Piss off.' Caroline thumbed back a reply.

Living with bloated idle rich all very well but will be back when house is cleaned up. Dinner and underpants both sound extraordinarily good x

Connie had knocked back her gin and let the glass fall onto the floor. 'Tired,' she said. 'Can I have some sweets? Is it time for breakfast yet?'

Caroline looked at Ruth. 'Leave it,' she said, 'it's not fair. She can't remember anything—'

Ruth hesitated. 'Let's just—'

She came and sat beside her mother, picking up the glass and setting it gently on the table. 'Mum,' she said, touching Connie's face so the old woman turned to look at her. 'Mum, Caroline wants to ask you something. Is that okay?'

Caroline said, very gently, 'Did you know someone called Lizzie Sixpence?'

Connie was looking at the door. 'I want to go home,' she said.

Caroline swallowed, hard, the movement setting up a twinge in her throat that wasn't entirely due to the smoke. 'Okay, Aunty Connie,' she said. 'Don't worry. It isn't important.'

Connie turned her head, very slowly. Her eyes fixed on Caroline's. 'Lizzie Sixpence?' she said, frowning.

'Yes.' Caroline was so startled that she squeezed Connie's hand. 'Do you remember her?'

'Oh yes. Lizzie.' Connie giggled. 'Busy Lizzie. Lizzie's in the greenhouse. Bad girl, Lizzie. All that blood. Naughty Lizzie, bad Lizzie…'

Caroline's heart started to thud; this was it, a real, breathing link to that elusive ghost girl, the name in the wall, the sobs in the night. 'Do you know what happened to Lizzie?' she said, very quietly.

Connie gently pulled her hand free and brought it up, cupping Caroline's face. Her eyes were suddenly bright and happy.

'Oh yes, love,' she said, beaming. 'Your granny killed her.'

27

Betty, 1980

God, the way she's looking at me.

All these years of work, building up my contacts, getting known… and here I am, finally able to say it. Come with me, darling, come to Spain, we'll live in a little flat and go to the beach at the weekend and you'll learn Spanish very quickly, you're such a clever little thing. It'll be wonderful.

And she just stands there, all awkward teenage lumps and angles, her socks pulled up to exactly the same length on each side, and says no.

'But why not?' I protest. I'd thought she'd be pleased. After all, how many times had she asked to come with me? How many times had I seen her face go tight with the effort of not crying when I said no, sweetie, it was too difficult, Mummy needs to concentrate on her paintings, I'll be back soon, Granny will look after you?

She casts a quick look at Frances, sitting silent and watchful in the corner.

'I want to stay here.'

'But, sweetie—' I feel helpless. 'Don't you want to get away? Away from all – from everything here?' I look up, towards the rooms where the latest victims are waiting to escape. 'We'll be free, we can do what we want.'

'It's not sensible.'

'Sensible? Of course it's sensible. I've got a job.'

'You said it's only for a year.'

'Yes, well, I know, but something will come up.'

'What if it doesn't?'

'Well, can't we deal with that then? Come on, Caro, I'd love it if you came with me. I can teach you to draw—'

'I don't want to learn to draw. I want to do my A levels, I want to go to a good university.' She looks into the corner again. 'Granny always says, don't let anything—'

'Disrupt your education. I know.' Now I look at Frances too, that old implacable face staring back at me, her expression almost pitying. For the first time I find myself wondering what made her like that, what turned that unassuming schoolmarm into this formidable, intensely practical old woman, who took over my life and the lives of so many others without so much as a blink. 'You can go to school in Spain, you know.'

'I can't do A levels in Spain.'

'I didn't get any A levels,' I say, trying to make a joke of it.

'I know,' she says.

'And look, everything's worked out, hasn't it?' I reach out for her but she jerks away.

'No, it hasn't. You can't just pretend that running off to somewhere else will make it all right because it's not. It's never all right.' She almost shouts it. 'You always ran away and you left me behind and now it's too late. You didn't even let me have a dad—'

That slashes into me like a whip. 'You know it wasn't like that,' I say, 'It wasn't my fault—'

'Nothing's ever your fault! It's always something else making you do it, making you leave, making you leave me here.' She takes a great shuddering gulp of air. 'And I don't want to be like that. I don't want that, I don't want to be like you. I don't want to be always changing and never knowing what's going to happen and just running away all the time.' She takes a deep breath. Her face is scarlet and for one appalled moment I think she is going to sob. 'I want to be a lawyer,' she says instead.

That's new. God, I never thought she'd want to be an artist – can't draw, and that's the simple truth – but she's bright, could do anything, go anywhere, but she's just a kid and she's saying she wants to bury herself in dusty books and boring courtrooms? That doesn't make sense.

'What's brought this on?' I ask.

'I want to be—' Her face twists for a moment as she hunts for the word. 'I want to be safe.'

'But Spain's safe,' I say, misunderstanding her. 'It's a lovely part of Madrid, there's a park and some beautiful shops – look, I'll show you on the map – and I'll be there all the time, we can do things together.'

Caroline shakes her head. 'Not that kind of safe,' she says stubbornly. 'I mean safe for myself. Safe for ever.' Her voice cracks, just a little. 'Safe from other people,' she says. 'The law keeps us safe, I want to be part of that.'

I can only look at her in bewilderment and I swear she actually stamps her foot.

'Oh I knew you wouldn't get it! Don't you see? See what happens to the people who come here? You were abandoned here, and then you left me here, this house where all these people come and it's all horrible and I want to get away and stop any of it happening any more!'

And then Frances speaks. She leans forward and takes my hand, and I am startled – and a little afraid – to see tears in her eyes.

'Oh my dear,' she says. 'Whatever has this place done to you both?'

28
Caroline

The last cleaner had been wringing out a cloth into a bucket full of black and greasy water.

'I'd open a window if I were you,' she said in a sepulchral voice, while brandishing a large white spray bottle emblazoned with a skull and crossbones. It had taken the best part of three days, but the combined efforts of glaziers and cleaners meant that the fire's last traces had been all but eradicated. The house smelled powerfully of some astringent lemon cleaner, and the cushions had a suspicion of dampness about them, but there was no sign of the smoke, the fire or the tenants. Caroline was relieved; there was too much else to do before she wanted to see those sharp and watchful faces.

She and Ruth watched the woman go, putting buckets and mops into a van emblazoned *Lloyd's Household Services - Cleaning up in West Wickham since 1952*. Caroline thought of their enormous bill, and was inclined to agree.

'What's that nursery rhyme?' she said as she closed the door. 'Ding dong dell, pussy's in the well? Or in the greenhouse, I suppose. I can't get it out of my head.'

Ruth turned from where she was looking out over the garden. 'Who put her in? That's the question. Assuming she's there in the first place.'

'Exactly. Oh, none of it makes any bloody sense. If Granny – well, you know, if she really did…' The sentence was tangling on her tongue. Caroline started again. 'Why would she say she was lost, if she knew where she was all the time? If she'd—' She lifted her hands in a little helpless gesture. 'What do you think?'

Ruth shook her head. 'I don't know. Honestly, I don't. If it was anything else I'd say it was just the dementia speaking, but Mum was so specific. So – so lucid. You saw how she sort of lit up. She hasn't been like that for months, so there must be something in what she was saying.' She turned back to the window. 'D'you reckon the greenhouse was even there in 1947?'

Caroline joined her. It was a grey, windy morning, and the lawn lay flat and subdued. At the end of the garden they could just see the greenhouse, and beyond it the churchyard wall. 'Yes,' she said. 'Look.' She went over to the table, where she'd left one of the photographs that had been hanging in the hall. 'I saw an old one of Maud in your library,' she said, 'and it reminded me of this. I must have seen it so many times I'd forgotten it was there. You see?' She pointed. It was a shot of the Grange, and the presence of a horse and dog cart on the drive, driven by a formidable-looking woman in an enormous hat, made her think it had been taken in the early 1900s. The rounded wooden finial on the greenhouse roof was just visible, a grey dot behind a row of trees that had since doubled in height. 'I mean, it proves that there was something there back in the day, so why not in the forties? "Dig for Victory" and all that?'

Ruth looked at the photograph and back down the garden, comparing. 'It certainly looks the same,' she said at last.

They were silent for a moment. Connie had carried on talking for another ten minutes, a rapid and excited babble, and her words were pounding in Caroline's head: *Buried in the greenhouse, bad Lizzie, in the greenhouse in the snow…*

'Are you sure you want to find out?' Ruth said.

'Yes. No. I don't know. All of the above.' Caroline rested her forehead on the cold windowpane. 'If Lizzie's body is down there – well, if I ever do manage to sell and the place is developed they'll find her, and I know this sounds stupid, Ruth, but if she is going to be dug up then I want it to be me. Someone who actually gives a toss about her and what happened to her, not somebody who'll chuck her in a skip rather than delay the build.'

'So that's a yes, then,' Ruth said. 'We'd better get down to the garden centre and see what they've got in the way of shovels.' She flexed her arms. 'Though I'm not sure that I'm up to much in the way of digging.'

'Leave all that to the rugged under-gardener, do you?'

'I should be so lucky. We get Dennis from the village two days a week, and he's nearly sixty. Oh, the things I could do with a horny-handed son of the soil.'

'There's a register for people like you.'

Ruth's grin faded. 'But seriously, what if you do find something? Do we have to call the forensic people, or what?'

The doorbell rang. 'I don't know,' Caroline said. 'But I know a man who does.'

Rob had brought everything they hadn't realised they'd need. A groundsheet, a tarpaulin, a camera, some plastic boxes, and garden tools. Laid out on the floor, the things made a sombre little tableau, made somehow more chilling by stickers bearing a cheery little cartoon trowel that winked up at them.

'You're right,' he told Ruth, as Caroline made coffee. 'If there is a body there then you'll need to call the police. It'll be a lot of upheaval. Tents and floodlights and all that malarkey. Thanks.' He took a sip, warming his hands on the mug. 'And in that case, you might want to think about asking your vicar friend to be on hand. People get funny about bodies.'

Ruth was handling a trowel with fascination. 'Do you go on digs?'

'Not with my knees. No, these belong to an old uni mate of mine. I let him store some of his field trip stuff in my loft.' Rob nudged the rolled-up tarp with his foot. 'We'll need this in case it rains, to preserve anything. Though even if someone was buried out there, there might not be much left. We can't guarantee we'll prove anything.'

'At least we'll have looked,' Caroline said. 'We'll have tried.' She'd known she wanted to do this ever since Connie had lapsed into thumb-sucking silence. It felt like she was suddenly holding a map and could find the centre of a maze. She looked out again, at the wide blank sky. It was as if the whole world was waiting. 'Shall we get it over with?' she said.

29

Lizzie, 1946

'M R CLAPTON. GOOD TO SEE YOU. COME in, come in, we've got the fire lit and I do believe there's a drop of the good stuff waiting. Lizzie, take Mr Clapton's coat.'

The thick, soft mohair almost swamps her as Kenny Clapton drops it carelessly into her arms. Mickey, taking pity, helps her to hang it on the hall stand, earning a frown from Sid as he ushers the newcomer into the living room, where June is waiting with a glass and a cigar. 'Take a seat, take a seat,' he says, pulling out the best armchair.

Clapton stays standing. The firelight gilds his blond curls and makes his eyes look so pale it is as if he is sightless. 'Who's the new girl? I thought we'd agreed, just our own people.'

'Lizzie? She's no bother,' Sid says quickly. 'She's staying here for a bit. Me and her go way back. Come and say hello.' Sid took Lizzie by the hand, squeezing it with a quick, vicious warning that made her gasp. 'This is Mr Clapton,' he says. 'He's going to help us all become rich.'

Lizzie's voice is quiet and thin. She keeps her eyes on the worn hearthrug as she speaks. 'How do you do, Mr Clapton.'

Kenny stares. 'How do you do?' he repeats mockingly. 'Where'd you get her from, Sidney, Buckingham Palace?'

Sid laughs, although his grip on Lizzie's hand becomes even tighter. 'We had her set up with some toff up west. Must have picked it up off of him. Good little earner, she brung us a fiver a week no problem. Then the silly bitch got herself knocked up, so he kicked her out.'

'And you took her back? Very gentlemanly of you, I must say. Not many would keep their damaged goods.'

'Well, she ain't showing much yet. I can still get a few quid out of her for the time being. And she's a decent little tea leaf, she can earn her keep that way when she's got too big for anyone to be interested.' Sid shrugs. 'Then once it's born I reckon we can find someone to take it, you know, some rich tart who wants a kid. That'll be a coupla hundred quid, easy.' Sid looks momentarily anxious. 'That's if it's all right with you, Mr Clapton,' he adds.

Kenny Clapton finally sits down. June steps forward with the whisky, but he waves her away. 'I don't care what you do with her,' he says. He reaches up suddenly, grabbing Lizzie by the arm and pulling her down onto his lap. She sits there awkwardly, not moving, like a doll that has been thrown aside as he traces his finger across her lips. 'What I want to know is whether you'll keep your mouth shut. This job we've got coming up, it's a big one, and I don't want to run any risks. You understand me?'

She nods, once, twice, but he doesn't let her go. Instead he runs his finger down her chin, pressing it against the tender flesh of her throat. 'I said, do you understand me?'

Her hands clench across the soft swell of her belly. 'Yes, Mr Clapton.'

'You'll be a good girl?'

'Yes, Mr Clapton.'

'Well done.' He pushes his finger harder into her neck. 'Because believe you me, if you so much as breathe a word to anyone about anything you hear or see, I'll have that brat cut out of you and put on a bonfire so you can watch it burn. You hear me?'

'Yes, Mr Clapton.'

'Good.' The finger lifts. He smiles, the smile of a deranged angel. 'I'll have that whisky now,' he says.

30
Caroline

The greenhouse door had once been painted a soft, spring-like green, but it had long since faded to an ethereal silver. Flecks of pale colour drifted down as Caroline's cold fingers closed around the knob, catching on the wind and floating away, reminding her of the ashes she'd sent spinning into the night.

Lizzie, are you there?

She pushed at the swollen wood. For a moment the door resisted, then with a resentful groan it gave way, scraping its way through the weeds and brambles that had grown up across the threshold, creeping in through the broken and cracked panes and taking over the interior as if they were reclaiming some ancient and ancestral land. Inside, the light was dim, almost muffled, green from the lichen and moss that had covered the glass of the roof. It felt as if they had entered some otherworldly and silent place, a cathedral made of weeds and wood. Mould and wet earth, sap and autumnal damp; the air was heavy with the smells of rot. When Rob pushed gently against one of the panes it bent and flexed, creaking, sending a shower of dust and dead seeds cascading across his boots.

'Looks like that bramble's the only thing keeping this place upright,' he said.

One of the thorns snagged in Caroline's hair. She swore and tugged herself free. 'We should have brought some secateurs.'

'A flame thrower would be more use.' Ruth dumped the plastic boxes and stood looking around at the weeds and dirt. Wooden staging ran around each wall, piles of terracotta pots stacked on the slats, their sides stained with moss. A zinc watering can hung on a hook, and a heap of weedkiller tins sprawled across the bare earth floor by one wall. A long-dead butterfly swung in a cobweb. 'Where do we start?'

'Put ourselves in their shoes. Whoever they were.' Caroline could not allow herself to imagine Frances creeping into this dank, hidden place, bringing with her – what? Who? 'Where would you go if you were trying to bury someone in here?'

'Depends on how much time you thought you had.' Rob came to stand beside her. 'Was the greenhouse ever used?'

'We used to get told off if we came anywhere near here.' Ruth was leaning on the wooden staging, testing it, making it creak. 'Mr Harris used to tell us he kept poison in here.'

Rob bent over the pile of tins. 'Not surprised. That one's paraquat.'

Caroline pulled on a pair of gloves. 'Maybe there's something underneath.' She lifted the first tin. Some oily substance had leaked out, corroding the metal and making it stick to the one beside it. 'Jesus, we'll need to get a skip.'

'You'll need to call the council.' Ruth was gingerly holding a plastic bottle, which she dropped into a bin bag. 'Though I suppose a load of hazardous waste would put anyone off if they came snooping.'

Caroline picked up another tin. The lettering had bleached into illegibility; it reminded her of the graves she had walked on in the churchyard, the names of the dead smoothed away. 'Let's at least shift these ones.'

They worked in silence, the only sound the clank and scrape of metal containers being dropped into bags. But when they'd moved the last tin, there was nothing to see underneath except compacted earth, stained with rust, the soil cracked and rough like dead skin where it had been left barren and bare. Caroline scraped at it with the trowel, which rang as it hit something hard. 'Paving stone,' she said.

Rob was kicking at the earth under the staging, scuffing it up with his boot. 'Another one here,' he said. 'Probably a line of them that goes all around the edge.'

Ruth carefully tied the last bin bag shut before dropping it near the door. 'So where else?'

'What about there?' Caroline said, pointing to a spot in the opposite corner. It was full of tall, lush weeds. There were more shadows here, the light blocked by a sheet of sacking that had been nailed over a broken pane as a rough repair. 'Nettles like disturbed ground.'

'Let me guess, you once prosecuted a murderer?' Rob said.

'Saw a documentary on Channel Four.' She slashed with a bamboo cane, flattening the plants so they lay cowed and broken. 'The space looks big enough,' she said doubtfully. 'What do you think?'

Ruth considered. 'Your gran was only small,' she said. 'I can't see her taking out anyone who was much over five foot.'

'If they buried her before rigor set in she could have been bent over to fit,' Rob said. 'I've got a *Silent Witness* box set,' he added, as the women turned to look at him.

'It might not have been a deep grave,' Ruth said. 'If we're talking about 1947, it was a bloody awful winter. The ground would have been frozen solid.'

Rob picked up the spade, handed it to Caroline. 'You want to do the honours?'

Caroline nodded. She stood for a moment, hefting the handle to get a feel for the weight. It felt right, as if she and she alone could do this, a strange and unlooked-for duty.

Then she sent the blade slicing down into the dark, crumbling soil.

A beetle scurried away in panic. The crushed nettles drooped as she lifted the earth away, dumping it to one side. She dug again, this time sliding the spade's head across in a more shallow direction. Straggling roots snatched at the metal.

'Hold on.' Ruth spoke sharply. 'What's that?' She scraped with the trowel, dragging dirt away from something white and hard. 'Just a flint,' she said, disappointed. 'There's a pile of them. Hold on while I—'

Caroline had already turned away, back to the hole. Her whole being was now rapt, focusing intently on the earth that spilled back into the hole each time she lifted the spade. Fine crumbs of soil were dribbling down the sides as if desperate to run back and hide whatever lay beneath. She dug again and again, moving so the hole became wider, stopping only so Rob could pull away a thick pale root that came writhing towards the light, then pushing the blade in again, going down two inches, then six, a foot—

A skull.

It appeared quite suddenly, the earth falling away from its yellowing round dome. The teeth gleamed in a broad grin, as if it was delighted to see them.

'Oh God,' Ruth said.

Caroline knelt, tucking her hair behind her ears. She brushed soil away with her fingers. Small, thin bones lay beside the skull; a hand, resting underneath the head, as a child will sleep. Tears pricked at her eyes.

Then Rob was beside her, a soft paintbrush in his hand. He handed it to her and she dusted the skull with gentle sweeps, ushering the dirt away from a great crack that ran across the back of the head, gaping wide like a second smile.

'Is it her, do you think?' he said softly. 'Is it Lizzie?'

But before she could answer, the door slammed behind them. A new voice, harsh and breathless, split open the darkening afternoon.

'Leave it!' The words were shrill with panic. 'Leave it now, or – or I'll bloody well shoot!'

31

It was a gun.

Caroline felt her whole body freeze, unable to look away, the black, implacable hole of the muzzle seeming to grow and swell, engulfing everything, so all she could see, all she could think about, was that round deep stare, so like the blind eyes in the ground that she felt she was tumbling forward into the grave beside the bones. The thought was unbearable, sending a fresh streak of terror snaking through her. She dragged her eyes away and up to the man's face, and recognition seared across her mind.

Him.

The watcher.

His dark hair was wild and the lenses of his glasses were spattered with rain. He held the gun as if it were a canker growing out of his hand, some alien and hateful thing that should be excised and cast away.

Caroline dropped the spade, her hands suddenly numb and trembling. The muzzle of the gun was a thing of infinite menace, wavering between them as the man took a step forward, stumbling slightly on the rough earth, his face deathly white and his eyes wide.

'Leave it,' he said again. He gestured with the gun. 'Get away from it, move!'

'All right, all right.' Rob somehow managed to sound reasonable. He held his hands out, fingers spread wide. 'Let's just all keep calm—'

'Shut up. I told you already, move. Right. Stop there. Stand still.'

Pressed tightly together, Caroline could smell Rob's fabric conditioner, Ruth's shampoo, sweet, synthetic scents that were piercingly clear above the dankness of decay. She wondered wildly if they could smell her – bath oil, coffee, the sharp spurt of terrified piss she had only just managed to hold in. Could they see her shaking? She felt for Ruth's hand, their trembling fingers interlacing. The leather of her glove made the touch feel alien and unnerving. She leaned back against Rob, feeling the thudding of his heart, hearing him exhale, his breath as ragged as the papery wings of the butterfly that hung above them in its dusty noose.

She heard Ruth start to speak, clear her throat, start again. 'Come on,' she was saying, 'there's no need for this—'

'Shut up.' The man was fumbling in his jacket pocket. The movement made the gun waver wildly, and he muttered to himself, 'For fuck's sake,' before dragging out his phone. His eyes darted between them and the screen as he scrolled awkwardly with his left thumb, jabbing at a number. The silence was so complete that Caroline could hear the buzz, buzz as the call tried to connect, the sound slicing across the dimness like a scythe. A thin, recorded voice sounded, faraway and unreachable.

'It's me. You need to call me back. Something's happened.'

'I can see that, you young fool.'

Mr Harris wore a long overcoat and a dark hat, and his eyes were as empty as those that stared from the soil behind them. He came slowly across the lumpy earth, feeling his way with his stick. When he reached their terrified little huddle he stood for a moment looking at them, considering, as if he were making some kind of calculation; then he turned to the man and shook his head.

'For crying out loud, Danny,' he said. 'Now what have you gone and done?'

32

The gun lay flat and malevolent in the old man's palm. He stood weighing it with little jerky movements of his hand, before sighing and dropping it into his coat pocket.

The man he'd called Danny sagged, although whether in shame or relief Caroline could not tell. 'I didn't know what else to do. They were digging. Over there. They found something.'

'Oh yeah?' Mr Harris turned to Caroline. 'What was that, then?'

'You know what it was.' She was startled at how firm her voice sounded. 'You know who it is.'

'Do I now?' Mr Harris looked down into the hole. 'Why'd you want to go and start bothering things that's best left?' His gaze was locked with those great gaping sockets.

'My grandmother lost Lizzie Sixpence.' She felt almost light-headed with the strangeness of it all, the familiar face of the old man, here, in this charnel house with its poisons and its secrets.

'And you had to go looking.' He rested both hands on the handle of his stick, looking like a heron as it waits to spear a chick. 'Them bones've been here a good few years. Why go digging it all up again now? Why couldn't you just let it be?'

She didn't know if he meant the bones, or the secrets, or whatever long-ago pain had led to this cold, damp place and the cold, sullied skull. 'I can't just leave her—'

'Her?' The old man let out a hoarse bark of what could have been laughter. 'Lizzie? You reckon this is Lizzie?'

'It's not?'

She told her feet to move, and managed to take the few steps forward so she could stand beside him, both of them now looking down at the white and fragile thing that lay beneath their feet.

'Course it ain't.' He turned away. 'My Lizzie ain't here,' he said. A tear fell out of his eye, disappearing into the crevices on his face as a shiver ran through him.

Danny put his arm around the old man's shoulders. 'Come on, Granddad,' he said. 'We best get out of here.'

It took Caroline a moment to realise what he'd said. 'Granddad? I thought this was about — is that why you've been spying on me? I thought it was because of Harriet?'

Danny shook his head. The light gave him a sickly greenish pallor, making it look as if he were about to vomit. He was older than Caroline had first thought, maybe in his early forties, with a face that in other circumstances might have been kind.

'Who the bloody hell's Harriet?' he said. His arm tightened around the old man.

Caroline stared. 'You're not… I thought… weren't you the one who yelled at me? You said you'd be watching me, that I'd regret…'

Danny took his eyes off Mr Harris for a moment, his expression a queasy blend of anger and bewilderment.

'My nan's dead,' he said. 'Who the bloody hell's Harriet?'

'Then who—'

Rob in turn took his own hesitant step forward. 'Maybe we should talk about this somewhere else,' he said. 'Somewhere we can be comfortable. Warm.'

'Tell us who this is,' Caroline snapped. 'Tell us why they're here. Tell me what has been going on in this bloody house and *tell me what happened to Lizzie Sixpence.*'

Mr Harris looked at her consideringly. Then he cast one more glance into the grave, before in an oddly angular movement taking off his hat and standing there for a moment with his eyes closed and his head bowed. 'All this bleeding time,' he said. Then he turned, looking at them as they huddled under the grimy glass. He used his stick to point to the door.

'No sense talking about it in here,' he said. He heaved a great sigh. 'I'll tell you. But I want to do it back in the house, back in your grandma's living room.' Another tear bumped its way down his face. 'Back where it all happened in the first place,' he said.

Part Two

1946–1947

The Laurels Boarding House,
Waldemar Crescent, Ealing
3 March 1946

Dearest Connie (or may I call you Your Ladyship?!),

Just a line to say thank you for the wedding cake. I haven't had anything so scrummy since 1939. I eked it out for three nights, such a treat.

How was the honeymoon? I imagine that in earlier times it would have been Le Train Bleu to the Riviera, but given the circs, I'm sure that an ordinary sleeper to Scotland was marvellous. Your hat was wonderful! Promise you'll show me some pics when I see you. I'm not going to enquire about the loss of maidenly modesty, you never had much of that to start with!

All here is much as it was. I sit in a smelly office with two smelly old men who constantly want me to make them tea and fetch them buns from Lyons every afternoon. They are snobs and prigs and insist on inspecting my work, even though they've not found an error yet. They are firmly of the opinion that a degree awarded to a woman is somehow ersatz, like I had to collect cigarette cards for it or something. One of them (Mr Poole) makes sneering references to 'your time in a man's job' — as if teaching in a boys' school is somehow forbidden to what his accomplice (Mr Rogers) calls The Gentler Sex. I sometimes think I will brain them both with the adding machine, just to see how gentle they think I am then. Incidentally, I heard from Diana last week. She says that the man they sacked me to make way for is terrible, and parents are complaining that their little angels won't get through the Common Entrance. Boys are apparently being removed in droves. Wrong of me I know but I couldn't help feeling very smug.

Oh, Connie, I am sorry to moan, when you're newly married and I hope so happy you could burst. If you really mean it I'd love to come and stay — I miss Shenstone Hall but not as much as I miss you. Who'd have thought the rotten old war would have in its way brought us such good times?

My fondest love to you and that lucky husband of yours,
Frances xx

Shenstone Hall,
Shenstone, Wiltshire
6 March 1946

Darling Fran,

You poor love, I am so sorry it's all so grim. That bloody school doesn't know a good thing when it sees one, I hope the governors end up having to scrub floors in a brothel for a living. They were bad enough when we were working there, the end of the war made them even worse.

But… are you sitting down? Prepare to cast aside the horrors of Poole and Rogers. Put down the adding machine this minute, because I've had an idea and even Ali agrees it's a belter.

Do you remember his aunt Maud? Batty as they come but I can't help liking the old girl. Family black sheep (or she was until I came along, ha ha!) – refused to be presented, was a VAD in the first war (God, how awful we have to say that now) and horror of horrors, is UNMARRIED, wears TROUSERS, BREEDS DOGS and DOES GOOD WORKS. I think you might have seen her at the wedding, she was the one who dashed out of the church as soon as we went to sign the register because she was so desperate for a fag.

Anyway, the point is, she's been ill (that awful flu germ that was doing the rounds, but being surrounded by snotty kids can't help – more on them anon) and it's really dragged her down. I suggested to Ali who suggested to her that she could use a capable, logical and efficient secretary-cum-companion, and we must have caught her in a weak moment because she said yes! Of course I said that you'd totally fit the bill and she's agreed to give you a go! What do you think? It won't be much money, but it'll be live in, a big old place just outside London, nice suburbs all around, and I don't suppose you'll find the work too tiring. She used to run the place as a home for unwanted evacuees, but now the war's over she takes in women whose hubbies have come home and gone bonkers. I'm being unkind, I know, but I have to say we all went through hell so why being demobbed should somehow make it okay for a man to beat lumps out of his wife is beyond me. I bet most of them never saw more action than an ack-ack gun anyway.

I am such a bitch. Never mind. Do you fancy it? If you do then write and tell her — Wickham Grange, West Wickham, Kent. Don't you dare forget to let me know too!

I miss you as well. Once you're at the Grange we can see each other loads more. Alastair's going to be like a blue-arsed fly getting the estate back up and running so I'll be glad of a bolt-hole.

Lots of love,
Connie xx

33
Frances, 1946

Good grief. Was that actually a gong?

I sat up, reaching for my glasses. The sound came again, ringing up the stairs. My watch said eight, and I recalled Maud's words: 'Brekker's at eight fifteen,' she'd said, best be sharp otherwise you'll have to make do with bread and marge. The thought was enough to make me scramble out of bed – surprisingly comfortable, if narrow – and into a utility skirt and a rather lumpy jumper I'd knitted when I was at Shenstone Hall. The thick stockings I used to loathe now seemed cosy and sensible, because the day was cold, and the WC colder still.

I'd arrived the day before, puttering up the hill in a taxi that smelled of wet wool and Woodbines. It had been raining – it's always raining, I don't think it's stopped since the end of the war – and the trees lining the lane were heavy with drooping leaves. I sat in the back, one small suitcase at my feet, an unflattering hat on my head, looking about me and wondering what on earth I'd agreed to do. We passed a little church, with a mason's van parked outside, two men struggling down the path carrying a gleaming white marble cross. I shivered, hoping it wasn't some kind of omen. I'm a logical woman, it's not like me to be superstitious, but when something seems to be too good to be true, like this job, I can't help crossing fingers and spitting at magpies.

The cabbie left me to clamber out by myself, clearly not wanting to get wet, and then had the temerity to charge me two shillings for a trip from the station that was barely as many miles. He held out a hand, but I withheld the coin until he said please, then turned around and looked at the house that was to be my new home. I don't even think I noticed him driving away.

I suppose a polite word for Wickham Grange would be eccentric. It's as if the architect had been paid by the right angle, because the place juts and turns in every direction, its pleasant red brick façade jerking unevenly up into gables, dormers, and chimneys. Windows blinked at me through the drizzle, the ones upstairs all open to let in the fresh air. I gave up counting them when I got to ten. From somewhere at the back I could hear children playing, and there was a welcoming smell of baking.

I stood for a moment, telling myself I wanted to get my bearings, although now I was here the truth was that I was suddenly nervous. Like everywhere, the house bore the scars of the war, with its weedy drive and flaking paintwork. From its position halfway up the hill it had what must once have been sweeping views down towards West Wickham, but the fields were now beginning to be dotted with the first hesitant signs of rebuilding, and the little lane we'd driven up was already home to two or three raw new villas that looked stark and gauche compared to the dusty bricks of Wickham Grange. Like me, the house found itself amongst strangers.

Enough of such nonsense. Time to pull myself together.

The bell-pull was cold to the touch, even through my gloves, although admittedly they are more darn than wool. But before I could ring it, the door opened and I found myself being surveyed by three pairs of eyes, all more or less at the same height.

'Saw you from the landing window,' said the Honourable Maud Shenstone. 'Glad to see you gave George Springer short shrift. Man's a rogue. Oh for God's sake, Haggis, get your paws off the windowsill. And you, Tattie. Let Miss Alleyn get through the door.'

I peered through the sea of snouts and paws. At their mistress's words, the two huge dogs dropped down onto all fours, and retreated amiably down the hall, where they waited in a tangle of grey fur and waving tails.

'Bloody hounds,' Maud said. 'Eat me out of house and home, and don't even bark when there's someone at the door. Here, let me take that. Come in, my dear, come in, I'm sure you're dying for a pee and a drink.' She pointed at one of several doors. 'Through there for the one, and when you're finished join me in the drawing room for the other. Down there on the left. Come on, you ridiculous animals, how many more times, don't just stand there.'

Feeling that to disobey would have been wildly impossible, I did as I was told. The water was erratic and the loo paper crackled, but when I tapped on the drawing-room door and went in I found it a beautiful room. Vases of rain-battered tulips stood on all the tables, and two long sofas flanked the fireplace, its marble surround topped with a gilt mirror that reflected the faded chintz of the curtains. There were French windows that gave a view of grass and trees; a crack ran across one of the panes, which was held together with what looked like tape left over from air raid precautions.

'Cricket,' Maud said, following my gaze. 'One of the boys we've got in at the moment is going to be a superb fast bowler, once we get his sense of direction sorted out. Not used to having this much space, poor chap, constantly over-shoots, but he's getting a real passion for the game and is going to try to get into a grammar so he can keep playing. I've said I'll buy him his first set of pads. Not bad for a snotty kid from Canning Town.' She smiled, looking like a happy child herself. 'This house does tend to be a place where people learn all sorts of things about themselves. Drink?'

Three in the afternoon? 'Yes, please.'

'Excellent. Sit down, Miss Alleyn, do, just tell Tattie to get out of the way. They do rather seem to think the furniture is there for their own convenience.'

'Please. Call me Frances. Miss Alleyn was for school.'

'Delighted. And when we get down to work there'll be no need to bother with all that honourable nonsense. Plain old Maud, in every sense, that's me.'

I sat down beside the dog, who was indeed sprawled over at least two thirds of the sofa, and took the glass my new employer handed to me. Maud sat opposite, and took a deep draught.

'Suppose you think I'm a frightful old lush,' she said. 'Truth is, it's been a pig of a day. Very glad you are here, you'll be a tremendous help.'

'I hope so,' I said. The whisky was dark and smoky and admirably untroubled by water. 'But I'm not really sure what—'

Maud cocked her head and blinked. She was a stout woman, much taller than me, and her cropped brown head gave her the look of a kindly hen. 'Ah,' she said. 'No. My fault, really. I should have told Alastair to give you the full gen. Your friend Connie's a game girl, by the way, she'll be the making of him, even if the local snobs disapprove.'

I couldn't help smiling. Alastair Shenstone had arrived home from his POW camp, thin and morose, shutting himself away in his room and only willing to see the doctor. We'd not really taken much notice, being too busy getting the children ready to go back to London; then three days after he got back, Connie and I led the second formers into what is now the Long Gallery but back then was our dining hall. Alastair must have just had a doctor's visit, because he was slumped in his wheelchair, trundling himself back to his room, and without looking round he barked at us to get out. Connie marched up to him and barked that he should make himself useful and hand round the plates.

Connie is blonde, buxom and Bermondsey, and she'd hit Alastair Shenstone like a torpedo.

'I think they're very happy,' I said truthfully.

'Bloody hope so. Poor old Ali, he's a good egg but he's like most men, needs a boot up his backside if he's going to get anywhere. Smoke?'

I shook my head.

'I shouldn't, but small pleasures in a wicked world, eh? Well, let me put you straight. I came here when the war broke out – the first war, I mean, I had a mad aunt who set it up as a hospital for wounded officers – and I've never left. It's always been the dumping ground for family waifs and strays, spinster daughters, disgraced sons and so forth, so in 'thirty-nine evacuees seemed a logical next step. One thing led to another, as is often the way.'

I was curious. 'Connie said you now take mothers as well?'

'Sad to say we do.' She blew an uncertain smoke ring, sending it wobbling up to the ceiling. 'Once the evacuees went home in 'forty-four we started taking in those women who couldn't take their children back even if they wanted to. Houses not there, husband killed, bomb injuries that meant they couldn't work, that kind of thing. I've always set my face against those societies that ship children off to the colonies, can't see any good coming of it, so having them here was a logical step. But things have got worse since the end of the war, I'm afraid. We're needed more than ever. Men driven mad by the things they've seen and done, women not wanting to go dutifully back into the kitchen, all sorts, it means families break up and often in the worst possible way. And when your husband's beating you to a pulp and your kids are starving and you've got nowhere to go… well, then you come here and we try to fix you up.'

'That's brave,' I said, and meant it.

'Is it? All I know is I can't stand unfairness. Maybe it's why I agreed to give you a try when I heard you were sacked to make way for a feller. Bloody cheek.' A clock chimed over the fireplace. 'I can't say I really wanted a secretary. But when Alastair told me you'd lost your job, I thought why not, let's give the girl a chance. Not her fault she was out on her ear just because some weedy little oik had been demobbed. Shall we say six months and see how we get on?'

She held out her hand, and I took it. Her grip was firm, no nonsense, the hand of a woman who rolled up her sleeves and sorted things out. I decided that I liked Maud Shenstone.

And now here I was, going down to my first breakfast at Wickham Grange. I could hear children's chatter rising above lower, more hesitant voices. Unbelievably, I could smell bacon.

I went down the passage to the dining room, feeling suddenly happier and more hopeful than I had done for months.

I wonder; if I'd known, would I have gone in, taken a seat, poured myself a cup of tea?

Or would I have run for my life, while I still had the chance?

34

That first morning there were three women and four children at the long mahogany table, the women all stiff, taut and exhausted, nibbling on toast and taking too long to stir their tea, while the children sat fidgeting, full of some adventure they were going to have in the garden that morning. It was like that every time, I learned, the broken boys and girls being quicker to sense the safety and protection of that house than any of the women who brought them. I'd seen the same thing during the war, when the children I taught could carry on complicated games even as the sirens screamed.

Maud was standing at the head of the table, pouring tea from a huge brown pot. She was in corduroy breeches and a man's checked shirt, her spectacles perched on top of her head.

'Come in, come in,' she bellowed, her voice matching her height. 'Everyone, this is Miss Alleyn. Malcolm, if you don't stop kicking your brother I'll make her teach you algebra. Ladies, Miss Alleyn is going to be my right-hand woman. Do ask her if you need anything.' She put the pot down and took a huge bite of toast, heading for the door. 'Take your time,' she said as she passed me. 'I'll be in the office down the hall. Young Maureen there can show you when you're done.'

As indeed she did. I tapped on the door some twenty minutes later, when the women had gone upstairs to make beds and stare at walls. Maureen skipped away to find the other kids. Maud let out a deep humming noise.

'Nicer than barking out the order to come in,' she said as I went in. 'These poor souls have had enough of being yelled at. Right, you sit here. You type? Excellent. Got fingers like sausages myself. Ready? This is about Mrs Garfield, she's the one with the two boys. Found her a nice place in Essex. Just need to do her a reference for the landlady. Only one room, but it's better than having her jaw broken, don't you think? Off we go. Dear Mrs Costelloe…'

I positioned my fingers on the keys. After a few moments of dictation I looked up, surprised. 'She's been here two years?'

Maud looked at me. 'Of course not. Six weeks, if I recall. But that doesn't look good enough, so we bump it up a bit.' She grinned. 'About the only time the old title nonsense comes in handy. Nobody thinks to question the quality.'

And so it began. There was always a steady stream of letters to type, forms to fill in, telephone calls to make to landlords, employers, councils and solicitors. If I was not chasing some official I would be writing to one of Maud's vast network, the silent army of women who not only sent cases to us but who would help with raising money, or who knew which country houses were crying out for housekeepers, who sat on the boards of hospitals and schools, who had run units and factories during the war and who were refusing to go back to afternoon tea and sales of work. The backbone of England, Maud called them, and it was to her credit that she included in that those women who had themselves stayed at the Grange and who kept in touch with news of openings and lodgings that could help those coming after them. Into my files they went, names and addresses and notes, snug in their cardboard folders.

Every morning, nine until twelve thirty: then two until four, with the rest of the day my own. In practice I usually stayed downstairs in the drawing room, where Maud played records and I read books, while the mothers either knitted or flicked through magazines, sometimes not turning a page for an hour. We had a daily, Mrs Lloyd, and a young woman doctor visited anyone who needed attention. I found she was someone I could respect, if not like, for she was brusque and abrupt, even with the children. But then she had been at the relief of Belsen, and one must make allowances.

I had every second Wednesday off, and the weekends (Maud called them Saturdays to Mondays) were free as well, which meant I could walk down into West Wickham to find shops and tearooms and a cinema. Trams and trains ran to London, but I rarely went further than Croydon unless I was meeting Connie, when we would browse the meagre offerings in the London shops. Bless her, she would bring fruit and veg from the estate, and occasionally stayed over at the Grange, usually when there were builders at the Hall, or Alastair was having one of his many operations.

So spring became what should have been summer, the first summer of peace. The war had been over for a year, not that you would have thought it. Everything, even the June sky, was grey, hard, dull. Life pinched like a worn-out shoe. The women I'd met on my first day left. More arrived. I typed and signed and telephoned. I read and slept and wondered whether I should leave, and if I did, what I would do. The months rolled round to autumn.

And then it was a Wednesday, and I was in Woolworths, and I met Lizzie Sixpence.

35

Lizzie

I dunno why I chose her. It's not like she looked up to much. I've seen more meat on a butcher's pencil and her clothes, well, they might have been good once, but they were on their way out and no mistake. I should know. The major used to like dressing me up in his wife's things, pretty silk frocks and tweed suits. That's how he found out I was up the duff, when her wedding dress got tight and he couldn't play wedding night with me no more.

But anyway, there we were in Woollies, one chilly Wednesday afternoon in the October, the day already getting a bit dark early like it was practising for proper winter. Sid had sent me and Mickey out to see what we could get, because now I was starting to show there weren't no trade for me no more on the streets. I can't say I was sad, because I never much liked nicking stuff, either, but it were better than anything that Clapton bloke wanted so I did it, to keep Sid sweet. And anyway, I saw this woman in Woollies, she was just wandering about, browsing, and more to the point she had left her purse on top of her shopping bag. It was just lying there, like a great big shell. I saw a seashell once, when I was a kid. Not at the beach, no, this was in a garden, a long row of them there was, all down the side of the path, shining like teeth.

I've always wanted to see the sea one day.

Woollies wasn't busy, because half of it was still in ruins, and anyway they had bugger all to sell. I nodded at her so Mickey knew what I was up to. He shook his head.

'Too easy,' he said, 'maybe she's one of them narks.'

'Nah. I saw her coming out of the chemist.' I was pretending to look at a mousetrap, feeling sorry for the furry little necks it would break. 'She's just daft. More money 'n sense.'

He held my hand, very gently, just for a moment. 'Well be careful. Sid'll have your guts for garters…'

My bruises smarted at the name. He didn't have to tell me what Sid could do if anyone cocked up. Even June had a black eye, just because some bloke had run off without paying her. Mickey had a nasty gash and a bruise on his face, as well, from where he'd got in the way when Sid were lashing out about something or other.

We'd had thin pickings that day and looking back I think I was getting desperate. Beckenham had been useless, and one of the shopkeepers kept giving us funny looks, so we'd come over to West Wickham to try our luck. We didn't dare go back to the flat empty handed.

I think I sounded braver than I felt. 'I'll be all right. You keep an eye out. We'll make a dash for it, out the front, and straight on the bus.'

He weren't happy, but he let me go. Don't suppose he had much choice, really.

The woman was looking at compacts. Cheap rubbish they were, full of powder that clogged on your skin. Mrs Major used to have Coty's, which was lovely. I nicked her lipstick holder when he threw me out. I thought I deserved something nice, but Sid made me sell it as soon as I got it home.

I wandered down between the shelves, picking up bits and pieces, pretending to think about them. Egg cups. Baby bottles and nappy pins. That kind of thing made me feel a bit funny, so I hurried past them, and maybe that's where I went wrong, maybe the baby things made me get all hot and bothered, because when I got close and I reached out, ever so slowly, towards her bag—

My fingers brushed the worn leather of the purse and quick as one of them traps, her hand snapped round and grabbed my wrist and oh my sweet Jesus I was caught.

36

I swear I couldn't help it. As her fingers wrapped around my arm I yelped with the pain, but fair play to her, she didn't let go.

'What do you think you are doing?' she said. Very calm. The Ts and Ds and Gs rattled in her mouth like tin tacks.

'Sorry,' I gabbled, 'sorry, miss, thought you was my mum, wasn't looking—'

I used to watch the searchlights during the Blitz. Her eyes, behind her little round glasses, were just like them, raking across my face and then around the shop. Mickey was at the end of the aisle, his face white and hard with alarm.

'I can't see anyone who could remotely be your mother.'

'She must have gone, sorry, miss, I'll just—'

'What seems to be the trouble, madam?'

Oh my Christ, it was a big bloke, in a pinstripe suit. Cheap stuff, as shiny as his face. He had a little moustache, you'd have thought that by now he'd have realised it made him look like Hitler.

'I'm the manager,' he was saying, then he looked at me and his little eyes went all narrow. 'Oh, it's you. I've heard about you. Come here.'

He grabbed my other arm and this time I really couldn't stop myself, I gave an almighty scream because bloody hell it hurt.

'There's no need to manhandle the girl,' the woman said sharply.

The manager puffed himself up. 'There's a police warning out for her,' he said. 'She and her accomplice were seen in Beckenham, only this morning, and their description was telephoned through not an hour ago. They're quite well known to those of us in the retail trade. No need to worry yourself, madam.'

I can't tell you what I was thinking, because I was just a great mess of fear. Not of the police, though that was bad enough. No, I was scared for Mickey, who was hanging around at the end of the aisle looking petrified, and I was even more terrified to my bones of Sid and what he'd do to both of us if he knew I'd been caught, if he found out I was getting recognised. He'd only agreed to keep me on if I went out on the rob, if I brought in enough to keep him sweet, and if I couldn't even do that—

I know I was shaking. I felt dizzy and sick, but with them holding me I couldn't even clap my hands over my mouth. I could feel tears stinging my eyes as my throat heaved. I made some nasty little choking sound, feeling puke bubbling in my chest.

'Here,' the woman said. She handed me a hanky, not the silly little lacy kind, a proper, useful big white one. 'Take a deep breath.' Then she turned back to the manager, and so help me, she said, 'It's quite all right. My mistake. I know this young lady.'

I nearly dropped with shock.

'Oh you do, do you?' He was looking at her with a nasty glint in his eyes, and I thought, oh Christ, she'll crack, but no, she just stood there, all four foot ten of her, and she gave him such a stare, you could almost hear it crackling, like ack-ack fire it was.

'You're doubting my word? Or would you rather I called the police and explained how you assaulted my niece and refused to let me leave your shop? I believe I saw a constable in the street a few minutes ago, I'm sure he will be pleased to come in and hear my statement.'

There was a long pause. I could see the thoughts scurrying like beetles behind his face as he weighed it all up. Then, at last, I felt those hard, podgy fingers unpeel themselves from my skin. I winced again as the blood started to flow back down my arm.

'Very well.' He took a step back, his gaze flicking between us. 'But—' one of those fingers jabbed towards us – 'don't think I'll forget you. Either of you.'

'I'm sure you will remain equally memorable to us. Come along.' And still gripping my wrist – though a lot more gently now – she steered me out of the shop and into the high street, past the bombsites and into a tea shop, where she pushed me into a seat and, well, I couldn't believe my ears, she ordered me a pot of Rosie and a plate of sandwiches. Cheese and pickle. I swear I nearly dribbled as they were put down in front of me.

'How many can I eat?'

She raised an eyebrow. 'As many as you want. And is that your young man out there? The one with the bruise?' I nodded. 'He looks almost as hungry as you. Bring him in.'

So Mickey come in, with much wiping of his feet and twisting of his cap, and he sat awkwardly between us while the woman ordered more grub and another pot. She was quite calm, as if this were just a nice little tea party with some of her posh friends. I grabbed a sarnie, then another one, not caring that little bits of cheese were falling down my frock.

It was Mickey who finally said something.

'Look, this is all very nice and all that, but what's up? Why are you doing this?' A thought struck him. 'Here, you ain't going to want to pray for us, are you, like the Sally Anns?'

'Certainly not.' The woman stirred a couple of Sugarettes into her cup. Then she reached across the table and pushed my sleeve back.

'Who did that to you?'

I could feel myself blushing with shame. Both my arms were purple and swollen from shoulder to wrist, with little pink cuts and grazes scattered amongst the bruises like flowers growing on muck. Sid had been drunk, furious over the share Kenny had given him from some factory raid, and he'd used his belt on anyone who couldn't get out of his way. He'd got me stuck in the corner, yelling that I wasn't worth my keep no more. In the end Mickey had managed to get him off me, getting a smack himself for his pains, but not before I'd got all cut about with the buckle end.

But I knew better than to say so.

'Fell down the stairs,' I said.

She gave me another one of those stares until I looked back down at the tablecloth. I could feel my face burning and I thought she was going to throw me out for lying. Then she turned to Mickey, her eyes taking in the scabs and bruises on his poor face.

'And presumably you fell down after her?'

'Lizzie's a good girl,' he said uncomfortably.

'I'm sure she is. But by the looks of things she needs a doctor and a hot meal, in that order.' She looked at her watch. 'Dr Fairfax can probably fit you in—'

My chair scraped on the floor as I scrambled up. 'I ain't seeing no doctor!'

'Do sit down, miss – Lizzie?'

'Lizzie Sixpence.'

'Is that your real name?'

'It's what everyone calls me.'

'Then it will have to do. For heaven's sake, girl, you need medical attention. You're black and blue and judging by the look of you you're a few months along.'

I put my hands on the hard curve of my belly. The baby gave me a little friendly kick, and I patted her, letting her know it was all right. 'I'm okay,' I said stubbornly.

'Is someone stopping you from seeing a doctor?'

I shot a look at Mickey. 'We're all right, miss,' he said. 'I can take care of her.'

'Well, you need to get better at it.'

'Mickey does his best,' I said heatedly. 'He's a good mate to me.'

'I'm sure he is.' She shook her head. 'Oh, you're a pair of idiots. But I daresay you know your own minds.' She beckoned to the waitress and handed her a ten-bob note. 'I think my friends would like some more sandwiches,' she said. 'And keep the change,' she added, looking at me. 'Use it to look after yourself and that baby.

And as for you, young man, don't let her get caught again.' She stood up, adjusting her bloody horrible hat.

Mickey swallowed, and held out his hand. 'You're a good'un, miss,' he said. 'Thank you. Me and Lizzie – we're grateful, ain't we?'

I could only nod. The whole thing was starting to feel more and more unreal, like something you'd see at the pictures or in a book.

The woman opened her bag and took out a little square of card. 'If you change your mind, come here. Ask for Miss Alleyn. You'll be safe, I promise. Now. Good afternoon to the pair of you. And take my advice, steer clear of West Wickham for a week or two.'

'We will, miss,' Mickey said. 'And thank you.'

I watched her go, her thin little figure weaving in and out of the tables. She didn't look back, so she didn't see me pick up the card and read it. 'Wickham Grange', it said. It sounded nice, like a big warm oven.

'You keep this, Mick,' I said. He tucked it in his pocket, and we sat there smiling at each other, full of relief and tea and more food than we'd had in a week. There were three and ninepence left over, an' all, and that kept Sid sweet for a bit as well.

But that night, as I lay under my blanket, feeling the baby swirl and dance, I kept thinking about what Miss Alleyn had said, the promise she'd made. *You'll be safe.* For the first time in months I felt – not hopeful, exactly, but that there might be some way to make things better, some way to get through it all and come out the other side, me and my baby together.

She was a clever woman, Frances Alleyn. Educated, been to college and all sorts. Had more books than I'd ever seen in my life.

But as I was to find out, even she had made a promise she couldn't keep.

37
Frances, 1947

Connie arrived in January for a visit. She came in like a spring gale, bringing eggs and butter and a case of port, which she said was for building up our strength. The women looked at her as if she was some kind of exotic creature, a leopard in tweed, but she made them tea, dropped her aitches, and within an hour was as familiar with them and their stories as I'd been after a week.

'God, no, thank you, darling,' she said when I tried to tell her how glad I was to see her. 'I'm just glad I can get a bit of peace and quiet. The Hall's like Bedlam. Ali is always yelling at the workmen – mind you, last week he was so enraged about something that he got halfway up the stairs before he remembered he's supposed to be in a wheelchair, so it's swings and roundabouts.'

Her arrival was a bright spot after a grim couple of months; we'd seen nearly a dozen women come and go since September, together with children who'd brought measles, whooping cough and the never-ending nits. Since the New Year the weather had been bitterly cold, and even Maud, usually so indefatigable, had developed a hacking cough and been instructed by Audrey Fairfax to take a few days' rest. She had done her best, spending forty-eight hours reading or stomping across the fields with the hounds, before declaring herself perfectly sound and would we all please stop making so much damn fuss. I didn't bother arguing.

That night, the last of the ordinary nights, I was in the kitchen, grating cheese while my employer hacked at a National Loaf. Supper was to be rabbit stew, and the heads of the unfortunate creatures lay on the table, ears drooping, blind eyes looking longingly at the pile of carrot tops that were waiting for the pig bin. A lump of rather waxy Cheddar fell on the floor and one of the dogs immediately snuffled it up, looking pleased with itself.

The door opened and Mrs Lloyd came in, fastening her coat. She was a stout, severely practical woman, who smelled permanently of Jeyes Fluid. I used to wonder if she dabbed it behind her ears every morning.

'She's all settled in the drawing room,' she said, jerking her head towards the door. 'I've left her ration book in your office. She brung some sausages but they won't keep so I'll cook 'em up in the morning. I put 'em in the meat safe, out of harm's way.' She gave the dogs a disapproving look. 'So if there's nothing else I'll be getting along.'

'Do take care,' Maud said. 'There's already quite a frost.'

'My Bob's picking me up at the bottom of the lane. You want to bring a shovel indoors, mind. The wireless was saying there's a terrible cold snap coming.'

'Can't be as bad as 1919,' Maud said cheerfully.

'Well, don't say I didn't warn you. And watch that dog, it nearly got its nose in the marge.' She gave us each a brief nod, and disappeared into the winter twilight.

'Good grief, that woman gets gloomier with every day that passes.' Maud lifted down a pile of plates, setting them out on the table in a neat row. 'Now, would you be so kind as to go and make Mrs Brown feel at home? I'll get this dished up. Give the gong a bash as you go past.'

I did as I was told, enjoying the brassy bong, bong, bong as it echoed around the house. Then I crossed the hall and went into the drawing room, where I found our new guest sitting stiffly upright, perched like a fledgling on the edge of the sofa. Her hands were clasped tightly in her lap. The room was almost dark, the only light coming from one of the table lamps, and when I appeared she gave a violent start, even though I'd tapped on the door and opened it gently.

'Mrs Brown? May I call you Grace?'

She gave a small, wary nod. She was still wearing her hat, a little green felt thing that was, if possible, even less flattering than my own. The bandage on her leg looked grey and grubby.

'I'm Frances Alleyn. Please call me Frances. I'm Miss Shenstone's secretary.' I went over to the standard lamp and switched it on, although the current was so weak it didn't add much to the gloom. 'Have you been up to your room?'

She managed a nod.

'Good. I hope you'll be comfortable. We'll be having supper in a minute, would you like to come through to the dining room? There are some other ladies here at the moment, I'll be happy to introduce you.'

'Thank you.' She spoke so quietly I could barely hear her. She kept glancing at the windows, and I followed her gaze out into the darkening garden.

'It's quite safe,' I said. 'I'm assuming nobody knows you're here?'

'I didn't tell no one.'

'Good. But even if you did tell anyone, this is private property. Nobody can come in.'

'But they'll be looking for me.'

'Honestly, it's all right. Everything's secure and you can stay for as long as you need.' I drew the curtains, the brass rings jingling, then turned and gave her what I hoped was a reassuring smile. 'Shall we go and meet everyone?'

The women who sat at the table were all much of an age, all in the mid twenties, all much of a class. An unusually large group, but none had children, which was an oddity I have been grateful for ever since. Two — Grace herself and Harriet, who had been with us for a week — were Londoners. Vera had washed up somehow from Swansea, while Jane and Maggie were cousins who had both been sent from Plymouth. Naval towns gave us a lot of work in those days. I always wondered if those two were more than just relatives to each other, not that it was any of my business; I was just glad that they had found love somewhere.

The five of them sat around the dining table like guests at a party they had been forced to attend. Harriet eyed Grace, and for one chilling moment I feared some horrible prejudice against her skin colour, but to my relief she just said, 'Pleased to meet you. Come and sit here, I'll budge up.'

There was no need for it; the table had been made to seat sixteen comfortably, in the age of bustles and elbow-length gloves, but they seemed to find a comfort in sitting close together. Grace got halfway to a smile before edging herself into a chair, then Maud wheeled in an ancient trolley bearing the pot of stew. It tasted better than I'd expected, and I ate my own bowlful hungrily, while Maud and Connie chatted amiably about the dogs, bread rationing, and that British staple, the weather. But when we had cleared away, and Maggie had taken her turn to wash up, we gathered around the wireless for the news. The announcer's voice was grave as he read out warnings of heavy snow, hard frosts, freezing air… I looked up and caught Maud's eye. For once she was looking concerned.

'Hope the coke delivery gets through,' she said. 'If this hill ices up we'll be stranded, and it's not like we've got neighbours to pitch in. I'd best take the car into Wickham tomorrow and see what I can get in the way of candles. Maybe you ladies wouldn't mind being a foraging party for firewood in the morning, just in case? Honestly, it's enough to make you wish they'd never brought back the forecast.'

The women agreed, although with some understandable reluctance, and it was not long after that Maud suggested we all had an early night. I went to the linen cupboard to find extra blankets for everybody, because upstairs, away from the warmth of the kitchen stove and the big old fireplace, it was already bitterly cold, and I did not like to think of how it would be should we find ourselves imprisoned here by drifts and icicles and fog.

Just as she did every night, Maud asked if anyone would like to come with her to make sure everything was locked up, and everybody did, a fearful little procession that wound its way around the ground floor from door to window and then up the stairs to take turns in the bathroom and lav. Connie gave me a quick hug, then went upstairs, taking her fur coat with her. 'Learned the hard way at the Hall,' she said. 'Place is like a bloody glacier in this weather.'

'I remember it well,' Maud said cheerfully. She and I waited at the bottom of the stairs, listening as locks clicked on bedroom doors. There was a scrape as someone dragged a chair under the door handle. Maud sighed.

'Never gets any easier,' she said. 'Good night, my dear. Best get a good night's kip, I think tomorrow we'll be battening down the hatches. Thank goodness none of them has any kids for a change, imagine being snowed in with a pack of brats, eh?' She chuckled, and I had the feeling that she would, in fact, relish the chance for games of hide and seek and treasure hunts to while away the time. She looked back up the stairs. 'Doubt we'll get any of these girls off our hands any time soon, do you?'

I shook my head, already thinking of train cancellations and blocked roads. 'Shall I come with you when you go to Wickham? I can bring the ration books, we might as well see if we can stock up on anything.'

'Good idea. Right then, come on, you two.'

She clicked her tongue and the dogs bounded up the stairs after her. I followed, going quietly down the passage to my own room, which was full of cold, clear light, and when I looked out of the window, the moon was so bright that deep black shadows lay like gashes across the lawn. I am not a superstitious woman, but for some reason at that moment I thought of Lizzie Sixpence and, when I burrowed down into my blankets, I couldn't help but wonder where she was, if her friend Mickey were still with her, and whether, somehow, he was managing to keep her safe, out there in the violence and the pitiless cold.

<h1 style="text-align:center">38</h1>

In the end it was Connie and I who took Maud's car, an elderly Austin that we used for all the house's business, and edged our way down the hill. The snow had started at dawn, and although the fall was only slight, sullen clouds hung low and heavy overhead, bulging with menace. The air was thick with cold and we hurried from shop to shop, queueing at each, picking up tins of condensed milk, a bag of flour, a box of candles, not caring how many coupons we had to hand over, just anxious to get what we needed and head home before the sky split and the snow came in earnest. We did not speak unless we had to, keeping our heads down against the slicing wind, the snow that had already fallen splashing over the tops of our shoes and soaking our stockings.

It was only one o'clock, but when we emerged from the butcher's the day had grown as dark as dusk. Lights were coming on in windows and one or two people had lit torches, the thin beams bobbing erratically on the heaps of slush that dotted the pavement.

Connie hefted her parcels. 'Come on,' she said, raising her voice above the wind. Her face was red with cold. 'It's going to bucket down. Best get back before the hill's blocked.'

I was in no mood to disagree. We had parked in a side street and as we pulled out, the first fat flakes had started to sprawl across the windscreen. The wiper did its best but I drove slowly, the headlights picking up the thickening ranks of snow that were now parading insolently down onto the road, covering any tracks as soon as they were made. A bus laboured past, its windows steamed up, and at the next stop we saw the driver shepherding his passengers onto the pavement, their journey abandoned. I put my foot harder on the accelerator, feeling the wheels fumble for grip, and turned the car for home.

The bare branches of the trees were so weighed down with snow that they hung across the lane like the arches of a nave. The verges were already invisible, and had I not driven that way so many times before I shudder to think how I would have known where the bends and twists were. I found myself leaning forward, as if to encourage the car onwards, peering through the arc of clear glass that the wiper left before the windscreen was immediately covered again. The air was a great swirling mass of specks. Dark, muffled things that might once have been bushes or gates appeared and vanished as we crawled past.

'Jesus Christ!'

I don't know which of us said it. I stamped on the brake, sending the car slewing around, Connie slamming into me with the force of the spin. I heard something thud against the passenger door.

The engine sputtered and died. The thing we'd hit heaved and got up, staggering towards us. It was a man, a tatty scarf around his face, his head bare, only a thin jumper on his back.

'Help us,' he said hoarsely. 'Oh God, please, help us.'

He was leaning on the bonnet, his hands outstretched and imploring. I opened the car door, catching hold of him as he pitched forward.

'Shit,' said Connie, crouching beside us. 'Is he hurt?'

But he was shaking his head, struggling to sit up. I pulled the scarf away so he could breathe. In the gloom it took me a moment to recognise him.

'Mickey?' I put my hands under his shoulders and between us we helped him to his feet. 'Are you all right? What are you doing here?'

'You said – you said we could come.' He pointed down the path to the churchyard. He was panting but I couldn't see any blood. 'Lizzie. She's down there. She's… she's…'

'Oh God.' I turned to Connie. 'Can you get him into the car?'

Connie didn't even blink. 'Right you are. Come on, young man, in you get.' She looked at me, eyebrows raised. White stars were scattered across her furry arms. 'You're sure you'll be all right? What if the path gets blocked?'

'It's not far. If push comes to shove and we can't get back, well, we can wait in the church.'

'If you're not back in ten minutes I'll come looking.'

I picked my way down the path. I could just make out footprints where the hedge had provided some weak shelter from the blizzard, but there was a trail of darker patches that gleamed wetly and I felt sick as I realised that they must be blood.

'Lizzie?' I called. My voice was batted away by the wind and I shouted louder. 'Lizzie! Where are you?'

I wasn't sure I heard it. I stopped. Shouted again. The wind carried a thin mewing sound, pitiful and vulnerable. A girl's voice, no words, just a wail of pain.

I pushed through the snow towards the church, and into the porch. I took my glasses off, wiped the snow from them so I could see better. It took me a moment to make her out, huddled on a bench in the corner, a man's mackintosh draped over her so all I could see was her hair, hanging limp down her back. She was bent over, clutching at her belly. Blood stained the little ankle socks she wore and dripped off her shoe.

'Oh my God, Lizzie.' I went over to her, took her hand. She was shaking and her skin was clammy. She looked up, dazed. 'It's Miss Alleyn, we met in Woolworths, remember? Are you all right?'

Well, that was a bloody stupid question.

'We was caught in the snow,' she said. 'We couldn't find nowhere, it was so dark…' She looked wildly down the path. 'Mickey,' she said, 'where's Mickey?'

'He's all right. It's you I'm worried about. Can you walk?'

She was such a tiny, frail little thing, but she nodded. I put my arm around her and helped her slide forward on the bench so she could stand.

'Wait.' She reached back, picking up a cheap plastic handbag, slinging its strap over her shoulder. 'All right.'

'Come on, then.'

But we had only taken one or two faltering steps before she cried out and stopped, panting.

'Is it the baby?'

She nodded. She had bitten her lips so hard they were bleeding. I pulled her closer to me.

'If you can walk back to the road there's a car. We're nearly home. Come on. Lean on me.'

Dear God, those few yards felt like miles. The wind had grown even stronger, slapping at us with callous gusts that sent ice spiking into our faces. The path was inches deep in snow now, and I looked down at Lizzie's bare legs, seeing the flakes stick to her flesh. Twice we had to stop while she gathered herself inwards, her arm curving around her belly as it tightened, closing her eyes and letting out a sob of pain. She was shivering so violently I nearly dropped her. My own hands were numb and I could not feel my feet. The snow was blinding now, coming down in a vortex that would have been beautiful if it had not been so dreadful. For the first time I began to feel afraid.

'Just a few more steps,' I kept saying, but now I was not sure who I was comforting. 'Just a few more.'

We were nearly at the road when she slipped and fell. She went down so heavily I had no chance to catch her, and she landed in an awkward slump, her face catching on the hedge so a deep red scratch sprang up on her cheek. I tried to lift her but she was a dead weight, lying moaning in the snow.

'Lizzie,' I pleaded desperately. 'Lizzie, I can't get you up. Lizzie, I need you to stand up.'

She turned away, rolling onto her side.

'Oh for God's sake, Lizzie, please, you need to—'

'Come on, Liz, love. I've got you.'

Mickey knelt beside us. He was engulfed in Connie's coat, the fur lying wet against his face. Lizzie reluctantly opened her eyes, and he smiled at her. 'We're nearly there, Liz. Lady says as there'll be toast if we hurry. You like a bit of toast, doncha? All nice and warm. But you gotta do one more little bit. So come on. I've got you. Up you get.'

And somehow she found that last bit of strength and dragged herself up onto her elbow so he could lift her. Between us we got her into his arms and he carried her to the car, putting her onto the back seat so gently she could have been made of glass. Only when she was settled did he climb in beside her.

Connie was waiting, and when she saw me she gave me a gruff hug. I was trembling, though whether from the cold or shock I couldn't tell. 'You're a bloody idiot, Alleyn,' she said. 'Get in. Cross everything that the damn thing starts.'

She climbed into the driver's seat and pressed the starter. The car gave an apologetic cough. From behind us, Lizzie groaned.

'Come on, start, you bugger,' said Lady Alastair Shenstone. She tried again. There was the smell of petrol and then, oh thank you, God, the engine rattled and sputtered and finally caught. Connie swung the wheel cautiously, inching forward, and we went creeping up those last few hundred yards until at last, at last, we turned in through the welcoming gates of Wickham Grange.

39

Lizzie

I ain't never seen so much money in all my life.

It had been a hotel they'd done over, June said, some posh place up west where they'd pissed off one of the waiters once too often. He'd been only too happy to earn a couple of quid by finding out a combination and leaving a door open, and now Sid was like a pig in shit, grabbing fistfuls of fivers out of some old leather bag, striding about the house like he was cock of the walk and smoking a cigar so big it looked like he'd got a small tree sticking out of his gob. He'd lifted a couple of bottles of champagne from the bar, an' all, and we all got a swig, even me. I'd had it once before, that first night when the major were being nice, and like then I thought it was like drinking a firework, all sparkles.

Kenny Clapton was there, too, sat on the settee with his legs spread wide, a bottle in one hand and the gun in the other. I didn't like it. I kept my distance, staying behind June and some of the Clapton boys who'd turned up last night after the job and who'd been there all day, demanding beer and sarnies morning, noon and night. Me and June had been run off our feet looking after them. I saw them looking in disgust at my big belly and was glad of it, because they had June in the back bedroom one after the other and when she said no, Sid told her to shut up about it and do it on the house. She gave him such a dirty look I thought he'd belt her one, but he was too far gone by then and didn't bother.

It must have been gone ten at night when it all kicked off. Sid and Kenny were sat at the dining table, putting the money into piles, great heaps of the stuff, two, three hundred quid at least. There was a couple of watches and a pearl necklace, too, lifted from the hotel safe. Anyway, they started talking about who'd done what, who'd supplied the car, who'd paid the waiter, who'd taken all the chances. There was something about a night porter getting whacked with the gun, and for a horrible moment I thought they meant they'd shot him, but it turned out he'd just been clouted, though that was bad enough. They were talking about how much blood there'd been, and then it all got lairy, the two of them growling at each other, snarling about fairness and risk, danger and profit. Mickey and me took one look and went to sit on the stairs outside, but we could hear the shouting even out there, something about swindling and the like, and then Kenny come striding out with his coat on his shoulders and kicked us out of the way like we was rubbish. His boys went stumbling along after him, all yes, Mr Clapton, sorry, Mr Clapton, and we sat huddled together in the dark, too scared to go back inside because we knew how it would be if we did.

But in the end we was so stiff with the cold we knew we'd have to get inside or freeze, so we tried to creep in without Sid seeing us. But just our luck, he was coming out of the lav, buttoning himself up as he went, and when he heard the door click shut he looked round and his face went all dark. Mickey pushed me behind him, but it didn't make no difference, Sid come round and pulled me to stand in front of him, shaking me like a dog with a rat.

'How long you got?' His breath stank of whisky and the black market sausage and onion he'd had.

I was so scared I didn't know what he meant. 'Sorry, Sid?'

'Christ, are you stupid or summink? That brat. How long until you drop?'

Well, I didn't know much, on account of not having seen any doctors or nothing, but I could count to nine. 'Won't be long, Sid,' I said.

'All right.' He pushed me away, towards Mickey. 'Keep her inside. I want her resting. That kid's worth money.'

I must have made a noise because he rounded on me, giving me a slap, though he was so drunk it never hurt much.

'That bastard Clapton's taking the piss,' he hissed. 'Leaving me short. So you'll hand over that kid if you know what's good for you.' He yelled over his shoulder. 'June? You got them marks lined up?'

She came sulkily out of the living room. 'Yeah. Couple from Enfield. More money than sense. Oh don't look like that, you silly little bitch. How're you gonna look after it? Be grateful they want it.'

The baby gave a little swirl of fright. Sid jerked his thumb at the stairs.

'Get to bed. You're staying in now until it's born, where I can keep an eye on you. I ain't losing another hundred quid.'

I stumbled up the stairs to the crowded room I shared with a couple of the other girls. They were out, though God knows trade would be thin on a night like this. I crawled onto my mattress, not wanting to think of them on the icy streets.

I lay staring at the rafters for a long time. I felt like I was having hundreds of feelings all at once. Part of me was a little girl, screaming and sobbing with fright, clutching her baby, terrified and alone. But underneath all that was something else, something I'd not felt before. Something that I could warm my hands on. Something that I could burn.

I learned a long time later that it is called rage.

40

Frances

I've never been a religious woman, but when I saw Audrey Fairfax standing in the hall I could have dropped to my knees in thanks.

As it turned out, she'd come in to see how Maud was getting on after her cough, and when the snow started had decided to wait it out. When we staggered in, carrying Lizzie between us, she took one look and told us to get her upstairs, out of her clothes and onto – not into – a bed. 'And bring any newspapers you can find,' she said, rolling up her sleeves. 'It's a messy business.'

We started across the hall, but she stopped Mickey in his tracks. 'No place for you, young man,' she said.

Of course the other women had all appeared by now, and even in all the carry-on I remember that I was surprised to see that instead of running from this intrusion they came gathering around, pity and concern on their faces. Dr Fairfax surveyed them.

'Any of you got any nursing experience?'

'I done a bit.' That was Grace. She rarely spoke, and she looked as surprised as I was to hear her words. 'Back in Jamaica. I liked it. I'll help.'

'Good. Come with me.' She turned to Harriet. 'You, take that young man to the kitchen and fill as many hot water bottles as you can, we'll need things warm. You—' she said to Vera – 'can you go with them? Oh and fetch some bowls of water and clean towels. Any soap you can find.'

Vera nodded, and they went off to the kitchen. Mickey cast an agonised look over his shoulder, but Audrey ignored him, turning instead to the rest of us. 'Anyone else?'

'I helped Mum when she had the twins,' Jane said. She'd taken Lizzie's hand and was stroking it gently. 'Mags were there, too.'

'That'll do. Maud, which room?'

'Follow me.'

I suppose that when the house was built the room she led us to would have been a servant's room, narrow and stern, with a high window. There was ice on the glass and I went back to my own room, sweeping out the few bits of coal I'd laid in the grate, taking them back and getting a small, apologetic fire burning. Lizzie was on the bed, Audrey briskly pulling down her knickers, tutting at the blood. The girl twisted, crying out.

'Fuck, fuck, fuck!' She blinked sweat out of her eyes and looked at us, her eyes wide and rolling, like a frightened beast. 'I'm sorry,' she said in panic, 'I didn't mean it—'

'There's nothing nice about this,' Audrey said briskly. 'Even if you were in the best maternity home in the land it's all shoving and shit, so you yell as much as you like. Ah, thank you.'

Vera came in, tucking hot water bottles around the bed while Audrey washed her hands. She bent over Lizzie, probing gently, and when she washed them again the water went red. Without a word, Maggie took the bowl away. Maud and I only moved when Audrey snapped at Grace to hand her a towel or one of the strange, clinking things from her Gladstone bag, which gaped open on the nightstand.

An hour passed. Two. Mickey sat on the landing, his head in his hands, only for Vera or Jane to chivvy him down into the kitchen to drop towels into a pan of boiling water so they could be used again. Inside that high, narrow room, Lizzie arched on the bed, clambered off, walked around, crawled. We brought more water, more coal. The air stank of blood and sweat.

And then the bare bulb hanging from the ceiling flickered and went out.

Darkness swamped the room, drowning what little light was coming from the small flames that sulked in the grate. Lizzie screamed.

'Bloody power cuts!' Maud exploded.

'Hang on.' Connie had been there all the time, sleeves rolled up, pulling out stained bits of paper from under Lizzie's swollen, sweating body, taking them away to the boiler, bringing tea and a bit of toast, clearing up when Lizzie vomited it straight back up. Now she went outside, her footsteps hurrying down the stairs, her voice distantly telling the dogs to get out of the bloody way.

'Here you go. Fran, you hold this.'

She passed me the box of candles we had bought only that morning, a hundred years ago. Her gold lighter clicked, and tiny hesitant flames sprang up. We passed the candles from hand to hand, a ring of light forming around the bed.

Audrey bent forward. 'One more,' she said, 'make it a good one.'

We stood like figures from some Mediaeval Doom, our faces contorted by shadows. Lizzie closed her eyes, as if she were silently asking for help, then she reached out and grabbed at my hand, her grip as fierce as steel. Her face went scarlet and her mouth opened in a hoarse scream. Audrey tensed.

'Nearly there,' she said, 'come on.'

And then a pale little shape unfurled on the bed and Lizzie's baby girl was in the world.

41

Lizzie

What with them cleaning me up and finding me something to wear, it was a good half hour before they let Mickey in.

He came around the door like he was coming in to be shot. I were sitting up by then, feeling sleepy and warm, all padded up down below and with bigger knockers than I've ever had in my life. The baby had nuzzled at me for a little while, but I think she was tired too, and now she was lying in my arms, her face like a new painting, waiting to dry.

'You all right, Liz?' he said. He looked terrified. 'Only you was carrying on so.'

'Carrying on?' the doctor woman snorted. 'Only a man—'

'Not to worry, miss,' I said. 'I don't mind.'

'Just as well.' She was rolling some metal things in a towel. 'Right, I need to get these as clean as I can. You're in luck, young lady, doesn't look like I'll be going anywhere any time soon so you'll have my undivided attention.'

'Thank you, miss,' I said humbly as she went out.

The moment she was gone Mickey came to sit on the bed beside me. 'Can I have a look at it?'

'Her. It's a her. She's called Iris, like them flowers we used to see.'

'That's nice. Can I have a look at her?'

He reached out and very gently pulled back the corner of the pillowcase she was wrapped in. 'Oh,' he said, and his eyes, God bless him, they went all swimmy. 'Oh, Lizzie.'

'Do you like her?' I asked shyly.

'She's pretty.' He looked up at me. 'I ain't never seen a baby this close before. She's got little ears, look.'

'And little hands.' I lifted one of those tiny stars, letting the fingers curl around my own.

'You was ever so brave.'

'So was you. Oh, Mickey, when you give me your coat and said you was going to get help…' I could feel a tear running down my face.

'Ssh, girl. S'all right now. Miss Alleyn told me to tell you not to worry about anything. We can stay as long as we want and then, listen to this, Lizzie, she said as her and that fat one will help us find somewhere to live.' He looked up. 'I mean, that's if you want. You don't have to…'

'Course I want to. We used to talk about it, di'nt we? Darby and Joan.'

'I can get a job, a proper job.'

'You won't have to.' I felt a little shiver as I said it.

He frowned. 'What d'you mean?'

I managed to sit up a bit. 'Pass us that bag,' I said, pointing to where my clothes had been left in a neat pile. 'It's under me dress.'

He gingerly pushed the stained thing aside. Miss Alleyn had said they'd get me something better, something that wasn't covered in blood and piss. He picked up the bag, passing it over. 'You want a lippy or something?' he said, smiling.

'Not really.' I opened the little metal catch and held the bag out to him. 'Have a look.'

He looked down. His face twisted in horror.

'Oh, Lizzie,' he whispered, 'you never—'

'It's for us,' I said stubbornly. 'You and me and Iris. Sid owes us, Mickey.'

He looked inside at the notes in their neat paper folds. 'How'd you get this?'

To tell the truth I wasn't sure how I'd had the neck to do it, but I had. I'd waited until they was all asleep, then I went creeping out of the room and along the landing. They was all used to me needing the lav three times a night, nobody took no notice, and I got dressed in there, pulling on the few clothes I could still get into. I'd forgotten my suspenders so I had to make do with socks, but I didn't think it would matter. Give it a few days and I could have silk stockings.

I don't think that I meant to steal the money. I was just going to wake Mickey up and tell him I was running away, see if he wanted to come too, but when I went into the living room where he was asleep on the sofa I could see the satchel, lying there on the table. Banknotes were spilling out of it like sick. And June's handbag was on the floor and I don't know, I found myself scooping up handfuls of notes and shoving them into the handbag, then hiding the lot under my dress. The plastic scratched my skin but I would have eaten burning coals to save my baby.

'He left it on the table. I come to wake you up and I saw it there and I just thought, he owes us.'

'How much is there?'

'I dunno. Forty quid, maybe?'

He flicked through the notes. It was gloomy in there with just the candles but I could see him going pale. 'Christ, Lizzie, there's a hundred and fifty here!'

I held the baby a bit tighter. 'He was going to sell Iris, Mickey!'

'I know, love, I know, but oh Jesus he'll kill us, he'll bloody kill us.'

I had that strange feeling again, of something stirring and coming alive. Something fierce and pitiless that was not going to let Sidney Parker or anything he'd done get in the way of me doing what was right for my baby.

'He don't know we're here,' I said. 'And as soon as this lot's melted we'll be gone. We can go anywhere we like. Scotland, Liverpool, you name it.'

He didn't look convinced, so I tried to talk some more, but I couldn't help it, my eyes were getting heavy. He held Iris while I limped off to the lav, then helped me back into bed and pulled the covers up over me. He lay the baby in a drawer by my bed, where she snuffled and mewed contentedly.

'You want anything?' he asked as he straightened up.

'Can you pass me my cardi?'

'You cold? I can get you a blanket—'

'Nah. Just something I want.'

It was folded right down in the pocket, all scrunched up. I brought it out, feeling its familiar softness, the nicest thing I'd ever had. I was so glad I'd managed to keep it hidden away all these months.

I leaned down and tucked the little dog in beside my daughter. Its velvet nose was as soft as her skin. 'Here you are, Iris,' I said. 'Your first toy.'

Mickey helped me back up, put a pillow behind my head. The last thing I remember was him bending down and dropping a wary kiss on the baby's forehead.

'Sleep tight,' he said, looking down at her. 'Me and your mum, we'll make sure you're all right, don't you worry.'

Which I suppose we did, in the end.

42

Frances

The snow fell and fell, settling over the house and the land like an eiderdown. We became hermits, all of us huddling in the drawing room for much of the day, wrapped in blankets and coats, eking out the coal so there was always a little bit of a fire to take the sting out of the air. Lizzie and the baby had a deep armchair nearest the grate, and the other women would fuss over them both, bringing soup and tea and cotton wool. It was as if this was their first step in gaining strength for themselves, through the care of someone even more helpless and needful than they were.

Maud, of course, was in her element, going out to bring in wood, coaxing the boiler when it faltered, organising rotas for making meals. Connie played the piano, I shared out books. Dr Fairfax nagged about fresh vegetables, only mildly placated by a few wartime bottles of plums we found in the pantry. Mickey, I suspect to his own surprise, proved to be a useful handyman, able to wrench open frozen taps and lag pipes, lugging in coal scuttles and fetching cans of hot water for bathing the baby. When the power failed, which it did at least twice a day, we lit oil lamps that sent smuts floating around the room like greasy ghosts.

Despite everything, it was a curiously peaceful time. While the outside world drowned in snow, the old house stood sturdy and safe against the wind and the bitter, bitter cold. We became a little family, the eleven of us, the wireless our only connection to the rest of the human race, gathering around to hear stories of villages cut off and rivers frozen solid. And in the middle of it all, serene and unconcerned, lay the baby.

I think Maud saw her more as a human-shaped puppy than a child. She would ruffle her silky strands of hair, or chuck her under the chin, calling her a good girl and giving gentle pats on the head. 'Never saw the appeal, myself,' she would say, when offered the chance to hold and cuddle, 'not sure I won't drop her. Best you take her back. Right, I need to go and see if we're going to get any coke delivered, the pile's getting a bit low.'

And how did I see that tiny person? I wasn't sure. I know I didn't share the fierce protectiveness of the other women, who would take it in turns to heat bottles or change napkins. But I took my turn to watch over her while Lizzie slept or bathed, and more than once offered to pace around the drawing room with her late at night when she wouldn't settle. It was a practical way to help, and I liked those quiet and companionable hours when I would walk to and fro, enjoying the last warmth of the fire while Iris nestled against my chest and regarded me with wide, knowing eyes.

Connie would join me sometimes, and at those moments I would see a gentle wistfulness on my friend's face. One night, when it was just the two of us, she looked so sad I couldn't stop myself asking if she was all right.

'Oh, I'm just moping,' she said. 'Missing Ali. You know.'

I looked at the way she was cradling the baby. 'D'you think you'll ever—?'

'Have one of my own? God, I hope so. Not just for the estate and all that, though it'd get the bloody dowager off my back. But it'd be nice. All right, all right, shh, shh, that's right, back to sleep.'

'You're a natural.'

'Am I? Tell that to Mother Nature.' She said it with unusual bitterness. 'It's been a year now.'

'Does Alastair—?' I asked awkwardly. 'You know.'

'Mm. Well, he does his best. Though it's getting better the more he heals up. It's more in the mind, the doctors say, give it time, but they say that about anything, don't they?' She grinned, the irrepressible Connie breaking through, though whether in earnest or just to move away from the subject I couldn't tell. 'Mind you, it's fun trying, which is the main thing. Anyway, what about you? Seen any handsome young devil who's caught your eye? No desire to tie the knot yourself?'

I thought about it. 'Honestly? No. I never did. And working here—'

'I can see how it would put you off.'

'It's not just that, though it doesn't help. It's – oh, I don't know. I like being useful. And besides, can you imagine any man wanting a wife who did all this, rather than dashing about in a pinny to have his dinner ready?'

'They'd be few and far between, that's for sure.' She yawned. 'Oh, thank you, God, she's finally dropped off. Do you want to take her? I'll sort out the fire.'

I took the baby, who stirred a little but did not wake, and carried her gently up the stairs. It was snowing again, and I paused by the big stained-glass window that looked over the drive, watching the flakes as they drifted from blue to green to amber before falling into the drift of white that covered the grounds and the lane and the world. In my arms, Iris snuffled and nestled closer, her little fists tucked under her chin, as if she were ready to take on the world in a fight. I held her closer, cradling her head in one hand, as if just for that split second I could keep her safe from everything that waited out there, beyond the glass. Then I gently opened the door to Lizzie's room and put the baby in the drawer that lay by the bed where her mother, another tired child, was already asleep.

Mothers and babies, babies and mothers. They filled my life. But however much I cared about them, however valuable I thought my work to be, I had told Connie the truth. Marriage and a family were not things I wanted. No, I wanted to stay free, unfettered, uncontrolled. I could not think of anything that would make me veer off the path I had picked when I was not much older than Lizzie herself.

Of course, I did not know then that any choice was about to be taken from me.

The next day was – I'm not sure. A Saturday, perhaps? Without anything to keep us on track, the days had blurred and without the wireless I am not sure we would even have remembered that there was a world outside the walls of Wickham Grange. It had been weeks, certainly, almost the end of February. By mid-afternoon it had stopped snowing, and we were daring to talk about the prospect of a thaw, how it would be good to get some fresh air and stretch our legs, that surely this terrible winter could not go on for ever?

Vera was saying something about how she'd seen the buses were running again. Maggie was putting a carefully allotted portion of our precious fuel on the fire, building it up with sticks and old newspaper.

When the loud peal on the doorbell came, the clang jarred in the quiet like a shriek. We all started, looking at each other, uncertain. This was out of tune, out of step. It was as if we were being shaken awake from sleep.

Maud was not so disconcerted, instead slapping her hands on her thighs and standing up. 'The coke!' she said delightedly. 'I knew they'd not let us down. With any luck we can get the boiler stoked up properly again, we could all do with a good hot bath.'

'I'll go,' Connie said.

I did not miss the way the other women gathered nearer together, moving up on the sofa so they could sit packed in close. Even the baby sensed their sudden unease, and let out a little whimper. Lizzie had just fed her and was still buttoning her dress, so I picked her up, cuddling her solid little body against my own. I could hear voices in the hall, Connie's high and surprised, another low and deep.

There were footsteps on the hall tiles, then the drawing-room door opened. Connie came in, a faint frown on her face. A man I did not know was following behind. He stopped on the rug, then turned to face our startled little huddle. He wore a long overcoat, a smart hat, and town shoes that were soaked with snow. He was young, but his eyes were ancient.

'Afternoon, ladies,' he said genially.

Maud stepped forward. She looked sturdy and indomitable, but did not hold out her hand. 'How can we help you, Mr—?' she said.

'The name's Parker. Sidney Parker.' He smiled, the blandest, emptiest smile I have ever seen on a human face. 'I've come for my girl Lizzie,' he said.

43

'LIZZIE?' MAUD SPOKE GENTLY, GOING ACROSS TO where the girl sat and perching on the arm of her chair. 'Lizzie, do you know this man?'

Of course she knew him. Her face had gone the shiny, slick grey of putty and even from where I stood I could see she was shaking.

'Lizzie, do you want to go with him?'

'No!'

It sounded like the howl of some wounded animal. The other women flinched, clutching at each other. The baby in my arms started, her eyes flying open and her body going rigid.

'Then I'm afraid, Mr Parker, that I'm going to have to ask you to leave,' Maud said. 'Lizzie does not wish to accompany you.'

'It ain't a question of what Lizzie wants,' Parker said. He pulled out a chair and sat down, spreading his legs wide and comfortable. He took his hat off and tossed it onto the table, then looked around the room and nodded to himself. 'Nice place you got here,' he said. 'She's fallen on her feet again, I see.'

'Mr Parker—'

'You see, missus—'

'Kindly address me as Miss Shenstone.'

He ignored her. 'There's a little matter of the hundred and fifty quid she half-inched before she left. Don't suppose she mentioned that, did she? Didn't think so.' He leaned forward, resting his elbows on his knees. 'Did she tell you I took her in when she was just a kid? That I found her in some bombsite and give her a home? And this is how she repays me.'

'I ain't got it, Sid.' Lizzie spoke in a whisper so hoarse it was as if she was dragging each syllable over barbed wire. 'I ain't got no money.'

'Now, now, Lizzie, don't tell fibs, there's a good girl.' Parker threw a jovial glance at Maud. 'Honestly, what must these ladies think of us?' He turned back to the girl and his face shifted, hardened. 'Don't take me for a mug,' he said. 'I know it was you, you and that whining kid who was always mooning after you. Hundred and fifty. Mr Clapton wants it back.'

'Really, Mr Parker,' Connie said. She had really mastered the upper-class voice over the past few months and her vowels rang like crystal. 'She's just told you—'

'I ain't talking to you. I'm talking to that thieving little bitch.'

'I can assure you,' Maud said, 'that when we found Lizzie there was no money—'

I swallowed. She'd seen that cheap handbag, tucked neatly on the chair with Lizzie's clothes. We all had. It was still up there in the bedroom, on the chair. I remembered her panicked grab for it, that day I found her in the church porch.

'Then she's hidden it somewhere.' He lunged, swift as a cat, grabbing Lizzie by the hair and pulling her out of the chair and across the rug. She screamed. The other women cried out as well, five voices in unison, sharp with terror. Connie shouted, 'Leave her alone!' and Maud bellowed something I couldn't hear. From somewhere in the kitchen the dogs started to bay.

'Give me my fucking money,' Parker was shouting, shaking Lizzie like a rat. The noise made the baby squall and I backed away, cradling her, wanting to take her out of this nightmare, but I only found myself with my back pressed against the wall, cornered and desperate.

Maud was charging forward. Connie was close behind. The other women sat rigid, their eyes huge, their mouths open in silent horror. Audrey Fairfax was looking wildly around her, as if looking for some escape.

Parker saw us, and I swear it, he smiled, as if we had done something to amuse him. And then he threw Lizzie to the floor and oh, dear God, he put his hand in his pocket and when he raised it he was holding a gun.

The squat, grey thing swung its snout around to face us.

'Let's try again,' he said. He was not even out of breath. He looked down at Lizzie, who lay on the hearthrug, motionless. The back of her dress was stained with blood. 'You nicked that money. Kenny wants it back. And he ain't a man to take no for an answer.'

She twisted her head and looked up at him. Her face was so calm it was as if she were an effigy.

'Fuck off,' she said.

His face contorted. 'You little—'

He pointed the gun at her. There was a click that sounded like cannon fire.

All I could hear was the pounding of my heart and the jagged rasp of my lungs. 'Don't be a bloody idiot,' someone said, from a long way off.

It was me.

Parker didn't take his eyes off the weeping girl on the floor. 'You want to be next?' he said.

'If you kill her,' I said, 'you'll never get your money. We don't know where it is. She's the only one who can tell you.'

'Quite the clever one, ain't you?' But he straightened up, twitching his coat back into place, using his free hand to smooth down his hair. He looked straight at me and I gritted my teeth, making myself meet his gaze. *He's just a naughty schoolboy*, I tried to tell myself, *you can face him down*, but I could feel my knees shaking and my skin crawling as he took a considering step towards me, the eye of the gun implacable and deadly.

'Well, well,' he said. 'I'd forgotten all about you.'

For one wild moment I thought he meant me, then bile scorched my throat as I saw he was looking at the baby. I held her tighter against me but he just stood there, as if he was adding something up.

'Boy or girl?' he said.

'Girl.'

'Shame. I'd get an extra fifty for a boy.' He looked around the room, and let out a satisfied breath. 'Well, now,' he said. 'I'm a reasonable man. I don't want to inconvenience you ladies any more than I have to. If that little slut there ain't going to be sensible then I'm going to take my money some other way. Hand the kid over and nobody need have any more trouble.'

From the rug Lizzie let out a ragged cry. She was struggling to her feet, Audrey trying to help her up. Over Parker's shoulder I saw the door open.

Mickey, white with determination, came running in, a kitchen knife raised high over his head. He slashed viciously at Parker, but too soon, too distant, and the tip of the blade just snagged uselessly in the back of the overcoat before clattering down and away. Parker swung around, bringing the gun up in a wide sweep that smashed into Mickey's head, sending him staggering backwards to collapse on the floor.

The women on the sofa were screaming, a mass of terrified eyes and hands, clutching at one another. Maud jumped for Parker's arm, grabbing at his sleeve. Connie was at his wrist, sinking her teeth into his skin, but he didn't let go of the gun, just batted her off as if she were a moth, slamming her against the table so the lamp fell onto the floor and shattered. The smell of oil sprang into the air and a flame started to lick, so I shoved the baby at someone – Audrey? Grace? – and pulled the cloth down, stamping, feeling heat scorch through my shoes. Parker was roaring. He lifted the gun, pointing it wildly, its muzzle like some vast chasm that we were all plunging into—

There was a soft crunching sound. I watched, hypnotised, as blood sprayed bright and crimson, shooting upwards like a firework. Parker tried to swivel his eyes but they would not move, just widened in shock and pain. His roar becoming a sodden gurgle as blood spilled out of his mouth and down his chin, soaking his shirt. He folded onto his knees. The gun fell from his hand, lying grey and cold like some monstrous dead fish.

Then he pitched forward onto the rug and was still.

44

Lizzie

When he came in I thought I was going to be sick, right there in front of everyone.

He walked in like he was cock of the heap, all swagger, him in his fancy coat and his stupid shoes. I couldn't move, it was like I'd grown roots down into that chair, not even when Miss Maud come and asked me what was going on. I could only make that Godawful noise, my throat as tight as if he had his fingers round it.

I hadn't let myself think about what would happen if he found us. I'd been so scared, so determined to run away, and then there had been the pain and the blood and the baby… and now, seeing him sat there, it was like I was in some kind of fog, a pea-souper where everything's blurred and unreal and you don't know what's there until it hits you. Even the lies sounded strange as they came out of my mouth, though what was I supposed to say? That money, it was for me and Iris and Mickey, to get us away from this man, what he was and what he did. What he'd done to us and what he'd made us do.

Mickey. I was looking for him, hoping he'd have the sense to stay out of it, when Sid yanked me up and started on at me. I could hear them dogs, making that awful howling noise, and then I was on the floor and God help me Miss Shenstone and that other one, the one with the fur coat, they was looking like they was going to punch his lights out but oh no, he had to go and get that bloody gun out.

I don't know anything about guns but from this one's long thin snout even I could tell it was the one they'd used on the hotel raid.

It sat in his hand like some kind of wart. I couldn't see straight because I'd hit my head when I fell, and the room was spinning, and I was bleeding from down below, but I didn't care because this was just between him and me, now. All them years of thieving and starving and whoring. All that fear and pain and hunger. All to end up here on a hearthrug staring at his shoes.

And you know what? I finally stopped caring. I had the strangest feeling that I was floating. If he killed me then at least he couldn't hurt me no more. In a way, I'd have won.

I looked up at him, at the cowlick of hair hanging down over his face, his tie crooked and his face all sweaty.

Maybe it was the bang on the head that gave me the guts to do it, but I told him, I did, I told him to fuck off, and it was like I was snapping some kind of chain.

He did something to the gun. I craned my neck, trying to get one last look at Iris. She was snuggled up with Miss Alleyn, who was stood with her back to the wall like some kind of guard. I could see my baby wriggling in her blanket and then Sid was walking towards her and he was talking about her like she was some kind of a thing.

I can't remember much of the next bit. Mickey was there, with a knife, and there was blood and shouting and fire. Dr Fairfax was holding on to me but I shook her off and that made me stagger, so I grabbed at the first thing I could reach to steady myself and it was a bloody great clock.

The stone it was made of was hard and sharp under my hands. It was heavy, I remember that, and the weight of it made me stumble, but I knew I had to get him away from Iris so I swung it round and lifted it and brought it down and there was a tiny little noise and the next thing I know I was lying on the floor puking my guts up.

Dr Fairfax was kneeling by Sid, her hand on his neck. She was saying something about a pulse, that someone should turn him over. Miss Alleyn was there, kneeling in the blood, tearing up a bit of scorched cloth. My baby was on the sofa, five people curling around her like armour.

A hand crept into mine. I blinked the sweat out of my eyes and saw Mickey, his face covered in streaks of blood, his mouth trembling. I sat up, pulled him towards me, cuddling him close, trying to get warm. I closed my eyes, not taking any notice of the vomit on my dress, the blood on my legs. I was tired, so very tired.

Something was happening but I couldn't decide what it was. There was a hand on my shoulder, shaking me, I knew that, but the doctor's voice over my head was oddly faint, shouting something about Emma, Emma Ridge, and I remember wondering who Emma was. I felt light-headed and cold, like when I was outside in the snow. Mickey's hand was still in mine and I squeezed it gently, trying to let him know it was all right, I didn't mind, I was happy. I was finally free.

45

Frances

Audrey Fairfax was gone for what felt like hours. Mickey and I had carried Lizzie upstairs, her little white face lolling against his shoulder like a star, and laid her down. Audrey barely glanced at us, but when she saw Mickey her eyes narrowed.

'Sort him out,' she snapped, before turning back to the unconscious child on the bed.

'Come on, Mickey,' I said gently.

He shook his head stubbornly, not letting go of Lizzie's hand. I pulled at his sleeve. Still he would not move.

Lizzie let out a groan and Audrey swore. I felt suddenly furious that this was happening, that everything had all gone so terribly wrong in just those few minutes of horror. I grabbed Mickey's arm and shook it.

'You want to hurt her?' I said fiercely. His eyes rolled round to me like some wounded beast seeing the hunter's knife. I felt a pang of guilt but went on relentlessly. 'You want to stop the doctor from helping her?'

''Course not.' He sounded what he was, a scared boy. My anger died a little.

'Then get out of the way and let her do her job. Come on.'

I led him down the passage to the bathroom, where I managed to sponge away most of the blood. He had a long gash along one temple that was still oozing, but he sat motionless on the lavatory even when I dabbed at it with what I hoped was iodine and taped on a rather musty wad of lint. 'I'll find you an aspirin,' I said.

'I want to go back in—'

'Mickey, if you want to help Lizzie, you need to come down with me and help us sort this out. All right?' He gave the smallest of nods. I felt as though I were back at school, sorting out some childish squabble, a most incongruous and ludicrous sensation. 'Good. Take it easy. You're going to have a monumental black eye.'

'Won't be the first time, miss,' he said.

God, it really was like the fourth form common room. But instead of a fight about tuck or football there was a man lying dead on the floor. His blood was drying on my stockings.

We went slowly down the stairs. I could see movement in the dining room and we went in to find Maud passing glasses of brandy around the table, where the women sat silent and grey-faced. They looked dazed and bewildered, like people emerging from a bomb blast.

'Have a drink,' Maud said, pressing a glass into my own hand. 'I think we need one.'

I sat down. Connie was beside me, holding a wet cloth around a badly swollen wrist. She caught my eye and managed half a grin. 'You all right?' she said.

'Just about. You?'

She rubbed the cloth. 'Think it's sprained. Lucky I don't have to be driving anywhere any time soon.' And indeed it was snowing again, heavy flakes meandering down to form fat pillows on the lawns outside.

'And for you, young man.' Maud handed Mickey a glass, which he took warily. 'Not sure if it's recommended for head wounds but you deserve it. That was a very brave thing you did.'

'Didn't do no good, though, did it?' He swirled the brandy suspiciously, then took a small, wary sip.

'You tried.' Maud looked around the table. 'You all tried. I think you were all rather marvellous.'

'So was you,' Maggie said. She had both hands wrapped around her glass, but I could see tremors in the liquid that showed me she was still shaking. 'I've never seen anyone stand up to a bloke like that before. And he had a gun.'

Maud turned to Mickey. 'Do you feel up to explaining?' she said. 'Clearly he knew Lizzie. Who was he? What was all that about money?'

Mickey closed his eyes. 'He was the boss,' he said. 'Of our – our…'

'Gang?' Connie said.

'I s'pose. I knew him when I was a kid. He used to let me run messages for him, penny a time. Then when the war come he looked after us, got us extra rations and that.' He took another sip, a slightly bigger one this time. 'I never had nobody else,' he said. 'Neither did Lizzie. So we stuck with him, even when he got nasty. Made us do stuff – nicking, looting. He made Lizzie…' His voice trailed away. 'That's how she got knocked up.'

I felt sick. 'She's just a child.'

'Yeah, miss. I know. He said there was blokes who'd like that.'

'So I assume the money he wanted was from some criminal activity?' Maud said, breaking the chilled silence that fell at his words.

'Yeah. They done over a hotel. Stole stuff out the safe.'

Connie said sharply, 'They?'

'Him and Kenny. Christ, you think Sid was bad, Kenny's evil. A right bastard. Sorry, miss.'

'Don't you worry about me,' Connie said. 'If he was a bastard then let's call him one.'

Mickey looked up suddenly, his eyes wild. 'Oh my God, what if he comes an' all? He'll bring his boys, he'll—'

'We'll deal with that if it happens.' Maud handed me the decanter. I couldn't remember if it should be passed to the right or left, then decided it didn't bloody matter. 'They probably don't even know he came here. Why should they?'

'I dunno. Sid wouldn't have said nothing. He just wanted the money.'

'I think the less you say about the money the better,' Maud said sharply. 'What we don't know can't hurt us.'

Someone let out a whimper. I couldn't tell who. The door opened and we all jumped, but it was only Audrey. Her hair was coming down and she looked exhausted.

'How is she?' Mickey's chair went scraping back as he scrambled to his feet. 'Can I go—'

'No you may not.' The doctor sat down. Connie pushed a glass towards her. 'Thank you. She's through the worst, I think, but she needs rest and quiet. I've put some stitches in and given her a bromide, so she should get some sleep. More than the rest of us will, I fancy.' She looked at the five women who sat at the end of the table. 'Any of you need anything?'

They looked at each other. Harriet shook her head. She was holding the baby, giving her gentle little pats.

'Good,' said Audrey. 'Not that I've got much left. If the snow doesn't ease up soon I'll have to risk a walk down to the surgery.'

'Well, sufficient unto the day,' said Maud. She leaned forward, her elbows on the table. 'The big problem is what do we do now. There's a dead man in the drawing room.'

'Do we call the police?' Audrey said.

Jane gave a horrified gasp. 'No! They'll make us go back – they've done it before, they took me back to him, and I can't, I won't!'

'Nobody will make you go anywhere,' Maud said calmly.

'But we were all here, we all saw, we're all part of it!'

'We'll make it perfectly clear it was nothing to do with any of you.'

'You promise?' Grace asked. The others were watching Maud intently, their eyes huge in the growing dusk.

'You have my word,' Maud said. 'Whatever happened here today will not change anything for any of you.'

'It might not be that easy,' I said.

They all turned to look at me. It was as if I'd spat at their feet. I'd been sitting silently, not speaking, because a small speck of fear had been growing in my mind, roiling like a thundercloud.

'Go on,' said Maud.

'Before I came here I had a job in barristers' chambers,' I said. I could not shake off the vivid memory of Mr Poole handing Mr Rogers a thick sheaf of papers, chuckling about the fee the case was likely to incur. *At least two weeks' pre-trial hearings*, he'd said. *Oh, Miss Alleyn, might I trouble you to fetch me an iced finger?*

'Two smelly old men,' Connie said, with a sharp flash of her old self. I looked at her gratefully.

'There was a case I had to type up,' I said. 'I can't remember what the legal principle was called, but I know that it was about three men who went out and got each other drunk. There was a row when the barman tried to stop serving them and one of them stabbed him. Killed him outright.'

'How on earth is that relevant?' Audrey demanded sharply. At least she was feeling more like herself, I thought grimly.

'They were hanged,' I said. 'All three. For murder.'

There was a silence so heavy and horrified I could almost feel it pressing on my head.

'How—' Connie broke off helplessly.

'The judge said that they were all responsible. Even though only one of them had used the knife, they were all part of it. They'd all egged each other on, they'd all got into the argument.' I looked at Maud. 'I'm scared that they'll say the same about this. That we're all part of it.'

'Joint enterprise,' she said unexpectedly. I nodded, hearing Mr Poole's thin voice saying the words. 'That's it.' I swallowed. 'And even if we aren't – aren't involved, there's Lizzie. She's the one who – you know. She's only sixteen.'

'You're saying my Lizzie could hang?' Mickey said, his face contorted in horror.

'I'm sorry,' I said. 'I'm not sure, I can't be certain.'

'But there's a chance,' Maud said flatly.

I nodded miserably.

'Oh, Christ.' Connie got up and went over to the sideboard,

bringing back another decanter. We passed it around in silence. The baby stirred and shifted, and Harriet passed her over to Vera. We all watched that little helpless bundle, her whole future hanging on whatever decision we took. Lies, truth, freedom, death – they sat around the table like unwanted guests at dinner.

I swallowed, trying not to think of a rope tightening around my throat.

'Looks to me like we have a decision to make.' Maud sat back in her chair. 'We call the police, we risk everything and everyone, or…'

When I spoke, my voice sounded like it belonged to a stranger. The words hung in the air like stones falling down a well.

'Or we get rid of him,' I heard myself say.

46

We needed Mickey to help us, but by dusk it was done.

If I close my eyes I can still remember everything about that terrible couple of hours. Connie, Maud, Audrey and I went out into the grey grimness of the snow, stumbling down the path to the greenhouse. We had agreed, sat around the table, that only the five of us would know where the grave would be. Nobody voiced the thought that what was not known could not be told.

The greenhouse was half-ruined, damaged by the V1 that had landed in the churchyard. The remaining part looked sickly and weak, as if it was going to collapse at any minute, but there were a few bits of gardening gear propped in a corner, left over from Digging for Victory, so at least we had a shovel and a pick. That part of the garden was shielded by trees, and although they were bare the weather was so bitter there was little chance of us being seen as we trudged through the snow and shoved open the door. The glass walls bowed as we went in and for one awful second I thought they would collapse, but they held. Under cover, the earth was slightly less frozen than it was outside, which was why we'd chosen this place, but even so, we each carried two cans of water, which we boiled on a small, secret bonfire before pouring it onto the ground so it softened enough for Mickey to start digging.

Then it was back to the house. Maud wouldn't let anyone else go through Parker's pockets – 'Did worse things in the VAD, my dears, no need for any of you to be distressed' – turning out an identity card, a train ticket, a five-bob note and a few coins, and then a familiar scrap of card I'd last seen in a tea shop a thousand years ago.

'Oh Christ,' Mickey whispered when he saw it. 'I hid that, I swear I hid it, he must of found it – it's all my fault, all my—'

'Bollocks,' Connie said briskly. She'd picked up the gun and was shutting it in a drawer. 'Is that everything? Oh, sorry.' She stepped aside so Maggie could get past with yet another bucket of water. The room smelled damp and scrubbed, like a child being got ready for church.

'Everything.' Maud stood up, wiping her hands on her skirt, and handed me the papers. I dropped them into the fire, shuddering as they caught and smouldered. We had become filthy, elemental beings of blood and water and dirt, blank-eyed witches hunched over our secret. The dead man lay on his back. I noticed that Maud had straightened his tie.

'All right. Harriet, could you and the others please go and wait in the kitchen. Mickey, you can join them if you'd rather.'

'S'all right, miss. I'll come, if you don't mind. I want to see him put away safe.'

'Very well.'

We waited while the cloths were wrung out and the bars of yellow soap were picked up. We could hear buckets clanking as the women trailed out, like the tolling of a cracked and discordant bell, and knew they would be back once the thing on the floor was gone, to remove the last few traces of the tattered shell that had once been Sidney Parker.

Then we lifted the body, hoisting it onto the table where we could get a better grip. I gasped at the weight of it, and Audrey looked at me.

'Put your back into it,' she said. 'It's got to be done now, before rigor sets in. Otherwise we'll be stuck with him until it wears off, which in this weather could be a while.'

'All right,' Maud said sharply. She had her hands under one armpit, Mickey the other. Connie and I took a leg each, and Audrey held the head. 'Let's take it slowly. One step at a time. Everybody ready?'

Oh God, that walk. We'd left him in his coat and suit, but I swear I could feel his flesh, soft and ripe, as if it was already squirming with decay. I felt bile scratch at my throat. I risked a glance at Connie, but her face was set, her eyes fixed on the ground, making sure of every step on that treacherous ground. It was still snowing, the inexorable flakes landing on that dead face, settling on his open eyes. It was as if he was being wrapped in a shroud of snow. I remember I took a swift glance back at the house, as if I was expecting to see men with guns and truncheons in pursuit, but all I could see was that impenetrable veil of white. Our footprints were already blurring away.

'Damn.'

We paused, panting. Despite the bitter air, I had sweat running down my back and wondered vaguely if it meant I'd catch flu. Audrey dropped the head, letting it jerk abruptly in a way that made me wince.

'Door's too narrow. We won't get him through like this. You two, put his legs down, come and take his arms. Watch out for that step.'

Those ridiculous shoes left twin tracks in the snow as we dragged him the last couple of yards. Mickey had left a lantern burning inside but the air was still stiff with cold. The hole gaped like a wound.

We carried the body across, lay it on the earth beside its grave.

'We'll have to fold him,' Connie said. 'Lift his knees up – oh shit!'

We all grabbed, but too late. The body had rolled down into the hole, ending up curled on its side, one hand under its head, one leg out, the other bent, like it was doing some grotesque dance. A pas de deux with death.

'Can we move him?' Mickey said.

'Leave it.' Maud sounded unbearably weary. 'It doesn't matter. He's there now. Let's just get him covered over and leave him in peace.'

I picked up a trowel. It felt ridiculously small and delicate as I lifted little heaps of hard, cold soil and dropped them into the grave. A stone hit the face and left a streak of dirt but it was soon gone, hidden just as our footprints had been, only this time by the dark, gritty earth.

I don't know how long it took. I can only remember my back burning and my hands growing numb, until eventually the heap of soil was gone and there was nothing left but a pile of loose earth.

We all stood there in silence. I swear the snow was so heavy you could hear it sticking to the glass roof.

Maud took a ragged breath. 'Does anyone want to say anything?'

We all looked at each other. In the dim light we looked haggard and exhausted. Audrey Fairfax cleared her throat.

'In the camps—' she said. Something happened to her voice and she paused, closing her eyes for a moment before carrying on. 'One of the women wanted to go to the burial trench. To place a stone for her mother. She said it means that they remember the grave is there. That the person existed. And she said that the stones keep the soul from walking.' She looked round at us, then bent and picked up a white, round flint, before dropping it on the heap of soil. 'So. Let's keep him there. Where he belongs. And let's not ever forget.'

As if we will, I thought grimly.

But I too dropped a stone onto that new and unloved grave.

47

Lizzie

Haemorrhage, not Emma Ridge.

I saw it on the notes the doctor kept about me. I couldn't make head nor tail of it, all them 'r's and the 'a' and 'e' that should have said 'ay' but didn't. Anyway, when she saw me looking she spelled it out and told me what it meant. Blood, she said, and I'd lost a lot. That was why I was so tired, and why I had to stay in bed.

I started to ask about Sid but she just give me a look and told me I didn't need to worry, it was all sorted out, and would I please just lie still as if I burst the stitches she wouldn't be responsible for the outcome. I didn't mind, not really. It was sort of nice being told what to do by someone who was trying to look after me for a change. She let Mickey in, a couple of times a day, and he wouldn't tell me anything neither, just said him and the ladies had cleaned everything up and we was safe. He wouldn't quite meet my eye when he said that and I could see he was still thinking about Kenny and the money, even though he'd said Miss Maud had told him not to say nothing about that. So I just started talking about where we could go and what we could do, silly things, really, like having a cottage with roses and a vegetable patch.

Not that we were going anywhere just then. It must have kept on snowing for a month or more in the end, because it was still coming down when I finally stopped bleeding and Dr Fairfax let me get up.

I must say I was a bit scared about going back into that room, but Mickey was right, there was nothing to see. Even the clock was back on the mantlepiece, and although there was a crack in the glass that hadn't been there before, it just went on, tick, tick, tick like nothing had happened. There wasn't even a stain on the rug. Grace and Jane and them were all ever so nice, as well, telling me how they'd loved looking after Iris while I was asleep, that she'd kept them going and given them something to be happy about. I'm not stupid, I could see they was still jumpy, and I felt bad because it was me as had made Sid come here and scare them in the first place. But nobody ever said his name. Nobody said nothing. Ever.

And then at last the weather began to change.

It was still perishing, mind you, but we went one day, then two, without any fresh snow. The icicles that had been hanging outside the window began to drip, ever so slowly, their sharp points going blunt as they melted. The grass started to peep out again, all brown and mucky as the snow thawed, turning everything into a great big dirty puddle that swamped the garden, drowning the plants and the lawn. Them great big dogs loved it, leaping about and getting so muddy they weren't allowed out of the kitchen any more. I liked watching them, though. I even found a bit of paper and started trying to draw them. Miss Alleyn found one of the pictures and said I had a talent for art. It was the first nice thing anyone had ever said to me, though I thought art was only for posh people and didn't really believe her, but I did start a little picture of Iris, cuddling her toy dog, just because I loved her.

Then one morning Miss Alleyn asked me and Mickey if we had made any plans, and what kind of thing did we want to do, because she could start making enquiries. She was lovely, she didn't talk about us not being married or nothing, and though I thought she might know about the hundred and fifty pounds she never said nothing. I never mentioned it, neither. Safer that way, Mickey said, and I thought he was right.

Miss Alleyn did say two things though which I knew made sense. She said we should start a bank account, because Miss Maud had given Mickey a few quid for doing odd jobs around the place and it would be a good idea, she said, because having an account meant you didn't have to worry about it being nicked. And she said we needed to register Iris, because of the rations and whatnot. She could take us into Bromley, she said, now the roads was clearing, and we could do them both at the same time. Maybe she could take me shopping as well, she said, get me some decent clothes. She had some coupons she could let me have. And then we could think about where we wanted to go, when we left the house.

God help me, I couldn't wait.

48

Frances

I told Maud what I'd said to Lizzie, and she was energetic in her agreement. It fitted in well, she said, she had been watching the other women and in her view they should all leave at the same time, all one big group, nobody left behind to brood or to carry the weight of the secret alone.

'You're right.' I closed my eyes briefly. I was so tired. 'We can get them away in a day or two, surely? We've got places for them to go, we can just bring it all forward.'

'Good. Otherwise they'll bolt. You can see it in 'em, they're all so tight they'll snap unless we get them out of here.' She shook her head. 'I've had hounds the same, something spooks them and they're gone. And there were men in the first war—' She broke off. 'Anyway. They'll all be safe enough once they're out of here.'

'They're going a good way. Harriet's going to Barrow-in-Furness, Vera's got a job in Lincoln.' I frowned, opening the filing cabinet. 'I can't remember the others. Let me check now.'

'Leave it. You're worn out. If we can change their tickets they can be gone by the end of the week. There's bound to be hotels we can find for them until their jobs are ready.'

'All right.' I made a note, seeing, as if from a long way away, that my hand was shaking and the words were uneven and untidy. 'I'll sort it out in the morning. The wireless said the weather is improving a bit so it should be all right.'

'Good girl.' Maud patted my shoulder. 'Don't know what I'd do without you, I really don't.'

That, more than anything else, brought me near to tears. Without me she wouldn't have a body in her greenhouse, there wouldn't be the taint of fear in the air, we wouldn't have the threat of the noose swinging over us.

You brought her here. You made this happen. The words throbbed in my head and I knew that whatever happened, however long I had, they would be an unending counterpoint to my life.

Enough, I told myself sharply. If Maud could bear this, then so could I. I went to splash cold water on my face, then sat down at my desk with the five files, tugging out the tag so I could free up the papers – letters of introduction, case notes, addresses – and put them on the fire. I had caused them so much harm already; to shield them, to help them hide, was all that was left for me to do.

It took another two days, but by 25 March we were ready. The women – Grace, Harriet, Maggie, Jane and Vera; I will know their names and see their faces until my dying day – had been packed and ready for a week, anxiously listening to the weather forecast for the news they craved. There was still snow on the ground but no fresh falls, and we heard that trains were running again; I think they would have gone had they had to trudge through ice and mud, so desperate were they to get away.

On that last night, we held a little tea party as we did every time a woman left us. It was meant to be a celebration of freedom and new beginnings, and for many it was just that, but this time it felt like a wake, even though I had managed to get enough sugar and butter together to make a tiny cake, and Connie had helped cut finger sandwiches. There were daffodils on the table, looking vulgar and cheerful, making me think of piano music coming from a backstreet pub. I had picked them myself from a sheltered corner of the garden, carefully avoiding those which grew beside the greenhouse and which seemed lusher and fleshier than the others, for reasons I couldn't bear to consider. The tablecloth was white lace and we'd put an extra clothing coupon on each woman's plate so she could get herself something small and nice, something to make her feel pretty again.

None of it was any good. Since the day Sidney Parker died there had been a silent presence in the house. Not a ghost, nothing so mundane, no, this was different, this was the slinking sense of dread that reared up with every knock on the door, every ring of the bell. Now it drifted across the table like smoke, tainting the food. We sat there with smiles so tight it hurt our faces as we tried to nibble and sip, the conversation limping until it faltered. Mickey sat awkwardly at the end of the table passing plates and cups when asked, Lizzie pale and silent beside him. Even when Connie produced a box of chocolates they were handed around with tiny shakes of the head and brief, apologetic 'no thank you's.

It was Vera who finally spoke. She pushed her plate away, and it was like a signal, because the others put down their cups and sat with their hands folded on their laps.

'We – well. We want to say something. Before we go, like.'

Maud nodded. 'Do go on, my dear.'

Vera took a gulp of what must have been stone cold tea. 'Well, it's just this.' She looked around, getting little nods of encouragement. 'We know that what – what happened wasn't your fault. It wasn't yours, either,' she said, giving Lizzie a little pat on her hand before turning back to Maud. 'And we know that you've done more than good by us. So we wanted to say, we did, that we'll none of us say anything. Not now, not ever. And it's not just to save our own skins, mind. We'll look after you like you've looked after us. We hope that makes things easier for you. And for the little one, bless her.'

I swallowed, hard. 'Thank you,' I said at last.

Lizzie was crying, her face hidden in Mickey's shoulder.

Maud was polishing her glasses on the tablecloth. 'Awfully good of you,' she said gruffly. 'And goes without saying that our lips are sealed too. Mum's the word and all that. Nobody will ever know. It's like nothing happened. We've done our best to make sure you're safe and we'll keep it that way. Protect each other, safety in numbers, you know the drill. And you all get a fresh start, onwards and upwards.' She looked at me. 'The only thing we ask is that you keep in touch. Nothing more than a forwarding address, so we know where you are. So we can let you know — well, if there is anything you need to be aware of.'

That was it. Just a few stilted sentences around a tea table were enough to bind us all in a snare of secrecy that would go on for the rest of our lives.

49

Lizzie

I was like a little kid that morning, so excited I almost skipped down the stairs for breakfast. Miss Connie saw me and laughed, said I was full of beans. She was always nice to me, though I was a bit shy on account of her being married to a Lord. I never understood why she wasn't Lady Connie, and in the end she said just Connie would do. But that seemed a bit cheeky so I always added the 'miss' like I did with the others.

I don't know why I was so chirpy, not really. Maybe it was because once the doctor said I was well enough we could start to think about leaving ourselves and this made it feel like that was getting closer. She weren't too happy about me going to do the registering thing but I could go as long as I took it easy and came back to rest after.

We'd decided to get a paper while we were out, start looking for jobs and places to go. It had been a bloody awful time, what with me being ill and – well, Sid. I never liked thinking about it, to tell the truth. I'd done my best to forget about it, but it never went away, it was always there, a nasty little voice that kept saying, *You killed him, you're a murderer.* I had bad dreams, that they were coming for me with a noose, until Miss Maud told me it wasn't my fault and it was something called self-defence, and that he'd been an utter cad who deserved it. But that didn't change nothing. I'd killed him and that was that. I couldn't bear to go in that big room, where I'd done it, so I stayed upstairs or in the kitchen, but after a while, when I was better, that got a bit boring and God help me I was only a kid and I couldn't help wanting to go out and do something, so I was all ready when Miss Alleyn come in that Wednesday morning to say she were ready.

All the other ladies were there in the hall, with their bags and cases – nobody had much, it was kind of sad to see them all grown up with so little to show for it – and they reminded me of people when they first heard the siren, all twitchy and looking around for somewhere to hide. But they was nice to me, still, even though I'd brought all this trouble to their door, and they each give me their coupon from the night before so I could buy something pretty for Iris when we went to the shop. They was off to the station and when the taxi come they all squeezed in together like they couldn't bear to be on their own. The driver had a face like a slapped arse and was muttering about charging more for wear and tear on his tyres until Miss Maud give him a shilling and told him to stop moaning.

It took him two goes to get the engine started and I could see their faces freeze, as if this were some bad dream and they'd not be able to get away, but then it coughed and caught and they went rattling off out of the gates. Miss Alleyn and Miss Connie waved, but none of them waved back. I remember I felt a bit jealous, that I couldn't wait for it to be my turn, because although that house had saved me it had sort of damaged me as well.

So then Miss Connie started hugging the rest of us and saying she'd be back soon, and we could all go to the Hall as well if we wanted, only not just yet, it was like a bomb had hit it. I liked that idea, me, at somewhere called the Hall! It tickled me, it really did. Her car started first time, and I gave it a little pat to say thank you for carrying me and Mickey up the hill that time. The sound of the engine made Iris jump and I lifted her little hand so she could wave bye-bye too.

'You'd best be off,' said Miss Maud, and she reached out and took Iris, because she'd said she would look after her while we was out so me and Mickey could take our time. She gave Miss Alleyn a string bag and a shopping list, as well, so as to get the best use out of the petrol, and then we was off.

Me and Mickey sat in the back of that little car feeling like we was lords and ladies ourselves. It was still cold but the sun was out and I started to believe that there might one day be a spring. The trees down the lane looked like they was stretching, glad to be rid of the snow that had weighed them down all them weeks, and there was little clumps of white flowers beginning to show amongst the roots, like tiny bells gleaming amongst the ivy and the moss. Miss Alleyn drove slowly, on account of it being so wet with the thaw. There were streams running down each side of the road and when we reached the bottom of the hill one of the fields was flooded, so it looked like a little lake.

It wasn't far to Bromley, only two or three miles, but it was lovely riding along in that car. Mickey and me were sat close, and his hand rested right alongside mine, our fingers touching. I felt calmer than I could ever remember. It was as though I was bobbing along in some golden bubble, that great heavy weight of Sid and the life I'd been leading gone. I was so relieved to think that it would all soon be over, that we could get away and start again, just me and Mickey and Iris. I never said nothing to him about the baby, because after all I knew deep down she were bound to be the major's kiddie, or worse, and that she wouldn't be his, but he were ever so gentle with her and I thought that maybe, just maybe, it would all turn out to be all right and we could be Darby and Joan after all, somewhere nice where people didn't hit you and make you do stuff and where we could look after the baby and give her a better time than we'd had. I could even pretend we were a proper family. It didn't feel like too much to ask.

We parked the car and Miss Alleyn said that we wasn't due at the registrar until ten, so we could go to the shops first. I laughed at Mickey's face when we went into a dress shop and started looking at the undies, he looked like he was going to burst he went so red. Even Miss Alleyn smiled and said it was all right, he could get a paper and wait outside if he liked. I don't think I'd ever seen him move so fast.

The war had only been over a year and a bit, so there wasn't much to look at but oh, I felt like a bleeding duchess in that shop. I picked out a blouse and a skirt and a coat, nothing fancy but nicer than anything I'd had before, and even though the shop girl had a face like a dog's bum when she saw the state of me, Miss Alleyn was as cool as you like with her and said I should try them on.

I had to find a different blouse because since having Iris I'd got quite big up top, but in the end I got it all on. I looked at myself for a long moment in the mirror. I'd seen myself before, at the major's, but then I'd been all dolled up in his wife's things. Here I was just me, wearing clothes that nobody else had ever worn, and I met my own gaze and looked myself up and down like I was meeting myself for the first time, which I think I was, really, because I was a very different person to the one who'd arrived at Wickham Grange all them weeks ago, changed in oh so many ways by my weeks at that big old house. I nodded to myself. I thought I could get to like this new Lizzie Sixpence.

I put the coat on and picked up my bag. I wasn't leaving that lying around, oh no, because you see it wasn't going to be just Mickey's couple of quid going into that account. I pushed aside the curtain, heading back to the shop floor, where Miss Alleyn was waiting. I wanted her to see me, to tell me I looked nice. I realised that it mattered to me what she thought.

I could see her, a little way off, looking at some hats. She had her back to me and I had to go around a display of shoes to reach her. A woman in front of me was picking up a belt, holding it in such a way that I knew instantly she was going to drop it into her bag, and I remember that I felt cross, that I didn't want to be reminded of such things, not today.

She heard me coming. She hastily put the belt back on the stand, took a step backwards as if to decide where to go next.

Then she turned, and I felt fear streak through me like a blade.

50

Frances

The first thing I heard was the clatter as she knocked over the shoe display.

Then there was a shriek from one of the shop girls. I dropped the hat I was looking at and swung around just in time to see Lizzie running at full pelt across the shop floor, scattering customers and clothes as she went hurtling across the shop floor, before she shoved open a door marked 'Staff Only' and disappeared. There was a woman running behind her, tall and bony, but she was stumbling on high cork soles and Lizzie had a head start, fuelled by sheer terror, running like a hunted deer. I kicked the fallen shoes out of the way, and forced my way past a gawping mother, but by the time I pushed open the door there was nothing but an empty staircase. I peered over the rail, just in time to see the peroxide hair of the tall woman disappear around a curve and out of sight.

I followed the stairs down, until I reached another door that was propped open with a pile of boxes. Beyond it was a yard, an alley, and then the street, full of shoppers and traffic. I stood looking wildly around but I couldn't see or hear anything, no commotion or shouts to show me where she might be. I saw a flash of yellow, and thought it was the other woman, but it was just a man hoisting a small child onto his shoulders, its cardigan bright in the weak spring sunshine.

And then, thank God, I saw Mickey, sitting on a pile of rubble, the *Daily Mirror* open in front of him. I pushed my way past a couple of old men, and grabbed his arm.

'Mickey! Mickey, have you seen Lizzie?'

'What?' He dropped the paper and scrambled to his feet. 'What happened? Where'd she go?'

'I don't know. I was waiting for her and the next minute she was running out of the shop. I think something spooked her, and there was a woman, chasing her—'

'I ain't seen her.' He climbed up on a pile of bricks, scanning the street. 'I can't see her.'

'Do you know where she'd go?'

He shook his head. 'I dunno, miss. We never come up this way.'

'You take this side of the street, I'll go over there. Maybe she's in a shop.'

He nodded. 'All right.'

'If you find her, take her back to the car. Can you do that?'

''Course.'

'Good lad.'

I turned away, waiting for a gap in the traffic. A van trundled past, then a motorbike. I stepped off the kerb, ready to cross.

Mickey snatched my arm. I nearly fell as he grabbed me, dragging me into a shop doorway.

'Mickey—'

'Oh Christ,' he said. His face was white and his eyes were huge. 'Oh Christ. It's June.'

'June?' I rubbed my arm. 'What are you talking about?'

'Oh God, if she sees us…'

Fear was sharp in his voice. Its edge made me pull him right into the shop. 'Where?'

'Over there. See? In the green coat.'

I looked through a crowded window display of bottles and bars of soap. It took me a moment to find her, walking up and down, looking into doorways and up side roads. I felt acid rise in my throat as I recognised that tall, skinny shape, the harsh yellow hair.

'She went after Lizzie,' I said.

'Oh God,' he said again. His eyes were fixed on the woman, who was now walking slowly back the way she'd come, away from us.

'Who is she, Mickey? Mickey, listen. Pull yourself together.' I shook his arm. 'Mickey, tell me who she is.'

'June. She's one of Sid's girls. Well, she was, before—'

I glared at him. He swallowed. 'She must be with Kenny now.'

'Who's Kenny?' We moved out of the way as a customer reached round us for a tin of tooth powder.

'Kenny Clapton.'

I don't know why it took me a moment to remember the name; everything about that afternoon felt like it had been branded onto my brain. 'The Clapton who wanted the money?'

'Yeah. It were his hundred and fifty quid Lizzie nicked. Oh Christ, miss, if June tells him she's seen Lizzie – Kenny will come looking – oh my God, Kenny will come after us.'

I tried to calm him. 'She can't have been sure. She could only have seen her for a split second.'

'June's known Lizzie for years.'

'All the same. We don't know she saw her.'

'Then why'd Lizzie run?'

'Maybe she panicked.'

'We've got to find her.' Mickey was trembling, though I couldn't tell whether it was from fear or worry or shock. 'I can't let Kenny get her, he'll kill her, he'll kill the baby.'

'Will this June woman know you?' He nodded. I took a deep breath. 'Right, then. Can you get back to the car? Wait for me there? Here's the key. Get inside, stay down. I'll come back as soon as I can.'

He took the key reluctantly. I patted him on the shoulder. 'It'll be all right,' I said, trying to sound more confident than I felt. 'She's a sensible girl. We'll find her.'

'I hope so, miss.'

He pulled his hat down over his face. The shop bell tinkled as another customer went out, a woman with two lanky sons, and we took our chance, following them as closely as we dared until we were out on the pavement. I risked a quick look over my shoulder. June was standing on the kerb, her back to us, one hand shielding her eyes as she looked up the road. I nudged Mickey.

'Quick. She's not looking. Go.'

He dodged out into the traffic. I watched as he went, his thin figure weaving in and out of the crowd, staying close to the shops so he was hidden by awnings and signs until he rounded a bend in the road and vanished. I risked a quick look behind me, but the green coat had disappeared too. I tried to think calmly, imagine what Lizzie would have done, where she would have gone, but her terrified face told me she'd just bolted, blindly heading for the first escape she'd seen. She could be anywhere.

I looked. I looked everywhere I could go, everywhere she could have been. I went all around the market square, dodging piles of bricks and craters that had been left on the pavement. I went into shops, I went into cafés, I went into the public conveniences. I went down alleys, I stumbled across bombsites. I saw a policeman and wondered if I should ask him, but then realised this would mean statements and visits to the Grange and all the risk that would bring, so I just nodded politely as he passed and ducked inside a butcher's shop where a stout woman glared at me for jumping the queue. I went as far as the station at the bottom of the hill, even buying a platform ticket so I could run down the stairs and scour the waiting faces staring blankly at posters or announcement boards. There were men in demob suits, women holding up waving children, clerks and secretaries, tradesmen and lovers. People smiled, embraced. One man wept alone in a corner.

But not one of them was Lizzie Sixpence.

51

We searched for hours before we gave up. We had no choice. The baby would need feeding and we had nowhere else to look.

When I finally went back to the car, Mickey confessed that he too had been looking, going into pubs and backyards in the hope he'd find her hiding in a corner somewhere. But it was half-day closing, the shops were emptying, and we drove slowly home in a miserable silence.

Maud was waiting in the drawing room. I'd found a telephone box and called to let her know what had happened, and before either of us could say anything she put her hands on Mickey's shoulders and told him it was not his fault. His mouth trembled and he buried his face in her shoulder and wept, great racking sobs that reminded me for the first time that he was a boy, just a scared, lonely boy snagged in events and deeds that he could neither understand nor control.

I'd bought powdered milk for the baby, and Maud fed her while I went up to change. I stared at myself in the mirror, at my pale face and frightened eyes. All I could think was that I had let Lizzie down, I had lost her, that she was out there in the dark, alone and terrified. To have run from us, to have left her baby behind… I could not begin to imagine the sheer blinding horror that must have driven her to whatever lonely place she had found.

I did not dare let myself think about what would happen if she was discovered, and could not decide whether the police or Kenny Clapton would be more dreadful.

In the end, when it was dark, I had to go back down. Maud was waiting for me at the bottom of the stairs, and without a word led me into the office. I sank into a chair, my head in my hands.

'My dear girl,' Maud said gently. 'How utterly bloody for you.'

I looked up. I could feel tears, unfamiliar and unwanted, and blinked them away in fury. 'I'm sorry,' I said.

'You know there's no need for that.'

'Do I? I took her there, I left her alone…'

'And why shouldn't you?' I shrugged miserably and Maud went on. 'Think about it like this. You didn't exploit her. You didn't force her into that godawful life she was living. You didn't terrify her so much she'd run away, did you? Of course not. Put blame where it's due.' Maud pulled out the chair from behind the desk and sat down to face me. 'So stop torturing yourself. Focus on what matters, and that's what we're going to do.'

'What can we do? I've looked everywhere.'

'I don't mean that.' Maud leaned forward, taking my hand. 'We can't help Lizzie right now. If this Clacton fellow—'

'Clapton.'

'Really? Must get Audrey to syringe my ears. Whatever. If he comes looking for her we need to be ready. Now and in the future.'

'Oh God, do you think he will?'

'The big problem of course is the baby.' Maud said it as if she were discussing some domestic snag, a blocked pipe or patch of damp. 'I mean, obviously we can keep her fed and clothed, but you saw how that odious little oik Parker was with her. No reason to suppose this Clapton chap'll be any different. If he wants the money he'll not baulk at how he gets it. Maybe he'd even think she could be bait, lure Lizzie out that way.'

I had at least got something to say about that. 'I was thinking we could ask Connie and Alastair to take her,' I said. 'She'd be safe at the Hall, surely?'

'Good idea. Bound to be room and I daresay there'll be some village woman who'd be glad of a few quid to be a nursemaid.' She smiled faintly. 'Be like the old days, with dear old Nanny Miller. I can still taste her tapioca.'

'I'll ring and ask Connie in the morning.'

Those bright eyes met mine. 'And what about you, my dear?' she said. 'I can't expect you to stay. Not now. Totally understand if you want to look for somewhere new.'

I couldn't pretend I hadn't thought about it. To be away from here, from all this misery and loss – it was something I warmed my mind on at night. But then I looked at Maud, her sturdy, determined figure and her weary, brave face and I just said, 'Maybe. But not yet. I'll help you get through this and then we'll see. Is that all right?'

'Bravo.' She put her hand on my shoulder for a moment. 'We'll win through,' she said. 'You just wait and see. Now get off for a nap, you look like death warmed up.'

'All right. And Maud…'

'Yes, my dear?'

'Thank you,' I said.

She waved a hand. 'Nonsense. Just doing what needs to be done.'

I nodded and left her. I went out into the hall, looking automatically to see that the door was bolted. The old photographs on the wall seemed to watch me as I went past, my reflection wavering across the frames. From somewhere upstairs the baby had started to cry.

I jumped as the phone rang. The receiver was cold and hard in my hands.

'Hello?'

There was silence. A deep, ragged breath. Another. Then a click and the line went dead.

I hung up, my hand trembling.

Maud had followed me out. She saw my face and raised her eyebrows.

'Frances? Who was that?'

'I don't know. Just breathing. Then they hung up.' I looked back at the squat black bulk of the telephone. 'It could have been—'

'Yes. It could have been.'

Maud gave a little nod. 'Let's talk in the morning. I'd try to get some shut-eye, if I were you.'

'All right. Good night.'

'Sleep well, my dear.'

I went slowly up the stairs, pausing only to glance back down when I reached the landing. I could see into the office; Maud was at her desk, a pile of paperwork in front of her. The dogs had appeared, trotting in to stand beside her, tails waving and heads cocked in hope of a treat.

Maud put her pen down, leaned forward, wrapped her arms around one of the shaggy necks. She buried her face in the grey fur, and I suddenly felt as though I were watching something private and raw, something almost naked.

I turned and ran to my room, locking the door behind me. I curled up on the bed, clutching the pillow to my chest, unable to get warm, unable to shake off the sense that I had just seen the most frightening thing of all.

Maud Shenstone was weeping.

And I think it was at that moment I first realised that Lizzie and her baby had to die.

52

How do you hide a tree? Put it in a wood.

It's an old joke, but it's true.

How do you hide five women? Tidy them away in a crowded filing cabinet.

And how do you hide a baby?

I think I'd always known there would only be one way. Only that wasn't a joke at all.

She'd grown – of course she had, I don't know why I was surprised to see her change, she was two months old now – her face already losing that crumpled look she'd had when she first squirmed her way into the world. She had a fuzz of blond hair, like pussy willow, and eyes of the clearest blue that would stare into mine as if demanding to know what I was thinking. The first time I fed her, that day I lost her mother, I was surprised by the strength of her grip on the bottle and the determined way she drank, taking her time, doing it her own way, the decisive way she turned her head when she'd had enough.

Such a tiny thing to have an enemy like Kenny Clapton.

'Do you think he'll really come looking for Lizzie?' I said. We were in the office, early the next morning, the house feeling scoured and empty around us now the women had all gone. Outside, the March breeze pulled at the bare branches of the trees, which were still bent and stunted from their recent burden of snow, and when the sun did glimmer through the clouds it was hesitant and unsure, as if it had forgotten how to shine.

Maud considered. 'I can't imagine he won't,' she said at last. 'It's only the snow that will have kept him away. He'll be missing that Parker creature by now, as well.'

'Will he know to come here?' I don't know why I asked, really. I knew that there was every chance that Sidney would have told Clapton that he knew where to find Lizzie; for all I knew, he'd been the one to find the card that Mickey said he'd dropped. But I wanted Maud to say something reassuring and calming, to take away the gnawing fear that growled in my belly every time I thought of all that had happened.

But she didn't. She couldn't.

'It's all very convenient for him, I have to say,' she said. 'If he turns up and finds young Iris here he can either take her — now don't look like that, we have to face facts — and let it be known he's got her, in the hope it makes Lizzie show up, or he can do what that Parker fellow threatened and sell her. It makes my blood boil, it really does.'

There was a gurgling sound from the basket where Iris was lying, watched over by an enormous old teddy bear. Maud had greeted it with a cry of 'Hello, Harold, old bean!' when it had arrived in a parcel the day before, sent up from Shenstone Hall with a letter from Connie that at any other time would have filled me with joy for my friend, but which now had shut off one last chance of hope.

Maud was still speaking. 'And at the moment, let's face it, if anything happened to her here we wouldn't have a leg to stand on. Clapton could say he's her father, that he's adopted her, that she's any kind of relative, and who are we? Total strangers.'

'We're all she's got. I know Mickey wants to do what he can, but—'

'He's not up to it,' Maud said bluntly. 'And anyway, a lad like him turning up with a baby in tow? He'd be the talk of the town. No, what we need is somewhere to hide her. Maybe one of the ladies… let me see… what about Gertie Hassett? She was a nice woman.' She dragged open the filing cabinet and rifled through papers. 'Oh, bother. She was a gardener. Wrong kind of nursery. Maybe I'm mixing her up.'

'Would that be fair? If Clapton found out we'd sent her away we'd just be getting someone else involved. Putting them at risk, and there are too many involved already.'

'We can warn Maggie and the others. In a roundabout way, of course, we don't want any careless talk costing lives as we used to say, but it won't hurt to let them know that Lizzie's gone missing. I'll drop them all a line, we've got forwarding addresses.' Maud brightened. 'Who knows, she might find her way to one of them. That'd be just the ticket.'

'That would put them in harm's way.' I swallowed, hard. 'This is my mistake, I need to sort it out.'

'Oh, my dear young woman, whatever are you talking about?' Maud stared at me. 'Mistake?'

'I brought Lizzie here. If I hadn't—'

'Stuff and nonsense.' Maud swung round, all fourteen stone of her, hands on hips and a steely glare on her face. 'I won't hear any more of it. For an intelligent woman, Frances, you are being remarkably obtuse. What were you supposed to do, leave her out in the snow? Leave her to be beaten black and blue by that little beast Parker? You did what was right and I'm surprised I have to point it out to you. So stop whining and feeling sorry for yourself and concentrate on how we are going to put this right.'

She was angrier than I had ever seen her, and it brought me up sharp, as abruptly as if she'd slapped me. For a second it made me furious, too, and we stood there bristling at each other until Iris set up a wail.

I took my time bending to jiggle Harold around for a bit, until she calmed, and when I straightened up the fight had gone out of me. 'You're right,' I said, and I sank into a chair, exhausted. 'I'm sorry. You've been so kind…' I could feel my voice wavering and bit my words off before they could crack into tears.

'Not at all. I told you the first day you came here, I can't bear unfairness, and it's not fair that Lizzie led that kind of life and it's not fair on Mickey or the others and it's not fair that we've been left to deal with it, but that's where we are so we need to pull our socks up and get on with it. I'm delighted for Alastair, he and Constance will be marvellous parents, but all the same it means we've got to look elsewhere and we need to do it sharpish.'

'I don't want to send her away,' I said stubbornly. 'I need to know she's safe, I can't bear the thought of her being miles away where we don't know what's happening.' I swallowed, hard. 'Maybe Lizzie will come back.'

'Well, I have to say I think that's unlikely. She knows Clapton and his crew are after her and if she's got an ounce of sense she'll lie low. And if she does eventually show her face, then we can help her like we've helped all the rest. But in the meantime—' Maud looked at me, her glasses glinting – 'I know there's adoption,' she said. 'But personally I think that's out of the question, don't you? I don't mind telling you, I think we owe this little lady a bit more than just passing her on to some society or other, not knowing where she'll end up.'

I was suddenly back on my first morning at the Grange. *I've always set my face against those societies that ship children off to the colonies…*

'Absolutely,' I said firmly, and saw Maud nearly smile. 'She needs a family,' I went on, suddenly certain. 'Somewhere she won't stand out from the crowd, where she'll just be ordinary.'

'A shame we haven't got a great pack of brats here at the moment,' Maud said. 'Like last summer, do you remember? This is such a terrific house for children,' and for a moment she sounded wistful.

'Maybe she doesn't have to go anywhere,' I said slowly. 'Maybe I…'

I paused, feeling suddenly dizzy. I didn't know where the words had grown from, why this solution was suddenly there in my head. Had the idea always been in my mind, since those nights walking and rocking while Lizzie slept? Had my months at the Grange given me this sudden new courage?

This does tend to be a house where people learn all sorts of things about themselves.

'Are you thinking…?' Maud sat down heavily. 'Oh, my dear. Such a big step.'

'If there's a mother then surely Clapton won't risk anything?'

'You could be putting yourself in a lot of danger.'

'Iris is already in danger.'

'But have you thought it through? The world can be a very cruel place. Especially for women who are thought to have transgressed, which is what everyone will assume you have done. You don't need me to tell you that, surely?'

'I know. But this is how I can make it up to Lizzie, to the others. I can keep her daughter safe and then, who knows, maybe one day she'll come back and it'll all be all right.' I looked down at the baby, who had fallen asleep, a thumb half in, half out of her mouth. 'It has to be me,' I said. 'I let Lizzie down – no, I did – so I have to do this. For her. Please, Maud. I'll leave if you want me to but this is the right thing, I know it is.'

There was a long pause. Then Maud reached out and caught hold of my hand, chafing it in both of hers.

'There'll be no talk of leaving,' she said, her voice rather thick. 'You're doing a very remarkable thing. And I'll be right beside you, my dear. You're not on your own. Whatever happens, whatever the world thinks, you and young Iris—'

'Iris Elizabeth. That's what I'm going to put on the certificate.'

'Really? Well, that's rather nice, I must say. Two names to choose from.'

'It's a connection. To Lizzie. I was thinking I could call her Betty.'

'She's a look of a Betty about her, certainly.'

'And if I register her now, it will be a different date, so if Clapton ever does come—' The idea made my voice crack, and I swallowed – 'if he does come it'll be proof it's not the same baby. It'll help keep her safe. Safer, anyway. Don't you think?'

'No.' Maud shook her head, and I felt sick, but she said thoughtfully, 'It'll be better if I do it. I can say her mother is one of my cases, staying here, very unfortunate, so on, so forth. Just in case there's anyone asking questions. I hate to paint you in that light, my dear, but if you're sure…'

I nodded. 'Yes. I want to do this.'

Maud bent and picked the baby up, but she didn't wake, knowing herself to be in capable hands. 'So, young lady, that's all settled. We'll look after you.'

'Oh, Maud,' I said, unbearably moved. 'I can't thank you—'

'Nonsense. We'll stick it out together. All three of us.' Maud smiled suddenly, handed me the baby and stood up. She rested her hand on my shoulder, warm and reassuring and so, so strong. 'After all, it's what this house is for,' she said.

53

'In the midst of life, we are in death.'

I could hear the stonemason muttering this to himself as he slopped mortar onto his trowel. The vicar had just said the same thing, though with slightly more conviction.

The stone was rough and the lettering shallow. All they could get, Maud had said regretfully, the good stuff's been requisitioned for housing. I could tell it had been a rush job from the way the edges were left sharp and uneven. I watched anxiously, thinking that it could give someone a nasty cut if they weren't careful, although with luck after today nobody would remember that it was here at all.

The mason stepped back. 'This about right? That better?' He shifted the stone slightly, making sure it was straight. 'There. That do you?'

Maud nodded. 'Thank you, Mr Walker.' Then she turned to the plump man standing beside us. His face was as smooth and innocent as an egg. 'I hope this is satisfactory, Mr Clapton?'

The man looked thoughtfully at her, then at the stone. 'Nice of you to do this, vicar.'

Reverend West bowed his head graciously. 'It is a sad duty,' he said. I thought of the ten pounds Maud had given him, ostensibly for the Poor Box. No doubt it would help him make the best of things.

Over his surpliced shoulder I could see the marble memorial to the V1's Lost Dead, sticking up stark and white amongst the weathered graves. The vicar made a wavering sign of the cross at Lizzie's stone; the gesture took in the trees, the blue sky, the greenhouse. A tiny bit of borrowed ceremony for Sidney Parker, given that he would never have any of his own.

There were three other men too, standing alert and watchful. They had arrived with Clapton, been introduced as his 'boys', each of them lean and hungry and hard, and despite their polite handshakes and their deference to the older man, each of them terribly, terribly dangerous.

Of course, being British, we could not let the occasion pass without tea. So we had all walked the few hundred yards back the house, to sit uncomfortably in the drawing room and wish that our guests would leave and never come back.

'We are just glad we could do this small thing,' I said. On my lap the baby was sucking on a rusk. 'I know the municipal cemetery holds a brief ceremony when they hold a – well, a pauper's funeral – but it's nice to show her some respect. In the circumstances.'

'In the circumstances,' Clapton repeated. The three 'boys' had declined tea and were standing in a row behind him, like a firing squad.

It was his second visit to Wickham Grange. The first had been a week after we lost Lizzie; his car had purred onto the drive like some enormous cat. Thank God, I'd been in the office, had seen his bulky figure climbing out, had just had time to send Mickey running up the stairs before the bell clanged. 'So sorry to bother you,' he'd said, 'I'm looking for a young friend, reason to believe she'd come to this house.'

Mrs Lloyd had brought in tea. Maud poured.

'I am afraid I have some very bad news for you, Mr Clacton.'

His lips narrowed. 'It's Clapton.'

She raised her eyebrows, patted her ear. 'I beg your pardon. Deaf as a post. No, I'm so sorry to have to tell you—'

He leaned forward, taking his cup. 'Tell me what?'

'A young woman did come here, during that awful snow. Terrible, wasn't it? We were cut off for weeks. I've never known it so cold, not since the last war—'

'Yes, yes. But this girl – Lizzie.'

'Well, she said her name was Elizabeth. Tiny little thing. Would that be your friend?'

'Sounds like it. She was up the – in the family way.'

'Then it sounds like it was definitely her. Milk? Poor child, she was extremely ill.'

'Did she have anyone with her?'

'A young man came,' I said, frowning as if trying to remember.

'No one else? Did any lanky bit calling himself Mickey turn up as well?'

'A Mr Parker, I think he said his name was.'

'Sidney. One of my lads. I'd sent him to find her.' Clapton tried to look concerned, but the expression slithered off his face like a snake crawling under a stone. 'She'd nicked something of mine that I wanted back, and I sent him to fetch it.'

'He certainly seemed very anxious to see her. But I'm afraid I don't have good news.' Maud shook her head. 'We summoned a doctor but I'm very sorry to say the girl had lost a lot of blood. We did all we could, given our limited resources – I was a VAD, you know – but she never regained consciousness. My sincere condolences.'

He stirred his tea very slowly. 'You're telling me she's dead?'

'I'm afraid so.'

'And the kid?'

'It was never born. As I say, we would like to extend our sincere sympathy.'

'Thank you.' He said it almost absent-mindedly. You could see the thoughts swirling behind his eyes.

I passed a plate of rather pallid biscuits. Clapton waved them away. 'When the ambulance finally arrived she was taken to hospital, but it was far too late and she died that night.' I paused. 'They arranged a burial in one of the municipal cemeteries. I'm afraid it will be an unmarked grave. We had no idea of her surname or if she had any relatives.'

Clapton waved a hand. 'Nobody did. She called herself Sixpence, no idea why.' He shifted in his chair, impatient to get back to what mattered most to him. 'You said Parker come — came with her? Didn't he say anything?'

'He arrived shortly after she did, yes. He didn't say much, as soon as he heard she was unconscious — well, I'm sorry to say he was a bit of a cad. Ran straight out again.' Maud broke a biscuit in half and passed it to one of the dogs, who licked it politely before letting it fall onto the rug. 'He took her bag with him,' she said suddenly, like someone having a good idea. 'Maybe there were some details in there that will help you trace her people?'

His head reared up. 'He took her bag?'

'Yes. I do so hope it will help you find her family.'

'I'd rather it helped me find him. There's a small matter of a lot of money that's gone missing. My money. I want it sorted out. You say he had the bag?' He was watching us intently. It was like being raked with fire. Then he narrowed his eyes. 'Only I have a friend,' he said, and I felt a slash of fright run through me, 'who's sure she saw the young lady in Bromley. Just this week.' He stretched his legs out in front of him, idly crossing them at the ankle. 'So you might I say I'm a bit surprised to hear she's brown bread.'

Maud and I had talked for hours about how we would answer this, but in the end there was only one chance to take.

I thought of Mr Poole and Mr Rogers, and put one of their condescending smirks onto my face. 'Forgive me for saying so,' I said. 'But Elizabeth was a very — ordinary — young person. I think your friend must have been mistaken.'

'Perhaps.' He put his tea back on the table untouched, and stood up. The boys snapped upright as if he had tugged on a leash. 'Though I have to say she was pretty certain. Maybe I'd better go and ask her again. Just to be on the safe side, as you might say. Then we can have another little chat, if need be.'

The threat was like a razor blade wrapped in silk. I pretended to be fussing over the baby, because I knew that if I tried to speak my voice would betray my utter terror.

He looked around the room and I had the sudden nightmarish fear that there'd be a speck of blood we'd missed, a smear of grey slime on the rug, the smell of death caught in the curtains.

But he just put on his hat and picked up his gloves.

'It's actually fortuitous that you've called,' Maud had said as she showed him to the door. 'We were planning to put up a memorial. We've never had a death here before and, well, we feel it, rather. It would be so nice if you could be there – someone she'd known, the closest thing we can find to family.'

He'd nodded, said something polite.

So here we were, back again, drinking tea again. *And please, God,* I thought, *this will have worked, you will believe us, now you've seen that this death that never was has been marked with a stone and not just a heap of pebbles.*

The vicar murmured something about writing his sermon. The dogs whined to be let out. Maud got up from the sofa. 'Of course, Reverend, thank you so much. Yes, on Sunday. Tattie, get down. Mr Clapton, may I fetch your hat?'

Kenny Clapton stood up slowly. In my arms, Betty wriggled and mewed.

'Please excuse me,' I said. 'I'm afraid my daughter is getting hungry. It was a pleasure to see you again, Mr Clapton, I just wish it had been—'

Clapton reached out. Before I could move he flipped down a corner of the shawl, making the baby blink up at him in protest.

'Pretty little thing,' he said conversationally. 'A shame young Lizzie's kid didn't make it.'

'I know.' I swallowed, hoping he'd think it was from grief and not fear. 'It makes it rather painful. Knowing that she had died so young, when I was about to become a mother myself…'

Maud patted my shoulder. 'Buck up. At least they're together.'

'Funny they should be born at near enough the self-same time, innit?' Clapton was still looking at Betty. 'Where's her pa?' he said suddenly. 'You ain't wearing a wedding ring.'

'I'm sure you know, Mr Clapton, that this house is a home for unfortunate women.' Maud spoke sternly.

'Little bastard, is she?'

I took what I hoped was an offended breath. 'We were engaged,' I said stiffly. 'I had his word of honour.'

He shrugged, dropping the shawl back into place. 'Be a shame if anything happened to her,' he said. 'I'll have to see what I can do for her. I think I'll send the boys round now and then to keep an eye on her. Just in case you hear from anyone who can help me find what I want back, if you follow me.'

Maud opened her mouth but I spoke first.

'You do that, Mr Clapton.' I met his stare and for once he looked away. 'We'll be here. We'll wait for you.' I pulled the baby closer, patting her back with little soothing taps. 'I'll be here for as long as it takes,' I said.

It was the only truth I'd told all morning.

54

Lizzie

I can still remember the first time I saw the sea and oh, in spite of everything, I thought it was bleeding lovely. It was a cloudy afternoon and there it was, all spangled with the reflections of the lights that hung along the prom, like some great big necklace. Everything smelled of salt and chips and warm beer and the sound of the waves was like someone hushing a child. I stood there on the pavement and I stared and stared and stared.

I hadn't planned to end up in Brighton. When I ran out of the shop I'd just gone haring down the hill, the bag bumping against my legs, the unfamiliar skirt bunching between my knees so I nearly tripped and fell. Sweat stung my eyes but I didn't dare stop because I could have sworn I heard June behind me, clacking along on her heels, her skinny claws reaching out to grab me and pull me down. I barged into a man with a dog and he yelled something at me, but I was already away, my shoes slapping on the pavement as I ran. I think I had some mad idea of getting on a bus, but there was stops all down the high street and I was terrified that she'd catch up and get on, trapping me. I wanted Mickey, I wanted Miss Alleyn, but they were far behind me now and I didn't dare turn around, I didn't dare go back. So I ran and it was only when I smelled steam that I realised I was outside the station.

I ducked inside and looked wildly at the signs. The words seemed to jump about because I never learned much reading, but I recognised one and went up to the little window where a bored man give me a ticket to London. I fished in the bag, found a pound note and handed it over. He raised his eyebrows but I was too scared and too winded to say anything, so he just scooped out all the change he had and slid it through the little trough towards me.

I didn't stop shaking until the train was dragging itself out of the station. I had a seat on the far side of the carriage, as far away from the door as I could manage, and I pressed myself into the corner so I was as tiny as I could be. The whistle blew and I jumped, thinking it was the coppers, but nothing happened and off we went.

London was just like it had always been, full of dirt and rubble and tired, hurrying people. When I got off the train I stood still for a long time, not knowing what to do, where to go, letting myself be carried along by the crowd. I felt dizzy, like I did when Sid clouted me round the head one time. I couldn't think. I wanted to go back to the Grange but I didn't know how to get there and I didn't know if June was there waiting for me. My knockers ached and I wanted my baby, but I thought of Kenny getting his hands on her and I felt sick. I wanted to lie down and sleep, I wanted something to eat, I wanted a piss. In the end I thought, *I know, I'll go somewhere and lie low for a day or two and then I can find out what's what.* I heard a man calling out about a train to Brighton and I said out loud, 'Why not', and I bought a ticket and got on and that was that.

It was early in the spring so I got a room in a guest house easy enough, even though the woman give me a funny look when she saw I didn't have no bags. I'd never slept in a room by myself, not until I went to the Grange, and this one weren't up to much, just a little narrow bed and a table with a Bible on it. But there weren't no bugs, which was something, and I had the ration book Miss Alleyn had sorted out for me, so at least nobody asked questions about that.

After I finished staring at the sea I went off and bought some chips and a cup of tea, and I ate them sat on a bench by the beach. There was music coming from somewhere and I thought, *Well, this ain't bad. Maybe Mickey and me can come here one day.* The thought of him made me smile in a sad kind of a way. I hadn't been on my own, without him, for ever such a long time and

I missed him, his nice smile and his kind ways.

I didn't want him to fret, like I knew he would, so I found a phone box and I asked to be put through to the Grange. The operator woman made a right old fuss about getting the name right, but in the end I could hear ringing and I imagined Miss Alleyn or Miss Maud coming across the hall to pick it up.

'Hello?'

It was Miss Alleyn. Hearing her voice made me come over all funny, my throat going tight and my mouth going dry. I wanted to say I'm here, I'm sorry, I'm so sorry, but the words wouldn't come, I could only give a big ragged gasp and then oh God I could hear Iris and I couldn't bear it, I slammed the phone down and put my head on it and I cried and cried and cried.

After that I kind of stopped thinking for a bit. I stayed in my room as much as I could, though I had to go out and buy a toothbrush and some knickers, and the landlady asked a few nosy questions about why I was all on my own. I told her I'd left an orphanage and was trying to get myself sorted out, and that shut her up for a bit, especially when I said I was looking for a job. My tits stopped hurting after a while and that made me cry again because I knew it meant that when I went back I couldn't feed Iris no more. I bought little toys and put them in a bag ready to give to her, and when I were in the toy shop I got a pad and some pencils and started to try to draw things ready to show her.

I think it was that what gave me the idea of writing. I'd never been much good at that but in the end wanting to talk to Mickey hurt so bad I thought I'd give it a go. It weren't a long letter but I put it in the post and when three days later I got a reply, I hugged it to me for a long time before opening it. It took me a long time to work out what it said, and longer to think about what I wanted to say in return, but in the end I sat down and I started.

Dear Micky,

You was ever so kind to write back. And to say you ain't angry with me. I'm so sorry I done a runner but I was so scared and then it was to late.

I was scared when you said Kenny had come and that he says he is still after his money and oh Micky that makes me sad cause I know it means I can't come back just yet cos it ain't safe for you or me or Iris. He said he'd come again and that made me so feel sick I had to stop reading for a bit because I am so scared he'll take my baby.

But then I read it a bit more and you say she ain't called Iris now. She ain't even mine no more because I'm dead. I'm not cross, honest. I know as Miss Allen is doing what's right to keep her safe and it's so kind of her to pretend she's had a baby even though everyone knows she ain't married. I got to face it, I won't be able to do nothing for my girl, not for a long time. So in a way I'm glad she's Miss Allen's baby now. It's sweet she's called her after me and if she ever asks why she was called Elizabeth I hope you'll tell her it was after someone called that who was a nice person and loved her a lot.

I'm reely glad you're staying at the Grange. It's nice and you're good at mending stuff. And Micky I mean this I want you to meet a nice girl and have fun. Don't you go worrying about me. I've got plans. There's this place called the Workers Education and they've said I can go there and they'll help me learn stuff. And the landlady here says as she'll pay me to do the laundry and then one day when it's safe I'll come back.

Can I write to you again? Don't tell no one where I am. Not even Miss Allen. I don't want her worrying. It can be our secret.

I'd like that, one secret that's nice and not anything nasty.

I miss you.

Love from Lizzy

I read it back but it said everything I wanted it to say and my hand was aching. I folded it up and put it in the envelope. Then I found a stamp and wrote the address, all nice and clear in big letters:

Mr M Harris
Wickham Grange
West Wickham
Kent

Part Three

2006

55
Caroline

It was only when the old man's voice finally petered to a halt that Caroline realised darkness had crept into the room while they listened. Everything was swathed in shadows, grey shapes that did not seem to belong to this time but instead had somehow come from across the years to hear the story being told at last.

She opened her mouth to speak but there were no words, no words at all.

It was Ruth who at last stirred and turned on a lamp. The soft light felt unbearably bright, and it took Caroline a moment to gather herself and look around. Rob put his hand on hers.

'You okay?'

She managed a nod. Opposite them, Danny sat awkwardly on a dining chair. Mr Harris – Mickey – was sitting on the other sofa, Dr Fairfax very straight beside him.

Danny shifted in his chair. Caroline had the distinct sense that he wanted to put his hand up. 'Look, can I have a drink? Only it's bloody weird hearing all this—'

'I think we could all do with one.' Rob got up, found glasses, brought over a bottle. Caroline sipped. The wine tasted rich and alive.

'Why were you watching me?' she said suddenly.

Danny looked down at his boots. 'I didn't want to scare you,' he said. 'Only Granddad said you might want to sell the house. And I was worried, because I've only got a one-bedroom flat and I don't know where he'd go if you kicked him out, so when he asked I said yeah, I'd keep an eye on you, let him know if you did anything.' He looked at Mr Harris. 'I only hung about a bit. Nobody said anything about a dead bloke,' he said accusingly. 'If I'd known—'

'I never told you to take that bloody gun!' Mr Harris said sharply.

'Yeah, well, you wasn't out there watching three of 'em digging up a bloody body! What was I supposed to do, ask 'em nicely to leave it alone?'

'All right, all right.' Mr Harris took the gun out of his pocket and put it on the table. 'Don't suppose I need it no more, anyway.'

'You kept it? You kept Parker's gun?' Audrey Fairfax was staring at the ugly metal thing. 'Good grief, boy, what were you thinking?'

'I wanted a bit of protection.'

'You thought you'd have a shooting match? Here? Dear God.' She took a mouthful of her wine, shaking her head.

'Did Clapton ever come back?' Caroline asked.

Mr Harris nodded. 'Oh yeah. Few times, over the years. Him or one of his mob. Never said nothing, just arrived, saying as he was looking out for your ma. And he always asked if your gran had remembered anything about the money. Like he knew and was just waiting for us to get something wrong.' He looked across at her, his face carved into slabs of darkness by the gathering dusk. 'I caught him once, did you know?'

Audrey sat bolt upright. 'You never said anything!'

'What you don't know can't hurt you.' He turned to Caroline. 'He'd found your mum on her swing in the garden. Got her to take him inside and show him round the house. Little, she was, only six or seven, bright little love, loved to chatter. He were asking her all sorts of questions, what's her mummy's name, does she get lots of pocket money, what bank does her granny use and all that. Thank God Miss Maud were nearby, she come out and told him to sling his hook.' The old man looked exhausted but he sounded stubborn. 'So yeah, I kept the gun. I had to do something. I had to keep things safe. For the baby.'

'The baby.' Caroline was having trouble with her words. They didn't seem big enough for the enormity of what she needed them to say. She cleared her throat, tried to smother the flood that was swamping her mind. The clock – the clock! – on the chimney-piece was ticking steadily, and she counted off ten seconds before trying again.

One thing was slashing through her confusion, a stark, sharp thought that was clear and distinct, like a beam of light slicing through darkness. 'The baby,' she said again. 'Lizzie's baby. Was that – was she – my mother?'

'Of course she was,' Dr Fairfax said irritably. 'Though why Frances had to let her call herself Betty I don't know. Iris seemed a perfectly pleasant name to me.'

'Then – then Lizzie Sixpence is – was…' Caroline was getting annoyed with herself now. 'Was Lizzie Sixpence my grandmother?'

'Yes, love.' Mr Harris spoke unusually gently. 'She was.'

'Granny – Frances – said she lost her. She said it was a terrible grief.' Caroline looked up, like someone suddenly seeing sunlight. 'She was worried the body would be found after she'd gone. That's why she didn't want the house sold. The restriction, the protected tenancies, it was all she could do to keep it hidden.'

'Nobody would have found nothing if you'd left well alone and not gone sniffing around,' Mr Harris said. 'Only with you saying you wanted to sell up – we couldn't risk you finding anything. Me and the doctor, we was all right, nobody would have known we were here that day, but them other ladies, well, they was different. People was already looking for them.'

Audrey Fairfax sniffed. 'And they were women who'd run away. Don't forget the way they'd have been treated. How they would have been treated, if it all came out. They'd all have been blamed. Maybe even hanged.'

Caroline remembered the letter in the *Standard*, its reference to trousered harpies, and nodded.

Mr Harris sighed. 'We had to do what we could. For them as well as us.'

'So you cut off the internet and burned the files to stop me contacting them.'

He looked embarrassed. 'Yeah, well, that got out of hand…'

'We could have been killed!'

'That'll do.' Audrey held up her hand. 'There'll be plenty of time for recriminations. The main point now is to determine what you intend to do about – about…' She gestured to the dark garden.

'What? Right now I don't give a rat's arse about Sidney Parker.' Caroline leaned forward, her face intent. 'You've just told me that I had a grandmother I never knew about,' she said. 'That there's this whole bloody awful story that's now my story. My mother's story.'

'Not surprising you're a bit het up,' Mr Harris said.

'A bit het up? A bit—' She put the glass down on the table and clenched her fists. 'For God's sake, is that it?'

'It's understandable—'

'I don't mean about me!' Caroline almost shouted. 'I mean about Lizzie. Who she was. What she did. My mother never knew her. I can't not tell her all this, what am I supposed to say? She was here, she killed someone, she ran away?' She had a sudden picture of cream paper, curvaceous copperplate and couldn't keep the anger out of her voice any more. '*What happened to Lizzie Sixpence?*'

'That really is not our most pressing priority.'

Caroline almost missed Dr Fairfax's words. She was feeling light-headed, as if she was floating in a web of questions and feelings that was winding around her and dragging her into the dark, making everything shift and slip out of shape. All she could think was how Lizzie, Lizzie Sixpence, had started out as a shadow, a ghost hiding in a letter, and yet now had a life, a presence, a reality. It was as if she were standing there in her cotton frock and ankle socks, watching and waiting and judging.

'What?'

'We need to decide what we are going to do now you've disturbed everything.'

'It's obvious,' Caroline said sharply. 'We call the police.'

Danny jerked upright in his chair.

'God, no!' he said in alarm. 'I'll go to prison, I'll lose my job!'

Mr Harris looked at him, then at Caroline. 'No. Not after all this time. You can't—'

'I'm a builder, not a bloody gangster.'

Audrey Fairfax had gone pale. 'This is not what your grandmother wanted,' she said. 'You'll destroy everything she did.'

'You can't want me to just pretend this hasn't happened!' Caroline said fiercely. 'You want me to go back out there and just bury it again? Act like it's not there? It's a fucking dead body!'

'I'm supposed to be doing a loft conversion next week—'

'We know.' Mr Harris's voice was harsh. 'We've known for seventy years. And we've kept it a secret all that time.'

'And you did everything you could to stop me finding out.' She took a deep, ragged breath. 'Didn't you think I had a right to know?'

'Didn't you think we had a right to be safe?' Audrey said. 'That we all did? Parker was a monster who would have done terrible things if we hadn't stopped him. Would you want us in prison for that?'

Mr Harris leaned forward in his chair. He suddenly looked very old. 'Please,' he said simply. 'Please. No. Not this. Not now.'

'Wait. Give me a minute.' Caroline sank her head into her hands and closed her eyes. She could hear her heart pounding. Her breath sounded harsh and loud in the sudden silence. But above everything, clear and stern as steel, was the thought of how her grandmother must have sat in this very room, made the same kind of choice, stared down two futures and decided which one would be hers. And Caroline could feel the weight of those years, the burden of that decision, knowing that what she said would change everything forever.

A burning sense of justice. My legacy to you.

She thought she understood, now, the old lady's words. Frances had been a woman driven from her job, thrown into a world of violence and grief, and yet had given up her life to protect a child, had spent decades keeping a stranger's secret. She had lied and defied, she had held her ground and made her stand, and all because it was the right, the honourable, the just thing.

Caroline looked up. Across the room the old people were sitting and watching her with a pitiful kind of hope. The idea that had started to form in her mind grew firmer, more distinct.

'We call the police,' she said, and closed her eyes so she did not have to see their faces.

56

DS Maria Hughes was round, plump and had a Somerset accent so thick it could butter a scone.

She had arrived in a van with three or four others, who climbed down onto the drive where they struggled with boiler suits that flapped and wriggled in the wind. The sergeant stood watching for a moment, then came over to where Caroline was waiting.

'Afternoon,' she said pleasantly. 'I hear you think you've got a body for us.'

'Just down there.' Caroline pointed. 'Would you like coffee first?'

'Don't mind if I do. Thank you. Trev, you and the others crack on, all right?'

She ignored their resentful glances and followed Caroline into the flat, where Rob was waiting with mugs and a plate of Marks and Spencer biscuits. Caroline took two, feeling she'd need the sugar, and gestured to the dining table.

'Nice to see someone with a good appetite,' the sergeant said approvingly as she sat down. 'And who's not worried about her figure. Now then,' she went on, before Caroline could say anything, 'you say you've found some bones.'

'That's right. A skull.'

'I see.' Through the French windows Caroline could see spectral white figures plodding across the lawn. 'And you just dug it up.'

'Yes.'

'Down there.'

'Yes.'

'In the greenhouse, it says here.'

'Yes.' God, thought Caroline, now I know why clients get annoyed when I tell people to just say no comment. 'It's Victorian,' she added, inconsequentially.

Hughes dunked her chocolate chip cookie. 'And it was you who found the skull?'

'Yes. Well, we did.' She looked at Rob, who leaned across to shake Hughes' hand.

'And you'd be, sir?'

'Rob Sayers. I'm a – a friend of Caroline's.'

'Ah. Friend.' Hughes gave them a disconcertingly shrewd glance.

'And my friend Ruth was here, too. She's had to go home, but you can contact her there. Ruth Shenstone, Shenstone Hall.'

'Shenstone Hall? My other half's cousin's from round those parts. We went to his wedding there. Very nice, all that country estate and stately home stuff. Especially for us poor country folk.' Another dunk, which gave Caroline time to reflect that anyone taking Maria Hughes for a bumpkin would very soon learn to regret it. 'Anyone else?'

'No. Just the three of us.' *If you don't count the old man, or his grandson with the gun.*

'Well, I daresay we can get in touch with Ms Shenstone. Or would that be Lady?'

'Just the Honourable.'

'Just. The. Honourable.' Hughes wrote it slowly. 'Good. Now pardon me for asking, but I'm a bit puzzled as to why the three of you should be out there digging around in an old greenhouse. Not exactly gardening weather, is it?'

'My grandmother died recently.' Caroline thought about another biscuit, then decided against. 'I inherited the house and I'm thinking about selling. My friends are helping me to sort out Gran's things and we decided to see what state the house is in. And the grounds.'

'Looks in pretty good nick to me.' Hughes smiled briefly. 'Are those de Morgan tiles?'

'Yes,' said Rob. 'And there's some William Morris.'

The sergeant got up and wandered over to the fireplace. Outside there was a sudden flare as a spotlight was switched on. 'I do like my Arts and Crafts,' she said. She looked at the clock, tapping it approvingly. 'Oh, and a nice bit of Art Deco. Shame about that crack. You could get the glass replaced, no bother. Anyway, so you go down into the greenhouse and then what?'

'We could see the ground had been disturbed,' Rob said. 'The door must have blown open and we thought a fox might have got in. So we went to look and – well…'

'Ah. Foxes. Bane of my life, always in the bins. Crisp packets all over my garden. Let's hope they don't go finding any dead bodies there, eh?' Hughes came and sat down again, turning over a new page of her notebook. 'I saw that there'd been a fire here recently,' she said.

Caroline registered the sudden change of tack and was reluctantly impressed. 'Well, I'd not call it a fire as such,' she said.

'No?'

'Just some papers and garden waste being burned. One of my grandmother's tenants. He's rather elderly…' She let her voice trail suggestively.

There was a tap on the door and a white-hooded head appeared. 'Sarge?'

'Yes, Trev?'

'Definitely human. Adult male, by the looks of things. Been there a good while, I'd say.'

'Any idea how long?' The Somerset burr was suddenly muted and the question snapped out sharply.

'Hard to say until we get him out. But I'd say at least fifty years. From what I've seen so far he's almost completely skeletonised.'

'Ah yes.' The sergeant nodded energetically. 'Any obvious injuries?'

'Bloody great crack on the head. Can't be sure without getting it under the microscope, but no obvious sign of healing, so it's a good bet that's COD.'

'Well now.' Hughes leaned back, folding her arms across her bosom. The accent dialled up again. 'Bit of a turn-up, isn't it? A body like that in your greenhouse? Any thoughts?'

'The place hasn't been used for decades,' Caroline said. 'Certainly not since I was a child.' She turned to the man in white. 'Could it be anything to do with the churchyard?'

Trevor shook his head. 'Unlikely. It's a whole skeleton, and it's in a funny position. If it was a grave he'd be straight. And rabbits only move the odd bone or two.'

'Rabbits eat bodies?' Caroline couldn't keep the horrified tone out of her voice.

'Nah. They disturb them, though. Now, badgers on the other hand, they'll tuck right in. I found a whole foot in a sett once, up to then we'd thought we were looking at an amputee but no, there it was, all chewed—'

'All right, Trev,' Hughes said reproachfully. 'Well, get him out and we'll see what else we can find.'

'Sarge.' With a final longing look at the biscuits the man disappeared.

'Anyone else who might be able to give us a clue?'

Caroline, her mind still on badgers, said, 'There are two tenants, in the flats upstairs—' she hesitated, wondering how to describe the third resident, before settling on – 'and a guest. But they're away at the moment.'

Unwillingly, reluctantly and mistrustfully, but away.

It took the police another hour to bring Sidney Parker back into the light, his bones carefully wrapped and put in a box. Caroline was surprised at how small it was, how light, a cube of blue plastic that looked too modern and ordinary for its cargo. One of the forensics team, a woman, carried it slowly to the van, the others standing at a respectful distance, and Caroline found herself bowing her head as it passed.

'What happens now?' she asked, as the van doors were being closed.

DS Hughes put her notebook into a pocket. 'Well, we get the medical people to take a look. Decide how old it all is, whether it's likely to have been foul play. When we know that, we know whether we'll need an investigation or not, although given the head wound it's probably worth looking into. We'll check the missing persons database, get DNA if we can. Which reminds me—' The accent was sharpening again – 'seeing as you found him we'll need a sample from you. So we can tell you apart. Elimination, they call it, don't they? You don't mind?' It wasn't a question.

Caroline could only nod. Hughes grinned, and beckoned to Trevor, who was already pulling on fresh gloves. 'And then if our man – assuming Trev's right—'

'I'm right. Just open wide please—'

'If our man turns out to be really old, we'll give him to the archaeologists to play with.'

It was a moment before Caroline could speak, and even then she had to swallow hard to get rid of the taste of cotton wool. 'Well,' she finally managed. 'Thank you. It all seems very straightforward.'

Hughes shrugged. 'Made a nice change,' she said. 'Still a ton of paperwork, mind you. But we'll find out what happened to him, don't you worry.'

Trevor was dropping the swab into the tube, sealing them both away. 'Any idea of how long it'll be before there's any news?' Caroline asked him, but Hughes spoke first.

'Depends on the lab. How busy they are, whether we get anything more urgent.' She beamed. 'Not to worry. If he's been there this long he'll not mind waiting a few more months.'

Probably not, thought Caroline as she watched the van pull out of the drive. *But oh God, I will.*

57

It was nearly ten by the time she arrived at Shenstone Hall. Caroline was surprised to be greeted by Eddie Shenstone. She liked Ruth's brother, but at eighteen years older than the two of them he had always seemed impossibly adult, a kindly but distant figure who would pull your hair one minute and give you ten pence for sweets the next. Connie had, Caroline knew, suffered many losses after his birth, waiting years before Ruth had come along, yet they had both somehow avoided being spoiled and smothered, something much to the family's credit, and were instead level-headed and kind. You could easily mistake Eddie for a genial insurance broker or bank manager, rather than the owner of several hundred acres and a house with twenty bedrooms.

'Come in, come in,' he said, giving her a pat on the shoulder. She almost expected him to offer her a biscuit for being a good girl. 'Ruth's just settling your waifs and strays upstairs. Rum bunch, aren't they? That doctor woman told me to lay off the port, can you believe it?'

'She says that sort of thing to everyone.' The remark about her blood pressure still stung.

'Really? She's a game old bird, I'll give her that. Come into the Blue Room, Ruth's sorted out some supper, you must be ravenous.'

'How are Polly and the boys?'

'Fine and dandy. She's up in town for some show or other. She'll be sorry to have missed you. Tom's out with his girlfriend and Adam's just started his third year at Durham. Time flies, eh?'

'It certainly does.' Caroline sank gratefully onto a sofa and accepted a glass of wine.

'Starting without me?'

Ruth came in, looking tired. Eddie picked up a sandwich.

'Well, I'll leave you to it. Need to check on the puppies before I turn in. Oh, and I've arranged for Fingal to go over to Monica's tomorrow, their bitch is coming into season, so fingers crossed we'll get another litter as well. Don't forget to put the fireguard up, sis, okay?'

'Have I ever?'

'There's always a first time.'

With a grin he bade them goodnight and went out. Ruth picked up a plate and brought it over to sit beside her friend.

'You okay?' she said.

'I think so. You?'

'I think so.'

Caroline felt as though she'd never finish apologising. 'I'm so sorry,' she said, 'I never meant for—'

'Of course you didn't. Don't be silly. It's not your fault.' Ruth pulled a sandwich apart and picked out the tomato. 'It was bloody scary at the time, but now – it feels like some kind of dream. Or a bad film.' She smiled faintly. 'That Danny's not bad, really. Kept saying sorry all the time he was helping to load up the car. Said he'll come and sort out the summerhouse roof to make up for it all.'

'Make sure he gives you mate's rates.'

'Damn right.' Ruth abandoned the sandwich and moved on to a fancy little cake. 'And how was your Mr Sayers?'

'He's been… good.'

And he had. They'd stood together on the drive, watching the bones being carried away down the hill, before going back in and standing, suddenly rootless and uncertain, in the flat.

'God,' she said. 'It's only six thirty. I thought—'

'Feels like we've been here for a hundred years, doesn't it?' Rob said.

She tried to remember how to smile but something was wrong with her face and her mouth wouldn't stop trembling. 'Oh God,' she said, 'Rob—'

'Shh.' He gathered her in a hug, his jumper warm and soft against her cheek. 'It's okay. You've had one hell of an afternoon.'

'So have you. I ask you to do me a favour and the next minute there's a gun and a skeleton and Christ knows what else.'

'I've had duller Sundays,' he said.

She managed a laugh, but that made snot bubble in her nose and she broke away in search of kitchen roll. 'Everything's gone completely batshit,' she said. 'I thought I was just trying to sell the house, that it'd be easy and I'd get it all done and I could start up on my own and now – oh God.'

'You're in shock. Tea. Lots of sugar.'

She couldn't stand still. She followed him to the kitchen and stood playing fretfully with a spoon while he filled the kettle.

'Do you think I did the right thing?' she asked abruptly. 'Getting them out of here? Not saying anything to the police?'

He paused, teabag in hand. He nodded.

'Yes,' he said simply. 'And by the sound of it, it's what your gran would have wanted you to do. Pick up where she left off, so to speak.'

Caroline looked up. Tears were threatening again and she blinked, hard. 'It's weird. It's like I can suddenly see her properly. All my life she was this stern, determined figure. I can remember thinking she cared more about the women who came here than she did about my mum or me. And now she turns out to have done this incredible thing, taking on a child so it stayed safe.'

Rob handed her a mug; the tea was toothache sweet. 'Are you going to tell your mum?'

Caroline nodded. 'I'll call her later, when the gallery's closed. I'll get her to come over; I want to tell her face to face. God knows what I'm going to say.' She put her mug down and went across to him, picking up the hug where she had left off. 'I really am sorry,' she said, her voice muffled against his chest.

'Shh. Don't be. No harm done.'

'Thank God. When I saw that gun—'

'Yeah. I know.'

They were silent for a moment. Then Caroline lifted her head. 'D'you want to come with me? Down to Ruth's?'

He shook his head. 'I would,' he said. 'Honestly I would. But I've got classes tomorrow. And it's – well. You know. Family time.'

'Okay. If you're sure. Can I call you?'

'You'd better.' He grinned. 'I want to know what you've got lined up next. We've had fire, guns, skeletons—'

'I'll make dinner.'

'No mad axe man in the cellar? You're letting me down.'

'You've not tasted my cooking.'

He laughed, and she thought how grateful she was that he was here. 'Thank you,' she said. 'I really am grateful, you know. For everything. I know I'm asking a lot—'

'Give over. I'm having the time of my life.' He looked down at her. 'Honestly. All the old sad stuff aside, I've had more fun this last week than I have for ages. And for what it's worth, I'm glad I came. Lizzie's story – well. I'm glad I can be a part of helping.' He dropped a kiss on her hair. 'So go on. Do what you need to do. Then come back and we'll see what happens. Maybe have some more fun. Okay?'

'Okay,' she said, and for the first time since she'd gone out into that bitter garden, she finally felt warm.

58

Caroline woke early, her head heavy and muzzy from a broken and restless night.

She lay in the pretty blue and silver bedroom she'd always used when she came to the Hall. There were the familiar smells of coffee and old books and woodsmoke, the sounds of radiators creaking, doors opening and closing, Eddie calling for one of the dogs. Outside in the woods she could hear the rasp of a pheasant. Calm, reassuring, timeless things that felt out of place on this day, when she had to tell her mother what had happened and what she had learned, and when Betty's life would change forever.

She went down to find the tenants were already at the breakfast table, sitting in an awkward silence while the housekeeper fussed around with toast and teapots. Caroline tried to make conversation, but every attempt wilted as soon as the words were uttered; it was as if everyone were exhausted, too battered, to chat about the weather or the Jacobean panelling or the coffee. The atmosphere only lightened for a moment when Ruth came in, followed by Flora, trotting in with her puppies, even Audrey Fairfax giving a small smile as Barnaby advanced across the rug towards them with a hesitant wag of his stubby little tail.

'Is there somewhere I can take him for his walk?' she asked.

Ruth managed not to glance out of the window at the enormous grounds. 'Of course,' she said. 'If you like, you can take him along the terrace and down to the lake. Let him have a run. It's nice and flat,' she added reassuringly. 'Lovely views. You might be able to see Salisbury Cathedral if it's clear.'

'Thank you.' The doctor nodded. 'We'll all go. Breath of fresh air will do us good.' She glanced pointedly at Caroline. 'Take our minds off things, perhaps. The police, and so on.'

Caroline felt the sting of that, and knew she'd not be welcome to go with them. She'd told them what Maria Hughes had said, the guess about the age of the bones, the threat of DNA and investigations and databases, and it had felt that with each word she was striking them with a whip. She knew that they still didn't understand her reasons for calling the police; she'd tried to explain, that it was the best thing in the long run, that if she hadn't and the bones had been discovered some other way there would have been even more problems, but she could see they didn't believe her. And she tried to convince herself, too, that it had to be done, that it was right, necessary, exactly the choice that Frances would have made, but even in her own mind there was a treacherous little voice saying, *look what you've done... you've put them right in the danger they've avoided all these years...*

'Good idea,' Ruth was saying. 'Just go straight down the passage and through the door at the end – Mrs Grady will be around if you get lost.'

They gathered up cardigans and walking sticks, Barnaby yapping as his owner dragooned them out of the room. Caroline poured her third cup of coffee.

'What time's your mum's flight?' Ruth asked once they were alone.

'She gets in at four. Oh, Ruth, it's so good of you to let us come here – especially after all that crap yesterday.'

'Don't be daft. You know you're welcome any time. I seem to remember telling you that only recently.'

'That was before I brought those three.' The old people had appeared on the terrace, Barnaby bobbing excitedly ahead. Caroline watched as they stopped to look at a bed of chrysanthemums that blazed yellow and gold against the sky like a sunset. *Let them enjoy this moment,* she thought, *while they can.* 'I just think I should try to shield them as much as I can. Just in case.'

'You did the right thing,' Ruth said gently.

'Did I?' She took a bite from a piece of toast, then put it down again. Flora materialised hopefully at her side.

'I think so,' Ruth said. 'And Mum was right, really, wasn't she? Lizzie Sixpence did die. In a way.'

'And my grandmother really did kill someone. Even though we'd thought it was Frances killing Lizzie, not Lizzie doing away with—' Caroline broke off, not wanting to say the name.

'Yes.' Ruth looked sober for a moment. 'Can't say I blame her though, do you? Self-defence. Anyone would say so. Even a jury, if it comes to it.'

'It's what I'd argue, certainly. Sixteen, post-partum, abused and trafficked. It'd be a good case. There's not a judge in the land would convict of mur—' She bit the word back, already hearing the prosecution's response: *A known criminal with a lengthy history of offending; a cheap prostitute, who ran away with stolen money; really, ladies and gentlemen of the jury, what else might she have done in the meantime? And is age really an excuse to let a killing go? Can we ever exonerate a cold-blooded offence like this?*

Ruth rubbed Flora's ears thoughtfully. 'I mean, you're the lawyer. Surely they wouldn't prosecute someone who was really old?'

'I don't know. There's no statute of limitations. Besides, we've only got their word for it that there's no ID on the body. What if they find out who he was? There might be arrest records.' She thought of the papers Rob had shown her. 'In fact I know there are. That'd lead them straight to Lizzie. Assuming she was ever nicked. And assuming that they can find her, she could be anywhere.'

'Don't tell me they'd go after the others, if they're still alive? Not that poor Jamaican lady, what was her name, Grace, even if she was there?' Ruth sounded appalled. 'That'd be awful. They'll all be nearly a hundred.'

'They try Nazis in their nineties.'

'Yes, but this is hardly the same.'

'Tell that to the CPS.'

Ruth nodded. 'I suppose so. But if they found her, they found Lizzie, and they did decide she'd done it, would it be, what do you call it, in the public interest to investigate?'

'The police can't just put their fingers in their ears and go la, la, la, we can't hear you,' Caroline said. 'Not when there's an actual skeleton to deal with.'

'It still doesn't prove he was killed. Maybe they'll think he had an accident or something.'

'If they'd found him in the woods or under a hedge then I'd go for that. But in a greenhouse? It's obvious someone put him there, isn't it? Oh for crying out loud—' Caroline picked up a crust and gave it to the dog, whose imploring gaze had been fixed on her plate. 'I wish *I* could make people do things just by staring at them,' she said.

'It was all so long ago,' Ruth said gently. 'They might not find anything at all.'

'I know. But it's the not knowing that's so bloody awful.'

Ruth finished her coffee. 'Well, if you're going to be like a cat on hot bricks all morning you can help me sort out the pantry,' she said briskly. 'Or hoover the orangery and count the cutlery. Or iron twenty-four tablecloths. Up to you.'

'I'm all yours.'

But Caroline knew that she'd rather rearrange tins for the next five years than face what was coming.

After the quiet of the Hall, after the familiarity of Wickham Grange, the arrivals lounge was like a slap. Caroline flinched at the noise, the brightness, the crowds of fractious, sticky people with their bulging suitcases and grizzling children, the staff in their cheap nylon uniforms. She sat on a bench, staring at the rank of screens, almost tempted to buy a ticket and escape to anywhere where she didn't have to do this.

The doors swung open. The first passengers began to stream through. From somewhere on her left a little boy shrieked 'Daddy!'

Caroline stood up, went to the barrier. She could already see her mother, striding easily along with just a leather holdall and a handbag, her face fresh and bright, her hair caught back in a multi-coloured scarf. Long earrings swung lazily as she moved. When she pulled Caroline into a hug she smelled of cigarettes and expensive aftershave.

'Darling,' she said. 'How are you? What's wrong? You were so mysterious on the phone.' She tilted her head, looking closer. 'Are you all right? Sweetie, I don't want to sound unkind but you look terrible. Do you use that moisturiser I sent you? Maybe you need the menopause one—'

'Hi, Mum.' Caroline mustered a smile. 'I'm okay. It's just been a tough couple of days.'

'Did you say you're staying at Ruth's place?'

'Yes.'

'Has something happened? Why aren't you at the Grange?' Betty frowned in concern. 'I'm worried about you,' she announced.

Caroline swallowed. Suddenly, more than ever, she wanted this maddening, infuriating woman to be here. 'Mum, I'm glad you came. It's important.' She caught herself thinking, *Please, please don't say you can't stay long, please don't say anything about the gallery.*

'Well, so you said, darling. But you're all right? That's what matters.'

'Oh, Mum.' Why did Betty suddenly seem so intensely loveable? 'Something's happened, that's all.'

'Has anyone hurt you?'

'No. No, Mum, I'm all right,' Caroline took a deep breath, 'but there's stuff I need to tell you. Important stuff.'

'Are you pregnant?'

'Mum! No.'

'Thank God for that. I'm not ready to be a grandma.' Betty hoisted the holdall. 'Well, Caro, you're making it all sound very sinister. But you're a clever girl, I trust you. All right, lead the way.'

'Thanks, Mum.' A clever girl. Had Betty ever said anything like that before? Caroline couldn't remember. Or had she just chosen not to hear it? She said in a rush, 'It's so good to see you.'

'Well, between you and me, sweetie, I was glad of the excuse. Mateo's being a bit annoying. Terribly attentive, wants cuddles all the time, it's like having a hamster. I could do with a break, to tell you the truth.'

Tell you the truth? That's just what I'll be doing, Caroline thought as they emerged into the car park.

I only hope you can bear to hear it.

59

They'd been having tea in the library. There had been tea in a big silver pot, cakes on a stand, little fancy meringues nestling like cygnets on a glass tray, a fire burning and leather-bound books; a scene of tradition and comfort, but Caroline knew it could only explode when she finally spoke.

'This is really lovely, darling.' Betty was eating an éclair with gusto. 'And how lovely to see you all again.' She swept the old people with a smile, the blob of cream on her lips only adding to her charm. 'Honestly, I feel like a girl again. I think Dr Fairfax must have given me my first jabs, didn't you? And do you remember teaching me to ride a bike?'

Mr Harris nodded. 'You was a natural,' he said gruffly.

'And Mrs – oh what was her name, used to come in to help with the cleaning.'

'Lloyd.'

'That's her. Used to moan about how you couldn't get proper furniture polish any more. Didn't she set up some kind of business? Very bold for the fifties.'

'Mum.' Caroline leaned forward. 'Mum, we really need to talk to you.'

'We *are* talking.' Betty beamed. 'Though I don't remember you, Miss Tanner. Did you come to the house later?'

'I came and went, dear.' The old lady gave a small smile.

Betty frowned. 'Have we met?' she said. 'I don't usually forget a face.'

'Not for a long time, love.'

'I'm sorry.' Betty held out a hand. The old lady took it in both of hers. 'I'm Betty Alleyn. Do you know what all this mystery is about? I'm getting quite excited.'

'Mum.' Caroline came and sat beside her mother. 'Mum, I've got some stuff to tell you. You know when Gran died? Well, I got a letter from her. Telling me I couldn't sell the house without – well, that's not important just now.' She swallowed. 'Mum, she said she'd lost someone called Lizzie Sixpence.'

'Oh yes!' Betty took a cream horn. 'I remember you asking me about it. Did you have any luck?'

'You could say that. I'll tell you the rest of it later, but, Mum, I don't know how to say this, I did find out about her, and she's well, she's – she's your mother.'

'She's my what?'

The pastry fell to the floor. Barnaby scrambled up and snatched it before Audrey could grab him.

'Lizzie. Lizzie was your mum. She'd had an awful life, there was a gang, she was being controlled all through the war by some vile men, and she ran away so Frances could help her when she had her baby. When she had you. You were born at the Grange and then Lizzie – well, she had to leave.'

'Had to leave? What do you mean, had to leave?'

Caroline swallowed. 'Oh, Mum, I'm so sorry. There was a man called Sid, one of the gang, and he was her – he controlled her, and he came looking for her, so she ran away and—'

Betty had said, loud and disbelieving: 'This is mad—'

And then there had been more words, that became shouting, and a door had slammed, and Caroline had followed her mother out into the shadows of the autumn night.

It took her eyes a moment to adjust to the growing darkness. Then she saw Betty, striding along the side of the house and through a gate. Caroline, wishing she'd brought a coat, went after her, her heart thumping in dread at this conversation, what it would mean and what it would change. The gate creaked as she pushed it open and went down the path to where her mother was sitting on a bench, her body stiff and her face set.

Betty didn't look up as her daughter approached, just lit a cigarette and blew out a stream of smoke.

'Fuck,' she said.

Caroline sat beside her on a wooden bench that was damp and cold. Moss glowed like green damask on the armrests. Around them, the kitchen garden was nestling down for the winter. Stems and stalks had been clipped back and tied with twine, so they poked up starkly from amongst the blanket of leaves that covered the soil, and a forest of bamboo canes had been stacked neatly in a corner. Around the garden's edge, a wall that had been built before Waterloo stood tall and reassuring in the twilight, shutting out the house and grounds. From the espaliered pear tree a robin was watching them with pert, interested little eyes.

'Are you okay?' she said hesitantly.

'What do you think, darling? I've just heard that my mother – my mother…' She took another long drag. 'Fuck,' she said again.

'I'm sorry,' Caroline said. 'Oh, for God's sake. Why do I keep saying that?'

'Not much else you can say.' Betty was staring straight ahead, her eyes fixed on the gates. A thin mist was coming down, blurring the hedges. 'And this all came out because Frances left you a letter?'

'It was with her will. The solicitor sent it to me.'

'Why didn't she tell me? Why you?'

Caroline had thought about that. 'I think,' she said carefully, 'she wanted to protect you. In case I found out what had happened. Better I dug it up than you.'

'You did, though.' Betty flicked a quick glance at her daughter. 'But then she knew you would. You always do. You're like a bloody terrier. Never let go.'

Caroline shrugged. 'I didn't think it would – it would mean all this.'

'No, sweetie.' Betty sighed. 'Who would?' She looked back down the garden. Something was moving, coming slowly down the path. 'This Sid person,' she said abruptly. 'Was he my father?'

'I don't think so.' Caroline had hoped to gloss over this part of the story, unless the DNA results brought further horror. She decided that that particular nightmare could wait. 'He was the — the pimp.'

'What a bastard.' Betty tapped ash onto the grass. 'Do you remember that day I was leaving for Spain and Frances asked what the Grange had done to us? Maybe she meant all this.'

'Maybe. Or maybe she meant that we'd both grown up in that house, that all the sadness had rubbed off on us. Being with those women. Hearing all their stories.'

'God, I used to hate that.' Betty stubbed out her cigarette. 'I used to think I'd be trapped there.'

'Trapped there with me?'

Betty looked at her properly this time. 'Seems to be a day for revelations,' she said drily. 'So honestly? Yes. I'd been living it up, glad to be out of there, and then I was stupid enough to get knocked up. I was eighteen, I had a whole life suddenly in limbo, when I had things I wanted to do. And I had to stay there, in that bloody house.'

'At least you had somewhere to go,' Caroline said. 'You were safe there. Not like Lizzie.'

'Safe? I suppose so. Though it explains why Frances told me I had to be careful about who I talked to, why I was kept under wraps.'

'Did she ever tell you about Clapton?'

'No. Though I suppose it's why she eventually told me about my mother. She must have thought I was old enough to know.' She twisted her lips, and Caroline couldn't be sure if she were trying to smile or trying not to weep. 'You know Frances,' she said, 'never one to shy away from the truth, even if it was bloody awful.'

'Too much for a child,' Caroline said. 'It must have been so hard. I wish I'd known…'

'Why? Do you think things would have been different? We'd have been some lovey-dovey family?'

That brought tears to Caroline's eyes. 'No,' she said at last. 'No, we'd never have been that.'

Betty tilted her head back, staring up at the sky. 'At least I went ahead and had you,' she said.

'Did you seriously think about—'

'No. And that's the truth. I could have done it, there were people who could arrange it back then, but no.'

'Why?'

'Because I didn't want to be like your bloody father. And I didn't want to be like her, just running off because I couldn't be bothered.' Betty looked back towards the gates, where the figure was clearer now, coming slowly down the path. 'It was bad enough being let down once, let alone twice. I wasn't going to do the same to you.'

'But you did. You were gone for weeks at a time. And I wanted you.' Caroline pulled up a bit of dry grass, started twisting it around her finger. 'I used to have to ask Maud to do my hair for school.'

'I came back.'

'But you weren't there.' Caroline's throat was tight. 'Not when I needed you. The other kids asked where my mummy and daddy were and half the time I didn't know.' She swallowed. 'I don't even know his name.'

'You never said.' Betty paused. 'You never asked about him.'

'I did, once or twice. But you never answered me, so I gave up. That time we went for ice cream, remember? And when you were leaving to go to Spain.'

'You said you wanted to stay behind.'

'It was too late. I'd decided that I wasn't going to be like you, always dashing around, never settling. I wanted to be secure. And you should have known, you should have stayed.'

Betty made a harsh sound that could have been a laugh or a sob. 'Christ. Abandoning our kids must run in the family. Is that why you never bothered? Probably just as well. Shit mothers are us.'

'Oh, don't say that, love.'

They both started. The old woman wore a white coat; with her white hair and pale face, it was as if she had been formed out of the mist.

'May I?'

She sat down beside them, her hands in her lap. The robin gave an uncertain little trill.

'You should have stayed in the warm,' Caroline said. 'Look, let's go back inside—'

'In a minute.' Betty turned to the old lady sitting beside her. 'Were you there?' she said. 'Were you one of the women at that bloody house? Did you know about this?'

'Oh, yes, love, I knew.' Miss Tanner sighed. 'And so did the doctor. And Mickey, Mr Harris, I mean. We knew.'

The garden was utterly still, as if the very earth was listening.

'That's the bit I don't get,' Betty said. 'I could have only been a few weeks old. And I was just left behind. Abandoned. How could that happen? Did this Lizzie woman say anything to you?'

The old lady winced at the raw anger in her voice. 'It was dangerous,' she said at last. 'You can't understand what it was like in those days. Men like Kenny Clapton were cock of the heap and the police were bugger all use, most of them taking backhanders right, left and centre. If Kenny'd known who you were, he'd have seen you as a way of getting his money back, not as a baby. You'd have been taken and sold off and God knows where you'd have ended up. So Frances took you, and kept you. Hid you.'

'Kept me stuck there, spending my whole bloody life wondering who my mother was and where she'd gone.' Betty lit another cigarette, drawing on it so hard that the tip glowed an angry red. 'Christ.'

'Safer for you not to know. And you were better off there than where you could have been. What if it hadn't been some couple from Enfield? What if you were sold and sold and sold, like Clapton's other girls? Did you think about that?' Miss Tanner leaned forward and put a tentative hand on Betty's arm. 'Did you never stop and think that leaving you at that house was giving you a better life than you'd have had otherwise?'

'Oh, much better,' Betty said bitterly.

'Mum,' Caroline said, but the other women ignored her.

'And you did all right, didn't you?' Miss Tanner said. 'Being there, at that house, it meant you got the chance to do your own thing, go your own way. As did you.' Caroline was startled when that serious face turned to her. 'I don't suppose that's been easy. So maybe something else runs in the family. Guts, passed down the female line.'

'Right. So if this Lizzie's so bloody brave, why did she never come back?'

'Oh, she wanted to. But it wasn't safe. Not for her, not for you.' The old lady brushed at something on her cheek. 'And then when it was, it was too late.'

Betty stood up. 'It's been sixty, seventy years, for God's sake. Those gangsters – or whatever you call them – must be long gone. But she stayed away.'

'Everyone thought she was dead. Then things changed, you were settled…' The frail voice faltered. 'Mickey got married – it was better to stay away.'

'Right. So where's Lizzie fucking Sixpence now?'

A yellow moon was easing itself into the sky. From the other side of the wall a fox shrieked. The old lady reached out a hand, caught Betty's sleeve. Her voice was very quiet but it cut across the air like a knife.

'What's another name for a shilling?'

Betty tried to shake her off, but the other woman held on, her knotted fingers suddenly very strong. 'Go on,' she said. 'What's the other name for a shilling?'

Caroline said helplessly, 'I don't know. I was five when they changed the—'

'A bob,' Betty said. She was not looking at them, her eyes instead fixed on the moon.

'And what'd you call a pound?'

'A quid.' Caroline was looking from one to the other. She had a dizzying sense of things shifting, changing, that this swirling moment would—

'And a sixpence?'

'Oh God. Oh my God.' Caroline felt her heart jerk. 'A tanner,' she whispered. 'A sixpence was a tanner.' It was as if the three of them were the only people in the world. 'You were there all the time, up in the spare flat. You're – you're—'

'That's right,' said Lizzie Sixpence.

60

'I ALWAYS LIKED THIS ONE.'

Lizzie Sixpence – Lizzie Tanner – picked up the picture and stroked it with a finger. It was a black-and-white snapshot, only a couple of inches square, showing Betty on some long ago Christmas morning, agog at the sight of the tree. Maud was in the picture, too, beaming as she held out a present.

'That was a set of colouring pencils,' Betty said. She was standing stiffly beside her mother, clearly making an effort, but her rage had gone, replaced with a kind of wary acceptance. 'And a sketch pad. I was so excited, I spent the whole day drawing and by the time dinner was ready I'd used up all the paper.'

They were back in the breakfast room, rain pattering against the windows and the trees that lined the terrace shifting sulkily in a fitful wind. It felt as if the night before had been a century ago, an evening full of long silences and hesitant questions, matched with reluctant answers; how Lizzie had moved around the country for years, never daring to settle down, only coming back when Mickey told her that Frances had died and that the house might be sold.

'Didn't know what else to do,' he'd said to Caroline.

Then Caroline had brought out Frances' letter, had told them of how she had made the calls to Maggie, Jane, Harriet and Vera, the visit to Grace. She did not mention their distress or their anger. There had been enough of that.

Lizzie wept all the same. 'They were all so good to me,' she said, 'they were like mothers.'

She had brought down a great pile of photographs and papers, and spread them all out in a fan amongst the coffee cups and toast racks.

'Mickey always kept them for me,' she said, laying another photo on the table. 'Sent them to me whenever he could. I've got ever so many. Take them everywhere.' She smiled tentatively at Betty. 'You've always been so pretty.'

'Got some more back at home,' the old man said. 'Never got a chance to send them.'

'Including my graduation photo?' Caroline said drily.

'Found 'em when I locked up your gran's flat,' he said, shrugging. 'She'd not have minded.'

No, thought Caroline, *I don't suppose she would*. She picked up a photograph of Betty standing proudly by a snowman outside Wickham Grange, Maud Shenstone helping her drape a scarf around its neck. In the background, caught unawares, Mr Harris brandished a shovel full of snow.

She took it across to where Connie sat in her wheelchair.

'Aunty Connie? Have you seen this one?'

Connie took the picture, staring at it for a long moment. 'Snow. Come on, start, you bugger,' she said. Then a smile broke across her face, her eyes suddenly warm. 'Candles,' she said. 'Baby. Lovely baby. Was it my baby?'

'Your babies are Eddie and Ruth,' Caroline said. She touched the picture, then pointed across the room to where Betty was bending over a photograph, Mickey and Lizzie either side of her. Lizzie was looking at her daughter and not the picture. 'That little girl's my mum,' Caroline said. 'Betty.'

'Betty. Iris.'

'That's right.'

'Frances' baby.'

'In a way.' Caroline took her hand. 'Frances was very brave. You were all very brave.'

'Made us happy,' Connie said. 'Babies. Iris and Eddie and

Ruth and Caroline. All the children.' She smiled, a smile of pure happiness. 'Safe as houses.'

'Yes,' Caroline said. 'We were safe.' And so was everyone who had been sheltered and protected by Frances and Maud and that big, sturdy house.

At the table Betty had picked up a piece of paper. 'This is one of mine!' she said, surprise taking some of the caution from her voice. 'God, this must have been done when I was eighteen or so.' She looked closely at it, a charcoal sketch of a woman with white hair flowing across her shoulders. 'Is that you?' she said. 'I knew I'd seen you before.'

'Mickey told me you were at art college,' Lizzie said. 'And I saw they were looking for models and I thought, I wonder, I might see you, so I came along and there you were.' She took out a handkerchief and wiped her eyes. 'I was so proud of you,' she said. 'And I thought I'd take a chance and ask if I could have it.'

'I remember.' Betty put the picture down. 'I'm glad you liked it,' she said, her voice uncertain.

'Maybe you can show me a few more pictures one day,' Lizzie said tentatively.

Betty looked down at the sketch. She swallowed. 'Maybe,' she said.

Lizzie picked up something else; a fat scrapbook with a tasselled marker. 'And I got you this.' She passed it to Betty, who took it gingerly. 'I used to dream I'd be able to give it to you,' she said, her voice breaking.

'Come on, girl.' Mickey put his arm around her, giving her a kindly little jostle. 'It's worked out in the end. You're here, and your girl's here, and that's something we thought we'd never see, ain't it?'

Lizzie nodded, and Ruth produced an enormous handkerchief so she could wipe her eyes. Caroline, over by the fire, couldn't bear it any longer and took refuge in practicality.

'We'd better start getting packed up,' she said, her voice louder than she'd meant it to be. 'It's a long drive and I want to be back before dark.' She got up, heading for the door. 'Mum, are you coming with us? It'll be easier for the airport.'

Lizzie looked imploringly at Betty. 'I'd like that,' she said, 'ever such a lot.'

Betty took her time, but at last she nodded. 'All right. I have to be back by Friday but I can do another couple of days.'

Relief flooded Lizzie's face, but Caroline, heading up the stairs, wasn't so sure that the two of them at the Grange, with all its memories, would be the best idea. But there wasn't really any other option, despite Ruth's assurances that they could stay as long as they liked. Sid was gone, taken away in his blue plastic coffin, his malevolent presence cast out. But at the Grange they could be found, at the Grange they could be confronted and challenged.

And at some point soon she'd have to go back to work, back to Charles and the rest of her colleagues, back to Oxford. It was not an easy thought. The idea of leaving the old people alone and unprotected worried her more than she wanted to admit.

She opened her holdall, putting away the few things she'd brought, retrieving her toothbrush from the bathroom and her shoes from under the bed. She took her time, folding more neatly than she would normally bother to do, making the bed, even though she knew perfectly well that the housekeeper would be stripping it as soon as she was gone. Mundane, dull tasks that failed to distract her from the heavy block of unease in her stomach, the prickle of worry that poked at her mind.

But time was implacable, as always, and now it was time to leave, to go back to the Grange, and deal with what could come next. She picked up the bag and took one last look around before going downstairs. It felt like she was checking that nothing except her old life had been left behind; but the room was empty and she had no reason to stay, so she went out and closed the door behind her.

61

'I CAN'T FIND MY LIZZIE,' SAID MICKEY Harris.

They were back at Wickham Grange. Everyone was exhausted, even Betty's ebullience dimmed and subdued, as if the enormity of the past days had drained the fizz out of her. In the car she had sat in the front with Caroline, staring out of the window as the car trudged up the grey, flat motorway, and even when they stopped for a coffee she didn't speak, just went into the ladies' with the others and took longer than she needed to at the sink. When they'd finally turned in through the gates of Wickham Grange, Caroline felt relief wrap itself around her like a hug, and wondered whether it was for the end of the journey or because she was back in the sanctuary of the big house on the hill.

The old people had not lingered, and after some painfully polite conversation had carefully climbed up the stairs and into their flats. Betty had gone out for a cigarette, saying she needed to call Mateo; as soon as she was gone Caroline had taken out her own phone and dialled Rob's number, leaning gratefully into his reassuring voice.

'Yes,' she said. 'Oh God, yes, dinner would be wonderful. Saturday? And I'd love to meet her. Thank you. I mean it. For everything.'

'You're the cat that's got the cream,' Betty said as she came back in. 'What's his name?'

'Why do you assume it's a man?'

'Because it usually is, darling. I hope he's nicer than that Dan or whatever his name was. I really didn't like him.'

'You never said.'

'Would you have listened?' And Caroline had to concede that no, she wouldn't have done, and that admission was something new in itself. So she'd told Betty about Rob and they'd opened a bottle of wine and lit the fire and ordered a curry and now, the next morning, she felt as if something old and raw had started to heal.

Now, though, they both snapped their heads around to look at the old man. He stood in the doorway, his tie peeping out over his pullover, his mouth working in distress. Caroline took his arm, led him to the sofa.

'I can't find her,' he said again. 'I went and knocked at number four to see if she wanted a cuppa and there was no answer, so I thought she'd gone over to the doctor's but she said—'

'No sign of her upstairs.' Audrey Fairfax – who in extremis was still the doctor to Mickey – came in. 'That ridiculous girl.'

'Where might she have gone?' Betty asked.

'No idea,' Dr Fairfax said. 'She can't drive, and she wouldn't know the bus routes. Honestly, not coming out when the place was on fire was bad enough – you should have listened when she told you to get a shredder.'

'All right.' Betty was surprisingly practical. 'You two stay here. I'll check the garden in case she's just gone out for some air or something. Caro, you look down the road.' She patted Mickey on the shoulder and for a moment sounded just like Maud. 'Chin up,' she said, and went to get her shoes.

Caroline's trainers were where she'd kicked them off at the door. The morning was still, overcast, and she remembered that rain was forecast so took a jacket before heading out of the house. She stood at the gates for a moment, deciding whether to go up or down the lane, then reasoned that an old woman would not realistically choose the climb, however gentle it might appear to anyone younger. So she turned right, going down the path and around the curve of the road, hurrying, her eyes flickering into the fields and hedges, fearful that she'd see a body lying collapsed on the grass, but there was nothing, just trees and bushes and – there.

Five, six hundred yards ahead, an old woman, heading for the main road, where the buses ran. If she got on one she could end up anywhere; so Caroline broke into a run, her feet and knees protesting as she forced them into the unfamiliar movement. The white-haired figure kept moving, determined but slow. Caroline gritted her teeth and kept running, ignoring the screams from her lungs.

'Lizzie!' she managed to call. *For God's sake*, she thought, *I don't even smoke.*

The old woman stopped. She was wearing her coat and carrying her handbag and when Caroline caught up with her she squared her shoulders as if for a fight.

'Where the fu— Where are you going?' Caroline leaned on the churchyard wall, panting. The blood yelling in her ears became a steady roar, like a faraway crowd. 'Everyone's looking for you.'

'No need. I'm all right. I know where I'm going.' The old lady started to walk again, with slow and determined steps. 'Don't you worry about me.'

'Well, we do.' Caroline coughed. 'Jesus, I haven't run anywhere since Millennium Night. Can you at least let me get my breath back?'

'I used to run everywhere,' Lizzie said unexpectedly. 'Away from the bombs, away from the wardens – away from June…' Her voice trailed off. 'And I'm not running any more. I've decided, I'm going to go to the police and tell them the truth. Mickey said there's a bus stop down here somewhere, I'll find my way.'

Caroline said, appalled, 'You can't. You can't do that.' She coughed again. 'Oh, for God's sake, let's at least sit down and talk about it. Look, we can go in there, we can sit quietly…'

She gestured to the church porch, but Lizzie shook her head. 'Not in there,' she said vehemently. 'Not in there, not again.'

Caroline was startled at the vehemence in Lizzie's voice, not sure what she'd said to cause such an emphatic refusal. 'Oh. Oh, okay.

How about that bench?' And she was going through the lychgate before Lizzie could say anything, leaving the old lady to trail rebelliously in her wake.

The bench had a little plaque explaining that it was in memory – just plain memory, Caroline noticed, no mention of love – of someone called George Springer. Lizzie lowered herself carefully onto the seat and looked down over the churchyard, which, despite the clouds, was still timeless and beautiful. The greys of the headstones, each at its own angle, were mottled with yellow lichens and the trees were beginning to be blurred by autumn, old leaves curling up and unveiling Wickham Grange; Caroline could just see the roof, a window, one of the chimneys. To their left a blackbird, its eyes ringed with gold, stood warily on the top of a table tomb before springing into the air, its song soaring up after it, and over by the tap a patch of amber was a young fox, watching them with bright and curious eyes.

'It's just so lovely here,' Lizzie said quietly. 'I've always thought so. I liked it when I heard there was a stone for me here.'

Caroline said hesitantly, 'Do you want us to get rid of it? Only—' she tried to think of a gentle way to say it, then realised that if anyone was tough enough it was Lizzie Sixpence – 'it might help. If we need to persuade the police about anything, I mean.'

Lizzie looked at her granddaughter. 'You'd do that? You'd let them think I was long gone?'

'It's an option. If they find out who he was. If they make any connection to you.'

The old lady shook her head. 'It's not just about me, though, is it? Grace, Vera, Jane – what about them?'

'They'll be all right. Nobody knows they were here then. Nobody knows their names.'

'You sure? I know Mickey burned the papers, or at least tried to – and I'm sorry for that night, I really am, it was all just too much, the noise and that house and knowing what you might find…' Her voice wavered for a second, but she rallied, and said quietly, 'But what if they did find out? What if they did go looking, knocking on doors?'

'They won't,' Caroline said. 'And even if they did, I can't see how they'd find anything.'

'It doesn't matter. Like I said,' said Lizzie. 'I'm going to tell them.'

'You've stayed hidden all this time. You can carry on—'

'No, love.' Lizzie raised her hand. 'I know, I know you're trying to protect me and it's lovely, really it is.' She sighed, and suddenly looked very tired. 'But I want this finished. I've got my girl back and that's enough for me. I just want an end to it.'

Caroline said sharply, 'You can't let that bastard Parker win now.'

Lizzie shook her head. 'There's something you don't know,' she said. She looked back at the path, as if to be sure nobody except the fox could hear them, but it was curled up in a patch of sun, asleep like everyone around it.

'Oh Christ, what now?' Caroline couldn't help it, the words burst forward.

Lizzie smiled. 'Been a bit of a bumpy ride, ain't it?' she said. Then her face settled, falling into a pattern of old hurts and lingering pain. Her eyes were focused on the big white cross. 'The forgotten dead,' she said bitterly. 'Only he's not forgotten, is he? Even now.' She took a deep breath. 'I wasn't going to tell you,' she went on. 'I didn't want to hurt my girl any more than I already have. But you said about DNA.'

'Only if they can get it.'

'But if they do…' She reached out a hand and Caroline took it, feeling the thin fingers curl into her own. 'Oh, love, I wish I didn't have to say this. But if they've taken yours then they might find out.'

'Find out what?' But Caroline thought she could already guess.

'Sid…' Lizzie closed her eyes. 'Sometimes, back then… if I went out but didn't get a trick… when I got back he'd… he'd make me…'

There was a long silence. Even the blackbird was quiet, as if out of respect.

'What a complete and utter shit.' Caroline squeezed the old lady's hand. 'I'm sorry.'

'No need for you to feel bad, love.' There was a tear on Lizzie's face and Caroline very gently wiped it away with a fingertip. 'It was only a couple of times, and then there was the major and it was all right after that.'

All right. How could being with a man who wanted to play wedding nights with a fifteen-year-old girl be all right? But Caroline stayed silent, letting Lizzie ride her memories.

'But you see what I'm saying?' the old lady whispered. 'He could be Iris's – he could be your…'

'And if he is and they've got my DNA…' Caroline said.

'They'll know. And you'll know. I'm so sorry, love, I really am.'

'Don't you dare apologise,' Caroline said fiercely. 'But even if he is – I'm not going to even say it – well, it doesn't mean anything. There's still no link to you.'

'But you'll be dragged through it.' Lizzie tried to smile but her mouth twisted the wrong way. 'Mickey said you're ever so good at your job,' she said. 'So what about you? They'll come knocking at your door too. How will that look, you being a lawyer and all?'

'That's my problem.' Caroline allowed herself a small grim smile at the thought of Charles Dudley's face if he ever found out that his pet partner was involved, however obliquely, in a murder investigation. But a small, quietly mean part of her, that was not as small or as quiet as she would like, whispered in her head, *What about starting up on your own? What if everyone knows?* And the voice became Charles', dropping words in all the right ears, knowing they would spread like mould… 'Of course, she's able. Very able. And I don't want to speak ill of anyone. It's just that matter of the family background. Not the most stable, you know. You'll have seen the reports in the papers? Grandfather some wartime crook, murdered by the grandmother? An actual skeleton, though not actually in the closet, ha ha. Not the best look, you have to admit. And genes can be funny things. Just thought I'd mention it. You might want to think about taking your business elsewhere… but of course, you mustn't let me influence you in any way. Here's my card, in case you'd like to discuss further. Now, they do an excellent port here, shall we?'

'I don't want Iris to know.' Caroline felt as though she had been slapped awake. Lizzie was crying, her whole body shaking as sobs rolled through her thin bones. Caroline, helpless, put an arm around the old lady, who still sat upright, looking straight ahead while decades of pain trickled down her face. 'I want her to think her dad might have been a good man, a decent man, not someone like – like him.'

'He might still be,' Caroline said. 'He might—'

'There's a chance, though. A big chance. Isn't there?' Lizzie pulled a handkerchief from her pocket and wiped her eyes. 'And I want to protect my girl from that. I haven't been able to do anything else for her. Let me do this. Let me tell them I killed him, that it's nothing to do with anyone else. Let me protect her.' She gave one last sob. 'Please, Caroline,' she said. 'Please. Help me protect my daughter. Protect your mum.'

Pick up where your gran left off…

'There must be something else we can do,' Caroline said stubbornly. Her phone buzzed in her pocket. She ignored it.

'You're such a clever girl,' Lizzie said wistfully. 'You'd better get that. It might be important.'

'This is important. Promise me you won't—' The phone buzzed again.

'Go on, love. Don't worry about me.'

'Give me a minute – oh. Mum? Yes, I've got her. We're just sitting for a bit. We won't be long. Tell him she's fine. I'll look after her.' She looked at Lizzie. 'We'll head back in a minute. Honestly, it's okay. Bye.' She put the phone away. 'Mickey's having kittens,' she said. 'Come on. You can't just walk out on him. Not now.'

'He doesn't deserve all this.'

'He's here because he chose to be. Let him make his own decisions.' Caroline sighed. 'If anyone's to blame it's me. I wish I'd never dug Sid up in the first place.'

'You were looking for me,' Lizzie said gently. 'And you found me. That's a good thing.' She turned away, looking down over the churchyard where the fox was still asleep and the blackbird was singing again. 'It's so lovely here,' she said again. 'A nice place to end up. Do you think they'll bury him here when they're done with him?'

'I don't know,' Caroline said. 'We could ask Mel – the vicar. She'd know.'

'It'd be peaceful.'

'More than he deserves,' Caroline said tartly.

Lizzie tentatively placed her hand on her granddaughter's arm. 'I used to sit in the window when your mum was a baby,' she said. 'I'd cuddle her and look out and it was all covered in snow, so deep that the only thing you could see was that big white cross down there. So beautiful. After the war and the blitz and everything – well, I thought it was the most wonderful place I'd ever seen.'

They fell silent. Caroline found herself wondering if what Lizzie had said was true; whether this really was a place of peace, or whether all the dead who lay here had taken their own secrets, their own dangers, their own shames, to the grave with them. And even then they had not lain there undisturbed, there had been new burials, ashes interred, bombs that splintered bones—

She shivered.

Behind them, the ivy stirred in the wind. Beyond the church the clouds were thickening, as if they were gathering to see what would happen next. Caroline stood up.

'We'd better get back,' she said. 'It's going to rain.'

She held out her hand. Lizzie took it, and for a moment they stood looking at each other. Caroline said gently, 'Please, don't do anything yet. Just give me some time. You'll be safe.'

'Oh, love,' said Lizzie. 'That's what Miss Alleyn said. And look what happened.'

'I know.' Caroline helped the old lady to her feet. 'So I'm going to make it up to you,' she said. 'I promise.'

62

The departure lounge was quieter than the arrivals hall had been. A group of elderly tourists stood chattering excitedly on the concourse, ignoring the harassed travel rep who was trying to make sure they all had their boarding passes ready. As Caroline watched, three of them staged a breakout and headed for the bar where she was sitting with Betty.

'Go on,' Betty was saying. 'Have a bloody cocktail.'

'I'm driving.'

'My flight's not for another hour. You'll be fine. Yes, please,' she said to the waitress. 'I'll have a Cosmo. And she'll have a—'

'Oh, all right. I'll have a G and T.'

They lapsed into silence again as the waitress walked off. Caroline touched her arm.

'Mum? Are you okay?'

'Hmm?'

'Are you all right? You seem really – distracted.'

'Got a lot on my mind, sweetie.' Betty pulled out a packet of cigarettes, then saw the No Smoking sign. 'Bugger. I keep forgetting the health police are in charge.'

'Mum…' Caroline paused as their drinks arrived. Her gin was so weak it would have made John Cooper weep. 'Mum, did I do the right thing telling you about Lizzie?'

'How'd you think you'd have managed for the next twenty years or so, keeping that little gem quiet?' Betty knocked back half of her drink. 'God, they have the nerve to charge seven quid for that? Daylight bloody robbery.'

'I'll take that as a yes, then.' Caroline looked away, blinking hard.

'Oh, God, sweetie, I'm sorry.' Betty took her daughter's hand and rubbed it. 'Look, give me a bit of time, all right? It's a lot to get used to. It's only been three days.'

'I know.'

'For you too. I'm not so insensitive that I don't realise that.' She managed half a smile. 'Feels like we've spoken more now than we ever have.'

'It does. That's got to be good, hasn't it?'

'It's taken long enough.' Betty pushed her hair off her face. 'I'm sorry.'

'Don't. I am too.' Caroline swallowed. 'I found a grandmother and got my mum back too.'

'I suppose we both did.' Betty finished her drink and beckoned the waitress over to order another. 'Anyway,' she said briskly when the girl had gone, 'I meant to show you this last night.' She reached into her holdall. 'Then I thought it would be better now. Go on, take it.'

It was the black scrapbook that Lizzie had given her. The cover was soft, creased leather.

'"What Lizzie Sixpence Did Next",' Betty said. 'She said she kept it all for me in case she could ever see me again. Can you imagine?'

Caroline opened the book. Old photos, handwritten notes, little fragments of a life telling their tale. Betty pointed at a picture of a tall, flat-fronted house advertising *Vacancies*.

'She got a job as a chambermaid in a B and B in Brighton, then worked in a shop – and you see that? She went to night school and got O Levels. More than I ever did.'

'Oh, look.' Caroline touched a small piece of paper, cut out of a newspaper. 'The first Open University degree ceremony. Did she—'

'BA in English. But she didn't dare go.' Betty finished her drink. 'She was still running scared after thirty odd years. Jesus.'

'It must have been terrifying for her,' Caroline said. 'Coming back, I mean.'

'There are letters, too.' Betty took a pile of envelopes out of her bag. 'Postcards to Mickey, mainly, from wherever she was living. Just her address, no signature or anything. Some are years apart. He kept them all, only gave them back to her when she moved back to the house. No wonder the poor old sod got married to someone else in the end.' She pulled out the one she wanted. 'But he always wrote back. This is the last one.'

Caroline took it.

You got to come home, Lizzie, come home, just until it's all sorted out, then you can go away again if you want. Oh I do miss you. You can have one of the empty flats, if anybody asks we can say you're just visiting. But we've got to decide what to do — Betty's girl was at the funeral, she was talking about selling — I'll get Danny to keep an eye out if she comes but oh, Liz, love, what are we going to do if they find it?

'At least they know that Clapton's dead.'

'He's not the stiff they need to worry about, though, is he?'

Caroline put the papers down. 'It'll be all right, Mum,' she said, with more confidence than she felt. 'I'll sort it out.'

Betty looked at her consideringly. 'Yes,' she said at last. 'You will.' She finished the rest of her drink, grimacing. 'So, I'm going to invite her over for Christmas. Get to know her a bit. Think she'll come?'

'She will if you invite Mickey and Audrey as well.'

'Fair enough. And you? Do you want to come too?'

'Maybe at Easter. I think you need a bit of time with her first, don't you?'

'Probably.' Betty was fiddling with her lighter, little staccato clicks on and off. 'About the house,' she said abruptly. 'I think you should leave off trying to sell for a while. At least until all the police business is over and done with.' She looked accusingly at her daughter. 'Don't you dare start going on about bloody tax or whatever.'

'I wasn't going to.'

'Good. Because I know I'm probably being stupid.'

'You're not stupid, Mum. Far from it.'

'Say that in a year's time when HMRC are knocking on the door.'

'But why? You always said you couldn't wait to get out of there. You called it a trap. The first chance you got you were off.'

'Yes, well. I know.' Betty put the lighter down, reaching for the book. 'But last night, when I was looking at this…' She flipped open the pages, Lizzie's black-and-white face peeping out at them. 'She had a whole life doing things she'd never have been able to do if she'd not been at that house. And there's me, being a painter like I always wanted to be, setting up the gallery. You got your career, the one you set your heart on. Something gave us what it took to go and do that stuff. Something in us that made us think, to hell with it, I'm going out there to make it happen. Makes you wonder, doesn't it?' She caught Caroline's expression and shrugged. 'Oh, it's all a bit airy-fairy, I know. Maybe I'd just had one nightcap too many.'

'It's not airy-fairy.' Caroline could hear Grace's voice: *I found out who I was at Wickham Grange…*

'But anyway, hang on to it for a bit. At least then you won't have to worry about that restriction putting a spanner in the works. What d'you think?' She shot her daughter a shrewd glance. 'You could work from there, so no need for any expensive offices. Your chance to finally set up on your own,' she added.

'Maybe.' The thought was new, and Caroline found herself wondering, could it work?

There was an electronic chime and a distorted voice gargled something about Barcelona. Betty stood up.

'Gate One,' she said, with a trace of her old briskness. 'Right, sweetie, I'm going to head off,' she said. 'Get some duty free.' She picked up the letters and stowed them in her bag, but handed the book to Caroline. 'You take this,' she said. 'Read it properly. Bring it over when you come.'

'Okay.'

Betty stood for a moment. 'She's done such a lot,' she said suddenly. 'All on her own. After everything that had happened to her. I – I really admire her.'

'You did a lot, too. You had a goal and you went for it, and that took guts, like she said. I just never realised it until now.' Caroline smiled at her mother. 'I admire you too.'

'God, don't, sweetie, you'll make me cry. Look, I'm going to go.' Betty hesitated, then said, 'I don't know if you'll want this. But take it anyway.' She took a piece of folded paper out of her pocket. 'Don't look now,' she said, as Caroline started to open it. 'Read it when you're at home.'

'What is it?'

Betty looked away. 'It's your father's name,' she said. 'I might not know who mine is, and I'm not stupid. I know it could be any one of those arseholes who liked little girls back then.' Caroline opened her mouth, startled at how close her mother was to one of the possible truths, but Betty went on. 'Anyway, there's no need for you think the same about yours. Well, I mean, he was an arsehole, but he wasn't in that league, which is something. You'll be able to find him, if you want to. I thought I owed you that, after all this. So you can decide what you want to do.'

She bent, gave Caroline a sudden fierce hug. 'Call me later,' she said, and was gone.

Caroline sat for a long moment, turning the paper over and over in her hands. She could feel the indentations from the pen strokes of Betty's elaborate and decisive handwriting, curves and loops that swirled like fingerprints.

Lizzie had wept at the thought that Betty could learn her father had been a man like Sidney Parker. And now Caroline had the chance to learn her own background, to find out what kind of man had fathered her, that careless, uncaring, faceless being who had created her. After forty-five years she could know.

I found out who I was at Wickham Grange…

Her parking time was nearly up. She stood, tidying their glasses for the waitress.

And then she tore the paper in half, dropped the pieces into the dregs of her drink, and walked away.

63

Rob's house was a 1930s semi on a quiet cul-de-sac near Beckenham, with an unexpectedly neat garden and the original front door. It was opened by a young girl of seventeen or so, with bright purple hair, a long floral dress and a nose ring, who stood looking at Caroline critically.

'Finally, his taste's improved,' she said. 'I'm Ellen. He's through there – don't worry, I'm not going to be the third wheel, I'm off out. Dad! Caroline's here.' She flashed a sudden smile. 'He's said a lot of nice things about you,' she went on. 'You've really cheered him up. I like you for that, so it's a good start.'

Before Caroline could speak, Rob appeared in the hallway. 'Get out of it,' he said, flicking a tea towel at his daughter. 'And don't spend your cab money on cocktails, I've got a really good Merlot so I'm not coming to pick you up.'

'I'm crashing at Tolu's, anyway,' she said.

'Since when?'

'Since, like, ten minutes ago, her brother's out so I can have his room. So I'll be back tomorrow. Bye, Caroline, see you, Dad.' She grinned, and was suddenly very like her father. 'Have fun and if you can't be good, be careful!'

She skipped past in a waft of perfume and was gone, leaving them staring after her.

'Is it me or do I suddenly feel like I'm about ninety?' Caroline said, following Rob into the house.

'Tell me about it. One minute she's asking me to leave the light on because she's scared the big bad wolf is coming to get her, the next she's – well. Anyway. Come here.' He pulled her into a hug. 'How are you? I didn't want to call in case it was all going belly up, but I've been thinking about you, I really have. Do you want to tell me about it?'

Caroline did. The story took them through the Merlot and a rather good lasagne and on into the lounge, where they ate chocolate mousse on the big, squashy sofa. The walls were covered in prints and paintings, mostly landscapes, with a photo collage of Ellen in pride of place.

'So that's where it's all got to,' she said. The mousse had been delicious and she tried to unobtrusively scrape up the last few specks with her spoon. 'All we can do now is wait. See what the police say.' She reluctantly put her bowl down on the coffee table.

'All right. Say they prove there's a family connection. So what? They don't know where Lizzie is and even if she fesses up there's not going to be any evidence, surely? Just an old lady, maybe a bit forgetful.'

'She's so desperate to protect my mum, she thinks that if she confesses she can keep all that side of it quiet.' She didn't say anything about the possible damage to her career; that felt shamefully selfish, but she wouldn't mind betting he'd have thought of it for himself.

'Have you told Betty about it?' he said.

'No. I promised Lizzie. I said I won't say anything and nor will she until the police come back to us. Then if they do identify him, she says she's going to confess and that I have to respect that.'

He topped up her glass. 'You can't let her do it,' he said. 'Poor old lady, after everything she's been through.'

Caroline sighed. 'I wish we could try to persuade the police the body's too old to investigate so they wouldn't bother. But what does that mean? At what point do they say it's not worth it?'

'I don't know.' Rob sat up. 'But I know someone who will. You want me to give him a call?'

'Really? Who?

'My mate Marcus. He's a history prof these days, he's supervising my PhD, but he still has a – what would Ellen call it? – a side hustle with an archaeology consultancy. I borrowed some of his stuff that time when, well, you know.' He took out his phone and glanced at the time. 'Which reminds me, I need to replace that tarpaulin, the police trampled it to bits. Hold on… hey. Marcus? Rob. Yeah, good, you? Caught the second half… oh, clearly offside… no, no way was that a penalty either. I know, but the ref's from Manchester so what do you expect?' He caught Caroline's eye and went on hastily, 'Anyway, look, mate, can I pick your brains? I need to know something about police investigations. Oh God, sorry, you should have said. What's her name? Bingo? You're kidding. Well, look, enjoy. You're sure? Okay. Tomorrow. Yeah, eleven should be fine. Cheers.'

He put the phone down, looking pleased. 'I should have known,' he said. 'Old Marc's got a date. He's totally shameless, could pull at a nun's funeral. Anyway, he said we can drop round to his office at the uni tomorrow if you're up for it?'

'Yes.' Caroline took a deep breath. 'But look, I should have said this before.'

'That sounds ominous.'

She took his hand. 'I'd not blame you if you didn't want anything to do with all this. I've already got you into enough trouble. I mean, it's a big ask, getting you involved, and I don't want to make any problems for you.'

'What problems?' He put his arm around her shoulders and they leaned back against the cushions. 'I like you, Caroline Alleyn. I really like you. And I think you're brave and gutsy and you're trying to do the right thing, so if I want to help with that then let me, okay?'

'You're sure?'

'I was sure the minute I heard you shout bugger at the library. You looked like you wanted to give the microfilm reader a good kicking and I thought, I say, she looks like she'd be interesting to know.' He kissed her. 'So. Fancy another bowl of mousse before bed?'

In her last year at school Caroline had done a week's work experience in a barrister's chambers. Christopher Churchill ('Well, we're all related at a genetic level' being his usual response to the usual question) had been a big, florid man who swept along the corridors at various Crown Courts with his gown flapping and his wig clinging to his toupee like a baby marmoset riding on its mother. His tuition had mainly involved leaving Caroline to sit with instructing solicitors and their clerks, from whom she learned enough about how the legal system worked to confirm her in her choice of career. The other thing she had learned was when Churchill sent her to collect his dry cleaning, and she saw at first hand just what a really good suit looked like. And even that marvel of tailoring was nothing compared to the one Marcus Lewis was wearing.

He wheeled himself around his desk to greet them as they were shown into his university office, shaking hands with a grip that spoke fiercely of years holding trowels and spades and whatever other hefty implements she imagined that archaeologists used. Slightly older than Rob, he was fair haired, with skin creased and wrinkled by the weather, and huge black spectacles on a gold chain around his neck.

'Come in, come in,' he bellowed. 'Caroline, fantastic to meet you. So good to see you both! Did Rob tell you he was the one who saved my life when I did this?' He gestured to his legs in their wonderful trousering. 'Crashed my bike, no helmet, own stupid fault, six months in hospital feeling sorry for myself, planning to end it all as soon as they let me out, but old Sayers here came every bloody day and kept me going. He was a year below but he still helped me catch up with essays and all sorts. He's a good bloke, Caroline, but don't tell him I said so.'

As all of this had been at top volume, Caroline didn't think she'd have to. But she smiled anyway and accepted the cup of coffee that Marcus handed her. The office was large, untidy, with piles of papers and boxes of things ranging from stones to bits of clay lying on a long shelving unit. Marcus saw her looking and grinned.

'Fruits of my labours,' he said. 'Great thing about a catheter and no feeling from the waist down is that you can lie up to your bollocks in mud for eight hours at a time without caring. This little beauty—' he undid a box and handed her a tiny bronze mouse – 'was buried in a Roman villa two thousand years ago. Nearly got missed because it was right at the end of the trench, but because it was at face height for me I spotted it. Isn't it lovely?'

His voice was suddenly gentle and Caroline realised he had a genuine love for the things he found. And he was right; the mouse was beautiful, its perky little ears so well cast they almost twitched.

Marcus spun the chair and went back behind his desk where he picked up a mug that bore the winking trowel logo and the legend *Trench Art Archaeological Consultants.* 'Anyway, you said you wanted to pick what few brains I have?'

Rob looked at Caroline. 'Do you want to tell him?'

She put her own mug down. 'It's a bit tricky,' she said. 'Only I have a client who found some remains in their garden.' It was true enough, in its way. 'A body. And the police are investigating and they said that if the bones are really old they call in the archaeologists. So before she spends a lot of money getting me involved if she doesn't need to I want to know at what point would they decide it wasn't worth following up and call you guys in?'

'Wow. A lawyer who wants to save their clients money.' But he was grinning and it was impossible to take offence.

'I mean, I know there's no statute of limitations or anything,' she went on, 'but how old would it have to be for them to say it wasn't something they were interested in?'

'Depends.' Marcus steepled his fingers in front of his chin. 'What kind of condition was it in? Still squishy?'

'Bones. I think. They only uncovered the head and a hand, but the police said it was mostly skeletonised.'

'Well, the rest could have had tissue still in place. Depends on the soil and the local wildlife.'

'We've heard about the badgers,' Rob said. 'Who knew?'

'Don't know what's worse, them or crows. Anyway. They'll have to weigh up the resources needed against the likelihood of finding out who it was and how long they'd been there. No point throwing money at a murder that was done a hundred years ago and everyone involved has shuffled off the old mortal coil, but one where the killer could still be around? Different story. So the age of the bones is going to be important.'

Caroline couldn't help sighing. 'I thought you were going to say that.' She looked at Rob. 'At least we know,' she said.

'Although,' said Marcus, 'there's always context.'

'Go on,' Rob said.

'We had a dig a few years back. Found a body under where they wanted to build a warehouse complex. All very sinister, until they found that the site used to be a prison and it had had its own graveyard. This poor sod had been missed when they relocated the bodies.' Marcus shrugged. 'What I'm saying is that the context might mean they don't have to look into it.'

'But the forensics guy said the fact it was next to a churchyard didn't mean anything,' Caroline objected.

'Well, I've not seen it so I can't be sure, but who knows?' Marcus said. He looked from one to the other, shaking his head. 'If you get any reports from the Bill I can have a look if you like.'

'You're a mate.' Rob finished his own coffee. 'Maybe we should do dinner one night – you could bring Bingo.'

'It's a date.' The computer chimed and Marcus clicked his tongue in annoyance. 'Caroline, it's been an absolute pleasure, but time and students wait for no man. Rob, mate, we've got a meeting next week, yeah?' He smiled, his sheer vitality radiating off him like summer. 'Good luck with it all.'

*

Out on the London street the sky was the same indeterminate grey as the office block behind them. Pigeons bustled about on the pavement, pecking at invisible crumbs, deftly dodging the feet of commuters and the wheels of delivery riders. Rob smiled as one found a whole crisp and scuttled into a corner to enjoy it.

'They were the first thing that got me into history,' he said. 'I was nine and read Samuel Pepys' description of the Great Fire, when he talks about how the pigeons flapped about trying to find somewhere to roost. I realised that the world then was just the same as this one, only with different clothes.'

'And TB. And cholera. Plague.'

'You've got no soul.' He pointed over the road, to what even she could see was a very old pub. 'That's one of the only buildings in the city to survive the fire. They do a good pie – fancy lunch? Without the cholera?'

Caroline agreed, letting him take her hand and lead her into the bar, which was tiny and busy and patrolled by a huge black cat. It was early, so they found a table, but after only a few minutes the place started to fill with men and women wearing dark suits and serious expressions, and she realised that they were right opposite the Royal Courts of Justice.

'I haven't been up here for years,' she said.

'Best bit of London. I found this place when I started my PhD – would it surprise you to learn that Marcus is a regular? – and I love it.'

Caroline thought that if she wasn't so preoccupied she might well love it too. The food was excellent, served by a magnificent landlady, and she was just starting to feel some of the tension ease out of her shoulders when her phone, which she'd left on the table so it was out of the way, buzzed.

'Shit,' said Rob.

He was looking at the screen. It bore a single imperious name: *DS Hughes.*

For a wild second she thought she could just stab at it, shut it off, make it all go away. But her eyes met his and she knew she had to—

'You'll have to—'

'I can't hear in here.' She stood up, uncertain for a moment, then started to push her way through the throng to the street where the smokers were huddled together in a defiant crowd. The phone in her hand continued to shake, and she could picture Hughes sitting at a desk with an implacable expression on her face, knowing that Caroline would eventually crack and—

'Hello?'

Was it her imagination or could she hear a smug grin breaking out at the other end? But the accent was as warm and guileless as ever.

'Ah, Ms Alleyn. I was just about to give you up for lost.'

'I'm in London. Is there something I can help with?'

The faint hope that Hughes would be reproved was quashed immediately. 'Ah, well, not just yet. But maybe one day, you never know.' Was that a threat in her voice, gleaming like faraway lightning? Then the accent fuzzed again. 'This is just a courtesy call, really. Thought I'd let you know that the lab has had a look at your bones, and they're in good enough condition for them to get a DNA sample. So that's a step forward, isn't it?'

A pneumatic drill started pounding and Caroline raised her voice so she could be heard. 'Did they say—'

A woman in a barrister's gown and bands turned to fix her with a pained look, and she realised she was shouting; the drill was her heart, smashing against her ribs. Caroline took a breath, which caught in her throat and made her cough. 'Sorry. Did they say how long they'll be before any results?'

'How long's a piece of string?' Hughes said breezily. 'But the boffins say a good few weeks. Depends how long it takes them to rinse out the test tubes, I dare say. Still. There we are. At the mercy of the Bunsen burner. I'll be in touch if I hear anything else. Unless there's anything you want to tell me?'

The question rapped out like a knock at a séance. Caroline looked in through the window; Rob was watching her, with such a look of concern on his face that she could have wept.

'Nothing at all,' she said, and cut the call before Hughes could say anything else.

She glanced up at the courtrooms, their Gothic certainty such a contrast to her own tumult. A bike courier raced past in a blur of Lycra. Someone climbed out of a black cab, grumbling about the fare. A couple of students ambled past, not caring if they were late for a lecture, chatting about a band she'd never heard of.

A line from a half-remembered poem came into her head, something about merciless, hurrying Londoners. Betjeman. Had she studied it for O level? It was all so long ago. The words' melancholy fitted her mood, a counterpoint to the thoughts in her head that were as loud and insistent as the traffic and the burst of voices that followed someone out of the pub.

'You okay?' Rob asked gently.

'They found DNA. Or they will, at any rate.'

'Damn.'

'I know.' She shoved the phone back into her pocket. 'But they won't get any results for a while.'

'That's good. So there's still a bit of time. You want to go back in before someone nicks our table?'

She made an effort. 'I'm more worried they'll nick my chips.'

He pretended to smile, and they went back inside, to even more noise than before. They talked about Marcus, and the accident and Rob's loyalty, which he shrugged off but which had deeply impressed Caroline, who knew the value of someone being there when you had nothing and nobody. They even had ice cream, and a slow walk back to Charing Cross, with Rob pointing out odd little scraps of the city's past that nobody else paid any attention to. The pavements were crisp with the leaves that were drifting off the plane trees, and the spire of St Clement Danes cast long shadows in the late afternoon sunshine, as if trying to make the most of what warmth was left in the year. The chess board over the door at Simpson's was still poised in its never-ending game, children scampered in the fountains at Somerset House, and the unfortunate angle of Nelson's sword was making a group of tourists snigger. London swirled around them, restless and unheeding, and Caroline was grateful for its contempt. It gave her the briefest respite, a feeling that here, nothing mattered, and nobody cared.

But underneath everything, following them like a stalker as they walked through the centre of the heartless city, was the dark and brooding uncertainty that now hung over Wickham Grange.

64

It was not until she closed the front door that she realised.

It was a week before Christmas. Two long months had dragged past, eight interminable weeks. She had started to have a recurring dream, in which blank-faced scientists opened the blue plastic box containing Sidney Parker and took out his skull, before laughing and putting it back untouched, leaving her to wake to another day of anxious waiting. Two months of not knowing, two months of dread. Not even Christmas, which with Rob should otherwise have been a happier one than she'd known for years, could quite shake the weight off her shoulders.

Outside, frost was already decorating the house, scattering glitter across the roof and furring the windows. The moon had risen while Caroline was on the motorway, where the garish yellow lights of the M23 had made it a dull little speck in a featureless sky, but here on the hill its alabaster gleam was sending deep shadows across the lawn and the drive, and the cold was pinching her face like a spiteful parent trying to put colour into her cheeks. She was glad to get out of the car, stiff from an hour sitting in a mysterious traffic jam, desperate for a pee and a glass of wine, but as the door clicked shut behind her the thought struck her with such immediacy that she paused, startled.

It was the first time she had ever, ever, been alone in Wickham Grange.

She kept it in her mind throughout coat off, shoes off, bathroom, corkscrew. The house was quiet, warm, wanting to be friends, and she wandered out into the hall with her drink, listening to the creaks and sighs that had been threads in her personal tapestry for so many years. The stained-glass window on the landing was dark, its colours swallowed by the winter's evening, but she bent to switch on the fairy lights on the tree she'd put up in the hall, bringing the orange, red, and greens to glow down here instead.

The flight had been on time, and she'd left Audrey in charge of passports and boarding passes. Mickey and Lizzie had been like children on a trip to the seaside, watching wide-eyed as planes taxied past like so many buses before lining up to fling themselves into the sky. Betty had texted to say she hadn't forgotten and would be at the airport to meet them. Lizzie asked yet again if Caroline really thought that she would like the earrings, and Caroline had answered truthfully that yes, they were lovely. She hadn't missed the fact that a box of the same size and shape was under the tree with her own name on it.

And now they were all somewhere high over Europe, and Rob was at a PhD supervision meeting with Marcus and wouldn't be here until later, when he was bringing Ellen over for Christmas. They'd invited the Coopers for Christmas lunch, a suggestion which Mel had accepted rapturously – 'I've got three services on the trot to do in the morning and then I don't care if it's the second coming, I'm not going out again until New Year' – but for now she was here, utterly alone.

She stood at the foot of the stairs for a moment, not really thinking, just letting the silence settle, before she crossed the hall and pushed open the door to the office. There was a brass lamp on Frances' desk, which cast a small pool of light but left the shadows undisturbed, where all those useless files were roosting peacefully. Caroline understood now that they had been kept for all these years for no real purpose other than to hide the five that mattered, the five that had been buried here for so long and were now nothing more than ash.

She sat down on the old swivel chair and took a sip of wine. There was a little spider on the typewriter, picking its way between the G and the H and the J, going steadily on its way, up and down the keys, its destination known to itself alone. From their silver frames on top of the desk Frances watched her dispassionately, Maud with a beaming smile; Betty, in miniskirt and white boots, was looking out sideways, her expression half challenge, half giggle.

The street lamp in the lane shimmered as it came on, and in its light she could see the drive, the frost turning the gravel into sugarplums. This was where Sidney Parker had come, one monster sent on an errand by another. She could picture him as he trudged up the hill in his cheap suit and thin shoes, his cold eyes narrowed against the snow and his shoulders hunched with the violence he meant to deal out, but that had instead been turned against him in one terrified moment of horror.

And then afterwards… that long dark time in the earth, in the silence and the mould. She couldn't find any feelings of pity for him, not really, even knowing that he could be her—

No. She wouldn't allow that thought to form. That new tragedy had not arrived, not yet.

She finished the wine, putting the glass back carefully on the desk, watching the darkness as it curled around the house. The radiator gave a comfortable little clunk. How many nights had first Maud and then her – yes, her grandmother, for that was what Frances had been – sat in this room, each in her little pool of lamplight, while upstairs strangers lay awake for fear of nightmares? Was it in here that the choice to hide Betty had been made, here that her mother had come for help seventeen years later when her world had fallen apart? Caroline thought it must have been.

She had not heard anything else from DS Hughes since that day in London. For these two dreadful months she had watched her phone, even in court, getting a pained query from the magistrate: 'Are we boring you, Miss Alleyn? I do so hope not,' and a cold rebuke from Charles: 'You'd better not be slipping, Caroline, we've no room for dead wood.' She'd stared at his departing back, longing to tell him that yes, she was slipping, slipping off to a whole new forest of her own, but there had been no news, nothing to tell her whether Sidney Parker's blood ran in her veins as well as between the floorboards of her house. Nothing to tell her that she would have to keep her promise to let Lizzie confess as one last act of love for her daughter. Caroline felt as if she was floating on gossamer, as the spider was now doing on its way to the floor, everything suspended on something impossibly fragile.

The thought of Lizzie made her take down the scrapbook from where she had left it, tucked into one of the pigeonholes. She opened it at random. Here was Lizzie in a 1950s frock, smart behind the counter of a shop, here was Lizzie looking up at a cathedral somewhere. Who had taken them all? There was no clue, but Caroline was glad that there must have been friends, even if they were only fleeting substitutes for the child Lizzie had surrendered. In this one – Lizzie on a park bench – she had the same tilt of the head that Betty had when she was thinking of a painting, but Betty had a more angular nose and wider eyes that hadn't come from Lizzie's thin, delicate frame. Caroline lifted down the picture of her mother, tracing the shape of her face with a fingertip. There was something…

Grace's voice, startled and startling, came unbidden into her mind. *Just for a moment I thought you were—'*

Caroline flicked back through the scrapbook. She found the pictures she wanted, a birthday party, the snowman, a new swing in the garden. She propped them up on the desk beside the silver frame, looking at them for a long, long time.

It was only when her phone buzzed – Rob, on his way – that she sat back. Then she tucked the photos away, tidily, pulled down the roll-top, put Betty's picture back, making sure it was straight, then walked out of the office and back into her flat. She moved slowly, deliberately, taking her time as she picked up the keys from their bowl on her dining table.

And then she went upstairs.

65

2007

She was in an end-of-year budget meeting, one of early spring's boring chores, when the call finally came. Even though she had been expecting it for nearly six months now, she still jolted with shock as she saw the number, sending her untouched coffee slopping into the saucer. She jabbed at the screen, cutting off the call.

At the head of the table, Charles Dudley raised his eyebrows. 'Everything all right, Caroline?'

DS Hughes flashed again.

'Sorry,' she said, pushing her chair back, 'I've got to take this—'

It felt like it took hours to clamber past chairs and bags and make it out into the corridor. She cursed as the green icon refused to slide up the screen, had another go with fingers that felt swollen and ungainly.

'Hello?' She prayed it didn't sound like the croak it felt.

The sergeant sounded more rural than ever. 'Good morning,' she said breezily. 'Hope I'm not dragging you out of an important interview?'

'Not at all. A rather dull partners' meeting.'

'Oh, partner, are you? I didn't realise that.'

Don't give me that. You probably know my bloody bra size. Caroline let the silence itch and for once Hughes blinked first.

'Anyway, I've got a bit of an update. Sorry it's taken so long. Must be, what, six months?'

Five months, one week, two days, she wanted to say, but instead just said: 'Something like that.'

'So, I was wondering if I could drop in.'

Caroline paused, as if she were leafing through a diary. 'I'm coming home – up – this weekend. I'll be there on Friday afternoon if that's any good?' Was that casual enough?

But the sergeant just said briskly, 'By all means. See you then.'

Caroline hung up. She suddenly felt oddly calm. It had happened. The waiting was over. There was no more time for fear.

She looked at the phone. He'd be teaching. She tapped out a text. *Hughes coming this Friday. Says she's got news. x*

He texted straight back. She hoped his students didn't notice. Maybe he was as keyed up as she was. *It'll be fine. Trust me. x*

Oh, I do, she thought. *The trouble is, everyone else is trusting me.*

She looked back into the meeting room. Charles was pointing at a slide where rows of figures marched across the screen. She thought of her own simple spreadsheet of five names, five addresses, which meant so very much more. Around the table her colleagues were looking smugly pleased with themselves, glad to be thinking about their bonuses; they'd not been so keen on the first part of the meeting, where they'd discussed current cases, talking about that assault, that stalking, that harassment, as coldly and impersonally as she or Rob would have said, this kettle, that bit of carpet. Her throat had ached from the effort of not shouting in protest.

Inside the conference room Charles changed the slide. More figures. A heading about legal aid cases not bringing in enough money. Her colleagues were nodding.

Not one of them glanced up, or turned to see where she was. Not one of them would care where she went.

Twelve thirty.

She could be in West Wickham before the shops closed.

*

Later, when Caroline looked back on that Friday afternoon, she could only see it as a series of vignettes, little images that stood sharply distinct from each other, each a separate picture, as unconnected and disjointed as a pile of bones.

The first of these scenes, these snapshots, was the arrival of DS Hughes, on her own this time, pulling up in a vast Range Rover that sat on the drive like a duchess. Its paintwork gleamed in the weak sunlight, and a solitary leaf slid off the roof as if it knew that untidiness would not be tolerated.

'Afternoon,' the sergeant said, rubbing her hands. 'Not getting any warmer, is it? The clocks go forward this weekend and I'm still scraping ice off the car in the mornings.'

They went inside, but Hughes declined coffee. 'I'm on my way to a meeting, thanks anyway. I just wanted to bring you up to date with what's going on.'

Caroline gestured to the three old people, who were sitting tight together on the sofa as if they were waiting for a play to start. 'You don't mind if my tenants join us? I feel that as residents they deserve to know. And you remember Mr Sayers?'

Hughes shrugged. 'I don't mind if you don't,' she said.

She took an armchair and Caroline brought over a dining chair for herself, wanting its firm support for her treacherous, shaking knees, then wished she were sitting next to Rob's solid warmth but knowing it would look odd if she moved.

Hughes opened a briefcase, pulling out sheets of paper and fanning them on her lap. 'Let me see,' she said. 'So. We got the report back from the forensic people. Looks like your body was buried some time around the mid-forties.'

Yes, February 1947, if you really want to know. 'Oh. How could they tell?'

'His clothing, mainly. Fabric from a British Warm overcoat, braces, woolly vest. Scrap of what could have been a Utility label, brown leather shoes that had been mended more than once.'

Drag marks in the snow.

DS Hughes was still reading. 'No ID card or paper money, but that would probably have rotted away over time. Funny that there weren't any coins, but there you go.'

'Not much cash around in them days,' Mr Harris said. 'All the metal was used for planes and such.'

'Is that so?' Hughes ran her eyes down the printed sheet. 'Teeth not good, a couple of fillings that look like they were done in the thirties. Something about the amalgam they used.'

'Mercury,' said Dr Fairfax. 'I do hope your laboratory has a suitable fume cupboard, sergeant.'

'They'd better, the amount they charge.' Hughes chuckled. 'So, that's the preliminary findings. Took them long enough, eh?'

'It doesn't seem very much to me,' the doctor sniffed.

'Yes, well, there we are in agreement.' The detective sat back, nodding. 'But that's just the first report.' She tidied the papers on her lap, tapping them into a perfect pile. She wasn't looking up as she said, 'But of course, there's the DNA to consider, isn't there?'

The record player had been over there, next to the fireplace. When Caroline was eight and ill with chickenpox, the room smelling of Lucozade and calamine lotion, Frances put on some old LPs – *The Sound of Music*, some Gilbert and Sullivan – and Caroline had amused herself by speeding the records up and then down, so the music boomed or squealed under the needle.

Hughes' words seemed to be doing that now, swooping in and out of range, momentarily loud, then so soft she could barely be heard. Something about mitochondrial… that was to do with the mother, wasn't it? Oh God… bone marrow… teeth…

The sergeant paused, impassively waiting for someone to ask the obvious question.

Caroline swallowed.

'And did they get any results?' she said. Was that really her own voice?

'Ah. Now then.' Hughes pulled a sheet out of her fan, like a croupier finding the missing ace. The silence while she studied it was thick and oppressive, the crackle of the fire sounding like far-off gunfire in the quiet. On the sofa, Lizzie took Mickey's hand.

Hughes held up a sheet that showed columns of black and white blocks. A living, breathing, snarling human being had been reduced to these printed dominoes. Caroline felt her own pulse beginning to race, and wondered if it was recognising itself in that tower of chromosomes.

'This is your feller,' Hughes was saying. 'And this—' she held up another piece of paper, more random blocks – 'this is yours. Now, don't worry, we'll destroy all the samples once we're finished, you're welcome to come and see it all put in the incinerator if you want to.' She opened the briefcase again. 'I've got a form in here somewhere.'

Caroline looked at Lizzie. The world felt as if it were balanced on a pin and could fall at any second.

'Did they…' She felt her throat tighten, and took a sip of her cooling coffee before starting again. Four words. That was all it was going to take. 'Did they find anything?'

Lizzie Sixpence closed her eyes.

Hughes sat back in her chair. She beamed. 'Absolutely nothing,' she said.

From somewhere far away Hughes was saying something about poor samples and database searches and records not going back far enough, but all Caroline could think was a jubilant, *He's not your grandfather, he's not your—*

Rob was looking at her. She blinked, and the room came back into focus.

'Well,' she said. 'Thank you so much for letting us know.' She stood up, held out her hand. 'We really appreciate—'

Maria Hughes held out her own hand, but to stop, not to shake.

'Just one other thing, though,' she said. 'We still don't know who put him there.'

Her words landed like shrapnel. Caroline sat down again.

And in the silence that followed, Lizzie Sixpence said: 'I can help you with that.'

Everyone turned to look at the tiny, pale little woman who had been sitting so very still. Her skin was almost transparent, just two deep red spots that burned on her face like embers.

The detective raised an eyebrow. 'Can you now. And you'll be…?'

'My name's Tanner. Elizabeth Tanner. I've been staying with my friends here.'

Beside her, the other two old people nodded. The three of them were sitting so close together that their shoulders touched, a bulwark against the world as they had been for seventy years.

Hughes opened a notebook. 'And what can you tell me, Miss Tanner?'

'It was when you said the mid forties,' Lizzie said. 'And I suddenly thought, what if he was out there that day?'

'What day would that be?' Hughes was speaking patiently, but her eyes were fixed and sharp.

'Oh now, dear, I can't remember the date. Not after all this time. But it would have been forty-four, I'm sure of that, and that would fit, wouldn't it?'

'It would,' Hughes said.

Lizzie's voice was as thin and clear as a bird's. 'There was lots of people passing through back then. Some of them on their way to new postings, on leave, that kind of thing, and others, well, you'll know more about this than me, lots of them was up to no good. Deserters and the like. Looters. And round here, a good few burglaries, do you remember?'

Mr Harris nodded. 'They'd nick anything,' he said.

'So you think our man out there was some kind of crook?' Hughes wrote something in her book.

Lizzie looked shocked. 'Oh no, dear, though I suppose he might have been, when you come to think of it. No, what I was going to say was that I was in service here when it happened.'

'When he was buried?' Hughes sat forward.

'Good lord, what do you take us for?' Audrey Fairfax snapped. 'Murderers?'

'Then what?'

'When the bomb came down,' said Lizzie. 'What I think might have happened was this…'

A young man, out on his own, is wandering through the woods and fields. Perhaps he is on his way to fight, perhaps he is on leave. Or perhaps he is roaming with an eye out for anything that might come his way, whether it was meant for him or not. That's how he got his coat, stolen from a barracks when he deserted all those months ago, and he's going to steal again today.

This afternoon he finds himself outside a big house on a hill. The gates stand wide and the downstairs windows are open. At the end of the lawn is a greenhouse and he heads there, knowing it will be where he can find tools, a sack, maybe a ladder.

He is picking up a spade and munching on a stored apple, when he hears the faint puttering sound. For a moment he thinks it is a motorbike, and he wonders who'd be riding up here, where there's nothing but a field full of corpses; the very thing he has managed to avoid all this time.

He chooses a hammer. It'll break bones as well as glass.

And he is weighing it in his hand when the world explodes.

'My grandmother,' Caroline said carefully, 'always told me that blast did very strange things.'

Hughes looked thoughtful. 'I daresay it did,' she said.

Lizzie said, 'The house lost all its windows. I was livid because I'd just spent all day dusting and the place was filthy, soot blown down the chimney and all over everything.'

'And outside?' Hughes said.

'Well, once we'd picked ourselves up and made sure nobody was hurt, we went out to look. You could see straight away that the greenhouse had been blown over. Total wreck, it was. The mistress, Miss Maud, she was furious. Sacks of potatoes and apples there was, all lost, and as for the churchyard, well, that didn't bear thinking about. Arms and legs…' Lizzie gave a little shudder. 'There's a memorial, now, to them that got blown out of their graves.'

'I'll take a look.'

'It's a large white cross. You can't miss it,' Dr Fairfax said. 'Rather tasteful, for once.'

'And of course, back then, no chance of getting something like a greenhouse repaired, all that glass.' Lizzie smiled apologetically. 'I was long gone before they rebuilt it.'

'Weren't done until the fifties,' Mickey said. 'I helped out, but it wasn't much of a job, you couldn't get the materials.'

'And your man buried underneath.' Hughes was nodding thoughtfully.

'I suppose so. How awful.' Caroline hoped she sounded at least slightly regretful. 'What terrible luck.'

'Wasn't it just.' Hughes paused for a moment, as if she was going to say something else, then shrugged. 'Well, there you go. That's as good a theory as any. It's not like there's any evidence to suggest anything else.' And this time it was the detective who got up and held out a hand, taking Lizzie's with a surprising gentleness. 'I'll get you to make a statement, Miss Tanner, but no rush.' She gave them all a wide smile. 'Actually, that brings me to what I really came to tell you.'

Jesus, what now? Caroline thought. She could feel a bead of sweat trickling down her back.

But Hughes hadn't stopped speaking.

'We won't be taking it any further. There's not much chance of an investigation anyway, after all this time, money being so tight and this being such an old body. I was going to let you know that as far as we're concerned the case is over. Still, good to have – what do they call it – closure?'

'It is, yes,' Caroline said. She wanted to giggle.

'Well, if you'll excuse me then—' Hughes clipped her briefcase shut and headed for the door. 'No doubt you've got a busy weekend ahead.'

Caroline smiled as she showed the detective out. 'Just one or two things to sort out,' she said. 'Loose ends, you might say.'

They all stood in the hall to watch the Range Rover drive away. Sure enough, it parked for a few minutes outside the church, then started up again. Only when it had rounded the bend in the lane and was out of sight did Lizzie turn to Caroline.

'Did I get it right?' she said. 'Did I remember it all?'

'You didn't forget a thing,' Caroline said. 'You were perfect.' She looked at the others. 'All of you.'

'And it's over?'

'Apart from the statement? Yes. It's over.' *And he's not my grandfather, he's not.*

The old lady let out a long breath. She seemed suddenly taller, less fragile, as if she had vanquished something. Mickey hesitantly raised an arm, then carefully put it around her shoulders. Lizzie Sixpence smiled.

'At last,' she said. 'At last.'

66

Lizzie

Lizzie Sixpence smiles gratefully at the cabbie. She's a middle-aged Pakistani woman, whose hands are warm and firm as she takes Lizzie's own, no fuss, no dithering, just quietly and competently helping her out of the seat and onto the pavement.

'Would you like me to wait?' she asks.

Lizzie shakes her head. 'No, dear,' she says. 'I don't know how long I'll be. I'll manage.'

The cabbie does her the courtesy of not arguing. 'All right. I've got a pickup not far off, I'll come round in an hour anyway, just in case. You know where you're going?'

'Oh yes,' Lizzie says, though in truth she doesn't have any certainty over where this will lead, other than back to 1947 and to things that might not bear the pain of being woken.

She stands still until the cab has turned the corner and is out of sight. It's a bright, hopeful day in Levington Terrace. It feels that the street is sprucing itself up ready for spring; a window cleaner is propping his ladder up against Number 11, a proper window cleaner, she notices with approval, with a chamois leather and a bucket, not one of those hose things that leave everything dripping. A ginger cat sits on a wall, tucking its tail around its paws to keep them tidy, and a row of hyacinths in a window box send their crisp, acidic scent into the shining air.

But none of this is what she came for.

She remembers the number from the papers Mickey had said he'd burn, and she turns, walking slowly along the pavement until she reaches Number 28. For a moment she thinks of going straight past, of turning into the little café she saw a few streets away and waiting until the cab comes back, but she has never been a coward and she will not shirk this, not now. She has already posted four letters that took her a day and a night to write.

She pushes open the gate. Rings the bell.

And waits.

67

Caroline

The churchyard was a sea of buttercups. They pressed in close to the weathered old stones, sheltering from the brisk wind that sent their cheerful shiny faces nodding and bowing. Above, great galleons of cloud scudded majestically across a clean blue sky and crows flapped lazily around the stand of trees where they were building their ragged, lopsided nests.

The marble cross had been cleaned, so it gleamed white against the bright new grass at its base. A neat pile of soil had been covered with a dark cloth, and a few paces away, discreetly separate from the little group of women, stood the undertaker, his head bowed.

Mel wore a white surplice that snapped and billowed in the wind. The sun picked out the gold threads in the embroidery on her stole, making them glint like the handles on the box at her feet. The pages of her prayerbook fluttered like moths as the breeze caught them.

Everyone had agreed that the usual funeral service would not be right. Lizzie and Mickey had both wanted to be here, to see this final act played out, but when Caroline had asked what else they wanted, the old lady had just sighed.

'I want it over and done with,' she said. 'Finished. Put him somewhere decent and then let him be forgotten. He can't hurt us no more, can he? Let's just put him away and leave him be.'

Mickey had agreed. 'We've spent enough time grieving,' he said. His eyes met Caroline's. 'Shed enough tears.'

'But not any more,' she said, and it was true; no more of those deep, racking sobs had torn through the silence of the night.

'All right,' Mel said. 'Let me know when it's all been cleared with the police, and I'll think of what we can say.'

And she had. She took old and beautiful words that had been written in a land of heat and dust a thousand miles away from this gentle place, and she used them to mourn, not the dead man, but the loss and grief felt by those who had come to the house in fear, for so many years, and when she talked of resurrection she meant the rebirth of hope, of love, of family. Caroline looked at her mother and grandmother, and closed her eyes, if not in prayer then in gratitude for this moment and what it meant.

Only at the very end did Mel turn to the prayerbook. 'Earth to earth,' she said, and the undertaker stepped forward to lift the box and place it reverently in the hole at the foot of the cross. 'Let your servant go in peace.'

Lizzie held a small wreath of white roses. Mickey helped her to bend and place it on the foot of the cross, the petals brushing against the carved letters. *The lost dead.* Well, he had been found now.

Mel bowed her head. 'Amen,' she said.

'Amen.' Caroline said it without really knowing why. 'That was beautiful,' she said. 'Thank you.'

'My pleasure. Not to get all God about it, but I like to think we've brought him home. He can be at peace now, whoever he was.'

'So can they.' She was watching as the others began to make their way down between the graves. 'Did you want to come back for a drink?'

Mel shook her head, 'No,' she said. 'This is time for you. But call me when you're ready, okay?' She hesitated. 'I wish we'd been able to give him a name, don't you? So sad, to be forgotten.'

'Let's call him something, then,' Caroline said impulsively. 'Let's give him a name. Sidney, that'll do.'

'I like that.' Mel raised her hand, made a sweeping sign of the cross. 'Lord, I commend unto thee thy servant Sidney,' she said quietly. 'There. Didn't feel right not naming him. He deserved that, at least.'

'After seventy years – yes, he did.' Caroline gave her a quick hug. 'I'd better go. But come soon, okay?'

'Try keeping me away.'

'I'll give you a call.'

Caroline turned, starting to follow the others down the path towards that part of the churchyard holding the newer graves, smaller and less ornate than those of the longer dead.

Someone was waiting for her a little way off. Tall, erect, Martine a watchful presence beside her, Grace was standing by a yew tree.

'You go on, dear,' she said to Martine as Caroline approached. 'Miss Alleyn will look after me, won't you?' And when the younger woman was a safe distance away, she held out her hand, which lay warm and strong in Caroline's own.

'Thank you for letting me see this day,' she said.

Caroline shook her head. 'You don't have to thank—'

'You made it happen.' The old lady was looking up at the house, its windows gleaming in the brightness of the spring morning. 'I remember the first time I walked into Wickham Grange,' she said. 'I was so alone, so scared, so cold, but I knew, I knew that coming here was the start of a new life for me. And today is, too.'

'I'm glad,' Caroline said simply.

Grace smiled. 'And it's given you a new life too, I believe. A new grandmother. A new story.'

Caroline blew out a breath. 'It's certainly not what I expected when I came back,' she said. She glanced down to where the others were waiting. 'Do you think we should—'

'Just one moment. There is something else I need to say to you.' Grace's deep eyes were intent and serious. 'I have spoken to the others, to Harriet and Vera and Jane. Well, Lizzie and I did, between us. You'll have heard about Maggie?'

Caroline nodded. Grace sighed, and went on. 'Now they were phone calls to remember.' She chuckled quietly. 'But anyway.

Letters and emails have been exchanged. And when they knew I was coming here today they all agreed that I should be the one to tell you.' She patted Caroline's arm. 'Because of you, we are finally safe. And it's only right that you should know that we'll sign. You can sell, if you want to. Get that new office you were talking about.'

Caroline swallowed. 'I don't know what to say,' she said.

But Grace was watching her shrewdly. 'Oh, I think you do,' she said. And then, before Caroline could say anything else: 'Shall we?'

They turned slowly, Caroline matching Grace's pace as they followed Mickey and Lizzie, Betty and Audrey down the path to the newer graves. Two headstones stood side by side, one more weathered than the other, both only bearing short and simple inscriptions.

This time it was Betty and Caroline who placed the flowers: spring bouquets of bright and joyful tulips that they propped up against the stones, where the words had been carved deep and proud.

Maud Shenstone, 1894–1975
Frances Alleyn, 1920–2006

And beneath both names, two simple words.

Much loved.

68

For a moment she thought she could hear a faint siren from somewhere down the hill. But the sound was only children shrieking as they ran down the lawn to the marquee, where the band was playing softly, old tunes that echoed gently around the garden. Wickham Grange stood bright and hopeful in the sunshine, and the June breeze brought the scent of the roses and lilies that filled the garden with perfume.

It had been a perfect day. The church had been full for the quiet, reflective ceremony; from somewhere outside a blackbird had begun to sing as Mel began the words of the wedding service, her voice clear and compassionate.

'Dearly beloved,' she said. 'We are gathered together…'

Caroline looked round at the congregation. Her mother, seated in the front pew, gave her an enormous wink. The dark-haired man beside her raised an eyebrow, and Audrey Fairfax, in an unexpectedly frivolous hat, rolled her eyes. Amy and Ellen, now inseparable best friends, were standing in the aisle; they had begged to be bridesmaids – 'This is, like, just so romantic!' they had chorused – and so there they were, just about managing to keep straight faces. Rob, looking strangely formal in his suit, blew his daughter a kiss before turning back to the vicar.

On the other side of the aisle Ruth and Eddie sat with Connie, holding their mother's hands. Marcus and an elegant blonde – whose name, neatly printed on the RSVP, had turned out to be Fenella Housey – were there, and in the same pew was a woman with white hair and dark skin, sitting next to three more elderly ladies, all slow and frail now, but instantly known to each other. There had been little cries of recognition at the church door, outstretched hands that turned to hugs while husbands and children and grandchildren looked on, not sure what to think but glad to see the happiness that the moment brought.

Mel was speaking of impediments. Caroline thought of the cross in the churchyard, and knew that at last there were none. Rob squeezed her hand.

Mel smiled at them, then turned back to the bride and groom.

'Say after me,' she said. 'I, Michael, take thee, Elizabeth, to be my wedded wife…'

'It's been so lovely,' Lizzie Harris said.

They were sitting at a table on the lawn, listening to the band playing 'String of Pearls'; inside the marquee, Ruth was dancing in Danny's arms, a dreamy look on her face. Danny looked unexpectedly handsome in his best man's suit, and Caroline's heart swelled for her friend.

'I couldn't believe my eyes when you knocked on my door,' Grace said. 'After all this time.'

'I'm sorry,' Lizzie said. 'For everything.'

'Nothing to be sorry for.' Grace patted her hand. 'You were a victim, same as us. But it's all over. At last.' She turned to Caroline. 'And all because you went looking. Even though I told you not to.'

'I had to read your letter three times,' Harriet said to Lizzie. 'And then when Grace rang me – I nearly fainted.'

'Me too,' said Vera. She turned to the other old lady. 'I'm so sorry about your Maggie.'

Jane nodded. 'She'd have loved this. Real party girl, she turned out to be.'

They fell silent for a moment. The air was suddenly thick with memories. Above the garden, the evening sky was darkening to a rich purple; bats were flickering in the sky, while on the lawn the children were chasing moths, watched by indulgent parents. Harriet beckoned to one of them, a thin, scrawny man, five foot six at best, with sandy hair and a scared expression. 'Oh, and by the way. William has something to say. Don't you?'

He looked embarrassed. 'Yeah, well, that time you rang,' he mumbled, 'I was out of order. Sorry.'

'Not at all.' Caroline smiled as Rob handed her a glass of champagne. 'I was just glad I'd kept a spreadsheet with all your addresses.' She glanced wickedly at Mickey. 'After they got lost,' she added.

'Less of your cheek,' he said.

The caterer appeared, and coughed discreetly. 'We'll be cutting the cake in ten minutes,' she said.

'Blimey. Military precision.' Rob looked at Caroline. 'Do you want to—?'

She nodded. 'We need to get something from the house,' she said. 'Do you mind if we hold fire on the cake for a little while?'

Mickey smiled at Lizzie. 'Course not. Fancy a turn, girl?'

'Darby and Joan,' she said.

He led her off to the marquee while Caroline and Rob went in through the French windows to the sitting room. The table was piled high with presents and flowers. A waiter nodded to them as he carried out a stack of plates and a fearsome-looking knife.

From a corner there was a sleepy whine; a hound puppy lay curled up safely in a pen, worn out from an afternoon playing on the grass with delighted children. Caroline bent over and stroked the little dog, who gave her arm a contented lick before closing its eyes again.

'Wouldn't be Wickham Grange without a Shenstone hound,' Ruth had said. 'And now that you're staying…'

'I've thought of a name for him,' Rob said as they went out into the hall.

'Go on.'

'Ivo,' he said. 'I looked it up. Patron saint of lawyers and lost children.'

'Couldn't be better. And nor could you.' She kissed him. 'Come and see what I've done in here.'

She unlocked the office. It was tidy now, all the old papers and folders gone, replaced by a large, gleaming computer. A stack of neat files waited to be put into the old oak cabinet.

And a new brass plaque on the door glittered in the bright spotlights: *C. Alleyn*, it said, *family law services. Specialist Domestic Abuse advocate. Est. 2007.*

'Perfect,' he said.

She picked up an envelope that lay on the desk and handed it to him. 'You've not had a chance to read it,' she said.

There was a double helix on the letterhead. 'Kromo Zone?' he said.

'Don't let it put you off. Apparently they're very good.'

'I should hope so. "Dear Ms Alleyn, Thank you for your samples, which can be returned" – yuck, who'd want a toothbrush back? – "combined paternity index" – whatever that may be—' He looked up. 'Ninety-nine per cent. Can't say fairer than that.'

'I know.'

'So are you ready?'

'Yes,' she said simply.

'Come on then,' he said.

The garden was nestling in shadows. A soft wind stirred the trees, so it seemed that they were swaying in time to the gentle music in the marquee. From the churchyard came the call of a sleepy bird. The air smelled sweet and warm, and the moon gleamed like a pearl above the strong, reassuring presence that was the old house, standing sentinel behind them.

There they all were, Vera and Jane, Harriet and Grace, sitting safely with their families, bound together by a secret they no longer needed to keep. Beside them, Connie was swaying in her chair, her mind far away but her face rapt as the music swirled around her. And peaceful in the churchyard were Maud and Frances, their duty done.

Betty was standing with Mickey and Lizzie, looking at the cake. They saw her and waved, beckoning her to join them.

Caroline paused for a moment.

Then she went forward through the gathering dusk, to where her mother and her grandmother and her grandfather were waiting under the stars.

Acknowledgements

I've always loved the acknowledgements at the end of a book. They are like a window into the world of publishing, against which I pressed my envious nose, longing to be a part of it all. Now I actually have a book on the shelf, I appreciate just how well-deserved all the thanks are.

My agent, Emily MacDonald, and my editor Carolyn Mays, have been the best possible guides for my first steps as an author. Emily read the first thousand words of a long-ago draft and decided to take a chance on an unknown writer, and I will always be grateful to her for her patience, friendliness and expertise.

I am awestruck by Carolyn's laser eye for detail. She too has been unfailingly kind, supportive, and made marvellous suggestions for improvements, which were all exactly right, as well as putting up with my inability to keep track of dates and ages. Any mistakes which remain are entirely mine.

There are many other people who have brought this book to life – copy editors, cover designers, marketing and publicity teams. Thank you all.

Special thanks are due to the staff at Bromley Register Office, who took the time to tell me exactly where Lizzie would have gone to register baby Iris.

Closer to home, I have been blessed with love and support from my family – thank you, for everything. My parents have always encouraged a love of reading and history, and gave me the confidence to keep trying. My son Harry never fails to make me smile, as do the many friends who've listened and encouraged as this story took shape. You are all wonderful.

And lastly, my undying gratitude to my husband David, whose generous gift started this whole thing in the first place. You have your moments too.

Author's Note

Wickham Grange, St Anne's church and the vicarage are all figments of my imagination, although West Wickham itself is a real place. In this book, Maud and Frances are tireless in their efforts to help women and children who are at risk of harm from domestic abuse. If you have been affected by any of the troubles faced by Lizzie, Grace and their friends I would urge you to please, please reach out for help, either from your local authority or from the many excellent charities carrying on the work of Wickham Grange.

About the Author

Photo credit © Andrew Dunsmore

Zoe has worked in education services for nearly twenty-five years, but her heart has always been in writing. When she's not working, she enjoys baking, collecting antiques and gardening. She is also slowly decorating and furnishing a large dolls' house.

Originally from Medway, she has a grown-up son and now lives in London with her husband and their enormous dog.

Bedford
Square
Publishers